IMMORTALS: BOOK 1

1

THE BLOOD SEA

Published by: Wendiilou Publishing
                       Wendy Brown
Cover Artwork: © Chelsea Langdon
Line Art: © Andrew Munro

To connect with the author, and for more information and resources visit

www.immortalsepic.com

For more copies contact the Publisher c/-
Glenburnie Homestead
212 Glenburnie Road
ROB ROY NSW 2360
Mobile: 0468 998 268
Email: wendiiloupublishing@gmail.com

In memory of Ann. Thank you.

And to Tessy. A new beginning.

Special acknowledgement to:

Josie, Terri, Simon, Darren. Thank you for your efforts as friends and mentors to help prepare this book, and for the advice you gave to help me improve as a writer.

IMMORTALS: BOOK 1

THE BLOOD SEA

Andrew Wratten

PROLOGUE

Magic to influence and control the mind was of growing interest to the wizard, and his pursuit of such knowledge was leading him down strange paths. None more curious than the peculiar woman that resided in the basement of his tower. Her distraught family told him *the light had touched her*. Agreeing to investigate her condition, she was his guest now for five months.

He did not anticipate that his eccentric boarder would attract so many cats. The madwoman continuously fed and comforted the strays who seemed strangely drawn to her. Now the creatures not only infested the basement but made their way up to his study and lab. At least they kept his tower free from other vermin.

The wizard could only spend a short time with the woman each day before he felt that he might go insane himself. She always talked about the present in the past tense, and occasionally she would rant about the future as if it were the present. It was challenging to interpret, but there were enough known truths to what she said for him to be captivated by her words. Sometimes, when she spoke his name during her predictions, the words were like flames to an imp, and it became the focus of his record taking.

As he considered his progress with the experiment, the wizard flicked through his pages of daily notes.

> *Day 26: I am more certain now of a link between madness and cats. I have bound the essence of cat specimen B to the cap device, connecting it to the alarm, coded blue.*

> *Day 35: Blue alert, confirmed future tense. Repeated references to a sea of blood. Notation "Since coming to the sea of blood, you have become supreme amongst the casters".*

> *Day 72: Blue alert, confirmed future tense. Notation: "The Oracle's gift has given you great power." Unlinked notation: "The staff connects to the core; its energy is raw and unlimited."*

> *Day 132: No cats today. Alerted to blue, tense uncertain.*

The subject is in a rage, hot to touch. Suspect temporal hijack - unknown source. I am suspending the experiment.

The wizard closed his notebook and placed it on the shelf above his desk. Taking a deep breath and releasing it slowly to focus his mind, he reached for a blank piece of parchment and a pen. Dipping the tip of the pen into the inkpot, he reflected before jotting down his first task, *Travel to the Sea of Blood*.

Immediately, upon writing the words, he knew this was something he could not accomplish alone. Companions would be needed; people he had travelled with before and could trust. People that would not pry with unwanted questions.

Part One:

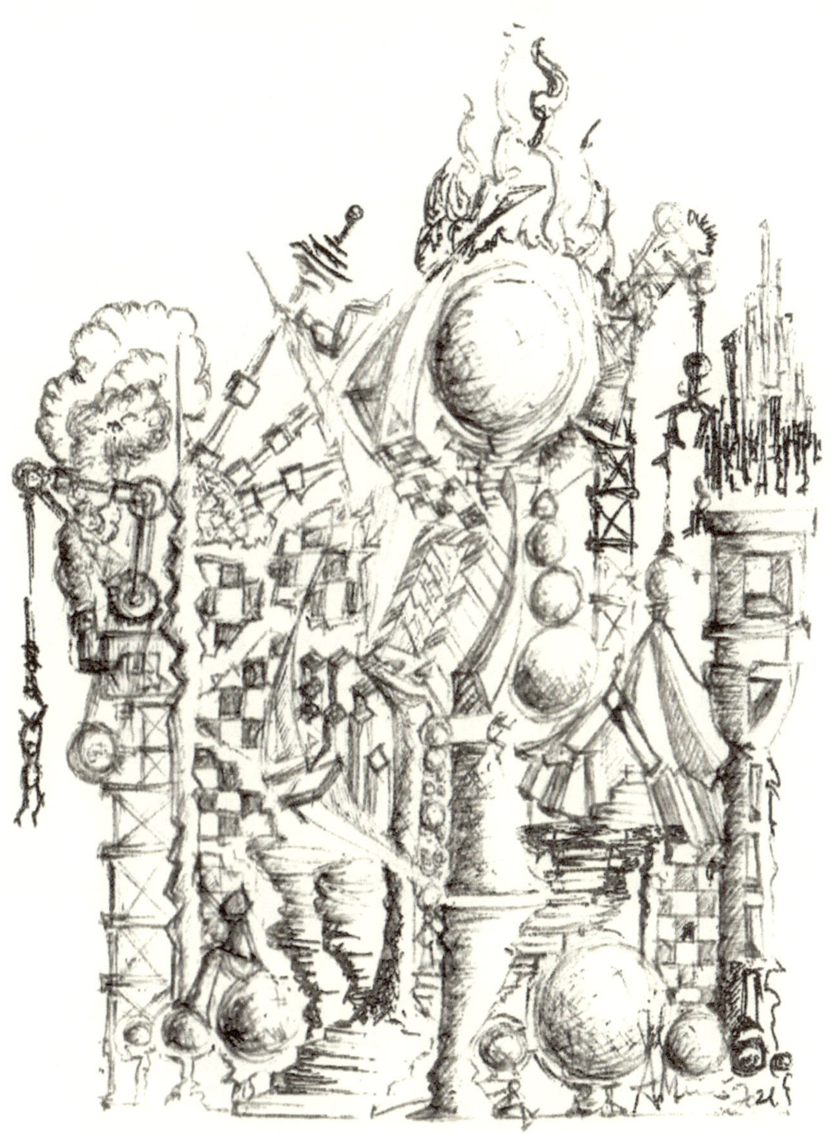

The Companions

A NEW LAND

Steam rose off his cotton shirt where, soaked at the arms and collar, it lay stuck to his damp skin. His sodden leather armour, propped up against the log he sat on, kept Mannace and his foul mood company. As he gazed into the campfire, the big warrior was indifferent to the flames as they rose and fell. He was sour at day upon day of abysmal weather. Irritable at having to navigate such murderous terrain. They were traversing the tangled stretch of wildlands that separated *The Spine*, a range of bleak and towering mountains, from the storm-swept ocean, known as *The Tempest*.

Jaal slouched against that same log. The warmth of the fire was doing little to raise the Dark Elf's spirits, and he ached from days of slashing a trail through dense forest and searching for paths through the waterlogged valleys. Jaal unwittingly discovered that the mud in the ravines could be neck deep, doubtless much deeper where the water pooled. For days, the only thing that stopped him turning back was the hope that their destination was closer than the lands they had left behind. Normally easy-going, tonight Jaal was at the end of his tether.

"Curse this miserable land. To the hells with you, Wizard, and your bloody schemes."

Across the fire from Jaal, Render looked up. He appeared no less exhausted, using the remnant of his energies to fuel the campfire, keeping the wet wood burning brightly with his magic.

"We've travelled worse paths, Jaal."

Jaal knew it for a lie, and his eyes narrowed as he stared at Render across the flames. Oblivious, the wizard rambled on.

"It is a hardship, but we will come through this. I have glimpsed the future, my friends. The rewards far outweigh the inconvenience. You will soon thank me for choosing this path."

Unconvinced of the pretext for the journey, it didn't matter to Jaal if the wizard had concocted some elaborate fantasy to entice them into his plans. Jaal had come on this adventure, as he had done many times before, solely for something to do. However, boredom was looking like an attractive alternative now. With bitter resentment, Jaal stabbed at Renders weak words.

"Sent to this hell by the rantings of a crazy woman. You are a pig's arse, wizard. A leprous cock that no whore would lick. We are as mad as that bitch to follow you!"

In a malicious, matter-of-fact tone, Jaal added, "You lack vision, and you embrace foolishness. You belong at your desk, Wizard, back in your gods-forsaken tower, where your uselessness is a curse only to yourself."

Mannace let out a brooding "Hmmph" in support. Looking up, he gave the wizard a disdainful glare then returned to watching the flames.

Render had known Jaal and Mannace for many decades as he often journeyed with them. In better circumstances, he enjoyed their banter and the bond they shared. Tonight however, the flames of the campfire flared as the wizard's gut tightened and his mind raced. Anger at the Dark Elf's disrespect churned his stomach, but his wisdom knew better of Jaal's malice and the big man's temper than to provoke their wrath by saying more.

Render was wiry and tall, though not as tall as Mannace. The wizard had a sharp, mean look about him with dark, piercing eyes. His practical travel attire was of the best quality, and even in this hell, he maintained a well-trimmed and oiled moustache and beard. Render's long hair was also oiled and tied back. He had been around long enough to know how to use the sword hung on his belt, but he had deadlier means at his disposal. Following years apart from his companions, Render looked forward to putting his full capabilities on show. Now, as they sat uneasily at the campfire, the wizard's brow drew deep lines as he imagined dealing Jaal a punishing sample of that expertise, to put the scoundrel on his arse and make him squirm like a cat in a trap. The mind-play gave him time to settle the inferno rising within him and remind himself of his larger purpose.

After three further days enduring the harsh wilds, the companions, at last, embraced a gentler terrain of rolling hills and wooded valleys. The rain was lighter here, and it lessened further as they moved inland from the hostile coast. Now, far from places they knew, they were pleased to be out from the damp shadow of The Spine and to enter this new land that warmed both their bodies and spirits.

Craving some time to himself, Jaal scouted ahead of the others, rewarded with the discovery of an old track in the hills that wound its way north. Following the trail for several days, the companions came upon campsites that had a look of regular use about them. One site had wisps of smoke still rising from its cook fires, with the smell of spilt fat wafting to them on the breeze. Horse dung, with its pungent aroma, was now commonplace at the campsites and on the road.

It was no surprise when, later that day, the companions caught up with a gang of armed men. When the band turned to confront them, of the three companions, Jaal and Mannace continued forward, while Render scuttled back and out of sight.

The men they encountered wore a uniform of sorts consisting of black trousers and shirts, and metal breastplates. The armour bore a stylised raven emblem, and they carried a variety of weapons, mostly axes and swords. A few wore helmets, while others had black hoods. Some of the fighters boasted old scars and dents in their armour, indicating to Mannace that these were seasoned warriors. Only one man was mounted, looking after a handful of horses that were grazing at the side of the road. Another man with a soured look pocketed a biscuit he was eating and came forward, while his crew drew weapons and spread out to outflank the two approaching men.

"What've we 'ere, a darkie and a baba? You're a long way from home - long way from places where your likes is safe. It ain't smart, ain't smart at all, to be wandering out 'ere, along the borders."

The man sniggered and took another step closer so that he was only a few feet from Jaal and glared at the Dark Elf with gut-seated menace.

"No tellin' what trouble ya might run inta."

Jaal's mood darkened. Matching the man's aggressive stance, he placed a hand on the hilt of his belted blade, fingers twitching. "Get off our path," he directed in a cold tone.

The response from the antagonist was an unfriendly laugh as he looked over his shoulder, purposefully taking in the group of armed veterans behind and to his side.

"We'll not be movin' for your kind." He turned his head slightly and spat at the ground.

Mannace estimated about twenty men, enough to present a challenge. Knowing Jaal's impetuous nature, Mannace stepped forward to be alongside the agitated Dark Elf.

"Move aside," he reinforced, raising his voice only slightly.

"What's a man doin' with a darkie?" was the response. "This is only gonna end one way".

"You'd be surprised".

With unusual speed for such a large man, Mannace reached forward and snatched the battle axe from the surprised fighter's grasp and extended the weapon towards him to prevent him from coming forward. On another day, Mannace might have embedded the axe-head deep into the man's skull. Today though, with considered restraint, Mannace coolly emphasised his dominance by tossing the weapon back. The man fumbled slightly but managed to bring the axe back to hand.

Mannace was a head taller than any others present as well as broad and muscular. Fitted out in light leather armour for travelling, he carried a wide-bladed, two-handed sword strapped to his back, another broad sword sheathed at his side, and a machete tucked into his belt next to a sheathed butcher's knife. Heavily bearded from his time in the wilderness, his scraggly dark hair hung loosely about his shoulders. Searing brown-green eyes, a strong jaw and broad smile all added to Mannace's intimidating demeanour.

"I'll take your fucking head," bellowed the antagonist, but when Mannace reached his hand behind his shoulder and wrapped his fingers around the hilt of his two-handed sword, his adversary stepped quickly back into the safety of his amused comrades.

Behind Mannace, the air shifted. Where a moment before there was nothing, Render now stepped forward to stand beside him. More than one of the men they faced took a step back and looked at one another, their amusement and confidence replaced with apprehension. Many took a defensive posture and bunched together.

"Leave now!" commanded Mannace in his most authoritative tone. Hesitating only for a moment, their opponents shuffled back then turned away. A few of the braver or more foolhardy souls among them cast baleful stares as they retreated but thankfully nothing more. The few riders retrieved their horses and mounted, following the rest of the troop away from the path.

Mannace allowed himself a relieved sigh. The big man knew from hard-earned experience that a poorly handled confrontation could turn to disaster. Once the troop were out of earshot, Jaal, whose temper was still aflame, broke the silence.

"Cowards and soft-cocks. Nothing about this land impresses me."

Mannace doubted that they were cowards. He was far more pragmatic, "I expect they have other priorities, as do we."

Picking up their gear, the companions continued forward. The road they followed was, in places, little more than a cattle track, but when they eventually came upon clusters of houses and farms, river stones were used to improve the thoroughfare. There was no friendliness to these frontier communities.

Squat hills and light woodland dominated the terrain they travelled through. Sometimes thicker forest came into view, and the occasional loftier peak would rise above the tree line. On the seventh day after their encounter with the armed band, following a gradual ascent, the land flattened into a broad plateau. By dusk, they had passed larger groupings of farms, and as darkness fell, they came upon their first village.

It was not hard to find the tavern. Light and noise led the companions to a building where men and a few women drank and laughed. As they entered, all eyes were upon them, and silence quickly enveloped the open hall. Unfazed, Mannace nodded at a pair of soldiers drinking at the bar. Both wore simple grey uniforms, with studded leather hauberks, and broadswords in leather scabbards at their sides. More astute than the armed men the companions had encountered previously, one of the soldiers returned the nod to acknowledge a fellow military man, and raised his mug in salute, even perhaps to recommend the local brew. The soldiers turned away and returned to their private conversation. The tension of the other locals eased, and the noise of conversation and laughter returned. The companions seated themselves, ordering food and ale from the keeper who had come to welcome them to his tavern.

Jaal eyed a pleasant-looking serving girl who responded with a sly smile. Mannace shook his head – there was something about Jaal that made women open their legs, something more profound than his fine looks and fighter's physique - a force of nature. There was a hunger in Jaal that raised his blood for any pretty girl. Often Jaal's ebony skin and Elven features would bring different attention, but surveying the room, this did not seem to be a factor here – an odd but welcome change.

With the dishes cleared, Render queried the tavern keeper about accommodation, and even with a silver piece in hand, the keeper merely shrugged and went about his business. A heavy-set man took hold of the hand with the coin, putting his other palm on Render's shoulder. "Hey bro, yous stay at my place. I'll take good care of yous." he beamed. "When yous fellas are ready, let me know."

Render looked at his companions. Jaal raised his eyebrows and Mannace shrugged his shoulders. The response was good enough for Render. He gave the bold stranger a nod, then returned to his ale.

It was much later when the man led them to a small dwelling close to the village where they waited while he ushered his wife and sons onto the road. "We'll be back in the morning, bro." He took the coin and left the door open. The house was simple but clean, one room with four beds and the necessities required for living. Mannace muttered to himself as he claimed the largest of the beds, which was far too small for such a large man. Jaal tested two of the other beds for comfort, also seeming displeased. Render's tone was cutting as he broke the silence.

"What did you expect? It's better than sleeping on a dirt floor."

"I'm gonna check around for a bit," an unsettled Jaal announced before he disappeared.

Mannace surmised his friend's unsaid purpose. He and Render shared a wry grin.

At dawn, they stirred, readied themselves, and were once again on their way. Usually, they trekked in silence, but that morning Jaal made conversation between chewing brick-bread. A unique crust preserved the black loaf for long journeys. It was so tough that it was almost inedible, but Jaal had become accustomed to the texture which softened quickly in the mouth, and he enjoyed the bitter taste.

"The girl says there are other Dark Elves in the city to the north. They're part of the priesthood at the Temple of War. She said that the ruler there took a Darkie as his bride."

Jaal snapped off another small piece of crust with his teeth.

"It's a large port, busy. We should try the pies at *Greenies*. We'll pass it when we're close to the city. She said not to buy a pie at the docks unless you've got iron for guts."

The thought of pies made them hungry for real food. Their dinner of spiced beef and potatoes at the Tavern had reminded their stomachs how good food tasted.

"Girl says if we have the coin, we can get *Nyx* in *The Smoke*," Jaal kept chewing as he talked. None of them knew what Nyx was. "It's another two days on foot if we follow the road.".

"That's surprising", Render interrupted Jaal. "You talked to the girl. Don't suppose you asked for her name?"

They all chuckled, and when Jaal went silent, both his companions laughed harder as they walked on.

As the region became more populated, the companions picked up essential information from locals: the region was Arenland, and they were nearing the port city of Ostoik. It was a place renowned for its industry, and it prospered on trade with other cities across the Blood Sea. They discovered that the group of men they had encountered on the road were *Ravens*, part of a mercenary company hired to patrol the southern border where the Two-Face Orcs were becoming more active.

There was a rise in the land before they reached the city so that when they came to the peak of the rise, they could see Ostoik laid out before them. Spread along a wide bay was an industrial area close to extensive port facilities.

Protected by a walled-off central district were structures marked with banners suggesting they may be military and government buildings. The off-white pennants displayed images of a ship, an anvil, and a fisted gauntlet – all illustrated in deep red and finished with black edging. Above Ostoik, a citadel loomed over the city, flying similar colours.

Smoke from tall chimneys lingered above the industrial precinct. A stiff sea breeze shepherded the smog down and through the city so that the buildings appeared dank and soot-covered. This industry was on a much grander scale to anything the companions had seen before, spiking Mannace's curiosity.

"What forge might create such a black cloud. It taints the air with its stench, even from up here."

Bursts of flame seen through the doors and gaping windows of some buildings gave the scene a demonic look.

"It's the Four Hells", piped in Jaal. "Made by men to worship the Forsaken."

Render, who knew something of the Four Hells, sniggered, earning him the Dark Elf's disapproving stare.

In addition to the thoroughfare they travelled, other roads were leading away from Ostoik along the coast, and Mannace pointed out smaller settlements nearby. Between the industrial and government quarters, Jaal took note of a large domed structure that was most likely their Temple of War. Looking beyond the city, this was the companions' first glimpse of the Blood Sea. It took its name from the red stain of its waters, a colour that seemed to darken and intensify as the day transformed into twilight.

They approached at day's end, and the companions settled into private rooms at a modest inn near the city's outskirts. Ale, food, and women were of a quality that pleased the three companions who were thankful to be back to city life. They had travelled a hard path and were relieved to see that things were similar to their homeland. As he retired to his room later that evening, Render's lips turned up slightly at the edges in a self-satisfied grin. In his mind, he placed a mental tick against the first task on his list; *Travel to the Sea of Blood.*

THE ORACLE

Ostoik was as cold and damp as a wet fish, and the smoke from the factories was as persistent and stifling as a nagging wife. It explained why so many people who worked there chose to live in the outer suburbs and why the more lavish homes were high on the hillsides overlooking the bay, not unlike their owners holding their noses up in disdain. It was a noisy city, with the machines of industry grinding and hammering throughout the day, and to a lesser extent, throughout the night. Mannace was fascinated by the boilers that fuelled the industry. Stoked with wood and coal, the steam from them turned large wheels, much like the windmills of his home province, that moved other wheels, which in turn powered all variety of machinery. The steam, like the smoke, vented above the city or leaked through pipes into the streets, adding to the dampness choking the air.

In the days that followed, the companions became more familiar with Ostoik's citizens. While the populace was predominantly human, other races also moved through the city. Mountain Dwarves operated local mines, with wagons of coal and ore trickling into the city throughout the day. The Dwarves appeared a dour type, getting about their dirty business with no time for conversation even amongst themselves. As expected, Dark Elves were amongst the priesthood of the War God, and surprisingly True Elves, also called Alani in their language, came and went from the city as part of the constant seaborne traffic. Mannace found the local term *True Elf* amusing.

"Didn't realise you weren't a True Elf, Jaal. Ears not pointy enough, eh? Not smug enough, maybe? Too much time with your spear spent in humans?"

Render laughed at the last jibe, but Jaal ignored his companions so that they couldn't tell if he found the term offensive. Mannace wasn't going to let it go.

"Not pretty enough, I expect. Perhaps your spear is not bent the right way?"

Render didn't particularly like Elves of any type, Jaal being a rare exception, and he was quick to add his cynicism.

"More likely missing the spear up your arse. Arrogant bastards, Elves, but the women are stunning, makes you want to bed them or kill them."

On quick reflection, he added, "Or both."

Render's friends looked at him sideways, and Mannace grimaced. They knew the wizard had a history of dabbling with Necromancy, and they were suspicious of his meaning. Seeing their stares, the wizard threw his hands in the air in exasperation: "For hells' sake!"

Jaal was indifferent to True Elves himself, and he was doing his best to avoid his Dark Elf kin. In his travels, meeting with other Dark Elves was rare, but when he encountered them, those senior to Jaal always expected to place obligations on him as was the customs of his people. The last Dark Elf he met was a merchant, of the type to conduct his business under the shadow, and who required Jaal to recover a contract from a rival. It took Jaal weeks to track the man down and complete the assignment. There was precious little thanks or compensation for his efforts.

In his exploration of Ostoik, Jaal discovered one tavern near the docks where Dwarves congregated and another inn where only men of the Guild of Engineers were welcome. Still, while there were tensions between the races or classes, it didn't seem out of hand, and Jaal felt under a less watchful eye than he did in most communities. The industrial district was particularly multicultural, with the local artisans working alongside men and women from many races.

The city had a reputation for the quality of its armour-making. Therefore, Mannace took the opportunity to purchase a new back-and-breast plate, as well as vambraces and greaves, to protect his arms and legs. Even with their weight, he felt much more comfortable in metal armour, more prepared to face anything the fates could throw at him.

Machinery that the companions could hardly have imagined was produced and in use. Three tall towers, each with a single long mechanical arm stood as a bold example on the docks, powered by steam and used to load and unload the ships. Another example was a boatyard at the end of the docks, where a ship of metal was under construction. The iron hull was in place, wider than a traditional vessel, with fins like that of a fish underneath. There were metal-smiths wielding tools and using flaming machines to shape and join metal beams to the construction. Mannace was unsure if it was a marvel or a misadventure. A view shared by the city folk who had been watching the project over the past year. They were used to answering questions about it from visitors to their city.

The Garrison of Ostoik seemed well organised and was ever-present on the streets or where there were crowds. There was an extreme sense of order.

One morning, Render returned excited from his reconnaissance after purchasing passage to a city called Rummond, only two days journey by sea. On the afternoon tide, they boarded a merchant ship and departed. Jaal was glad to be away from Ostoik and his kin. He had avoided the Dark Elves and was relieved to have escaped without being dragged into their arcane politics and convoluted schemes.

With no women aboard the vessel, Jaal seemed most comfortable with his own company. Likewise, Render was preoccupied – keeping to himself and deep in thought. In contrast, Mannace made an effort to talk with the merchants, and he was enjoying the captain's company. Captain Morgan Cain was sharply dressed and well-groomed. Mannace hadn't seen him with a weapon; nevertheless, the man had a fighter's presence and a confidence that only came with long experience. Both men were well-travelled and shared an interest in hearing of distant lands and each other's exploits. Morgan expounded on his encounters as a much younger man with the wild sea fearing tribes south of the Blood Sea and beyond the Teeth of Ranesh. During the day, the tribes would live peacefully and trade with one another, but at night they raided rival settlements to steal away their women. Joining a tribe on their raid, Morgan described how his crew took women for their own, but it was not the boon they hoped.

"I have never laughed so hard, Mannace. You should have seen the despair on the lads' faces. It was a night of torture like no other, nagged and abused and some were clawed bloody by the hell-spawn. Such beautiful creatures, soft to touch, yet harder than Aren steel. We abandoned the she-devils on a beach and fled back to more civilised lands."

Both men were chuckling, and Morgan revealed his stash of hidden liquor, bringing further smiles.

When Mannace told his stories, they covered a timeline that was inconsistent with a human lifespan. "How old are you?" asked the captain.

Mannace took a long breath before answering.

"I am of the Viletri, a race of immortals, also known as the *True Men*. I am one hundred and eighty-three years of age. My father, who was of the Viletri was a traveller, while my mother was a mortal woman of the city Kuros. Though immortal, my father was still of flesh and blood, slain by an enemy's spear during the service of our Lord, the Protector of Kuros."

Speaking of his father's death still sparked emotion in Mannace which caused him to pause briefly.

"I was age fifteen when my father died. My mother passed in her sleep at the age of sixty-seven. Morgan, I have had two wives but no children and served loyally as a soldier and commander for my Lord. My Lord died, and his son was not the same quality of man, so I left his employ and became a traveller as was my father."

It felt to Mannace as if he had already lived several lifetimes. He didn't want to appear arrogant nor insult Morgan by saying that he had found it challenging to reside amongst mortals.

"I know no other men of the Viletri and have not heard of the Viletri during my travels. Since leaving Kuros, I have pursued adventure across many lands. Often in the company of Jaal and Render, although we each have our separate paths."

The Captain, not new to unusual tales, shared an observation.

"I heard tell of a city on the coast of the Blood Sea. Legend would have it that the men there were immortal, like the Elves. The city was destroyed and plundered by Northern raiders many generations ago. I don't know more, but it may be of interest, and perhaps Elves that roam the Blood Sea may have visited that place in their lifetime."

Interest sparked, Mannace thanked the captain, though he felt a weight settle upon his shoulders, his curiosity demanded that he know more.

Morgan described the lands surrounding the Blood Sea and the vast continent that stretched north. The northern continent was divided by a great rift, with the people south of the breach embroiled in a lengthy war with those further north. Morgan had not travelled to these lands or the rift, though he had ventured to many other distant shores. The more Morgan talked the more Mannace felt that the world as he understood it was expanding and that with all his adventures he still had much to see.

When they arrived at Rummond, the companions found it to be more fort and town than a city. The port facilities were meagre, with a lack of urgency in the men who had come to unload the shipment of supplies for the local garrison. Morgan seemed unconcerned. He journeyed here often and was happy to guide the travellers to a place of accommodation. He joined them for a drink and then wished them well on their travels before returning to his vessel.

Happy to be back on solid ground the companions allowed themselves a day to recover their land legs and ease into the next stage of their adventure. It was an aspect of immortality that they didn't have the same sense of urgency as mortal men, that is, the need to cram as much as possible into such a short life. Morgan was a tremendous example of this, in his fifty years it astounded Mannace how far the sea captain travelled and what feats he accomplished. The more he dwelt on it during the day; the more Mannace felt driven and inspired to do something meaningful with his own life. Talking about his father with Morgan stirred something deep within him; even after so many decades, he still wished to make his father proud and sought his approval.

Render used part of his day to hire horses, and he commissioned a local hunter as a guide. Over their evening meal, the wizard shared the next stage of his plan with Mannace and Jaal.

"There's a monastery along the coast from here, two to three days ride.".

They nodded but were more interested in their roasted turkey, candied beans and ale, not prodding Render for more details.

Their guide, Rollo, was short and stocky with dirty blonde hair that clung to his shoulders, extending down his back in matted locks, matching his braided beard and moustache. He wore a simple leather hauberk and carried a metal-headed mace tucked into his belt with a compact hunting bow across his shoulder. Although Rollo seemed fit, he had a lazy belly that hung over his belt. "Follow me," he mumbled to nobody and walked ahead of the horses. He led them initially onto a quiet road headed away from the coast, then veered off to follow a well-worn track. It wasn't until the second day that the track petered out and their guide led them down less trodden paths. Often, they would need to dismount and navigate the more densely wooded regions, but where possible, Rollo kept to the high land, patched with tussock and brush. Occasionally there were glimpses of the sea to remind them that they were following a coastal route. On the morning of the third day, their destination was finally in sight.

A tiny wooden door, barely large enough to accommodate Mannace if he were to bend over, fronted a windowless, fortress-like building. The Monastery was perched atop a high cliff which dropped away to a rocky coast. The seaward walls of the abbey reached out from the height and descended into the sea. The companions imagined that the seaward side might have windows and possibly balconies, but it was impossible to know from where they stood. Making no real effort to hide, they watched as the small door opened and a group of men exited, passing close to where the companions stood. The group appeared to be hunters – human mostly, with an Orc amongst their number, which Rollo noted was unusual. Each was lightly clothed and carried a bow. Two also hoisted heavy spears over their shoulders and the Orc had bear-claw traps hanging from a large backpack. They glanced to where the companions stood but did not stop to acknowledge them, instead they continued their way inland. Mannace looked toward Render, who shrugged and started walking in the direction of the monastery entrance, followed closely by Rollo and the others.

A creak of hinges answered the hail of "Yo," from Mannace as the small door swung slowly outward. Two guards dressed in light armour holding spears greeted them.

"Don't make the mistake of thinking the monastery ain't well protected," warned one of the men, "all are welcome, make your way to the red room, that-away."

His comrade added, "Keep yer weapons sheathed and take the string off yer bow".

They waited until Rollo complied, then the guards moved to their alcove near the door and let the companions pass.

The red room was glaringly obvious, with red, crimson, and black mosaic floor and walls. Through one of many corridors that exited the room, an older man emerged unsummoned to welcome them.

"I am Syprus, may the light be upon you. How may I be of service?"

"We seek an audience with the Oracle," replied Render.

Syprus waved them towards one of the corridors that led them down a series of passageways and stairways. They came upon other people and glimpsed into many rooms as they passed by them. Render noted libraries and small chapels, in addition to domestic areas where people were mending clothes, weaving, and preparing food, He felt that the monastery had a hustle and bustle to it and was surprised, given its remoteness. The people they passed were tidily dressed. Some with brooms, baskets, and buckets seemed to be going about their jobs, while others with books or casually chatting, appeared to be visitors. More than once an unusual face would crop up amongst the human ones; twice, the tusked visage of an Orc, and once, the delicate features of a 30emalee Elf.

As the others continued ahead, Jaal stopped abruptly, stepping back. At the extreme edge of his hearing, there was a moaning – a distressed, tortured sound. Without hesitation, he deviated down a side corridor, took another turn and climbed up a short set of stairs. Jaal entered a different mosaic chamber, just like the red room but this was green and with fewer exits. Following the noise, he selected an unlit passage that opened into a dark, square-shaped space. A single candle burned on a shelf providing dim light, so that Jaal observed the outline of a cage. Within it and with her back to him, a naked, ebony skinned woman, let out a moan that reached into Jaal's soul and squeezed hard. He gasped.

The entrapped woman turned. She was of exceptional beauty, with flawless skin that glistened with sweat, and a grace of movement that seemed to exaggerate her exquisite figure. She came up against the bars of her cage, leaned into them like she might lean into a lover, and looked directly into Jaal's eyes. Her smile was inviting, promising. Her eyes were unusually dark with a tinge to them - at first green, then as their gaze met, red. These were eyes to get lost in.

The temptress hissed unexpectedly breaking the spell her allure cast. Her lips parted, exposing long incisors, and her eyes flared in rage.

Syprus stood alongside Jaal.

"I see you have found the Oracle's pet. The Oracle believes that good is in everyone. In this case, a work in progress."

Syprus beckoned toward the corridor from which they had both come, but Jaal remained transfixed with the she-devil. As his blood raced, the vice clamped to his soul increased its pressure. He stepped closer to the cage and experienced an intensity he did not want to release. There was tainted energy in the woman, or whatever she truly was, that was also within him. He wanted desperately to be with her and to be inside her.

Syprus placed a hand gently on Jaal's shoulder.

"What you want is not always what you need".

The older man's touch was oddly calming, and Jaal was able to take a step away. He locked eyes once more with the woman before turning and striding back the way he had come.

Together again, the companions were shown the dormitory and left to select their rooms. They regrouped in the common area set out with long tables and a kitchen with dried meats and wild fruits aplenty. They chatted with other visitors, many of whom, like themselves, were expecting an audience with the Oracle. It was daunting to hear that some of them had been waiting an extraordinary time, and none they talked to had seen the Oracle in person. Nobody seemed to question this, and there was an eerie calmness to the small community that the companions found disconcerting.

"Let's not stay longer than we need to," Mannace whispered to the others. Jaal seemed distracted but Render and Rollo nodded their agreement.

That night each of them experienced vivid dreams. As they talked over their breakfast of porridge and fruits, they realised that the dreams of Jaal, Mannace, and Render were similarly themed, they dreamt of a great battle.

In Jaal's dream, he looked out from a high place at a battle joined between two immense forces. The army he was aligned to was comprised of many parts - legions of differing races and types of troops - with numbers that stretched to the horizon. The enemy was also varied and immense. As the forces clashed, the sky filled with arrows and magic. In that dream Jaal had leapt into the thick of the fighting, moving with lightning speed as he wreaked havoc. He felt a surge of energy in his thoughts, so intense that the residue of that energy remained in him even now as he sat eating his breakfast.

While Mannace slept, he also dreamt a similar scene, but atop a hill and surrounded by soldiers that were loyal to him. He was conveying orders to a multitude of generals who in turn handed commands to others. He felt a massive burden of responsibility and an actual physical weight on his shoulders. Now awake, it was a hard feeling to shake off.

Render, within a related dreamscape, wielded fantastic magic - his body a channel for vast powers that he released as fire, force, and terror. Awake and at the breakfast table, he fidgeted, still feeling a sense of untapped potential within. The dreams were an intrusion linked to this strange place, and Render didn't like the thought of being manipulated. Agitated, he rose from the table and set out to find their host.

Syprus and Render met in the red room. "I demand to see the Oracle today!"

"Odd," replied Syprus, not liking Render's blunt tone, "Do

not demand of the Oracle, it is the Oracle who issues instruction. The Oracle serves the Light, the Light that rises over the world and keeps the night at bay. If you and your companions are here, so far from your homes, it is because the Oracle requires *you*, not that *you* need the Oracle."

Render had no patience for preaching. "Don't mix words with me, old fool. Let the Oracle speak for himself."

"Huh! You are all in your head, wizard. You think you see the world laid out before you, that you are the master. But you are blind in your heart, the truth is beyond your reach, and to you, the world will remain cloaked in night." Syprus' words had become heated, and he took a brief moment to check his temper. "Arrogance is an enemy. Light, wizard, is your salvation."

"Arrogance, ego, conceit, the wheelhouse of priests. Preach your pig-shit to the weak-minded, I can see through your tricks. I *know* what this place is, priest. The Oracle, now!"

"You know nothing! Your soul, wizard, is black. The Oracle is not available to you."

Render stepped closer to Syprus. Both men were tall, locking eyes in battle. Render took a deep breath, drawing power from his gut, his voice carrying deep malice. "I know about souls, priest. There is no mysticism to it, no blackness or light. Save your hollow rhetoric for the ignorant and weak."

Syprus, his temper ignited, no longer held back, "Weak, huh! Why did you come here, wizard, journeying all this distance? Because a thought wedged in your thick head fed your ego, and made you leave everything you held precious to arrive at this distant place. Who is *weak*, wizard! Why the Oracle has favoured you with a dream, a gift of light for one so dark is not my choosing. Nevertheless, I trust in the divine wisdom, and you will do the same. Your journey begins here."

"I am not a lackey to your faith. I'll follow no such path."

"You have no choice!"

Render despised priests, and Syprus' righteousness infuriated him. He could feel forces at work to divorce him of his anger, trying to penetrate his granite will. Render let go his gaze upon the man, turned, and stormed back the way he had come.

The wizard scarcely noted his companions who greeted him as he entered the common area. His thoughts remained deeply agitated and troubled, waving their questions away.

Later, as the four visitors prepared to leave the monastery, Syprus came to them, accompanied by an Elven woman. His calm demeanour had returned, though he looked past Render to engage the others.

"Casteel has often travelled the Blood Sea. She has agreed to be your guide." Addressing the group but looking directly at Jaal, he added, "*She* is what you need."

VILETRI

They waited four days at Rummond before boarding a ship headed for Yanth, an important port on the Blood Sea according to Casteel.

Casteel was of medium height, lean, and blue-eyed - typical of the Alani. She wore her dark hair tied back and interwoven with a leather cord. Casteel had a rapier at her belt, or a "child's plaything" as Jaal called it, with two long knives strapped to her calves. Gifted with natural agility, fitness, and confidence, it seemed likely to the companions that she would be capable in a fight.

Rollo asked to travel with them. Something about the monastery had changed him, and he seemed resolved to leave his old life behind and throw his lot in with the group. Because Rollo was resourceful on their journey in caring for the horses and keeping their bellies full, the companions quickly agreed.

Privately, Render was trying to reconcile between the mad woman's words and the Oracles manipulation. On reflection, it seemed to him that his objectives were still intact.

That said, for now, the group chose a new destination that was not within Render's considerations; Casteel was to take them from Yanth to Sylos, and from there they would journey on foot to the land that was once Viletri. When the Viletri race was vanquished, Casteel had been very young, but she knew something of the history of True Men, and she was confident of reaching their locale. Casteel and Mannace spent a lot of time in conversation. The information thus gleaned fuelled a growing desire within Mannace to pursue his Viletri heritage.

As they sailed to Yanth, Jaal and Render took the opportunity to discuss their monastery dreams. Both felt changed; something was unleashed within themselves during their visit to the Oracle. For Render, already an accomplished magician, it seemed as if the boundaries of the power he might draw on were no longer limited.

"I can feel it here, Jaal," the wizard had his hand over his stomach. "While magic is a talent of the mind, it draws energy from the gut … a wondrous cup of arcane power to carefully sip and channel to perform miraculous things. It takes decades of practice to enlarge that power and refine its use. Jaal, where there was a cup, there is now a pit, a great abyss alive with swirling energies, more power than I can comprehend."

Render laughed, although it was the type of cackle to make the skin crawl.

"If you find me cast across the deck turned inside out with my intestines thrown from bow to stern, put it on the Oracle for placing this darkness within me."

The wizards' words were disconcerting. It seemed odd to Jaal that Render would refer to his new-found power as darkness when the Oracle was supposedly of the Light, even though one element often embraced the other.

"So, it is the Oracles doing? A gift to accompany a dream?"

Render had been thinking about this, "I think it innate, unlocked by the dream, possibly amplified. I can't be certain."

That resonated with Jaal's experience. As a bladesman, Jaal had always been quick, and fortuitously, more skilful than any other he had battled thus far. Since his dream at the monastery, his speed was heightened, and he sensed untapped potential he could draw upon, a realisation that he might become even quicker with practice.

"I have the same sense. Wild dogs are chewing at my gut that must be tamed, or they will consume me whole."

The companions laughed in good humour. There was no doubt that the visit to the monastery revealed new abilities that would enhance their respective professions. It was in both their natures to relish the prospect of discovery and experimentation, further excited by the inherent dangers. Jaal voiced a shared concern.

"No such gift comes without expectation."

During the sea voyage, Jaal's various attempts to have an intimate conversation with Casteel were brusquely shut down by her. Casteel soon took to giving Jaal a hard time on other matters, and he was often on the wrong side of her wit. Rather than withdraw, Jaal relished the banter and gave as good as he got. It helped to pass the time as they continued towards Yanth.

Yanth was indeed an expansive port. The central city encircled a natural harbour, with busy wharves and a large merchant district. The residential area spread back from the port, over and beyond the hills surrounding the dock, so the full size of the city was not apparent. Even from a distance, the white-painted homes and their orange tiled rooves showed the travellers that Yanth had a sense of symmetry and traditionalism. Towers equipped with machines of war flanked the harbour entrance, and two sizeable forts looked down balefully from the hills above. Casteel mentioned that there was a naval base in another natural harbour a further two hours sail north and that the fleet Yanth stationed there was considered formidable.

Once docked, the companions disembarked and made their way into the city proper. The accommodation they picked was a large, two storey inn that, in addition to the typical offerings, also had a bathhouse, barbers, and laundry services which they were all glad to use. Mannace was a different man once clean and shaven, less barbarian and more the gallant military man.

After bathing, Rollo, who had never travelled far from Rummond, set out to see the sights. Mannace and Casteel further explored the dock area and were rewarded when they encountered Captain Morgan Cain and his crewmen. They were completing a delivery to Yanth and seeking their next consignment.

At the Kraken's Eye Inn, Mannace bought the sailors a few rounds of drinks, and after the small talk, he had a proposition for the captain and his crew. He stood up and banged a table to get their attention.

"Morgan, I like and trust you. I came to this Blood Sea as a wanderer, but I now feel a greater purpose. I intend to return to the territory of the Viletri and claim that land. At the monastery near Rummond, I had a vision; a foretelling of a great battle, one that I know will decide the future of the world."

Mannace knew some would think him insane, but ale had given him the confidence to say his piece and to the hells to those that might mock him.

"I feel a responsibility to prepare for that conflict, Morgan – something deep within me tied to the Viletri has set me on this path. I have funds to pay for your ship and all your crew. To you I offer a chapter in this story – a story we will write together. Are you with me?"

Morgan laughed. "If we hadn't talked previously, I would say you were mad, but I can see greatness in you Mannace. While there is an adventure to be had, I will stand with you. I swear by Ramthos, you will have a ship and crew, at least until your purse runs dry." The crew jumped up to celebrate as the two leaders laughed and locked their hands, the deal struck; sealed further with more liquor, drinking well into the night.

The next morning, Jaal was early to rise. As he stepped onto the street and took in the warmth of the early sun, he was surprised to see Casteel approaching, latched onto a giant of a man. The man appeared dishevelled, in a kilt, and an unbuttoned white shirt open at the front. He was thickly bearded, heavyset, and hugely muscled, one of his massive arms around the Elf. Before they reached the inn, he picked her up easily in a bear hug before putting her back down. She slapped him on his arse and sent him on his way. There was a big smile on her face as she winked at Jaal and sidled past.

Jaal looked genuinely perplexed; despite his best efforts, Casteel had shown no interest in laying with him. "I thought you preferred the company of women?"

Casteel laughed; nothing would break her good mood.

When Mannace arose, a maid informed him that a visitor was waiting in the dining area. Mannace stretched his arms to force himself properly alert, then made his way to the front of the building. Stopping at the door to the dining room, he could see that the stranger was the only one present. With his back to him, the neatly dressed man sat rigidly upright. He was drumming a finger on the table ... tap tap tap tap tap tap tap tap. Curious, Mannace approached and introduced himself.

"Greetings of welcome also to you, Mannace of the True Men. I am Kakos Agamos, and I serve the Council of Yanth. I am a loyal servant of this great City State." He smiled, "The Council were surprised that you had not approached them with your intended plans. It is poor form that they should learn of your claim through a surrogate's lips. Despite that, the Council wish you to know that after due deliberation, they will endorse and support your claim to the State known as Viletri."

It was a punch in the face. Mannace had not shown the caution he might have in engaging Morgan and his men the night before. Events were accelerating exceptionally quickly; he felt foolish and ill-prepared, which he surmised was the man's intent.

Now that the official held the higher ground, he looked to bring Mannace to ease.

"We understand the need for discretion. Before you depart, the Council felt it important you know that you have an ally."

"Why is that?" Mannace asked.

Kakos thought the reasons obvious. Seeing that Mannace was genuinely unsure, the official took a moment to consider his words and proceeded to present the information more transparently for the big warrior, in plain terms.

"Politics is sharper and deadlier than any sword. In diplomacy, like in combat, if you fumble your attack, your enemy will not hesitate to stab you through the heart. Fortunately, Yanth is not your enemy. The Council has decided that it is in their best interests that you claim Viletri. As an ally, they will support you. In return, when they need you, Mannace, you will be there to support them."

His attempts to keep it simple without being condescending were delicate, and Kakos was not able to tell if Mannace understood him. He had been beaten too many times by bigger boys when he was young to provoke Mannace's wrath deliberately. Kakos repeated the critical point.

"The Council will support you."

"What does that mean?" Mannace pushed back.

"What do you need it to mean?" A question answered with a question – Mannace had no patience for that.

Under the guise of a deep, thoughtful breath, Mannace took a moment to further assess the man before him. He didn't look like a bureaucrat, nor a soldier. He was wiry, fit and alert – somebody who got things done and could navigate a tough predicament. Mannace didn't get any sense of whether he could trust Kakos Agamos. Nevertheless, he decided to take a risk.

"Ships, troops, supplies."

It was a response intended to test the official. Kakos didn't hesitate before responding.

"How many?"

Mannace kept a straight face. He was right in the game now.

"Two transport ships, eighty men-at-arms who will obey

my orders, three months of provisions, tools, and materials for construction. Wait for my signal off the coast of Viletri, where the city once stood, before you deliver."

Kakos may have underestimated this foreigner. He liked decisive people.

"It will be done, Mannace of the True Men."

Back at the dock, Morgan was keen to be moving; therefore, they were at sea again by the afternoon, catching the rising tide just in time. Morgan's ship, *The Celestial*, was typical of most merchant ships trading across the Blood Sea. She had two main masts and a crew of twenty-four. The Celestial seemed a well-maintained ship though her age was difficult to discern, with paintwork relatively new and her halyards and sailcloth in excellent condition. She was also fast, particularly with little cargo in her hold, and with a pleasant breeze behind them, they were soon out of sight from land.

Handing control of the ship to his first mate, Morgan retired to his quarters and shared his well-worn captain's map with Mannace. Showing the Blood Sea and trade routes, it was a very detailed chart, yet it lacked any part of the lands beyond shore's edge or details of the ocean north of the Blood Sea. All the same, it gave Mannace a much better sense of the region.

"Who are my enemies?" asked Mannace bluntly.

It was a good question and Morgan thought about the politics of the Blood Sea before he responded.

"Of the Blood Sea nations, they may appear to be at peace with one another, but this is not always so. I would say that none pose an immediate threat, although the independent cities of Hindas and Sylos that are closest to the lands that were once Viletri may already have some claim to that region, or part thereof."

Morgan's finger was moving across the map, but now it rested over Hindas. Their leader, Akanidas, had a reputation as a tyrant.

"Also, they may not welcome a new neighbour. Hindas might see you as a threat. You have already visited the two largest nations on the Sea, Arenland and Yanth, and already have an ally in one."

Morgan stepped back from his map. His manner became even more serious.

"Mostly the enemy resides north of the Blood Sea, from amongst the nations of the Great Continent or any number of lands east or west of that. The land of the Viletri is on the southern tip of the Great Continent, so it is vulnerable to invaders both by sea and land, as are Hindas and Sylos."

It occurred to Morgan that the last point carried extra weight, possibly a curse or warning.

"Following the Viletri's demise, this may be why the region has not already been resettled or claimed by others.".

After seven days of travel at sea, five of which were in light rain and moderate winds that continuously rocked the Celestial from side to side, they were glad to have arrived at Sylos. As they disembarked, a plump young woman in a simple cotton dress approached Mannace. She relayed a message from 'a friend', saying that 'preparations are complete'. Mannace appreciated the efficiency and asked the woman how was it that the message was delivered so rapidly. "By bird, quicker'n magic", she replied. The comparison to magic was like a slap across the cheek to Render, who instinctively put his mind to work, considering ways magic might perform such a task more efficiently.

In appearance, Sylos was a coastal town and fort much like Rummond, although the port facilities were busier with another four ships tied up alongside Celestial. Grain silos, packed stockyards, a slaughterhouse, and timber yards all indicated a large and prosperous rural hinterland. The locals didn't seem to mind the smell or the manure on the streets. At least the odour was somewhat dampened by the rain that appeared to have followed them to shore.

While Morgan and Mannace intended to remain on the ship, Render arranged lodgings at an inn for the others. Even though the Celestial was a comfortable boat, they had no desire to stay on her any longer than need be. As they settled into their new rooms, Jaal seemed distracted, so Render, Casteel, and Rollo left him to his own devices. Ordering pork stew from the menu, the travellers settled into an afternoon of stuffing their bellies with good food and warm ale.

As evening arrived, they mixed with the gathering locals and Render wowed the crowd with simple magic tricks. When he reached into the fireplace, a small flame attached itself to his finger. From there, he passed the torch to the back of a chair, where it divided into four flames that moved and danced before flaring large - making those who were closest jump back – and then the glow disappeared. The patrons, none of whom had ever seen magic before, clapped and roared for more. Rollo sported a young wench on his lap, both laughing and cheering along with the others.

Meanwhile, Mannace and Morgan left the ship, making their way up a gentle hill to the fort. The stronghold utilised the natural defences, in this case, the elevation of the hill, which fell away steeply on the coastal side. It was home to the local garrison, with an area set aside for a noble's quarter, and buildings that housed the Lord of Sylos and his retinue.

After stating their origin and business to the Gatehouse guards, Mannace requested an audience with Lord Bisan Fitzlorgan. Surprisingly, one of the soldiers was gone only briefly before returning with a neatly dressed man who walked with purpose. He had the bearing of a man in charge. Lord Bisan strode up to the pair without speaking, his steward and a serjeant of the guard trailing behind him.

After an awkward moment, Morgan broke the silence, "May I introduce Mannace of Kuros, also of the Viletri?"

"You may," interjected Lord Bisan, "but I am sure that he is capable of introducing himself. Viletri, that is interesting. Come and talk." He turned, and the two visitors followed.

Lord Bisan led them to a small room with a table and an odd assortment of chairs; it was as if this was the place all variety of seats collected when they had outlasted their original purpose. There was a small pot-belly stove with a residual heat emanating from it, and a large copper kettle set off to the side. Mugs and cups were on shelves along one of the walls. Lord Bisan indicated for them to be seated.

"Viletri, that's not been a topic of conversation in these parts for a long time indeed. So, you are immortal?"

"I am," replied Mannace and gave the Lord a summary of his history.

"And why are you here, Mannace of the Viletri?"

"To reclaim the lands of the Viletri and reforge that nation."

Mannace's heart thumped heavily as the Lord paused to consider a response. It may have seemed rash to be so boldly stating his intent without first knowing more, but it was Mannace's style to confront everything head-on. He suspected that Lord Bisan might be of similar design.

"We will talk more tonight. You will be my guests and join me for supper."

Lord Bisan and his lackeys left, and the soldier returned to escort them to their accommodation. The evening meal was a small affair with the Lord and his garrison commander, Tasik Ataan. The commander was senior in years and stern of appearance, with the wiry toughness of one who had lived a long life of hard physical work. Mannace suspected that he also did not trifle with unnecessary words. Lord Bisan led the conversation, showing interest in both Mannace's and Morgan's adventures, asking many questions of the places, people, and details of their adventures. As the evening progressed, he also answered questions asked by Mannace and was forthcoming with greater detail where he could provide it.

Of interest to Mannace, Bisan could name five other surviving Viletri, including Syprus whom they previously met. Mannace was surprised that Syprus was his kinsman as he was like any other man in appearance, except perhaps that he held himself with greater confidence. Bisan also talked about the lands surrounding the Blood Sea, their leaders, and cultures. It was past midnight when Lord Bisan stood to signal that the evening was ending. Although they hadn't discussed Mannace's objectives further, he addressed him now.

"I support your claim to the lands of the Viletri. Not that it will be an easy task for you to resettle those lands, or to cleanse it of Orcs. I trust you to be a good neighbour." He turned to Tasik, "Organise thirty men to travel with Lord Mannace and make sure he has what he needs".

Tasik did not skimp in meeting his Lord's order. Mannace and his companions, with thirty of Lord Bisan's soldiers in convoy plus mules packed with supplies, headed out of the town and along the coast. Their officer, named Rowman, was a middle-aged man who seemed capable and kept them in good order. Two of the soldiers scouted ahead of the group.

The region of Sylos was a fertile land crisscrossed with fields and pastures. They passed through small villages and a garrisoned town. It wasn't until the fourth day of travel that the communities became interspersed with wooded and wilder habitats.

As they left civilisation, Rollo joined the scouts ahead of the main party as they made their way steadily west. A day later, reports came to Mannace of smoke drawing from fires. Rollo described an encampment of around twenty families, with four sentries and perhaps another thirty or so armed men within the camp. He pronounced the families as displaced. Mannace led the column onwards, riding ahead to alert the sentries to their presence.

After escaping from raiders who attacked and ransacked

neighbouring communities, the fleeing families were cautious but glad to encounter the soldiers. They had been travelling for almost two weeks towards Sylos, where they hoped to find refuge. Mannace asked them about their land. The leader, a broad-shouldered man who introduced himself as Tain son of Mason, described a wild, frontier region. As the men talked, an older woman approached Mannace and after a period of staring intently at him, waved a bony finger in his direction.

"Blackness stirs in the bogs and crannies of the blight. The Gru be unsettled, and Scalies gather in the night. In the night! We'll not be food in their bellies like the others. Mark my words, Lord returning, there be terrible nastiness brewin'."

One of the frontiersmen interrupted the old lady and gently led her away. Tain could see that Mannace was unsettled and looked to put him at ease.

"Best not worry about Martene, she's harmless. No sense payin' heed to the ravings of a crazy old woman."

Behind Mannace, Jaal let out a sharp laugh. Only Render seemed to see the meaning behind the outburst, shaking his head at his companions' apparent lack of respect. Unfazed, the frontiersman asked Mannace his purpose. Mannace was honest with them in his explanation, and then he wished them good fortune before returning to his camp.

The next day, the expedition came upon an old road, which they cautiously ventured down, discovering other signs of past civilisation; wrecks of farms and fallen ruins where there had been pillars or other stonework that hinted at elaborate residences or establishments. In the distance, the walls of a city appeared above the other rubble. Regardless of its derelict state, it was still a magnificent sight and one that again stirred Mannace's emotions. The father he remembered would laugh at him for thinking he might lay claim to this place, but Mannace also hoped that his father would be proud of his son for embarking on such a bold endeavour. Mannace ordered his force to make camp and sent scouts to observe the city ruins at night.

In the morning, there had been no signs of night-life within the city. However, from atop a hill near the ruins, scouts reported campfires dotted around the plains to the north. Rowman pulled his men aside and pushed for more detail.

"How many campsites?"

"We counted twenty-two in plain view sir, perhaps the glow from six others that were obscured by vegetation or the roll of the land. There are likely to be others, sir."

Rowman persisted, "Single fires or multiple fires at each camp?"

"Appeared to be single fires, sir. They're too far away to be certain or to make more of it in the daylight. Should we get closer sir?"

"No. Keep watching from the hill and stay out of sight. If it's Orcs, we don't want to disturb or alert them. Is that clear?"

"Yes, sir."

As Mannace, Jaal, and Rollo entered the ruins, Mannace could see that the bones of the city were still in place. The shells of houses and businesses were overgrown with vegetation and spread out from the city proper along the coast and inland. Viletri, in its day was perhaps the size of Yanth, and Mannace could imagine how it was once a thriving, colourful metropolis. A high wall that encircled it defined the city proper. The wall was mostly intact, although the vegetation that smothered the battlements indicated many decades of abandonment. Watchful for inhabitants, the group passed through a broad arch that appeared to be a gatehouse. Within was a mix of wholly ruined buildings and other still sturdy structures, as if the destroyers of Viletri had torched and toppled the easy pickings, but not had the time nor inclination to undermine the more robust buildings. Everywhere nature was continuing the destroyers' work. To Mannace, it was as if the elaborate gardens of the city had risen to consume it.

At one point, Jaal disturbed a small group of deer that drank at a fountain. The animals dashed down the main street and disappeared amongst buildings. All varieties of birds perched anywhere and everywhere, rising to the sky in a cloud of colour when disturbed.

Twice they passed areas that had been renovated and inhabited at some point; one very recently, perhaps within the last year. In that area, Rollo found bloodstains and small remnants of bone or clothing amongst the rubble on the streets. Jaal entered some of the reclaimed dwellings and in a few, the faded stains of dry blood and the presence of human bones, scattered by animals, painted a grim picture. He accidentally kicked a human skull that rolled in a circle and came to a stop, staring up at him. Jaal kicked it again to avoid its hollow gaze.

Moving cautiously, Rollo guided them to a sprawling area that was once a port. What was left had almost totally rotted away. It seemed to Mannace the most overgrown section, and in places, tangled trees rose higher than the city walls.

It was midday when the trio returned to the main group and shared what they observed. Mannace was surprised to find, waiting for them near the camp, the same refugees they met the previous day. Tain explained that the families had decided the best future was to throw their lot in with him. It seemed to them that frontier men were just what he needed, and Mannace agreed.

Venturing back to the ruins, Mannace was cautious about using the city's surviving structures without having them explored further, so established a camp in what was once the public square. He left Rowman and Jaal to secure the site and post guards, detailing Rollo and Rowman's men to scout around the immediate vicinity.

With his initial base in the capable hands of his companions, Mannace climbed his way to a ledge on the wall overlooking the sea. He smiled in relief as he signalled two ships a short distance off the coast by waving his arms at them. They responded and launched three craft. From the surcoats of the soldiers coming towards him, he knew that they were men of Yanth.

A weight lifted from Mannace's shoulders, and he was taken aback by how things came together so well and so rapidly. As he reflected, Mannace wondered how much of his initial success to attribute to the Oracle's influences.

"Early days," he reminded himself … "Early days…".

BLOOD AND TOIL

Within a week they cleared a small area of the city, making it habitable. Yanth soldiers were doing their best to repair a section of dock. At first, the soldiers of Sylos joined in the labour, but on the third day, Mannace instead ordered further scouting and short-ranged patrols.

On the sixth night, the scouts reported that the number of campfires on the plains doubled. And on the following night, they increased again. On the eighth night, there were many times the original number of fires, and in the dark early hours of the morning, a horde came silently out of the plains and fell upon the ruined city. Orc warriors streamed through the main entrance as others scaled the walls. They were of a fearsome breed; tattooed with tribal insignia and painted for war. Human-sized but more muscular, tusked jaws jutting from their large heads. While those with crude bows stayed on the walls, the others armed with clubs and spears charged down the streets in groups, yelling and seeking out their foe. Once in charge of the city, they hooted and howled, and they searched for the intruders.

Off the coast on board the ships, the companions, men of Yanth, soldiers of Sylos, and the frontiersmen silently watched the city fall. The noises of the Orcs yelling carried across the waters. Casteel, whose night vision was sharp, pointed out the movement to the others. By dawn, the city was again quiet.

Mid-morning, Mannace and his retinue cautiously returned to the ruins. The Orcs had wreaked what havoc they could, but thankfully the new inhabitants hadn't left anything of value to steal or destroy. The beasts returned to their camps on the plains.

Meanwhile, Rowman, accompanied by four of his soldiers, hurried east to retrieve the mules and their baggage handlers who were under instruction to push towards

Sylos. It would likely be three or four days before they returned.

Mid-afternoon, Mannace, Jaal, and Render travelled the short distance to the vast grassland where the Orcs resided. The plains were mostly of chest-high grass, yellow in colour, dry on top where it waved about in the breeze, with muddy patches underfoot. Bushes with spiked branches abounded, with small pink flowers, mostly as solitary vegetation although there were occasional dense patches. At the eastern end of the plains, near the ruins of the city, apple trees stood laden with fruit, some arranged in lines to mark the edge of a long-forgotten orchard.

Using his tinder, Jaal ignited the oil-soaked torch he carried, poking the flame into the grass. Reluctantly the fire spread from blade to blade. Render drew a deep breath, squinting as he focused his mind into the smouldering fire. The wizard spread his arms dramatically, evoking an inferno, fuelling it from the energy he controlled within. In dramatic response, the enchanted flames took on the shape of phantom horses that charged away from the wizard and across the broad plains, extending the sudden firestorm to the left and right of him. From behind the companions, a strong wind manifested, fanning the blaze, and pushing the fire out and across the expanse. Soon it was raging so intensely and broadly that they could no longer see what was happening.

As the companions retreated, Jaal commented, "Nice touch with the stallions." Being a showman and already on a high after drawing on his powers, Render lapped up the praise.

From atop the hill, Rollo and a Sylosian soldier watched the blaze as it quickly consumed the plains. With incredible speed and ferocity, the fire stretched from the foot of the hill to a distant mountain range north, and the western horizon. In the places where it had consumed everything that would burn, the land was left black and smouldering. Rollo felt sick in his stomach from the death it would have caused - he didn't give a pig's nuts for the Orcs, who would have massacred them all last night, but as a hunter, he felt an affinity for the multitude of animals that would have suffered and perished. Initially, the smoke blew away from them, but as the magic that fuelled the fire ebbed, both men coughed uncontrollably at the ash-filled air.

Later, two black dots appeared in the sky and circled. When they swooped closer, they were large, winged creatures, with four legs, black, and carrying riders. The scouts remained hidden until the flyers returned north, then headed back to the city to give their report. The news heightened Mannace's concerns for their safety, but it did nothing to quell his determination to resettle this land.

The next day, Morgan Cain arrived with his ship full of supplies. It was Mannace's back up plan if the Yanth ships did not deliver on their promise, so, for now, they had more food and equipment than they needed.

One afternoon, Mannace collected the leaders together, including Tain Masonson and a man named Mickell Agren who represented the contingent from Yanth.

Mannace started, "Well done to all of you. Through your efforts, the new city of Viletri is coming to life. We are putting flesh back on these old bones."

Rowman flinched at the dark metaphor, while it made Render smirk.

Mannace had sketched a detailed map of the city with chalk-stone on a wall. He circled the area of port that the men of Yanth repaired.

"This will be the enclave of Yanth. Within the enclave Yanth governance, law, and taxes will apply."

Mickell seemed pleased. In another area of the city, Mannace circled a small government building and part of a city block.

"This will be the enclave of Sylos".

Rowman wasn't expecting that, but it seemed that it would be a good thing for Sylos, and he nodded his head in acknowledgement.

"Tain, your people can claim what residence and buildings they need for their families and businesses. They may have land for farming outside of the city if that is what they desire".

Tain agreed. Mannace circled other areas that included government buildings, military buildings, some of the port facilities, and what had been the nobles' district.

"These will be needed".

Mannace indicated that the expansive unmarked areas were available to anybody willing to come to the city. Mickell offered to manage the process of allocating residences, businesses, and land. Mannace agreed.

Mannace, Jaal, Render, and Morgan chose residences that suited their purposes. Rollo and Casteel considered themselves guests and therefore were content to stick closer to the soldiers of Sylos.

Everybody set about the task of restoration. At Mannace's command, the two ships of Yanth and the Celestial set sail to take word to other cities of what had transpired at Viletri and to spread the message of opportunity. Jaal travelled on one of the Yanth vessels and Casteel on the other to act as ambassadors for the Nation of Viletri and their Lord Mannace. It was odd for Jaal to be in a position where he was answerable to Mannace. They were equals, and while Mannace portrayed the qualities of leadership, he never asserted himself over his companions. It suited Jaal to be away from the ruins.

At Viletri, there were many things to tax a leader's attention, and Mannace remained concerned about frequent sightings of the winged beasts. He feared the city was under scrutiny by other potential enemies.

He tasked his friend Render with the city's protection. It was an opportunity that interested the wizard who employed frontiersmen to assist him, giving them the task of capturing live animals. Of the first creatures to be seized,

Render selected a small deer, placing the bound animal at the foot of a stone statue of a woman dancing. He incanted and poked the deer and statue in several places. Following Render's instruction, one of the frontiersmen held their palms against the back of the tall figurine.

"Do not take your hands off, no matter what you see or what you feel," he instructed.

Then, drawing a long knife Render slit the deer's throat and pushed the creature firmly against the feet of the statue. The deer thrashed and died.

"Primitive methods, but you have to work with what you have," he offered as an explanation.

Render closed his eyes to focus on the complex spell. Cautiously, he kneaded the entrapped life force of the deer, skilfully merging it with the life-print of the frontiersman to give it human traits. Drawing on his power, the wizard imbued magic within the statue, forcing the particles to adopt his new design. Where the particles were inflexible, he morphed them into something new; not stone and not flesh, an amalgamation of both that was hard but flexible. Finally, he added the spark that gave his creation sentience.

The statue moved. Dust and vegetation fell away as it took a quarter step backwards and returned to its immobile state. Concerningly, small cracks appeared around the joints. Although light-headed and numb in his arms, the frontiersman kept his contact as instructed. He knew that Render was using him for more than holding the statue upright. By the time Render released him from the duty he felt numb down to his thighs, and he rested before taking the venison home as some small reward.

Render spent the rest of the day with the statue, incanting and sometimes sitting silently in deliberation. He would have preferred to have used a human life, but the animal's spirit was at least fresh and vibrant.

Render knew himself to be exceptionally intelligent and solving this type of complex challenge was where he excelled. The wizard didn't raise a sweat as he drew on power from his inner well to define further, shape, and fuel his creation. An additional two days passed before he was satisfied that the transformation was cohesive and stable. With great satisfaction, Render declared the archetype statue ready for trial. At first, it moved awkwardly, with a grinding noise as it loosened up. Eventually, it eased into more fluid, human-like motions. Render set his frontiersman helper to giving the stone creature commands. He left him to practice and experiment.

There were hundreds of statues about the city, about a quarter of which had enough definition and were in good enough repair for his purpose. The figurines had many forms and sizes, but for now, he would stick to those with human characteristics. The successful prototype was no fluke – it was a culmination of many years of research and exhaustive experimentation. Render relished the challenge of further refining and improving his animation design and technique.

JAAL

At Ostoik, Jaal departed the Yanth ship and took residence at the *Spikes and Chains* brothel situated well away from the docks. Over the next week, the ship's captain and crew had orders to spread the word amongst the local community of the rising nation of Viletri. Knowing the greed of humans, Jaal was confident it would raise great interest and wanted to separate himself from the extra attention it would bring.

Instead, Jaal slunk about Ostoik and made acquaintances of people in the know; shopkeepers, innkeepers, minor officials, and he listened. In a tavern near the barracks, he heard rumour of new skirmishes to the south with Two-Face Orcs. By coincidence, as he left to explore the nearby streets, he spotted the heads of Orcs on poles outside the Guild of Ravens. Jaal was impressed with the intricate tattoo work on the Orcs faces, which were unmarked on the right side but heavily tattooed on the left. From the large jaws and wide necks, he surmised the Two-Face Orcs were massive brutes.

At a pawn shop close to the brothel, the shop keeper was a man that liked to talk and prided himself on being well informed. He had educated Jaal on the history and politics of Arenland – details of that nation and its three major cities, its ruling lords, and the dominion of the Overlord. Today, the shopkeeper leaned into Jaal so that their faces were almost touching. His eyes were gleeful as he divulged the latest rumour.

"I've 'eard, through a reliable source, of open rebellion!"

After a dramatic pause, the shopkeeper leaned back just a little so that he could read Jaal's expression. None-the-wiser, he continued.

"Seems like one of the border lords in the east has been conspirin'. Doesn't like the Overlord's new taxes or some such, can't say I blame 'im. He's rasin' his forces, what good it'll do 'im. Overlords got his army on the way to sort 'im out. Wouldn't want to be at the end of that man's temper, bloody ruthless he is, but you never 'eard me sayin' it."

Jaal nodded. It was likely good for Mannace that the Arenlanders had their own politics to deal with and might not notice his recruiting. Jaal had plenty at the brothel to keep him busy, so he thanked the shopkeeper, surreptitiously passing him a small coin, before bidding him farewell.

On his final morning in Ostoik, Jaal awoke to a rhythmic *gooong, gooong, gooong* that resonated across the city and reverberated throughout his body and mind. His head spun from the *nyxiom* he had inhaled that night. Holding his head between his legs, foetal like, Jaal inhaled deeply and let out a slow breath to welcome in the new day. The two whores that shared his bed had already left, replaced by a breakfast of fried sweetbreads. He nibbled while slowly getting dressed. As the final *gooong* sounded, he made his way out of the building, settling his account with the brothel keeper who wished him a "Righteous Blood Sabbath and safe journey".

Jaal barely took twenty steps towards the docks when a tall and powerfully built Dark Elf approached. The Elf, dressed in black fabrics elaborately embroidered at the collar and sleeves, wore dark metal armour over his abdomen and chest that was moulded to enhance a muscular frame. On his back was an impressive two-handed war hammer, often the weapon of choice for a follower of the God of War. With coal-black eyes and oily hair tied back to enhance the angular shaped face, the warrior radiated power, wealth, and confidence.

In a deep voice, he spoke to Jaal, "Come and pray with me on this holy day".

This was an obligation in Dark Elf society, and even in this city far from his homeland Jaal did not have the option to say no.

The Temple of the God of War was a magnificent building with black stone pillars and walls supporting a huge domed roof. The entrance and central area of worship were immense, and around the walls were reliefs depicting battle scenes and heroic encounters. Polished black stone floors with grey flecks reflected torch and sunlight. More than once, when Jaal looked down, he could see ghostly faces that stared back at him in the mirror-like surface as if he were staring through the ice at terrified souls trapped beneath. Jaal reached down to touch one that flinched before it faded. At the outer limits of his perception was the din of clashing swords and battle cries. The God of War knew how to make its presence felt.

Entering a smaller chamber, the Dark Elf that led him here sat down in one of five ornately carved chairs. Three humans and another Dark Elf occupied the other seats. The humans were dressed and equipped much like the Elf he followed. The second Dark Elf was a woman, adorned in an elegant black robe with elaborate embroidery along the arms and at the hem. She wore a simple gold chain about her neck with a golden hammer pendant dangling between her ample breasts. Her jet-black hair was oiled and tied back in the same fashion as the others. Jaal tried to ignore the fact that she was stunning, even by Elven standards.

"Thank you, Dekon," she nodded at the Elf who had brought him there.

The woman introduced herself as Ahmeda Ravenborn, High Priestess and servant to the God of War. Jaal recognised the name; surmising she was also the wife of the Lord Ravenborn of Ostoik.

Wasting no time, the High Priestess asked Jaal questions about his time in the region of the Blood Sea and from his life before that. Sometimes the others also queried him to elicit more detail. Jaal answered everything accurately and held nothing back.

"Show us this quickness that you have been practising". The High Priestess turned to one of the human warrior-priests and calmly commanded, "Rugar, kill him".

Rugar put his hand over his shoulder to pull the Warhammer from his back, then leaned forward to get out of the chair. Jaal, adrenaline urging his body into action, drew his blade from his belt and in a fluid motion stepped toward the warrior-priest, then drew on the energy he felt within, pushing himself forward with his mind. Things slowed about him as Jaal surged towards the priest. Before Rugar was on his feet, Jaal already held his blade to the man's neck, a trickle of blood where he overextended. There was a moment where the War Priests eyes narrowed, and he snorted as if he might explode with anger. Jaal kept his sword at the priest's chin, shaking a little with adrenaline and dread at what might happen if the priest's temper overshadowed his reason. The previously faint noise of battle was now clashing violently in his ears as if the war god himself were in the room, scrutinising him. Reluctantly, Rugar let his wrath subside, and in a gradual motion, he sat back down.

"Impressive," commented the High Priestess, "and not magical".

After some more questions, mostly focused on his ability, Jaal was permitted to leave.

Back on board the Yanth ship, Jaal learned that two ships, one with passengers and the other a trader, had already left with the intent of travelling to the city of Viletri. People sensed a great opportunity there, and the crew were confident that a migration of sorts had begun.

The next stop was a short journey by sea. Lapthos Island was a flourishing port and town, with a busy fishing, sealing, and whaling industry. As they moored their vessel and disembarked, the smell from whale pots was thick and sticky, the foul aroma attaching itself to everything it met. Many people were coming and going from boats and buildings, and guards armed with crossbows kept a lazy vigil from wooden watchtowers along the waterfront. The dock near the ship was a mess of blood and guts where two young whalers washed away the gore with buckets of salt water. Jaal had seen battlefields less grisly.

They intended only the one night at Lapthos, and it didn't take long to spread Mannace's invitation. In the morning before they departed, the local Lord, a man who introduced himself as Caldice, came to the ship with two young men in tow. Jaal and the Yanth Captain spoke with the Lord, who then turned to Jaal and made a request.

"These are two of my sons Tumas and Harvor; both can wield an axe and handle a bow. Tumas is also good with horses. You would have the friendship of the Lord of Lapthos if you were to take these boys to Viletri so that they might find their way in the world."

It wasn't part of Jaal's plan, but as an envoy for Mannace, he played his role. The boys met his gaze and seemed eager for him to agree. He liked their keenness.

"Get on board, wait for me on the foredeck." As they bustled past and onto the ship, to Caldice, he added, "I will ensure they find good employ."

After another day at sea, they docked at Rummond. Upon landing, Jaal instructed the captain to continue the excellent work and advised that he had other business to attend to that might take him as long as a week. Tumas and Harvor were likeable and handled themselves well. Both boys had rusty coloured hair, were big-boned, healthy, and cared for their weapons and equipment as if they were trained soldiers. They weren't overly smart, which Jaal liked, and they didn't hesitate to follow his orders. Before setting out for the monastery, Jaal hired four horses, one for himself, two for the brothers, plus a fourth as spare.

It was an uneventful journey. The monastery was as bleak and enigmatic as Jaal's last visit. Recognised by the guards, the Dark Elf was granted entry and to go freely about his business.

Jaal made his way directly to the room with the caged woman, his heart racing as he drew closer. On entering the chamber, the cage was still there, but empty, the door ajar. A familiar voice snuck up on him from behind.

"Hello Jaal," said Syprus, "Come this way," he beckoned.

Jaal's temper flared. The intense yearning that pulled him back to the monastery now raged within him and demanded to see his desires met. He knew that this place would try to control him, and the thought of that manipulation panicked all his senses.

The Dark Elf reached to draw his blade and end Syprus' life right there, but as he feared, a calmness overcame him and easily set aside his violent intent. Jaal despised the manipulation but could not fight it. Reluctantly, reason replaced anger, and he followed Syprus down another corridor into an adjacent room. Bound and laying on the floor was the object of his obsession.

"Pick her up but do not untie or ungag her", Syprus warned. Clothed in a simple robe, Jaal could feel the warmth of the woman radiating against him as he picked her up. His body screamed for him to rip off her bonds and take her there. Instead, he drew on the calmness injected into him and carried the seductress through the corridor towards the entrance. Syprus picked up a bag of belongings and followed. When they reached the front door, the guards were surprised, but they obeyed Syprus' command to let them depart. Once back with the two brothers, they mounted their horses, Jaal with the woman across his lap, as they rushed toward the forest.

"I do not expect pursuit," said Syprus.

Jaal shot him a displeased look, and he continued at a quick pace. After travelling a short distance into the woods, Jaal stopped and ordered the others to go ahead. Even Syprus obeyed.

Jaal lowered the woman to the ground. She stared up at him with rage in her eyes. Her gaze pierced him with its fierceness, but he had no fear of her. He removed the gag from her mouth. With a knife, Jaal cut away the bonds and lifted the robe above the woman's head and tossed it away.

Consumed by her nakedness, Jaal kicked aside his boots and pulled off his leather pants. Now she stood and leaned into him. The woman reached down with her hand, and he gasped as she took control of his spear. She guided it inside her, already moist and sweet. Jaal inhaled again before pushing forward with his loins and descending into the depths of oblivion.

Exhausted, Jaal stepped back. In their passion, he felt the woman feed off him, drawing away his life force and consuming his soul. It was raw and on edge. She could have ended him but hadn't, and he loved how that made him feel. He looked at the woman who stared back. He covered her with the cloak, and then dressed, before setting off with her settled on the horse behind him, to re-join his companions.

CASTEEL

Casteel enjoyed time on the water. Her body easily aligned itself with the rhythm of the boat and sea. Putting her mind at rest, Casteel used the days of travel to rejuvenate and reset, often sitting cross-legged on the fore-deck in a deep trance. With her mind focused, she imagined herself in a fighter's pose and practised her movements, over and over until they were fluid and graceful. She did so with different weapons or no weapons and in response to diverse conditions. It was an Elven technique called *The Spirit Warrior* taught to her by her parents who had shared the philosophy that "To equip the spirit is to furnish the warrior."

Already the ship travelled to Hindas and Karanthos, where the crew spread word of the opportunities at Viletri. As they approached Loryan, a war galley flying the cities colours intercepted them.

"Lord Horick of Loryan commands you to depart". A man on the warship shouted. "Loryan does not recognise the claim upon the territory once known as Viletri."

They had no choice but to turn tail and move on to their next destination.

On arriving at Yanth, a group of officials greeted them at the port. The Captain of the ship went off with a senior officer to give his report, while Casteel stayed the night at the government apartments. During the next day, she met with ministers and officials who asked many questions about Mannace and developments at the settlement of Viletri. At the end of the day, when Casteel left the buildings and returned to the ship, her hosts wished her good fortune. The boat was full of supplies and ready for travel, setting sail for the next port, home of Casteel's people, the Alani Elves.

Their passage followed a length of coast where snow-capped mountains dipped their time-worn toes in the sea, presenting a rocky and hostile shoreline. They passed rugged islands dotted along the coast, then cut inland down a fjord that opened into a broad and sheltered bay. On one side of the bay, a narrow waterfall cascaded down to the sea from a rift high on the mountain, while on the far shore the Elven trading port of Alani Renai Del was alive with trading ships and fishing boats returning with their early morning catch. Except for the spectacular location, Alani Renai Del was not unlike human towns, and indeed humans were living alongside the elves.

Casteel left the ship's crew the task of spreading the word of Viletri to the townsfolk and took her leave to head inland to the city of *Alani Ruhen Efaari*. The land was rugged, and the river valleys often flooded, not conducive to a permanent road between the Elven communities. Instead, most of the distance was best navigated employing small river craft, or by foot using mules to carry goods and baggage. Casteel enjoyed the glorious scenery of mountains, forest, and cascading waterways. As much as she enjoyed city life, the chill air and noises of the wilderness tugged at deeper roots. Her spirit already felt uplifted in just the half-day it took to arrive at her destination.

Alani Ruhen Efaari, nestled in a broad valley, began at the end of a small lake, and stretched through an area of forest, pushing up against the side of a soaring mountain. Along the mountain slopes, in the few areas where there was enough purchase, homes were constructed. They commanded a grand view over the forest, back past the lake and down to the distant sea. In Alani Ruhen Efaari the buildings integrated with the surroundings. Rather than the statues and monuments found in a typical human city, the Elven community was a celebration of places of natural beauty; a creek running into a pool, a boulder of an unusual natural shape, and the area of trees that would welcome the first rays of the morning sun. Everywhere the colours of nature were at their most radiant and songbirds, tame enough to land on a shoulder or eat seeds from a hand, completed an idyllic, intricately choreographed, setting.

It reminded Casteel how different Elven culture was from that of the human lands where she spent so much of her time. While it was satisfying to visit her homeland, Casteel found Alani society too rigid with its continual homage to ritual, tradition, and ceremony. By comparison, in cities like Yanth, or Antigoth in Arenland, every dawn cast a new light. In the shadows of that light, new adventures abounded.

Casteel went to the home of her family. It was near the foot of the mountain and constructed of rocks and earth, rustic in appearance from the outside but inside was luxurious and exquisitely furnished, reflective of wealth and rare artefacts collected over hundreds of years. Her brother Rynolf was there, although her parents were away travelling. Rynolf was a traveller too, and Casteel had not seen her sibling for almost a decade. They swapped stories, and over the night and next day reconnected with each other. Rynolf had been part of an expedition that set out from Arenland and adventured through the borderlands into the region known as the Madlands. He collected many trophies and treasures from his adventures to show her.

Knowing his sisters' interest in carvings, Rynolf kept aside a gift for her. He opened a leather pouch and let several small objects, wrapped in cloth, fall out onto a table. One was a tusk that he presumed was Orcish, carved to be four Orc warriors wrestling with a mighty serpent. Another was a bone pendant shaped in the likeness of a fish. The other four pieces were small ornaments made from a bluish stone, carved in the image of creatures from the sea. Casteel was amazed by the detail in the craftsmanship. She hugged her brother tightly.

"Thank you, Rynolf. Your light is blessed and eternal."

Rynolf felt a tear run down his handsome cheek. As they stood embracing, he felt the chill of his time away from the city of the Alani melt away with his sister's touch.

"I have missed you, sister. I am reminded of the warmth of home and family."

Casteel laughed. Everything about Elves was so formal and pretentious; where they lived, how they lived, how they spoke. Old habits quickly returned, which made her laugh again. She liked herself better when she was around humans.

"There is a reason why the Elves are never at home. This city is a pretty cage, brother, and we are best to be free of it."

The next night Casteel caught up with other relatives and friends, then the following morning she and Rynolf made their way back to the port. Rynolf had no better plans than to travel with his sister. She was elated to have his company.

The next stops, Cavastock and the Isle of Malanos, went to plan. They met with locals and spread the message of opportunity at Viletri. Both were big enough towns that there was immediate interest from the more adventurous. Casteel was surprised that some people knew about Viletri before their arrival. Gossip and rumour travelled by the fastest roads.

The final stop was Freman, the mercenary hub for the Blood Sea. When they arrived at its port, they stumbled upon disruption. In the business precinct of the city, some buildings were alight, and there was fighting in the streets. Freman gave amnesty to any criminal or brigand travelling there, so Casteel was not surprised.

Casteel, Rynolf, and two of the sailors were at a tavern on the dock when a large group of men armed with weapons already bloodied from recent fighting, burst through the main doors.

"Drinks," demanded the gang's leader and the staff behind the bar hastily responded. One of the men looked in their direction.

"Bloody Elves".

Like his comrades, the man wore white pants and shirt,

with a metal breastplate on his chest. His black hair was oily and fell around a bearded face. He swaggered over to Rynolf and unhesitatingly spat on the Elf's cheek. Rynolf ducked and spun so that his leg swept the man from his feet, and he landed heavily on his back. Rynolf's sword was out and at the man's throat before the oaf had time to rise. Blades slid from their scabbards as the other armed men surged towards the Elves. Both siblings responded by dodging quickly backwards, using benches and chairs to slow their assailants. Weapons out, they parried blows from the men that came directly at them, but they were aware of others starting to encircle them. The two Yanth sailors, like the other patrons, scampered for the exits.

Casteel transitioned to her *spirit warrior*, letting her inner self take command. Diving and rolling left she came up under the swing of a mace to take its wielder with a rapier thrust into his side. She arched her body to the right and took another man with a quick poke to the neck, then shifted her weight sideways and re-balanced to face off three advancing foes. Her lunge at one of the men was knocked aside by his blade, unbalancing Casteel enough that his comrades rushed forward to strike with axes and swords. Rather than defend, Casteel dived to the floor and rolled under a table, clambering quickly to her feet on the other side. She stood back-to-back with her brother, who traded thrusts and cuts with two men.

Rynolf instantly regretted putting them in such a desperate position; he too often reacted without thinking of the consequences. As he fended aside more thrusts, out of the corner of his eye, Rynolf could see one of the bar keepers raising a crossbow. Time slowed as he tilted his head to bellow a warning to Casteel, then he turned back.

With the moment bought, Casteel bent her head to respond to her brother. But before she could speak, Rynolf's head jerked backwards, a crossbow bolt protruding through his skull. Shot in the face, the Elf dropped lifeless to the floor. Casteel's mind imploded, her inner warrior shattered, failing to defend as a large man grabbed her from behind.

Too late she struggled to reach the blades strapped to her shins, and now three men held her down on a table. She took a punch to the side of her face, an elbow stealing the wind out of her chest. Casteel raged to free herself from their grasp, but the struggle was lost.

Casteel awoke, lying on a dirt floor in a room void of any light. Her body ached from abuse and having lain there for an unknown time. Hands and feet were shackled, with the chain passing through a metal ring on the wall. In the blackness, the panicked Elf soon learned the small confines of her cell and the discovery of a door, cold and metallic, with no gaps for fresh air. She was desperate to take a clean breath. Casteel kicked an object. Reaching down, she retrieved the thing and in the dark felt its shape. It was a severed head, and with the sudden realisation, she threw it aside and screamed. Curling up into a ball, Casteel howled for herself and her brother.

The image of Rynolf dying returned to her; the splatter of blood that must still be on her face, the horrendous moment that he collapsed lifeless. Casteel's mind spun from the raw guilt and grief that overwhelmed her. In a sudden panic, she used her tears to wipe the blood off her cheek, accidentally scratching her swollen eyelid with a broken fingernail. Blood seeped into the slit that was her battered eye. The humiliation, the cruelty she had suffered, the despair and terror she felt in this moment threatened to consume her entirely. But she was a warrior, from a lineage of immortal champions, and even within this darkness of suffocating emotions, she had the sense to know that grief was a terrible enemy, that others had faced this same adversity and they had not succumbed. After a time, Casteel sat upright, focusing on the memory of her mother's voice, always calm and controlled, forever pragmatic. Casteel pushed her mind into its inner world, to a place of safety, and she waited.

MORGAN CAIN

Morgan Cain and his ship, the Celestial, sailed past the City of Hindas and turned north along the Cape of Knives. He chose a route that followed the coast of the Great Continent. For the first two days, the coastline was rocky but with numerous bays and inlets. It became rougher as they navigated the western end of the Icesleepers, a towering mountain range of inhospitable peaks and long glacial valleys. The crew was awed when they passed a vast glacier that loomed above the sea. This frozen river groaned as great chunks of ice fell away to tumble and splash into the saltwater below. As always, Morgan had a story for his crew.

"Behold the great works of the True Dwarves."

His crew looked at Morgan for further explanation, grinning and always interested to hear what he had to say.

"The True Dwarves once commanded this region. Their priests, giants amongst the Dwarves, controlled great powers over the elements and it was they who created the glaciers to block the passes and protect their rich cities from the outside world. Likely their sentries are still watching over the passes and out to the ocean. Keep an eye, lads - a silver to the first who spots a Dwarf. A gold if it's a giant."

The crew suspected the story to be their captain's imagining, but many looked anyway, wanting the tale to be true.

It took a day and night to pass the Sleepers and return to a coastline again dotted with long bays and inlets. They passed fishing villages and towns, eventually coming to a larger settlement where they made port. Landsborough was not unlike the towns of the Blood Sea, and they were able to talk to people at the docks and in the taverns, first small talk, then discussing Viletri. There didn't seem to be much interest. When probing the reasons why, Morgan found that the people here were wholly ignorant of the Blood Sea and its civilisation. It was much like the people of the Blood Sea, who typically knew nothing of those outside their domain. Recruitment here was a waste of his time.

"Well lads, the beers good and the sausages will put hairs on your spear, but she's a dead gull for migrants. Might as well be preaching to the forsaken."

One sailor spat into his palm, rubbing his hands together. It was a ritual to keep the forsaken at bay. He glowered at his captain for invoking the attention of the Four Hells. Morgan and some others of his crew chuckled.

"It'll take more than hell-spawn to put this old dog in the briny. Last beers, lads."

Morgan altered course to head west to regions he was more familiar with, starting with *The Fogmir*. The Fogmir was an expansive rain forest that covered most of a small continent known merely as *The Land* to its inhabitants. He had visited several cities there in the past, making directly for Xetaphastol, which was five days by the sea and another half day up the mighty Achna River. The lower Achna was so broad in places that you could barely see the far bank.

For the second time on this voyage, the crew were awestruck with what they saw. Xetaphastol was a magnificent city and river port. What astonished the sailors was the massive stone construction at the city's centre. The lowest level was a large square block upon which there were layers, organised to appear as giant steps leading up to a four-sided tower, broad at the base and tapering to support a small platform at the top. If people on the platform called down to those below, they would not be heard at such a distance. The building had several portals around its base and on the different levels. The construction was not pretty, but its immense size was certainly impressive. There were other smaller towers about the place, carved with runes and tapering to platforms at the top. When explaining what they saw, Morgan entertained his crew with stories of sacrifices, curses, and treasures – all with some truth, but embellished to satisfy the imaginations of his entranced audience. Around the city a low wall was constructed, to define it and keep wild animals out, and beyond that was the dense tangle of rainforest that stretched away to the horizon.

While there were some humans, they could see most of the population were part man - part reptilian. The crocodile people, also known as the *Rhalec* as Morgan called them, were taller than the humans but moved about bent over so that their reptilian heads were well forward of their broad torso. They had long tails that they dragged along the ground, and stocky arms and legs. Amongst them were soldiers armed with spears and shields, and civilians going about a variety of trades and activities.

At the docks, Morgan successfully located a Rhalec he had previous dealings with, a city official named Toal who controlled trade in and out of Xetaphastol. Toal spoke a broken form of the common tongue, slurred through a jaw full of jagged teeth. It allowed Morgan to explain to him the purpose of his visit and the history behind it. Toal asked for a day to ponder, confining Morgan and his crew to the port area near their vessel. With interest, they watched the Rhalec going about their business and noted a steady stream of small galleys coming and going upriver, carrying passengers or goods. Other humans visiting or running businesses also stayed within the port area. The inner city was exclusively the crocodile people's domain. As always, Morgan expounded.

"The wealth of the Rhalec is legendary. Though no man has ever seen it, I have on good account that deep beneath the tower is an ancient cave, once home to dragons, lined with sapphires and a lake of molten gold. Don't think of sneaking past the Rhalec, boys; they'll rip your throat out, eat your liver, and use your skin to make treasure bags. But they're good people if you keep your place."

Toal returned to meet Morgan the following afternoon with welcome news. He suggested there was interest in trade, fortuitously with an offer of gems and gold in return for items of iron or steel, notably weapons. Morgan felt comfortable agreeing to both.

Attracting migrants was not an option as Xetaphastol tightly controlled its citizens and the roles they performed in the city or abroad. Instead, Toal committed to establishing an embassy at Viletri to facilitate further negotiations. Agreements were signed.

Morgan spent an extra day at the port, before setting course north along the eastern shoreline. Winds soon blew them away from the coast, cutting back towards land on the third day. As they came closer to the region known to Morgan as Tarash Gormoth, three ships shadowed them, before converging on the Celestial, forcing Morgan to slow and allow them to pull alongside. Marines aimed crossbows at his crew, while a commander from one of the ships shouted at them.

"Ship's captain, state your name, nation and purpose".

"Morgan Cain, Envoy of the City of Viletri. I am tasked by the Lord of the Viletri to seek opportunities for diplomacy and trade."

After a moment's pause, the commander called out.

"We will escort you to the port of Tarash. Stay aft of my vessel and six lengths back."

Morgan and his crew sailed the Celestial into line.

RISING NATION

Kakos Agamos, the official of Yanth, arrived at the City of Viletri to see first-hand what transpired there. It exceeded his expectations, which was rare. Yanth were already investing heavily in the area set aside as their enclave. It had a growing port facility and a developing merchant district. Four ships flying Yanth colours were in port and workers from the ships were repairing or constructing the harbour and buildings. Kakos congratulated the Chief Architect and Quartermaster for doing so well in such a short amount of time.

As instructed, the Yanth contingent picked out a suitable abode for Kakos that was under restoration. He was again pleased. Of the grand houses in the noble's district, it was the one he would have chosen as it had views of both the main city thoroughfare as well as out to sea.

Mannace welcomed Kakos, making time to walk through the city as they talked.

"Thank you, Kakos, for being true to your word in delivering assistance. Thank you also for the investment Yanth is making in its enclave, it will be of mutual benefit."

As they meandered through the streets, Kakos observed the bustle of a community coming to life. Hundreds of people arrived to lay their claim to homes and businesses. Mannace could see that the official was impressed.

"People are drawn to the opportunity here. The rate of immigration increases each day."

"Lord Mannace," Kakos began, "Within the City-State of Yanth I am a senior official in a sea of bureaucrats. What you are doing here excites me. I have been with you on this journey not only as Yanth's ambassador, but to cheer you on. I admire your boldness and ambition. I ask, humbly, that you allow me to assist you in rebuilding this city and nation."

Mannace was immediately interested.

"What of your allegiance to Yanth?" he inquired.

"I am born of the Isle of Malanos and while I am a loyal servant to Yanth today, once retired from my position as an official of the City-State, I am a free man and can put my loyalty where I please. It would satisfy me greatly to place that allegiance here with the City of Viletri and with you. What greater challenge and reward could there be than to take a small beginning such as this and help to nurture it to greatness."

"I need assistance, Kakos. As people come to the city, the demands on my time are too much. Questions of water supply. Of sewage. Of law. Of trade. Your countryman named Mickell is efficient in allocating dwellings to new arrivals, but I know his own pockets are bulging. Twice, the Lord of Hindas has demanded a meeting. I am no fool, Kakos, but I am not expert at politics or running a city. I have no desire to be. Kakos, can you manage these things?"

"I can, Lord Mannace.".

"Then do so as soon as you are able. You will have my full support and authority."

Soon after, Jaal returned from his travels aboard the Yanth ship. Tumas and Harvor found a residence that suited them in the city. Settled in, they remained in the employ of Jaal who needed their help to keep the demon-woman under watch. It seemed a flawed plan, to say the least, given her mysterious allure, but thus far, she had not attempted to seduce the young men.

Jaal delivered Syprus to Mannace, who set aside the afternoon to talk to the Viletri immortal.

As the two kin walked about the ruins, Syprus spoke about the Viletri city of his childhood and middle years. It seemed to Mannace that it was of a different age before the other nations settled on the Blood Sea. In his middle years, Syprus found the Oracle, who he described as a place and power. He gave his service to the Oracle and Order of The Light. The Order built, and has existed at, the monastery for more than twelve hundred years. Syprus never revisited the city of Viletri during that time. Mannace was smiling.

"I will be honest with you Syprus, I was expecting the Viletri people to be larger, like myself; tall and powerful. It was something of a disappointment to find they differ little from mortal men."

The older Viletri seemed unimpressed by the observation, not sharing his kinsman's good humour.

"To the contrary, Mannace, the differences run deep. The Viletri are giants – look more closely, not just through your eyes but use your heart as a lens, and you will know the truth of it."

Mannace had no desire to be philosophical and changed the topic.

"Why have you left the monastery now?"

"To do this."

Syprus reached into his robe and pulled forth an egg-shaped device that he activated by passing a hand over a row of runes inscribed on the side of the contraption. Mannace felt sudden darkness fall over him. The world went black.

Part Two:

The Making of a Nation

MISSING FRIENDS

When it became evident that Mannace and Syprus were missing, Jaal and Render took charge of the search. The port and city entrance were locked down, while the garrison had orders to search every building in Viletri. A message was sent to Sylos to ask Lord Bisan to be watchful.

Render tried to discern if magic was at play, but he uncovered nothing. Although he didn't possess any enchantment for finding where Mannace might be, he had a sense that their friend hadn't passed into the realm of the dead. Jaal trusted his intuition that Syprus was more than he had claimed and suspected the Oracle might also have a hand in the event. He was not fearful that Mannace was lost to them, though he would not rest until this mystery was laid bare.

A day after Mannace and Syprus disappeared, the Yanth vessel returned from its voyage with news that Casteel was captured or possibly dead. Jaal was incensed. He put aside the search for Mannace to summon and interrogate the Yanth crew. He met them in the city, at a courtyard near the docks. Two of the crewmen described the fight where Freman White Shirts killed Casteel's brother and captured Casteel. Jaal could see that the sailors were nervous, and he found it hard to comprehend that they had left Casteel behind.

"Each day Casteel spends in Freman, know that you had a part in that fate. If she is dead, I will hold you to account."

He wrapped a hand around the hilt of his blade to be clear what he meant by that remark. The chill tone in his voice reinforced his disgust.

"Better you were dead at her side than to have lived with such shame. You should pray for death over the darkness I will bring upon you. Be away!"

The horrified sailors scrambled to be distant from the Dark Elf. Jaal moved to watch them scuttling down the street towards their ship. As marked men, they could have no doubt he would execute his threat. His justice would be implacable.

Jaal was resolved to rescue or avenge Casteel. It knotted his insides to consider the Elf's likely fate. Fuming to his core, these ignorant White Shirts unwittingly invited his wrath.

Jaal conferred with Render, agreeing that the wizard would continue the search for Mannace while Jaal journeyed to Freman to find Casteel. It took several hours to re-supply the Yanth vessel and assign a fresh crew. Jaal spent that time in the embrace of the demon-woman. His consuming lust and longing for her had not lessened; however, his compelling sense of duty to Casteel was such that he forced himself from the bed chamber and made his way to the Yanth quarter. He did not tell her his purpose, anxious to avoid her jealous rage. With final preparations made, Jaal boarded the ship and set sail once again across the Blood Sea.

In the days that followed, the search of Viletri for Mannace proved futile. Render's powers provided no clues, and the wizard was at a loss of how to further the search for his friend. Rather than dwell on his frustration, Render checked on Tumas and Harvor as Jaal had asked him. The young men were nervous about overseeing the seductress for what might be an extended period and it seemed to them that things were quickly turning bad in Jaal's absence. The woman hissed at Render when he approached her.

What challenge have you left me here, he mused? Indeed, a pretty one.

In the absence of Mannace, Kakos Agamos continued to administer the city. He worked with Mickell to raise funds from new immigrants, putting in place a small tax on businesses and trade. With the funds raised, Kakos employed some of the new arrivals to help restore the city's infrastructure and to put in place essential governance and law-keeping.

To help with the city's defences, Yanth and Sylos' soldiers patrolled the region. Render animated sixty statues that remained in place about the city in dormant states until they were needed. One unusually large figure of the Sea God, Ramthos, now stood at the main city gate. Experimentation proved the statues to make formidable defenders and Render continued to work with the frontiersmen on the guardians' refinement, development, and training.

A week after Mannace's disappearance, the search for him ended and work continued to rebuild Viletri while awaiting his return. The restoration lacked the same energy without Mannace to spur the populace, even with Kakos fervently organising and encouraging their efforts. Doubt and fear crept out of the city's dark crevices and were gnawing away at the foundations Mannace so carefully constructed.

THE RESCUE

After departing Viletri, Jaal travelled first to Yanth. He wasted no time, heading straight to those taverns where he knew he would find mercenaries. With several already in tow, he entered a bar and recognised a familiar face. Drinking with a group of locals was the large man that Casteel had tumbled with on their previous visit. Although he was reluctant to leave the company of his mates, Jaal coaxed him aside and shared the details of his mission.

The big man had a long frown upon his brow while he listened and steel in his eyes as he responded. "I am Khing. I will join you in this."

Khing was well known in the city and helped Jaal to collect more than thirty reliable sell-swords ready to sail on the afternoon tide. Jaal left the Yanth ship behind, not trusting their mettle or motivation for the job ahead. Instead, he hired the services of a large troop carrier, captained by a swarthy man named Urgar the Gull. Urgar was larger than life, always smiling and laughing. He seemed a popular leader with the definite look of a veteran, a missing ear, broken teeth, and old scars on his arms. His remaining ear had a large gold earring. With the mercenaries on board, Urgar waved to the first mate.

"Hymar, let her loose. To the sea, my fine flock, to the bloody blood sea."

The troopship had an enormous wheel on its side that dipped lightly into the water. As the ship moved away from the dock the narrow wheel turned, which, through a set of complex axels and turn-stations, drove a wooden bladed fan suspended behind the stern of the ship, pushing the vessel along at a quick clip. It was the genius of Fergis, a rotund Dwarf who looked more pirate than engineer – his bronzed torso covered only in the braids of a black beard, a tattoo of an octopus on his back, and gold chains that hung loosely about his thick neck. Fergis' inventions could be seen elsewhere about the ship; metal levers and winches to hoist the sails, cogs and brakes to help turn or hold the helm in place.

Standing at the prow as the ship passed through the wide sea gate, Jaal watched the soldiers patrolling the harbour defences. The men stared back, curious about the ship's odd propulsion, laughing amongst themselves.

Two days later when Jaal landed at the Freman port, he wasted no time in recruiting more fighters to aid him against the White Shirts. There were three mercenary guilds based in the Freman harbour district and its many taverns. Khing and Urgar, using gems given them by Jaal, secured the services of an additional fifty fighters. They also gained the attention of White Shirts who confronted them at the docks.

The White Shirts were a ragtag bunch much like the mercenaries, and although this group numbered only fourteen, their authority as the garrison and constabulary of Freman emboldened them.

"What are you boys about aye? And what's with the Darkie? - should be havin' a collar on that one. Let's be knowing ya business now. Out with it."

The speaker looked past Jaal, eyeing the mercenaries. One of the other White Shirts standing further back sniggered.

"A bloody Darkie. Fricking cheek that."

Jaal's fury had been simmering since he departed Viletri. With incredible speed, he drew his blade and stabbed the first speaker in the throat. Pushing the sword to the hilt, he twisted it so that blood splattered on the men behind. He could taste the blood on his lips. With superior numbers, it was a brief skirmish before eleven of the White Shirts lay dead, and three were pinned on the ground. Jaal stood over one of the prisoners.

"You are holding a female Elf prisoner, where is she".

"Junis will rip your fricking balls off".

Jaal pierced the man's hand with his blade, pinning it to the dock and with his boot, he kicked down hard, repeatedly, and cruelly, first winding, then crippling his victim.

"Wrong answer."

The mercenaries holding the White Shirt let go and Khing picked the man up by the neck with one hand and tossed him screaming off the dock into the harbour. Anguished cries abruptly ended with gurgling emerging from the brine.

Jaal repeated his question to the second man, who didn't respond, and as Jaal threateningly leaned over him, the other cried out.

"In the third barracks!"

Jaal let the tip of his blade rest on the speaker's shoulder, leaning down to look him in the eye. The talker was petrified, blurting out the response Jaal was seeking.

"In the cells of the third barracks. In the bloody basement."

Jaal killed the second man for his silence, while Urgar pulled the other to his feet. The mercenaries already knew how to find the third barracks, but they pushed the White Shirt along with them for now, in case further information was needed. The terrified man stank of fear and piss.

People around the dock were watching. To prevent his plan from unravelling further, Jaal ordered the mercenaries quickly into three groups, setting off at a jog to the city proper. As they moved through the streets, they twice encountered small groups of White Shirts that they dealt with mercilessly before continuing. Close to the fortress, Jaal saw ahead of them another band who were alerted to their plans. The bewildered White Shirts were backing away from the mercenaries and one of their number, smarter than his comrades, set off at a run to warn others. Jaal used his speed to outpace the messenger and impaled him from behind with a quick thrust of his blade. When he looked back, the mercenaries had dealt efficiently with the remainder. Some civilians were scurrying away or finding places of refuge, while others, used to violence in their streets, kept about their business and looked on with curiosity.

The mercenaries quickened their pace towards the barracks to a run.

By all accounts, there were more than four hundred White Shirts in the city. Many would be at the barracks or in the adjoining fortress. Jaal's plan was one of ambush; to cause panic and buy enough time to effect a rescue. The barracks were in a large compound with a high wall. Jaal knew that the gate was guarded but left open during the day. Their plan relied on surprise and Jaal was relieved to see the gate wide open as they approached. The first group of mercenaries ran through the entrance before the White Shirts could react. Urgar led them to keep the portal open at all costs.

Jaal's troop entered next. They headed for Barracks Three. Khing led the remaining mercenaries to assault the other buildings, confuse the garrison, and keep the courtyard secure.

Jaal and several mercenaries bashed in the barracks door and quickly killed two men who rushed to prevent them from entering. There were other entrances to the building, allowing more mercenaries in Jaal's band to force their way inside. Leaving them behind, Jaal sped through the common areas killing White Shirts and any other person that he encountered who was not his ally. The Dark Elf had a guiding philosophy that shielded him from any remorse; 'The friend of your enemy is also your enemy'.

Descending stairs that led to the basement level, Jaal discovered six dark cells that stank of faeces and decay. Frustratingly they were all unoccupied and with no time to spare Jaal exited the building, looking about desperately. Fighting was happening all around, and he could see mounting casualties on both sides.

Jaal charged at a group of White Shirts who joined the

battle in the courtyard. As they readied themselves against his attack, he surged forward, killing two before moving past them and pushing three more backwards. They tumbled to the ground, and Jaal stabbed one man in the abdomen. Mercilessly, he slashed at the other two as they started to rise and was assisted by a mercenary who cleaved the arm off one with a two-handed axe. Between them, they finished the job.

There was a shout from behind. Khing was carrying somebody over his shoulder that from her build and dark hair, Jaal assumed must be Casteel. The big man was giving the call to exit the fight, and the mercenaries near him began to run back the way they had come. Jaal remained to assist those caught in the melee, and it was not long before all surviving mercenaries were in full retreat. Behind them, more garrison troops were appearing on the walls, shouting and some firing bows. Other White Shirts formed into bands to give pursuit.

As they arrived at the dock, the exhausted mercenaries hurriedly boarded Urgar's transport ship, making haste for the open sea. Despite the mercenaries' losses, they were in high spirits. One of them put his arms around his mates and slapped them on the backs.

"Showed them arselickers a lesson, boys".

"Shit's gonna fly when they figure out what happened," said a man next to him. "Junis'll want fricking blood. Wouldn't wanna be the Masters having to explain why there's merc's killin' off his precious bully-boys."

They all laughed. Some of it was nervous laughter, knowing that the consequence might be blacklisting or even a knife in the night. Mercenaries attacking Whiteshirts went against decades of staying out of each other's business. They would need to watch their backs in the months to come.

Another mercenary further away joined the conversation, "Don't worry us; we'll be neck-deep in grog-n-pussy for the next two years with this payout, you better be good for it

Elfy."

Jaal nodded at them reassuringly. Later at Yanth, he paid the remainder of what he owed to the band.

Jaal was eager to keep some of the mercenaries in his service. To Khing and twelve others that he considered the best of the fighters he offered continued employment. His terms were reasonable, earning their trust. All but one of the mercenaries accepted. Urgar also approached Jaal.

"I know what ye be doin' and don't think you'll be leavin' me here at Yanth with the leftovers. If you dig a little deeper in those pockets, you'll have the best ship and crew on the Blood Sea."

Not sure that Jaal was convinced, Urgar changed tact.

"Think of the fun we'll 'ave. You, me, an' the big guy … I know this brothel in Cavastok, it's not much to look at on the outside …"

Jaal interrupted Urgar by putting a hand on his mouth. It was hard sometimes to shut him up.

"For Hells mercy, Urgar, we depart on the next tide. Don't make me leave you here just to have some peace."

The Sea Captain grinned and was silent. In place of words, he gave a mock salute.

In the days of sea travel between Yanth and Viletri, Casteel, a shell of her former self, regained a small fraction of her stamina and confidence each day. She came to Jaal when he was alone, sitting next to him in silence for a long while. In due course, Casteel spoke. It was soft and with genuine sentiment.

"Thank you, Jaal."

"You're welcome, Casteel."

THE VISIT

Render spent more and more time with the demon-woman. Her spark and energy drew him to her, more than just her powerful seductive lure. She also seemed to have an interest in him, not entirely predatory, but possibly because of his magic. He decided to explain the principles of spellcraft to her and see where that led. In their second session, he expounded.

"You cannot create something out of nothing. To create fire, you first must have heat, to create sentience you must have life, to create rain you need water."

Render checked that his student was paying attention before he continued. She seemed genuinely attentive.

"Fire, life, water, these are all things to dissect into their raw elements, their elemental particles, and reconstruct again in the way that you need them. The first step in magic is to see things as they are, the base components.".

Render reached for a nearby candle. It spluttered when moved.

"Look at this small flame. What is fire? It is light and heat, a transfer of energy from the wax to the flame, a wisp of smoke, a scent, a crackle."

He purposefully tilted the candle so that the hot wax spilt onto the floor and not onto his hand.

"In time, a person with the right abilities can look past these things to the particles, the codes, the essence that is the foundation of everything.".

Unexpectedly the candle flame burst to life, a small fireball that dissipated instantly but not before singeing the magician's eyebrows and fringe.

"Bloody hells!"

Render looked at the woman who stared back insolently.

"I expect an affinity for fire perhaps," he joked. More seriously, he added, "We need to find you a name".

"Saska".

Again, she looked him in the eye. He was surprised, but not as shocked as when her hand slid along his inner thigh and cupped his manhood. Her fingers massaged him. Keeping her hold firm, she stepped closer to the magician, slipping her other hand under his shirt to caress his abdomen and chest. Her eyes were intense as she met his gaze. His mind surrendered; thoughts of consequences evaporated.

"Light save me," he whispered.

Jaal, Casteel, and their entourage returned to the City of Viletri several days later. Jaal talked first with Kakos to arrange port facilities and housing for his followers, including Casteel who only felt safe in the company of the mercenaries. Their base was a sanctuary within the city that could accommodate two ships and several hundred men. Jaal tasked Khing and Urgar to keep an eye out for other sell-swords that might join them, but only those that they considered worthy and dependable.

Render briefed Jaal on the search for Mannace. Jaal was incensed that Render and others had wasted so much time. He brought Syprus to Viletri against his better judgement. Then the Oracle's agent used him, abducting Mannace for what purpose no one knew. The bubbling antagonism Jaal felt towards the Oracle was boiling over to be much darker feelings; shame at being duped by Syprus, and bitter anger at the arrogance of the Oracle in treating Jaal and his friends as if they were puppets in a show.

Jaal had planned to set aside the day to be with the demon-woman, but now his sexual desires were muted by other emotions. Striding to his residence, Jaal relieved Tumas and Harvor of their vigil over the seductress. The two young men were clearly under the woman's spell, and he needed to be firm with them to make them leave. It was just another thing to infuriate him.

"I, Saska," shared the woman as Jaal entered the bed-chamber. She let her robe fall to the ground and stood naked before him, enticing him with seductive movements. Jaal was abrupt.

"Put your clothes back on. I have business to attend to."

Saska's eyes flared with rage and Jaal could feel the air turn to ice. An unseen grip tightened around his heart, jolting him back to his senses.

"You will travel with me," his words were a reflex. "We will show the Oracle and its agents that we are not its playthings."

While the chill remained, the grip lessened. Saska walked over to a set of drawers and selected a full-length coat which she pulled around herself, leaving it unbuttoned invitingly at the front. She exaggerated the movement of her hips as she crossed the room to the door, then in the doorway, she leaned back against the frame, placing her arms behind so that they caressed the walls. The coat fell open to reveal her naked front. Jaal was mesmerised. Seeing that she had his full attention now, Saska raised her leg and set her foot against the opposite frame to bar Jaal's exit and further accentuate her exquisite shape. With one hand, she began to massage between her legs, lifting a finger to rest on her top lip, to take in the sweet taste and aroma of her juices.

"Mannace can bloody wait," Jaal whispered, his spear erect, and impulse taking precedence over neglected plans.

It was late in the day when Jaal and Saska made their way to the dock where Jaal met with Urgar and Khing again.

"Change of plans, Urgar we leave now, gather the men, set course for Ostoik. Tell Fergis to give it the four hells, let's see how fast this old bucket can go. Khing you stay here with Casteel and recruit like we discussed.".

He turned to Casteel who had joined them, "Bring Tumas and Harvor down here and get those boys in line.".

Soon after Jaal departed, there was an unexpected visitor. Kakos hurried to the port to welcome Akanidis, The Lord of Hindas, to the city of Viletri. His many rivals referred to Akanidis as 'The Tyrant of Hindas' or 'The Sea Snake'. He came without prior notice, with an escort of five large war galleys and his bodyguard of one hundred and twenty elite Hoplites who assembled after they disembarked from the ships.

Kakos made his own home available for Akanidis' stay and the Lord set up residence there, with forty of his guards stationed at the property. Kakos arranged for the statue of Ramthos to stand on the street, facing the front of his home. It was a display of strength but under the guise of the 'Visiting Lord's protection'.

The Lord of Hindas had his advisors, a warrior, and a magician present that evening when Kakos met with Akanidis at his home. Kakos calmly began.

"My apologies that Lord Mannace cannot attend. He has pressing matters away from the city."

Kakos suspected that Mannace's disappearance was known to Akanidis, and he enjoyed the fact that the conversation was already skirting around the events. The game was afoot. Nobody in the room was giving anything away with their expressions.

"I am empowered by Lord Mannace to represent the City of Viletri in all matters."

"This is a Lordly matter. If I required paper pushed and arses kissed, I would address you directly. Bring Lord Mannace to me now."

Akanidis was insistent. The visiting Lord locked his gaze with Kakos - as if by the force of his will Kakos would reveal either Mannace or more of the truth. When Kakos shrugged, the Lord's agitation peaked.

"I do not appreciate the propaganda targeted at my civilians by your spies. I have dealt with the traitors."

The Lord of Hindas was aggressive and accusing. Kakos became nervous, questioning his wisdom in coming to the meeting alone. As his mind raced, Kakos was unsure if he should challenge Akanidas on the term *spies*, for what Mannace would term *recruiters*. He knew that there was no chance of reasoning with bullies.

"I understand, Lord Akanidis."

"Do you? DO YOU! Is it right to steal from a neighbour, to undermine his rule?"

"It is not. How can Viletri and Hindas be friends, Lord Akanidis?"

The Lord laughed, his tone even more menacing. Kakos' nervousness became fear, a terrifying realisation that this was not a debate, but a reckoning. He cowered as Akanidas loomed over him.

"The Viletri are GONE. What you have here is a rag-tag of exiles and misfits. Without my help you will not survive. The might of the North will come, and this pitiful city will become rubble again. We will not be friends; Viletri will be my vassal."

Akanidis stood just inches in front of Kakos. Anger had distorted his face so that he spat through gritted teeth.

"I do not need stinking bureaucrats to talk to me of matters of state!"

Soon after, Render was resting in his lounge chair, a book opened but ignored on his lap, when two of the magical alarms in his house were triggered. It was a silent warning to him only of intruders, and enough for him to stop what he was doing and shift silently into *Nearspace* just in time. His study door opened and Hoplites with short swords in hand rushed in. They searched about then left.

Render had no inkling of why his home might be under assault. There were men all about his house. At the front entrance there was a Hindasian in robes, incanting and seeking him out. Render scoffed mockingly and passed before the wizard unseen. "What the Hells' going on?" he asked himself.

A PATH OF DARKNESS

Jaal spent much of his life in the company of humans, and for the most part, avoided his Dark Elf kin. Now he entered the Temple of War at Ostoik seeking them out. Ahmeda Ravenborn, the Dark Elf priestess, granted him an immediate audience and they met in her private chamber. He explained what had transpired and what Render had shared with him regarding Syprus, the device, and Mannace's disappearance. The Priestess could see the fury in Jaal; his passion and darkness were palpable. The War God was of the Darkness. The Oracle and the agents of the Oracle were of the Light. "Why do you seek me?" she asked.

"I would be the player, not the pawn," he answered.

As she came closer to him, Jaal became acutely aware that she looked and smelled remarkable. The priestess whispered in his ear and her voice, though soft and caressing, carried great power, "Awaken."

When Jaal returned to the ship, there were two other Dark Elves with him. One was the War Priest, Dekon Ruel, whom he had met during his previous visit to Ostoik. The other was Singer, a particularly lean Dark Elf. Singer was dressed in dark colours and carried an ornate bone bow with several quivers of arrows. Sheathed on his back were two curved swords. This dour Elf wore a hooded cloak and leather mask over his lower face. Deckon divulged to Jaal that Singer was mute, and as they walked, Jaal noticed the Elf also had an occasional limp. It reminded Jaal of a human term he had heard; Singer was every bit the 'thrice tortured soul'.

As soon as they boarded the Yanth ship, there was immediate tension between the newcomers and those already on board. By exception, Saska seemed at home with the new arrivals, and they enamoured with her.

At a cove several hours north of the Monastery, Urgar was surprised that only Jaal, the Dark Elves and Saska were disembarking. He hadn't talked with Jaal about the mission, but he guessed their intent.

"Jaal, surely the merc's 'll be of help? The Monastery will be rich, 'nough treasures for us all."

"Urgar, there are greater powers at play. At Ostoik, I made a pact with the Darkness so that I may be invisible to the Light. We four, the Elves of the Dark and Saska who is darkness born, are beyond the light and outside the Oracle's vision."

Urgar could smell shit when it was thrust under his nose no matter how it was perfumed. He remained unimpressed. Usually respectful of his employer, his greed encouraged him to push harder.

"Priests and monks. It's taking sweets off babies. A captain and his crew might retire from a purse like this. Jaal, you can't deny us this bounty."

The crew became unsettled, and through Urgar's persistence, they too were looking at Jaal as if he denied them a great reward. Jaal was losing patience.

"Urgar, this is not the time. You, the crew, and the mercenaries will remain on the ship. I have selected those I require. That is how it will be." To lighten the mood, he added, "What would you do if you retired – grow fat and ugly and bored. You have all the silver you need, enough to buy beer for your belly and a warm purse for your spear."

A few of the sailors chuckled, but others remained restless. Jaal turned away from them as he disembarked to a rowboat. The first rays of dawns light were dancing across the ocean behind the ship, lighting the rocks and steep slope they would need to ascend to escape the cove.

The Dark Elves and Saska stood before the monastery

Entrance. It was a chilly day made colder by the light breeze coming off the sea. Jaal preferred the cold to the heat; he felt alive and primed for what lay ahead. While incanting, Dekon raised his mighty hammer and with both hands, swung it hard at the portal. Jaal could see an energy building around the warrior and his weapon, a physical force that had a hint of swirling forms and spectral faces. There was that distant noise of battle at the edge of his hearing, like the temple in Ostoik. With a thunderous crash, the door blew inwards, breaking and splintering as it smashed against the far wall of the vestibule. Two guards appeared with spears levelled at the War Priest, but they fell quickly to Singer's well-placed arrows. The three Dark Elves moved swiftly through to the Red Room then down separate corridors. Saska followed and took the same passage as Dekon. Somewhere in the monastery, the ringing of bells sounded.

Jaal started with the areas he was familiar with, which led him into the visitor chambers and shared rooms. A man and a woman came out of a chamber into the corridor ahead of him. He accelerated and in a swift cut beheaded the man, then a moment later dealt the same fate to the woman. He liked to kill, the ritual in Ostoik had reminded him of that. Others now appeared, and he efficiently dispatched them too. The guards, attracted by the screams, were mediocre fighters and provided little opposition to Jaal's onslaught. His dazzling speed was hardly needed. At first, the massacre was easy because people were coming to him, but as the inhabitants of the Monastery became aware of the Elves bloody rampage, they scrambled to hide or barred their doors.

Then, as Jaal looked up from the carnage, Syprus stood staring back at him from the end of a corridor. Jaal moved with all the speed he could muster, but the older man eluded him and was now at the end of the next hallway. Jaal could not tell what magic or trickery Syprus was using to evade him. Whatever the means, Jaal's speed was not enough to close the distance. Again, the older man escaped down a different passage. Jaal continued the chase through chambers and corridors and down stairs until he came to a room where both Syprus and Mannace stood.

Mannace did not look like a prisoner, he had no chains or bonds, but Jaal had witnessed the older man's powers to subdue the spirit and dampen the mind. Jaal saw things as they were; he watched Mannace being drawn up like a puppet, standing and waving his arms at Jaal as Syprus pulled his strings.

"Jaal," Syprus started in a soothing tone. "Let me explain. I am your ally. I brought Lord Mannace here to protect him. I had seen through the Oracle the killing of Lord Mannace by the Hoplites of Hindas. He will return when the danger has passed.".

"Jaal," Mannace stated firmly. "Syprus shares our vision for the restoration of the Viletri he has..."

Mannace stopped his sentence short. Jaal moved with incredible speed across the room, and now his blade passed through Syprus' jaw, the tip breaking through the top of the older man's skull. Jaal turned to Mannace. There was a madness in his eyes that Mannace had not witnessed before.

"We are not toys to be played with. We will live and die on our terms.".

Jaal pulled back his sword and let Syprus' body slump to the ground.

"Let's go."

Initially, Mannace was dumbfounded; he considered Syprus a vital supporter and was shocked at his demise. But with Syprus slain, he could also feel the calming influence of the older man leave him and his steely resolve return. It felt almost as if he were awakening.

"Wait!"

Mannace moved down a corridor and took a door to an adjoining room. Jaal followed, finding Mannace collecting odd-looking devices and dropping them into a sack he pilfered from a basket in the corner. As they left the monastery, Mannace was shocked by the carnage they passed, but he said nothing. Over the years the companions learned to respect each other's choices, and they all had their moments in the shadow - this, however, was extreme and Mannace feared that Jaal was stepping too far into oblivion. He looked over at his friend hoping to see at least a speck of light, but what he perceived was the cool detachment of somebody determined to get a job done. At the building entrance, Jaal and Mannace waited anxiously for an hour until the other Dark Elves reappeared. Saska was the last to emerge. Seeing the group gathered did nothing to alleviate Mannace's concerns about his friend.

By mid-afternoon, they returned to the ship and a new course set. But first, they moved along the coast to observe the Monastery. On the seaward side, there were narrow windows through which smoke poured and rose skyward. Jaal was pleased. He did not know what magical fire might set ablaze a bastion of stone, though it satisfied him that the inferno would complete the job he had started. The crew and mercenaries seemed less impressed. They lingered for a while to watch the Monastery burn before Urgar steered the vessel away from the coast.

It was not the outcome Mannace wanted. As he watched Saska and Jaal, he could see her influence over him, the shameless manipulation of his friend. It was evident in the blatant way she fawned over him, making herself the centre of his attention. In his minds-eye, Mannace could see where this day had its origins. Darkness and light lived in balance. Today was a black day.

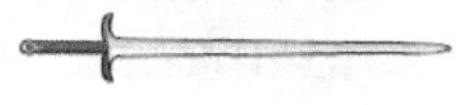

A RECKONING

The city of Viletri continued to grow, and it was hard to tell that it had been a ruin. Akanidis invested heavily in the restoration of the fortifications, with hundreds of labourers and artisans from Hindas in the city to execute his orders. The garrison increased to six hundred Hindasian warriors, plus eight war galleys docked in port. Akanidis ran the town like it was an extension of his military. During the day all children not at work attended a military school that he commissioned, and after dark, there was nobody on the streets except for the occasional patrol. As an exception, Render walked the streets unseen. That night, he visited Casteel and Khing. During the four months since Akanidis asserted control over the city, they moved to the Yanth enclave where they were safe for now. Akanidis was not so bold as to move against a major City-States enclave, and while their interests in the city were maintained, the Yanth forces would not escalate a conflict with Akanidis.

As Render, Casteel, and Khing talked, Kakos shambled into the room. After Akanidis killed Kakos, he had him strung up outside his compound as a blunt message to those who might question his authority. Several days later, when things settled down, Render retrieved the body and with his skills in necromancy brought the man back from the dead. It was still a work in progress. Kakos, forever pragmatic, was adjusting to his zombie form and he could move and talk, although both took more time and effort than he would like.

Render once served his apprenticeship under a Sorcerer named Zungrael who was a savant in *Undeath*. Render knew from helping his master that pulling a soul back from the recently dead was not demanding for an experienced necromancer. The trick was not pulling back something extra from the netherworld – something angry and vengeful. Animation of the body, restoration of the mind, preventing further decay, these were things he had helped his former master with many times over.

They were again discussing their options for opposing Akanidis. Casteel used the mercenaries for surveillance of the city.

"The statues are still in place, except for the statue of Ramthos."

When Khing raised an eyebrow, Casteel explained, "Akanidis had it dismantled. His wizard assisted the labourers."

Khing raised his other eyebrow which prompted Casteel to expound further, "I don't know why the other statues are untouched. Akanidis is smart enough to know they exist."

Render did not like the idea of another wizard tampering with his creations.

"The frontiersmen are fiercely loyal to Mannace. They will invoke the statues on my instruction."

All knew that it was a moot point without Mannace to lead them.

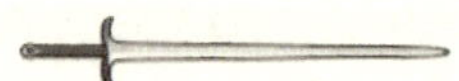

Unknown to the conspirators, Mannace sat on a rocky outcrop on a hill that overlooked a bay east of the city. It was a long inlet with a yellow sand beach and dunes. Watching the waves in the moonlight and listening to the sound they made relaxed him. At the end of the beach was a headland and beyond that, Viletri was tucked into a natural harbour. With Mannace were Jaal and his small band of mercenaries, grown now to thirty-one men. Following them along the coast, perhaps half a day's march behind were their allies from Sylos and a contingency from Ostoik, totalling around two thousand soldiers. Lord Ravenborn of Ostoik was not prepared to risk his ships against those of Hindas, as Hindas had a fearsome reputation for its naval prowess, so they made the long journey by land.

That evening, Akanidis was eating dinner when a returning patrol raised the alarm of an impending attack. Alarm bells sounded, and within fifteen minutes the first assault began against the city walls. Groups of soldiers were running through the streets to their rally points while their commanders gathered at Akanidis' residence, ready to receive orders. Akanidis excelled in the role of general, quickly organising the defensive effort. With the little information he had, he sent most units to the walls and gathered the elite Hoplites as a quick response force. Marines on the ships waited, as Akanidis was unsure how to commit them until he knew if an attack would come by sea. He sent messengers for the leaders of the Yanth and Sylos enclaves to form a defence at the city gates. To nobody in particular, Akanidas roared, "BRING ME MY ARMOUR!"

From his observation post on top of a hill near the City, Rollo watched the attack unfold. As a lookout, he should have seen the army of Orcs marching across the plains, but instead, they appeared suddenly, as if revealed. Now they moved amongst the outlying ruins very close to the city proper.

At a guess, there were perhaps as many as six thousand Orcs approaching, spreading out through the ruins so that their assault spanned the full length of the city walls. From what Rollo could hastily surmise, the Orc cohorts ranged in sizes from about twenty to a hundred warriors. His observations seemed to matter little though, with no way of returning to the city to report them, with an Orc army in his way. As dark a thought as it was, it seemed essential to Rollo that he might at least survive this attack to report and chronicle the event. As Orc commanders barked their orders, he watched groups carrying siege ladders make their way towards the defences. Another group with battering rams headed for the main entrance. The focus of the attack, however, was clearly at the western end of the wall where Orc numbers were most concentrated. These Orcs were well equipped and organised, nothing like the savages that attacked before.

Further down the hill from where Rollo sat, eight Orcs placed an elaborately carved log on Y- shaped stakes they hammered into the ground. With sticks, they beat on the hollow wood like a drum so that the percussion echoed across the landscape. The resonant sound gave Rollo a chill, each beat knocking upon his nerves. The Orcs seemed to acquire energy from the menacing tempo and shouted their battle cries as they quickened their pace.

Viletri came to life. Soldiers from the city mounted the defences and, in some areas, they were engaged with the Orcs. The clash of metal on metal and yells of men carried up to Rollo on the wind. At the western end of the city, Orc warriors poured over the defences and into the city streets. From where Rollo lay concealed, the assault looked overwhelming.

Night was quickly approaching as Akanidis, with his advisors, joined their soldiers on the wall, close to the main city gates. The defences here were hard-pressed but holding, and the Orc assault on the gatehouse was ineffectual; the battering rams the Orcs carried were not heavy enough to pound down the new iron reinforced gates. The primary battle was fought in the western districts of the city and Akanidis could see that some homes in that area were already ablaze. He turned to the runners that waited behind him.

"Tell captain Theros to engage the enemy in the Western districts. GO."

Yanth and Sylos garrisons had collected near the main gate as requested. As the first runner quickly departed, Akanidis barked orders at another.

"Tell the Yanth and Silos captains to wait for my orders. MOVE IT."

Beside him, Amnicles, his wizard, sent four spectacular

balls of light skyward where they hung above the city and intensified in brightness to provide eerie light to the troops below.

When the sky lit up from the globes, Rollo watched as a winged beast circling over the Orc army was joined by another that swooped down from its hiding place in the darkening sky. As they passed by his hill, it seemed to Rollo like they might join the attack on the walls, but to his horror, they came directly for his position and alighted on the slope nearby. Shaking in near panic at the fear of discovery, Rollo was greatly relieved when the creatures turned away from him, scrutinising the combat below. Rollo could not hear their words over the thumping of blood in his ears.

Although the flying beasts resembled a horse in body and hind legs, they were much more substantial. Their forelegs and head were those of a bull with magnificent horns that angled outwards from the skull before curving to point directly ahead. The wings were expansive and bat-like in flight but folded against the sides of their bodies once they landed. Upon the beasts were Orcs; powerfully built warriors wearing leather hauberks lined with fur, and helmets crafted from the heads of giant wolves. The wolf's fur coat hung as a cloak down the warrior's back. Like other Orcs Rollo had seen, their faces were broad, with wide noses and short tusks protruding from their bottom lip. One of the riders sported skulls hanging from his saddle, trophies of past conquests – not a fate Rollo wanted to share.

Embroiled in the fighting at the western end of the city, Casteel guided her rapier under an Orc's metal breastplate then stepped back quickly as it toppled forward. Harvor finished it off with a backhanded swing of his axe. Casteel, Khing, Tumas, and Harvor made haste to the area of the city where there was the most intense fighting. They made a good account of themselves, though it seemed that the number of Orcs increased, and it became harder to avoid the larger groups that rampaged about. Casteel watched the Hoplites fight. They were remarkable, using their formation and discipline to break and scatter the foe, but they were too few to protect the entire precinct. Around her, some residents put up a desperate defence of their homes, while others fled for safer parts of the city.

Five guardian statues ambled past with a group of citizens who gave commands. That was a good sign; the city was coming to life, and with that, it seemed to Casteel that it might be possible to turn this invader back.

Render moved about Viletri invisible to both the invaders and defenders. He sought out Tain and some of the other frontiersmen and worked with them to animate more of the statues. Now he hurried to a high vantage point amongst the government buildings where he could see Akanidis and Amnicles on the wall. The combat along the wall appeared a muddled brawl. In areas where things were going badly, marines from the ships in the harbour and soldiers from the Yanth and Sylos enclaves joined the fray.

After quickly assessing his options, Render reached out with his magic, touching Amnicles mind, giving it a flick. There was a mental flinch but no defences. Hack, thought Render, then he stepped easily into Amnicles' consciousness, taking control. Through Amnicles eyes, he could see Akanidis next to him shouting orders. Beyond the city walls, there were still many Orcs approaching, some with ladders and others with bows.

The possessed Amnicles grinned slyly at Akanidis.

"Watch this."

Leaning out from the battlements, he lowered his arms and sent a wave of force down the wall and into the earth. Ignoring the arrows that whizzed about him, he raised his arms dramatically and the ground before the walls responded with devastating explosions of rock and dirt. Hundreds of Orcs were tossed and thrown about, most not rising from the violence. Amnicles pointed at a group of Orc survivors who were struck by a broad ray of light emanating from the sky globes, disintegrating them, and scorching the nearby earth. The wizard laughed at the carnage he created and looked about for his next target.

Back on the hill, Rollo was relieved when the winged bulls and their riders again took to the skies. With great caution, he risked looking up from his cover to assess the progress of the siege. It looked bleak for Viletri. Whole areas of the western city were on fire, with large gangs of Orcs moving through the streets. On the walls, it was hard to tell who was winning as both sides were establishing strong-points. He watched a wizard unleash all hells on the Orcs near the city gate.

Suddenly the massive gates warped inwards and exploded. In front of the entrance, a mass of Orc warriors appeared; in the poor light, it seemed to Rollo as if they magically materialised at the location. Hundreds of enemies charged through the open breach. Even at a distance, Rollo could see that these Orcs were larger than those who already attacked the city and like the Orcs on the winged beasts, they were well armoured and manoeuvred like experienced fighters.

There was another movement to the east. Out of the darkness of the night, units of human soldiers became visible on the plains. Unbeknownst to Rollo, Mannace and his army of allies marched towards the city.

Mannace's plan was simple. The Forces of Sylos were to engage and clear the Orcs before the walls. The Forces of Ostoik and other allies would secure the main gates. On further signal, all forces would move into the city proper to re-establish control.

Keeping a careful eye on the skies, Rollo again scuttled between bushes to get a better view of the gatehouse and battle raging there. At first, the rampaging Orc warriors encountered little opposition and they were able to wreak havoc against the defenders on and around the walls. However, when the forces of Mannace and Ostoik arrived, the Orcs were surprised and forced to fight on two fronts. To Rollo, who watched with fascination, the Priests of War who fronted the Ostoik contingent seemed devastating combatants, wielding might and magic in a deadly union. One priest smashed his hammer into the ground in front of the advanceing foe unleashing a blast of force that threw the enemy back, broken and stunned. Another priest bathed himself in a radiant light; a spectral glow that swirled and reached out to consume others with its eerie luminescence. Those soldiers of Ostoik that it touched drew energy from the magic, fighting with unstoppable strength.

In the sky, Rollo noticed that the War Priests gained the attention of one of the bull riders who descended quickly on their position. There was no way for him to warn those below and Rollo felt the crunch as the bull rider crashed into the berserk priest and those who fought alongside him. The priest was crushed and trampled. Other soldiers were tossed back as the bull battered them with its massive wings. With a great leap, the creature was back in the air and headed for the sanctuary of the sky.

Following the War Priests, the soldiers of Ostoik fought in a loose formation, which matched the style of the Orcs. Some of the Arenlanders were equipped with vials that shattered when thrown, releasing choking gas that brought the Orcs to their knees in fits of uncontrollable coughing. The gas did not affect the Ostoik soldiers who had a cloth soaked in a neutralising fluid covering their mouth and nose. Jaal and his mercenaries also wore the material and fought alongside. Jaal was unstoppable, moving with incredible speed between combats and showing ruthless efficiency, his blades a whirlwind of slaughter.

With the odds against them, the veteran Orcs fell back to an area of the wall they still controlled, to make a valiant stand. When their defence could not endure the onslaught, the survivors retreated down ladders, hurrying back towards the plains. Some of the fleeing Orcs crossed in front of the possessed Amnicles who showed little mercy as he battered them with blasts of light and fire.

From his vantage, Rollo was optimistic that the soldiers of Sylos outnumbered and outclassed the Orcs who were not expecting this counter-attack. The battle in front of the wall quickly became an Orcish rout. Inside the city, Rollo could still see large numbers of Orcs, who continued to fight. As time passed, he was increasingly confident that, since the reinforcements arrived, the battle swung in favour of the defenders. Echoing his thoughts, the log drummers on the hill slowed their rhythm to a dull thud, thud, thud and in response, the Orc horde disengaged from combat and the attack transformed into a wholesale retreat. Some of the Orc warbands, loose in the city, continued the fighting, burning, raping, and looting. They were too far gone in their frenzy and bloodlust to heed the drummers' recall.

Rollo's attention turned to a small group of Orcs that moved away from the battle and back to the plains. From what he had observed of the battlefield, he suspected this to be the Orc command. He watched their movement across an open pasture, one moment they were there and the next they were gone. He was not sure if his eyes fooled him, but there was a shimmer to the landscape where they previously stood. Just as quickly, the land returned to its normal state. It made Rollo nervous about what other invisible things might be out there, but his sense of duty compelled him to learn more. Moving stealthily down the hill, he manoeuvred to where he last saw the group and in the dawn light, picked up their trail. Taking a deep breath to bolster his courage, Rollo followed the tracks north.

Gathered in the central square, what remained of the forces of Hindas had established a defensive position. Soldiers and marines stood side-by-side in a broad circle, with their wounded gathered in the centre and Akanidis still boldly barking commands. Soldiers of Sylos, who secured the lower districts by killing the last of the Orcs, were now purposefully blocking their way. They were cut off from their ships.

For those loyal to Hindas, their situation had only become worse. Even though one enemy was defeated, a second enemy, the forces loyal to Mannace, gathered and encircled them. Within this circle, Akanidis surrounded himself with his surviving Hoplites, faithful men whom he trusted implicitly. When Mannace appeared, Akanidis called out to him across the blood-thirsty throng.

"We finally meet. Today we kill Orcs together, and a bond in blood is made."

Mannace came closer, and the two men looked at each other fiercely. Mannace sneered; Akanidis' words were more that of a worm than Sea Snake. Jaal and others loyal to Mannace gathered behind him.

"Tyrant. You will not see the next dawn."

With that, Mannace stepped back while others advanced. Dekon Ruel, supreme amongst the War Priests, appeared to grow as he charged ahead of the others and in a mighty sweep of his hammer two of the Hoplites went down and two others reeled backwards. The final battle ensued.

VALLEY OF AGONY

The port city of Tarash was on a peninsula shaped like a bear's claw that sheltered a rocky bay and harbour. The peninsula was under siege from the mainland, and having been escorted into the sanctuary, Morgan met with an official who explained the situation. It appeared that while the sea routes were still secure, the city had enemies attacking its outer fortifications. Attempts over the last few months to storm Tarash were unsuccessful, but at a high cost to both sides. The official described their adversaries as a horde of evil men, beasts, and demons, though he was short on detail. He shared that the port of Sarcross on the distant western coast was already lost, and the capital city, Gormoth, was likewise under siege. Morgan had previously travelled to Gormoth, a great fortress in the mountains, and he could not imagine it falling quickly to any foe.

Once free to roam the city, Morgan and his crew explored the streets, and despite the conflict, they were able to purchase beer and food at an Inn. Unsurprisingly, amongst the locals they mingled with, there were plenty of civilians interested in the opportunities at Viletri.

Morgan also observed that Remman mercenaries were gathering into units at the docks. They were tough looking men; disciplined and professional. Morgan was most interested in the Troopships that brought them here. He met with the captains of two vessels and at an agreed price convinced them to deviate from their current task to transport migrants to the Great Continent. The seamen were only prepared to go as far as the beaches south of the Icesleepers. From there, the journey to Viletri would need to be completed by land.

Less than a week later, eight hundred men, women, and children were off-loading in a cove south of the Icesleepers as promised. What greeted them was a rocky land and bitter wind that blew down from the vast mountain range.

Unaware of the conflict with Akanidis, Morgan decided to move south to Hindas by foot, expecting it to be five to six days travel. From there he would reassess their options for transport to Viletri. Morgan would stay with this leading group while the Celestial and its cargo of the few migrant elderly, pregnant women, and baggage, would complete the journey by sea to Viletri and then meet them in Hindas afterwards.

For Morgan and those travelling by land, the first day went as planned. The region was tundra and grassland with small hills and minor waterways. On the second day, warriors on horseback appeared; fierce-looking men with fur trimmed heavy armour, fur cloaks, and horned helmets. Most held spears, and some had round shields on their backs. It was apparent that the horsemen shadowed them; backing away when approached and blatantly avoiding Morgan's attempts to commence any dialogue.

At mid-morning of the third day, Morgan, and the migrants from Tarash entered a valley between two hills. As they did so, more riders appeared on the ridges above, looking down at the refugees, while others cantered to block their path.

Of the eight hundred men, women, and youngsters travelling with Morgan, about three hundred carried a weapon, some being capable fighters and at least forty sporting bows or crossbows. The horsemen waited, which gave Morgan time to organise his defence, establishing a cordon of militia to protect the non-combatants.

As Morgan placed the last of his rag-tag troop, the mounted warriors turned to watch as other human-like figures entered the valley behind Morgan's rabble. The creatures that ambled closer resembled men and women but would be twice the height of a man if they were not bent over and running on all fours. Their nakedness exposed deathly white skin, tinged with green, and their eyes were a striking yellow. They did not need to carry weapons as their hands ended in bestial claws. Some howled as they ran past the horsemen and charged speedily towards the travellers. There were nine of these horrific creatures, one of which succumbed immediately to concentrated fire from the bowmen. The others crashed into the defensive line wildly bashing men and woman aside.

Panic amongst the refugees made their situation dire. In desperation Morgan yelled above the chaos.

"STAY STRONG AT THE FRONT. PROTECT YOUR FAMILIES."

Raking claws cut open flesh and sprayed gore in wide arcs through the air. Weapons bounced off tough hides, and only the crossbows of the few men still firing at the beasts seemed to cause them any wounds. Morgan looked to the reserves near him.

"To the centre. Slay the beasts, or we all will die. DEFEND THE CHILDREN."

The men raised their weapons and yelled as they charged into combat. Morgan was unused to leading men in battle, or inspiring their courage, but he did what was needed. The monsters' onslaught already seemed unstoppable, and Morgan couldn't help but think, "so this is how it ends"; knowing that even if he could find a way to extricate himself from the situation, he was not one to leave those under his care behind.

Another form swirled up from the ground, rising from the dirt as if stepping from a grave. The manifestation acquired a demonic, deformed shape. Naked, it could be presumed female, similar height and colour as the other monstrous attackers but standing boldly upright. One side of the demon was deformed, with a half-sized breast and a shortened arm, but extended rump and thigh. As soon as it appeared, it slouched melodramatically, releasing a surge of energy that enveloped those around it. Women and children caught in the turbulence fell to the ground and writhed in agony, most screaming, while the weak choked - dying. Others nearby shrieked as they fled in any direction.

While the monstrous beasts leapt about, battering the hapless fighters, the misshapen demon shambled towards another group of trapped civilians who backed themselves against a rock face, desperately scrambling to climb the impossible slope. Her magic emanated out once more as the innocents writhed in agony. This time the demons' yellow eyes grew wide. Under her penetrating stare, anyone caught in her gaze was moulded to the ground and rock face, turning black like obsidian statues, frozen together in poses of terror and anguish.

Elsewhere, another of the ghoulish creatures went down, again to missile fire - pierced in the neck by a lucky bolt, but it was a small victory amongst the bloody slaughter. Morgan knew he must act decisively.

"TO ME. WARRIORS TO ME."

With the fighters that rallied to him, Morgan charged towards the demoness and launched himself at the rampaging creature. Despite their ferocity, the few blows he and others landed impacted little before the demon drove them back against the valley wall with her diabolic magic, making them squirm like sun-cooked worms for her pleasure. Under her deathly glare, they froze at the point of utmost pain, the demoness perfecting a cruel sculpture. Again, panicked survivors scampered in every direction, and there were still too many men and women for the beasts and riders to chase them all down.

The horsemen who were now amongst the civilians picked out women, who they wrestled to the ground, bound with ties, and slung over their saddles. No mercy was shown to others as they butchered children as well as adults. The barbarians seemed unconcerned that some of the refugees were escaping. When they had what they wanted, the horsemen cantered casually away from the scene.

In the wake of the clamour, when the valley was again silent, the demonic woman and other beasts returned to the carnage, soaking up the ripe atmosphere and greedily feasting. The noise of chomping bones and chewing meat was a ghastly, lonely chorus amongst the still bodies and unheard screams of tortured souls trapped within obsidian forms.

ROLLO

Rollo made it safely across the plains and followed the tracks of the Orc command group into a wide area of marsh that backed onto foothills. Behind the hills was a range of grey, low-lying mountains. For a day and night, Rollo had avoided groups of Orcs headed north after their defeat at Viletri. At a marsh where the Orcs' route converged into a single path, he was forced to take cover until all the Orcs passed. Following a safe distance behind the retreating hoard, Rollo was watchful of the skies above, fearful of being spotted by the flying bull-riders.

The Orc trail wound through the foothills and turned towards the mountains where a river valley opened between two peaks. The valley widened and narrowed in places, but was easy going, and the Orcs used logs to construct makeshift bridges to cross the more difficult streams or ravines. At one point, Rollo had no choice but to cross the main river in plain sight, where it was broad and shallow, delaying him by half a day to ensure that the Orcs were well ahead of him.

The valley and mountains were wild and beautiful. In some locations, there was light forest and bushland, and at one point there was a long expanse of wood covered in giant spider webs. The Orcs gave this area a wide berth although it meant traversing some steep high ground. Rollo took the same precaution.

Further on, the pass opened onto a broad plateau. Behind the plateau, massive snow-laden mountains, much taller than the ones Rollo had already skirted, towered above the landscape. It seemed likely to Rollo that this upland was the Orcs destination, so he was reluctant to seek high ground and a better view for fear of being observed. Instead, he stayed within the wooded areas, setting about his exploration of the region.

To his surprise, rather than Orcs, Rollo encountered Dwarves. Until now there had been no indication that Dwarves might be living in the area. The Orc trail veered off to the east and entered another valley which Rollo did not investigate further. Instead, he spent his time inspecting the plateau where he found signs of long-abandoned farms and villages. Twice Rollo observed Dwarven patrols. The soldiers were short and broad, like the few other Dwarves he had seen throughout his lifetime but dressed very differently. They wore long grey coats, with knee-high black boots and simple metal helmets. He assumed that under the jackets, there might have been some armour. Each held a metal crossbow that appeared much bulkier around the grip and shaft than usual, with a wicked-looking blade attached to the front, clearly an adaption for melee combat. Each dwarf carried either a spade, hammer, or pick on their backs.

On the third occasion he spotted Dwarves, their forward scouts also observed him. Faced with the choice to flee or stay, Rollo boldly hailed the Dwarves and allowed them to surround him. Fortunately, they spoke the common tongue, and he explained to them his purpose and the battle that had taken place at Viletri. Their leader responded.

"First Orcs, now Humans. Where there's one, there's always more. Where's your mates, lad?"

When Rollo shook his head, the Dwarf seemed to lose interest in the conversation. Instead, he turned to one of his crew.

"Take his gear. Logthar will want to see 'im."

The patrol escorted Rollo to the western end of the plateau. There, against a rocky face at the base of a tall mountain, were four wide entranceways carved into the rock. They passed into one of them, and after travelling a small distance, the corridor widened so that it was large enough to house an iron bastion and gate. The bastion was a wall of steel that seemed to meld with the rock floor, ceiling, and walls to form a perfect seal. The gate, set at the base of the bastion, was in the shape of a half-circle and decorated with intricate designs. It was flanked on either side by wide pipes protruding slightly from the metal wall that Rollo guessed would spill some horrific liquid or gas into the chamber as part of the defence. There was a mechanical noise of cogs turning and metal grinding. Then with a spring set loose, the half-circle gate divided into many triangular segments that retracted into the metal wall. The group manoeuvred through the gap into a corridor that led further down into the mountain. As they descended, the triangular pieces of the gate snapped back into place, followed by more grinding of cogs and a final loud thunk.

Deeper inside the mountain was a labyrinth of corridors, some of which opened into large halls where Dwarves went about their business. Rollo could see markets, taverns, and workshops. One of the workshops caught his attention, where two artisans peddled timepieces of varying sizes. Rollo recalled an old clock of Dwarven manufacture at a pub near Rummond. It was a marvel of design that he had never seen the likes of anywhere else until now.

Eventually, they arrived in an area that seemed more the domain of soldiers. Accommodation and a ration of bread, cheese, and ale were provided. Hours passed before a Dwarf took him to a large chamber dominated by a massive rectangular table with ornately carved chairs. Two Dwarves and two men were seated at a corner of the table. Rollo sat with them.

"Rollo, welcome. I am Logthar of the Grey Dwarves. Meet my kinsman, Fedrin, and our guests Minhouas and Gideon of the Viletri. I am the spokesman for the Iron Halls, and Minhouas speaks for the Viletri beneath the mountain. Please, lad, share with us your tale and news of the outworld."

THE ELDERS

After the battle against the forces of the Orcs and Hindas, Mannace re-established his dominion over Viletri. His enemy, Akanidis, was dead, his army destroyed, and his navy fled. The Hindasian craftsmen continued their work, initially under guard and later by an arrangement where they could gradually earn their freedom with their labour. The forces of Ostoik and Sylos returned to their territories, though two War Priests stayed to establish a temple order within the town.

Mannace began recruiting young men and women from the citizenry to form the base for a standing army. He also funded Jaal, from the cities growing coffers, to continue recruitment of veteran mercenaries. Most of the living statues survived the battle against the Orcs, and Mannace asked Render to create more.

At Mannace's command, Kakos Agamos returned to his role of governing the city. Because of his unusual appearance, Kakos kept a low personal profile and used his appointed officials to deal directly with merchants, business owners, diplomats, and others. Kakos was finding advantages to his undead form; he never slept so was able to run the city day and night, people tended not to annoy him unnecessarily, and there was never any guilt when hard decisions were needed. Eating had its challenges, and Kakos went to some lengths to keep his dietary habits private.

Because the Ostoik troops had assisted in the retaking of Viletri, the nation of Arenland was given an area of the city like that of Yanth so that they could establish an enclave. The industrious Arenlanders immediately set about designing a district to outshine their Yanth rivals.

The Rhalec arrived at the city and established their embassy within a restored residence. Dwarves also came from the North and were provided with the same consideration. It quickly proved a profitable endeavour as trade in gems, gold and crafted weapons started to move through Viletri's expanding port.

As more migrants came to Viletri, the rejuvenation and new construction of the city and its surrounding lands became a significant industry, that further attracted artisans, guildsmen, labourers, and merchants from across the Blood Sea. Many of the migrant families turned themselves to farming, fishing, and new businesses. It wasn't long before Mannace felt that he no longer needed to push Viletri forward. Instead, his mounting challenge was to keep up with the pace of change and demands from a growing populace.

In the following month, representatives from the 'Viletri Beneath the Mountain' arrived at the city to meet with Mannace. There were five men and one woman, led by Minhouas, and they referred to themselves as the Assembly of Elders. When they met at Mannace's estate, Mannace had Jaal, Render, and Casteel join him.

"It is good to see the restoration of the city. You have done your people a great service Mannace of the Viletri," stated a very diplomatic Minhouas.

"I welcome my people, the Viletri".

An awkward silence followed. Minhouas continued carefully.

"In its prime, Viletri was a centre of culture and craft, the pearl of the south and the Blood Sea. One hundred and eighty-five years ago, not long in the life of an immortal, Viletri was sacked by a mighty and merciless invader."

The Viletri paused. By immortal standards, it was still a fresh memory.

"Our fleet and army were annihilated. The few survivors scattered. Two hundred and seven Viletri now reside under the protection of the Grey Dwarves. Mannace of the Viletri, we would return to our home."

"All are welcome."

Minhouas was quick to retort, "With respect, we are not migrants, this is our place of birth, a city that we founded, and for some, a place of residence for over two thousand years. We ask you to join your people, take your place at the Assembly and together let us restore the city to its greatness."

Mannace was just as quick with a terse response, "With respect, this is not the city you left, and you are not the Viletri nation of the past. You are two hundred and seven survivors. Already there are more than six thousand residents here, each invested in the new City of Viletri that they are building."

Another of the Viletri took up their case. The woman who spoke was steely faced and frank in her tone.

"We may be few, but do not underestimate the knowledge and capability of the immortals. Look at your own experience and skills. By our terms, you are short-lived. We have much to contribute."

As Mannace considered their plea, the six visitors did not interrupt. After a long silence, he gave them his decision.

"The Viletri are welcome to return to the city as equals to those already in residence here. Those with skills will stand on their own merits."

Mannace could tell by the scowls that his decision was not what the Viletri wanted to hear. Their displeasure gnawed at his insides; these were his kin, and he wanted to be on good terms with them. Mostly, he desired their acceptance. Mannace sensed that to achieve that he needed to give them more.

"We will have a new assembly. The six of you here will be part of that gathering, and you will have your say over the city's governance. As Lord of this city, I maintain supreme authority."

Minhouas looked at his companions, each nodding. They had little leverage for negotiation and agreed to Mannace's terms. Before leaving the city, the six Viletri met with

Mickell to decide residence and business allocations for their people. Jaal and twenty of his mercenaries escorted the Viletri delegation back to the mountain plateau.

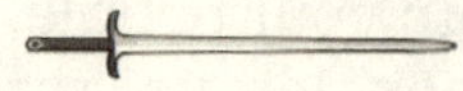

RENDER

Render was amazed at how quickly Saska picked up both the fundamentals of magic and the universal language. He suspected she may have always known both but never or seldom used them. The seductress was exceptionally bright and often challenged him. Today was no exception.

Render was trying to understand Saska's seductive power over men. It went well beyond her astounding physical charms. In her quickly developing tongue, she described it as an inner hunger and desire that she could project outwards into others. It did not create the lust in those affected; instead, it raised their yearning to a fever pitch that completely overwhelmed reason and even any thoughts of self-preservation. .

"And then you suck them dry," he asserted.

"I take what need". The conversation turned around, "like you".

"What?"

"I know how you live immortal."

"My magic sustains me."

"You like me. I take what need from men so live. Can take all man but here, now, I take enough survive. No kill. Killing bring attention. You same."

Render felt very uncomfortable and said nothing. Saska went on.

"See you steal life, not get noticed. How they feel? Secret, no?"

"Feel," Render turned the conversation back to Saska. "What do you know or care about feelings? You are a predator, manipulator, a creature of darkness."

Saska smiled smugly. "Same you."

Following this conversation with Saska, Render did not return to give further lessons. He took on two other apprentices. The first was Amnicles who he had extricated from the battle at Viletri after using him as a conduit for his spell casting. Amnicles had an insatiable hunger to learn more and expand his capabilities. He studied and practised tirelessly.

The other apprentice, Jesephene, was a healer amongst the first arrivals to Viletri. As a healer, she mostly used herbs and conventional methods to mend and repair wounds, and her patients experienced speedy recoveries that didn't go unnoticed. Render saw the potential in her and found that he enjoyed the process of teaching. After several lessons, their relationship moved from the study to the bedchamber, and the young, dark-haired apprentice was seen more often about his household.

SPIDER MOTHER

Jaal enjoyed being around the mercenaries. They were sturdy, professional and reliable, yet they didn't take themselves too seriously. While they followed commands from Jaal without question when it was needed, at other times they treated him as an equal and they included him in their humour. He only wanted the best fighters in his band as he couldn't tolerate people that needed to be instructed constantly nor those who would crumble under pressure.

Not all his crew were professional sell-swords though. A few, like the brothers and Casteel, liked the camaraderie, and their assignments gave them a sense of purpose. The band had grown to eighty-three and although still a small force, it had gained a reputation as an elite unit.

Jaal and twenty of the mercenaries returned from the mountain plateau. When passing the webbed forest, Jaal noticed an anomaly. Where the webs around the forest previously formed an impenetrable wall, some were pulled back as if to make an entrance. His curiosity was piqued.

His crew did not share Jaal's enthusiasm to investigate and rather than push the others to follow; Jaal sensed that this might be something better pursued alone. He ordered the others to make camp south of the forest and await his return.

The forest was confined. It stretched along the narrow river valley and deviated into two smaller side valleys. Where it could, it grew up the mountain until blocked by scree and bare rock faces. Its entirety was covered in giant webs so that it was not easily accessible by foot or air. Today, however, the entrance beckoned, and Jaal stepped into it. With the web covering, it was considerably darker than a typical forest and much quieter. Everything was damp. Mustiness overwhelmed Jaal's senses so that he had to focus on controlling his breath. All the while, he maintained a careful vigil of his surroundings. There were webs everywhere and sometimes he could see spiders that lurked on branches above, some the size of a large dog. He followed the path left for him. Jaal relished the danger, the sense of putting his head in the noose. He knew that with every step, the rope was tightening about his neck. Swallowing, Jaal licked his lips to give them some moisture. His senses and imagination were aflame so that every little sound and movement seemed exaggerated.

There was a strange enchantment to this place that intensified as he entered deeper into it. It prickled his skin but did not make him anxious as Render's magic often did. This place had a *rightness* that was natural and comfortable. While it looked like a trap, he had come far enough into it that he could but hope he was a guest.

Eventually, Jaal approached a clearing where the edges of the expanse were even thicker with webs, as was the canopy above. That odd definition gave Jaal the sense that he was nearing a large chamber. Above the glade, the sun's rays shone through the web in places, as if by design. It was much lighter here than along the forest trail.

Now, through the web and branches, he could see a woman standing in the clearing, naked and radiant in the filtered light. She was dark-skinned like Saska but more slender, small-breasted and with no hair on her body. Jaal's blood was racing. As he stepped into the clearing, the woman moved to be closer to him, until she was only an arm's length distant. Her voice was direct and commanding.

"Welcome. You are the first in many years to accept my invitation. In my home, you must put aside your weapons and your clothing."

Jaal complied. He could feel the tension and energy building within him. The woman pulled him close in an embrace. When he was in her arms, his vision instantly clouded, and a great motion enveloped him. Everything moved so quickly that his mind caught only distorted glimpses of the environment changing around him; the ground opening, a round tunnel, many eyes stared into his eyes, legs wrapped around him. Still, the woman embraced him tightly, and then came total darkness, so dark that even his night vision was of no use. The motion had stopped; the woman continuing to caress his back with her hands as if to put him at ease.

"I will have your seed."

There was significant meaning in that statement. Elven-kind could choose when a life seed would be shared. On a very rare occasion, the perfect coupling of the right people might result in the Fates releasing the seed, but for the most part, it was a choice that all Elves took very seriously. It was typically something an Elf might do once or twice in their lifetime, Dark Elves being no exception. Jaal walked freely into this trap and the intense sense of danger and knowing all was not as it seemed, excited him. He knew that his life depended on him delivering his seed, so there was no further consideration needed.

In the darkness, the ground beneath him seemed soft and springy. Jaal manoeuvred himself and the woman onto the silky surface so that they were lying, still partly embraced. He caressed her side, enjoying her shape, and she accommodated him as he explored further. After a time, she allowed him to part her legs, and he pushed so that she lay on her back with him atop, he prepared her softly with his hand then slowly moved his spear inside her.

After the coupling, Jaal lay on his back, exhausted. As he reached out his hand to where the woman lay, he could no longer feel her presence. The sense of danger was stronger than ever. Rising cautiously, Jaal moved about one small step at a time, blind in the pitch black. He felt a wall with an open passage and entered. The spongy floor veered upwards at a steep angle. After following it for some minutes, where it was almost vertical near the top, Jaal found the tunnel blocked. Upon putting his weight against the blockage, daylight appeared. Taking a moment to adjust to the light, he could see he was in a round, webbed tunnel. Shoving back the lid that closed the burrow to the world above, Jaal squeezed through, returning to the clearing where he quickly retrieved his clothes and gear.

South of the forest Jaal re-joined his troops. They were curious.

"So, what was in there?"

Jaal looked them in the eye.

"Giant spiders with bodies the size of dogs."

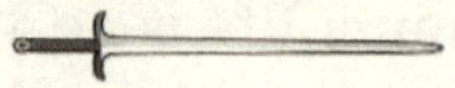

THE ASSEMBLY

A handful of the migrants from Tarash arrived at Viletri. They brought with them stories of the horror faced on their journey, Morgan Cain's demise, and the survivors' desperate flight to the territories of Hindas. Those that journeyed to Viletri looked beaten, but like others arriving at the city, there was a glimmer of hope. A trader, sympathetic to their plight, had given them sea passage, arranging employ for them at the docks.

The new arrivals and other travellers brought news of a Hindas population shocked and angered by their defeat at Viletri. Admiral Ithius Sartis was in command of the city, and reports suggested that the Hindas military were busy with the defence of their northern frontier from barbarian raiders. Mannace knew it would only be a matter of time before they turned their attention back to Viletri and thoughts of vengeance. It was just another trial to add to the many others. Foremost in his thoughts, was the manner of Morgan's death, but he tried not to dwell on it. Although Mannace hadn't known the explorer long, a heaviness settled upon his heart, darkening his mood.

The first city Assembly was in a grand chamber in the central government building. The members of the assembly gathered, seated in a semi-circular arrangement with Mannace sitting in a throne facing them.

The Viletri elders occupied six chairs. Mannace had already asked three of them to take up official roles, which they accepted. Titus Kane, a military man, was given command of the cities garrison and defence. Gideon, an experienced engineer, was put in charge of rebuilding and improving the city's infrastructure and roads. Mannace wanted roads built east to Sylos and north to the mountain plateau. He supported an idea that healer, Althea Kane, the wife of Titus, raised to commission a place of healing within the city. He also made her more broadly responsible for the city's health.

Jaal and Render took their seats. Neither desired nor would accept an official title or responsibility. If nothing else, Mannace wanted them at the Assembly for his personal support.

The War Priest, Demmal Fulstorm, an earnest man, sat proudly upright in a position of honour behind and above Mannace's throne. Mannace agreed to accept the War God as the city's patron, to remind himself of his long-term purpose, born of his vision at the monastery, to prepare for the conflict to come.

Kakos was seated too. The most gifted of the city's courtesans had applied her arts to his appearance. But no amount of skill with makeup could entirely conceal what Kakos was. Mannace knew that Kakos would be the glue that would hold all the parts together. Kakos was proven to be an outstanding administrator, responsible for the overall governance of the city. The zombie clasped the keys to the treasury, which gave him authority second only to Mannace. Demmal's religious order held some strong views towards the undead, and the War Priest eyed Kakos warily.

Each of the enclaves within the city; Sylos, Yanth, and Arenland, also had a representative present. A further six seats were left empty as a statement that the assembly would evolve and grow.

The meeting lasted the whole day. They talked about what they wanted to achieve and funding. It quickly became apparent there was insufficient coin in the treasury to support everything the Assembly sought to do. Mannace wanted progress and he refused to let this stymie him.

"Titus, Render, there are other ways. I trust your ingenuity to ensure the city's defence. The money will come in time, but for now, you must make the most of what we already have. Already we have walls and fighting statues."

Titus had some ideas, and he was not so arrogant as to

ignore the success of others.

"The military school started by Akanidis is working well. We should keep it going."

Others, including Mannace, were nodding their agreement.

As the conversation moved on, Gideon proposed approaching the Grey Dwarves and the Lord of Sylos, to collaborate on building and then patrolling roads between their cities. Mannace offered to travel with Gideon to garner support.

The topic that took up most of the day was the broader politics of the Blood Sea and the unknown threats from the North. They possessed little information regarding the Orcs that had attacked them or the Barbarians who raided Hindas to the west. To the northeast, the region was mostly uncharted. Further afield Tarash Gormoth was a land under siege.

Kakos, as the Assembly's self-appointed secretary, recorded three crucial decisions. First, Mannace would establish a company of Rangers to scout and secure the frontier.

Second, Jaal would travel with his mercenaries to aid Tarash Gormoth and better understand the foe that nation faced. Demmal offered two acolytes to accompany Jaal's troops.

Third, another of the Viletri elders, Shepherd, was given the responsibility of advancing cooperation among the nations of the Blood Sea. Shepherd was reserved but had a keen intelligence and a natural way with people. Mannace already noticed how the others often looked to Shepherd for his wisdom. The Yanth, Sylos, and Arenland representatives promised their assistance.

Unknown to the other leaders, Mannace commissioned another set of duties. Shylo, one more Viletri elder, was asked to be his eyes and ears within the city. Shylo was previously a teacher, with a sharpness and resourcefulness that Mannace liked.

Logthar of the Grey Dwarves had travelled to Viletri with the Elders to meet privately with Mannace. It was an informal meeting that allowed both leaders to familiarise themselves with each other. They found common ground in many things, and Mannace was eager to show Logthar the collection of contraptions he had salvaged from the monastery.

"Logthar, these are the inventions of a man who could see into the future. The Architect. He lived his whole life at the monastery, in body anyway, but his mind was well travelled. A traveller in time, Logthar, can you imagine what he has seen, what he might know. He based these creations on what he learned. They are a wonder, Logthar, a treasure beyond compare."

"Indeed, Mannace, a gift or a curse."

Mannace looked at the Dwarf sideways, unsure of his commitment.

"Logthar, you don't see these as a key to possibilities?"

"Don't get me wrong, lad, I am as keen as you to decipher these things, but I am wary of what we might uncover - a little caution to temper a bold hand. I know a smith who is particularly good with intricate designs. Let's see where these oddities take us."

TARASH GORMOTH

Jaal was happy to be away from the city. He had commissioned the Celestial as well as Urgar's unique troop transport and was taking all of his band with him. The Acolytes of War, Aleksander and Regan, mixed poorly with the mercenaries at first, but within a few days at sea, they were at least able to share a meal without there being a disturbance. The Acolytes were raised in the priesthood since they were very young and were used to a regime of order and discipline. The mercenaries' laid-back attitude and often crass humour were foreign to them. Within the priesthood, respect came with status. Whereas with the mercenaries' respect was earned on the field or through camaraderie. Khing took the young acolytes under his wing as he possessed a talent for lightening the mood and keeping the peace.

Casteel, while physically recovered, was changed in spirit. Her wit bit deep where Jaal was concerned.

"How's that demon woman of yours doing? Or should you be worried, who's she doing?"

"I expect she's baking some cakes and braiding her hair."

A couple of the mercenaries overhearing Jaal chuckled.

Jaal wanted Casteel to know that his bond to Saska was not some flash in the pan affair. Later, when Casteel stood next to him near the railing, he spoke privately to her.

"There is an order to all things, Casteel. I will always return to Saska. She will always be there waiting for me. Everything and everybody have a place and purpose. When you understand the order of things, then decisions and actions are made simple."

Casteel was unconvinced. She cared enough for Jaal to be blunt.

"You are led by your spear, Jaal. It blinds you to what is real and unreal. Are you a lovesick boy or the master in control of his own emotions?"

Anger flashed across Jaal's visage, his grip tightening on the ship's rails. Wanting to keep his emotions in check, he took a deep breath of the chilly sea air and let the animosity go as he slowly exhaled. He watched Casteel as she was staring out to sea. She was beautiful, radiant with her hair loose around her shoulders. Jaal looked back across the waters too.

"We will see."

The trip to Tarash Gormoth was uneventful. On arrival, the ships were guided into Tarash as the Celestial had been before. This time they flew the banner of Viletri - a golden war hammer on a red and white background. Tarash was far too busy, though, for a visiting diplomat's fanfare, and everywhere Jaal looked, people were creating chaos. To avoid the panicked crowds, Jaal got permission for a berth at the military docks.

Due to the mayhem, it took Jaal and his men much longer than expected to traverse the city streets and make their way down the peninsula. By the time they reached their destination, they were frustrated and in sombre moods. At the headland's narrowest point was a fortress stretched from a rocky cliff on one side to a beachhead on the other. Trebuchets and catapults inside the fort were launching their missiles against a foe that Jaal could not see. Off the coast, the Tarash navy was active, exchanging salvos with another unseen enemy onshore.

Units of soldiers and companies of mercenaries moved back and forth between the city and fortress. Those returning to Tarash were battered and wounded. They seemed exhausted from the fighting, nodding at Jaal and his mercenaries as they passed. A bloodied warrior looked up and grinned, "Your turn, mate."

One of the Jaal's mercenaries put on his steel cap.

"Time to go to work."

"Not today!"

Jaal's response was instinctive. Nothing seemed right or good about the situation, and Jaal decided to turn his crew around. He did not see himself as a hero, at least not the type that was needed here, and he did not expect his troop to risk their lives for no good reason. Looking around, Jaal realised he and his mercenaries were incidental to what was unfolding - their mission of diplomacy did not fit into the dire situation the Tarash people faced. If Mannace wanted to save Tarash, he would need to come himself and bring a proper bloody army with him. Jaal pulled Khing off to the side to confer.

"Khing, this feels like a death trap. We will make no difference here."

The big man nodded.

While the officials paid no heed to his arrival, it seemed that leaving Tarash was drawing more attention. One official called across the crowd to Jaal that he was not to depart. At the same time, desperate families pleaded with the mercenaries for passage and tugged at their clothes. People pushed past the soldiers who protected the military docks so that the mercenaries roughly forced their way back to their ships. When they were finally all aboard, the ropes that tied the vessels to the pier were chopped free with axes to make good their escape.

Urgar's troopship and the Celestial fled south for a day before anchoring in a bay next to the ruins of a fishing village. Burnt out huts were scattered about like knucklebones cast into a dirt bowl. Dead soldiers were left to rot where they had fallen. Both Casteel and Jaal were quick to notice Elven crafted arrows embedded in some corpses. The cadavers themselves told a story of two forces of men clashing, one with the armour and colours of Tarash, and the other barbarians with little clothing or protection. The state of the corpses suggested the skirmish occurred several months past. From the placement of the bodies, Casteel deduced that the Barbarians took the victory but were then ambushed and killed by Elves. She took into consideration that Elves would have had no interest in burying or burning the dead. It was a curiosity to Jaal that there might be a third player in the Tarash Gormoth conflict.

Keen to know more, Jaal climbed a nearby hill. From there, he could see grass plains and neglected farms in all directions. To the south, about half a day's walk was a deep forest stretching inland and down the coast as far as he could see. When Jaal returned to the others, a crewman from the Celestial offered some information.

"That's likely the northern reaches of the Fogmir, sir. It's three days sail to the forests southern end, where the Rhalec live. Up the river, sir, the Rhalec."

Jaal wasn't particularly interested in the Rhalec. Those few at their embassy at Viletri were an unadventurous lot, liking their traditions and keeping mostly to themselves - he was more curious to contact the Elves. Casteel, reading his thoughts, offered her advice.

"Chances are if we enter the forest, move along the edge of the woodland, that the Elves will find us."

Jaal laughed. He knew Casteel was right.

THE FOGMIR

Urgar remained behind in charge of the ships and crew while Jaal and the mercenaries moved into the forest, following the edge of the woodland west. In this part of the Fogmir, the wood was thin in places and a rough tangle in others. Where it was a tangle, the canopy was thick and little light filtered through to those on the ground.

On the second day, as they passed through a less dense area, Jaal sensed a presence amongst the trees, putting a hand up to halt his party and alert them to his concern. Silently they all waited, but there was nothing visible. Jaal could feel the hairs on his neck standing on their end. He knew to trust his instincts, and they continued to pause and watch.

A shape dropped from the trees, landing softly in a crouch then standing tall to face them. It was a female Elf, not young but not old. She was tall and lithe, muscular in the arms and legs. High cheekbones and steely blue eyes gave her a strong face. Straw-coloured hair was a wild tangle held back with ornate wooden combs. This Elf was striking rather than beautiful with a crouched pose best described as predatory. Her clothing was practical and straightforward, in the colours of the Fogmir. In her hands was a bow with arrow set, at her side a supply of arrows, and short sword. She looked directly at Jaal.

"Come here, dark one, let us dance."

Jaal drew his swords. As he did so, the Elf raised her bow and fired. Jaal ducked the missile and charged, already another arrow sped his way, this time aimed lower at his torso. He focused his energy, speeding his reflexes, deftly knocking aside the shaft with his blade. Channelling his power into the charge, Jaal covered the ground between himself and his adversary in a flash, prepared to deal a killing blow. The Elf responded, poking the end of her bow at Jaal's face and he instinctively leaned back so that his thrust to the woman's chest connected but only enough to cause a trickle of blood. Despite his speed, his next thrust was knocked aside by the woman's bow, and as he swung down with his other blade, the shortsword deflected it away. The woman stepped forward, giving Jaal no room for his next swing. Her knee connected with his groin, and for a moment, his energy left him. As he staggered back, Jaal desperately deflected two quick cuts aimed at his neck and only just sidestepped an attempt to trip him with the bow. Channelling his energy once more, in a flurry of slashes and thrusts Jaal forced the Elf back. She was not as quick as him, but she possessed an uncanny capacity for anticipating and countering his blows. Casteel came from the side to interpose herself between the two combatants.

"STOP THIS."

Casteel glared at the Elf and then at Jaal who both took a step back and relaxed their stance. More Elves dropped out of the trees. Their camouflage was outstanding, and the mercenaries had observed not one of them. There was no way to tell how many others there might be. The Elven woman spoke.

"An Elf and a Dark Elf in the company of men, what a strange lot you are. Is this boy your lover?" She quipped at Casteel.

"I'd rather lay with a slugfish".

Casteel's response was automatic. The Elf laughed.

"He's far too quick, not what you'd want in your nest."

This time Casteel laughed. Jaal thought better of entering the conversation, and now that his adrenaline ebbed, he felt sick from the blow to his groin. It was taking all his composure not to show its effects.

Casteel explained that they sought contact with the Elves after seeing evidence of their intervention in a battle near Tarash. They wanted to understand the nature of the enemy that attacked Tarash Gormoth and the position of the Elves in the conflict. The wild Elf took Casteel at her word, and before she would permit them to stay in the forest, she made Casteel accept responsibility for the conduct of the mercenary group. It was a responsibility with severe consequences if there was any miscreant behaviour. The Elves agreed to escort them through the forest to a place where such a discussion could take place, a three-day hike. A runner scurried ahead.

As they walked through the forest, Jaal was amazed how easily the wild Elves moved through the dense canopy above. He observed that the Elf he fought was held in high regard by the others, although she held no apparent rank. Her name was unpronounceable to him. Jaal wasn't sure, but he expected the war-band to consist of around ninety elves. In this terrain, he was glad not to be taking them on in a fight. Their enemies would find themselves turned into pincushions without ever laying eyes on an Elf.

Most of the Elves slept in the trees and some had a way of tucking themselves into the Vs of split tree trunks or large branches. It made them almost invisible. On the third night, Jaal got up to relieve himself well away from the camp. As he stood over a stream and while going about his business, a familiar voice came from directly behind.

"Nice night for a stroll, boy".

Two arms wrapped around him as he finished, taking his spear, and giving it a shake. The arms pulled back as he turned around. He was looking the Elf he had fought in the eye, and she smirked as she looked back. Jaal didn't know how to read the situation. He stepped to the side to walk around her, but she matched his step and blocked his way. He was sure now of her game, moving forward so that their forms touched lightly. She also pushed forward, so their bodies pressed against one another forcibly, and both exerted themselves not to give ground. Their hands gripped, wrestling to take the upper hand. The wild-eyed woman relented and let Jaal force her several steps back against the broad trunk of a tree, but as he relaxed his hold, she twisted him around and forced him against that same bole. She was remarkably strong. Jaal determined to be dominant, pushed back hard.

The Wild Elf abruptly stood back. Keeping eye contact, she removed her clothes, Jaal doing the same. Naked, she leaned into Jaal and raised her leg, pinning him once again against the trunk with her knee pressed into his chest. He didn't fight that, but he did win the arm-wrestle and was able to hold her arms at her side, pushing them behind her back. She was moist, and Jaal guided his spear into her purse, though she prevented him from finding a rhythm by again pushing with her lower body so that he had no room to manoeuvre. Jaal shifted his weight, toppling them both to the ground, still connected. He resumed his rhythm but only until she turned her weight so that they half-rolled and she was now on top. From that moment, she controlled the pace.

All the fortitude that Jaal possessed went into the wild encounter, and after a considerable time, it built to climax for them both. His birth seed was released and accepted. It was not a conscious choice for either. They looked at each other silently, to rest and to contemplate the consequence of their joining.

The next day, the travellers came to a glade that was clear of low vegetation and the canopy thinned out so that natural light lit up a meeting area. Four ancient carved logs formed a square. On one of the logs were wild Elves who beckoned for the newcomers to join them. There was space for many to be seated, while the others gathered behind them. Elves with baskets were walking amongst them, offering fruit and other food. When everybody was together and comfortable, one of the Elves raised a hand to silence the chatter, turning to Casteel.

"We of the Fogmir welcome the Elves of the Alani and those that come under their protection.".

The speaker's appearance did not mark him out from the others as a leader. He was perhaps older than most but wore similar clothing and carried the same equipment. His hair was wild and tangled like the surrounding forest. He was muscular and handsome, in a wiry, rugged fashion.

Casteel replied. "We of the Alani thank the Elves of the Fogmir for their welcome."

Inexperienced in formal rituals and not knowing the Fogmir Elves' customs, Casteel moved quickly into an explanation of their purpose in their land. She expressed the desire of the Lord of Viletri to assist the besieged forces of Tarash Gormoth. She introduced Jaal as the leader of their expedition.

The Elves were interested in news from the Blood Sea. It was evident from their questions that they had some knowledge of that region, although it seemed to be decades out of date. There was no hierarchy to the meeting, and anybody could and did contribute. Jaal was eager to get to the point.

"What can you tell us of the forces besieging Tarash Gormoth?"

"Ears can be deceived. Eyes will reveal more than words."

It was a mysterious response that did little to satisfy Jaal, but it was typical of the furtive responses he expected from Elves. His kin had their drawbacks, but at least Dark Elves got straight to the point. That said, the Elder Elf ended the meeting. Then, with the Elves leading the way, the whole group continued west for several hours and took a cautious route through a densely forested area. Finally, they climbed up a steep rise where the forest abruptly ended, and the land fell away into a broad vale. With guidance from the Elves, they made their way to positions where they remained hidden and observed a camp below them.

The encampment of a great host filled the vale and spilt over into the nearby hills. Harvor and Tumas tried to calculate how many warriors might be in a camp of this size. Harvor was first to hazard a guess.

"Thirty to thirty-five thousand. Mostly men, but some other

races.”

He pointed to one area of the camp where there were manlike creatures that were taller and broader.

“They look tough. See the others make way for them. Mean bastards, I expect.”

His brother Tumas was looking past the main camp, towards the end of the vale. “There are horse enclosures beyond the livestock pens. And back there, near the dwellings, those things have wings.”

Jaal could see that Tumas was right. As they continued to watch, a squad of winged creatures, human-sized, took to the air and flew into the distance.

Once satisfied they had seen enough, the group returned to the meeting area where they discussed the army in more detail. The force in the valley had amassed over the last month, appearing to be a collection of allies coming together. Other armies already ran rampant across Tarash Gormoth and besieged its cities, perhaps fifty thousand troops in total. Jaal expected that was more than could be mustered across the whole of the Blood Sea.

The Elves and the delegation from Viletri agreed that they shared a common interest in better understanding this invader and their broader intent. They gave Casteel a device and in a private ritual, the key that would allow her to communicate with them.

THE VILETRI RANGERS

Rollo was the first person Mannace selected to be part of the Viletri Rangers. The second was a trapper named Jediah who had come to the city with the original frontiersmen. As well as being a capable scout, Jed knew the lands to the northeast. The third recruit was of a race Mannace had not encountered before, a Daglari named Alsaborg. He arrived in the city with a group of mercenaries, and as well as having a reputation as a fierce fighter, his comrades joked that there was nobody better at sniffing out a trail. Alsaborg was a head taller than Mannace, broad at the shoulder with powerful arms and legs. Like others of his kin, he had a head that was more wolf than human. It gave him a fierce visage, more so when he bared his sharp teeth. The three Rangers reported directly to Mannace and enjoyed the freedom to operate as they saw fit.

The Rangers' primary task was to map the southern end of the Great Continent as far north as the Icesleepers, to patrol the region and bring warning of any imminent threats. It was an impossible territory to cover with just three men, so they collected information from local travellers, refugees, mercenaries, scouts from the Sylos enclave, Grey Dwarves, and labourers from Hindas. After working out the basics, they went to Mannace to share their initial observations. Mannace was leaning over a table, looking over maps and eating an apple. He looked up and gave a short nod to acknowledge his visitors.

Because of his familiarity with Mannace, Rollo became the Rangers spokesman.

"Lord, we have been thinking of ways to patrol further out from the city. The soldiers in Viletri only ever got as far as half a day's travel before returning. If we had forward bases, then patrols stationed there would range further."

Rollo paused to invite comment from Mannace, but the leader remained bent over his maps, so he continued.

"If we had outposts beyond that, one on the border with Hindas, another near Sylos and one on the Plateau near the Dwarves, these could be bases for patrolling the borders and scouting even further afield".

The idea resonated with Mannace. He looked up, briefly meeting Rollo's gaze. There was no friendliness in the stare.

"I will consider it."

With that said, Mannace took another bite of the fruit and returned to scanning his maps. The Rangers, apparently dismissed, returned to their barracks in silence.

The Rangers made their next mission the detailed exploration of the region close to Viletri; an area roughly three days in any direction from the city. They worked closely with foragers and others that already had local knowledge.

After returning from their first foray, a Dark Elf approached Rollo, interested in joining their troop. Jayne Azaren possessed a sharpness and presence that suggested he was more than capable, and Rollo suspected he was also more than he seemed. But that wasn't Rollo's place to decide, so he introduced the potential recruit to Mannace. The Lord was also unsure of Jayne's motivations or if he was the right fit for the Ranger Company, but when the Elf said that Jaal would vouch for him, Mannace decided to appoint him Ranger number four. Rollo paired himself with Jayne, to better assess the Dark Elf and to get him used to their ways.

Over the next two months, the Rangers worked closely with the city garrison to better secure the region. They quickly discovered and dispersed four camps of Orcs, who fled west rather than fight. In another area, a large pack of wild dogs were no match for the armour and steel of an organised troop. While Rollo and Jayne tracked the Orcs to ensure they did not return, Alsaborg worked with Jed to nurture young pups that they recovered, paying a farming family to build kennels to raise them.

It felt to all involved that they successfully pushed the frontier back, and the region of Viletri was now better defined and secure. Settlers could now farm the lands outside the city with some safety. Their next task, which was well overdue, was to find the lands of the Orcs that had besieged Viletri.

MIGHT AND MAGIC

Titus Kane and Render were given the assignment of building up the city's defences without spending a lot of money. Titus took the approach that everybody shared responsibility to defend their community. There was a sizeable cache of surplus weapons after the battle against Akanidis and the commander set about equipping and training a militia. With the memory of the Orc attack fresh in people's minds, it was not hard to garner support. Citizens agreed to maintain their equipment and attend training one day each month. For any new migrants: men and women over the age of thirteen, it became part of their path to citizenship to be marked on the militia muster.

An enterprising Dwarf sold crossbows to the citizens who could afford it. She set up practice archery butts and arranged training for those with the extra coin. After just two months the Militia started to participate in patrols and night watch activities.

Render taught his apprentices how to enchant and control the moving statues so that the number of animated defenders increased, still located about the town inert and in their regular positions until they would be needed. However, the wizard was not content with the creations, perceiving the need to manufacture defenders that were more capable fighters. Ideally, they would be able to act autonomously, but Render knew that would require more than animal sacrifices. After nights of discussing their ideas, Titus and Render agreed on a radical approach, one that only immortals would conceive. From the military school, they picked out twenty students between the ages of five and seven, selected for their potential as soldiers and willingness to take instruction. With agreement from their families and endorsement from the Temple of War, Render planned to infuse in them a magic that upon their natural death, their spirit would transfer to statues. They would stand guard over the Temple and the City. In return, the student's families would receive a gratuity each year. The students, through their adolescent and adult life, would be held in high esteem.

When selecting the boys, Render came upon one youngster that caught his attention; a blond-haired rascal named Kole, who impressed the wizard with his quick mind and fierce wit. He decided to sponsor the child and would take a personal interest in his development.

Render commissioned the Grey Dwarves to fashion twenty massive statues from bedrock and reinforced with steel, in the likeness of mighty human heroes. It required labour spanning several years and needed close collaboration between the sculptors, magicians, and priests.

The final consideration in the city's defence was how they would defend an attack by sea. Render was confident that magic was a good option. He had some ideas that interested him and started his research.

As if to emphasise the importance of coastal defence, the Hindas' fleet arrived at the city of Viletri and arrayed their armada of war galleys across the bay. On their decks two thousand marines stood to attention awaiting orders. Flying a banner of parley, a small craft carrying the Admiral of Hindas entered the harbour.

Admiral Ithius Sartis and Lord Mannace of Viletri faced each other. The admiral was accompanied by a small contingent of *Merthos*, his elite marines. They had the look of veterans about them and kept a watchful eye on the gathering crowd. Mannace was immediately aware of the contrast between the highly organised and disciplined forces of Hindas and his rag-tag militia and scattering of soldiers. As good a fighter as he was, Mannace felt vulnerable without Render or Jaal at his side.

The Admiral was a stocky man of average height with a neatly trimmed black beard. He wore soldier's armour and helm, with a billowing green cloak. He appeared sharp and arrogant, ready for a fight.

"I have come to collect the workers from Hindas that you hold in this city as prisoners of war."

Mannace liked that the leader went straight to the point, so he did the same.

"There are over five hundred workers, each paying off a debt of one hundred duracs. When they have paid their debt, they will be free men. Do you choose to pay fifty thousand duracs to set them free?"

"I would pay ten thousand."

Ithius looked immovable. Mannace countered.

"Twenty thousand, with the exchange to be made in three months, and a promise".

"What promise?"

"That Hindas will join the Council of the Blood Sea."

"I have not heard of such a council."

"A council of the nations of the Blood Sea will be called to unite them to be ready for conflict with the North."

Ithius surprised Mannace with his instant reply.

"We must stand together if we are to survive the wrath of the North. Sixteen thousand duracs, one month and not a day more, and a promise made."

"Agreed."

The transaction meant fewer workers for the roads but a much-needed boost to the treasury.

Following the encounter with Ithius, Mannace took steps to protect himself better. He evolved the role of the Rangers so that in addition to their duties as scouts, they would be his private guard. He commissioned another twenty

Rangers, bringing the company's number to twenty-four. He put them on a rotation where four of the Rangers would be with him at any given time, responsible for his protection.

His perceived vulnerability made Mannace think about other aspects of law and order, which he would discuss further with Kakos and the Assembly.

EXODUS

Jaal returned to Viletri and with him came an armada of vessels carrying civilians from the city of Tarash. The fleet was a jumble of warships and merchant vessels crewed by men and Rhalec. Once they unloaded their passengers, they set off again to retrieve more of the desperate families. For eighteen days there was a regular stream of traffic, and then nothing, until Urgar returned to Viletri with the Celestial and his troop carrier both empty. He hurried to inform Jaal and together they went to Mannace. Urgar seemed nervous in front of the Lord.

"Err, Tarash has been overrun, Lord. The city put its balls on the block, all credit to 'em, but they've had the chop an' been fed to the sharks."

Jaal gave a less colourful interpretation, "Mannace, Tarash is in the invaders' hands. The capital, Gormoth, remains under siege."

It irked Mannace that Jaal refused to address him as Lord when others were present. He knew that pressing the point would only make the Dark Elf more petulant.

As well as interrogating Urgar and Jaal further on the detail, Mannace sent a messenger to summon Kakos. When the official arrived, the Lord questioned him.

"Kakos, how many Tarash refugees have come to us."

"Over six thousand Lord. Most of the age are requesting citizenship."

"Urgar, does Tarash Gormoth still have a navy?"

"Err yes Lord. Their Admiral is Veroff Odari. Slippery bastard."

"Kakos, set aside port facilities and an enclave for Admiral Odari and his ships. If they have lost the seas then he may require such a haven. Make a place for the Admiral on the

Assembly. Jaal, ensure the Admiral knows he has refuge here.”

Kakos raised another point he thought might be of interest to Mannace.

“Lord, there were merchant ships amongst those that brought refugees to our city. For some, it was their first visit to the Blood Sea, and they are interested in returning. I have invited them to establish new markets.”

Mannace was smug. He knew Jaal believed the journey to Tarash Gormoth a waste of time, but the outcome could not have been more advantageous.

“Hah! It seems we grow strong on the backs of those that are weak. When Veroff Odari arrives, bring him to me.”

As well as the Tarash passengers, Jaal also transported three Fogmir Elves back to Viletri. In his time with the Elves, Jaal learned that many of them could not leave the forest, not for any good reason that he could see, beyond fear of being under an open sky. These three were young and fearless. They left their duty as Wardens to find adventure in new lands.

For a second time that day, Jaal returned to see Mannace, with the three Elves in tow. As he anticipated, Mannace offered them positions in the Viletri Rangers which two accepted. The third did not want to be bound by Mannace’s terms of service.

During the exchange, Jaal was taken aback to see Singer as part of Mannace’s Ranger bodyguard. Singer was dressed very differently, somehow lost his limp, and he seemed to have meat on his bones. He was talking to others around him. As Jaal stared across the room, he did not doubt that this was the same Elf he travelled with to the Monastery. Mannace saw Jaal scrutinising the Ranger.

“Jaal, you know Jayne Azaryn, he said you spent time together in Ostoik. I need to know that he can be trusted. Do you vouch for him?”

Singer's disguise was clearly enough to have fooled Mannace, which made Jaal smirk. He loved the sense of irony that Mannace embraced this Dark Elf that he previously, in a private conversation, condemned.

"I do Mannace. He will keep to his word."

Jaal had no option than to vouch for the capability and loyalty of his kin. Later, in private, he could speak to Jayne more freely.

"Why are you here, Jayne?"

"We are part of the Order, Jaal. I am here because I must be here. Do you want to know if I will kill your friend? I do not know. Only time will tell if my purpose is to help Mannace or to end him. Perhaps I am here for another purpose altogether? Why are you here, Jaal?"

It was a question Jaal often asked himself, though this was the first time he shared his thoughts.

"See how Mannace is at the centre of events, how the fates fall at his feet. Everything he touches shifts into place. Jayne, if Mannace were not pivotal to the future, you would not be here."

After a pause, Jaal continued.

"Mannace needs my help, or he will make a mess of it. I know him, he will destroy what he has built."

Jayne did not look convinced. He seemed agitated at Jaal's explanation, though rather than challenge the point, he changed the topic.

"Your agility and speed. Individuals have qualities that often lie dormant, and never awaken. You are young to be aware of your potential. Few mortal creatures have the time needed to understand and access their greatness and most immortals will go through their existence and never have that exceptional quality revealed."

When Jaal looked back at him blankly, Jayne lost his patience.

"With your gift, you are like a boy fumbling with a new toy.

Take the time to properly comprehend what you have and how to channel it, to evolve and develop it. Learn as well to see exceptional qualities in others. There will be adversaries that cross your path that will have talents and characteristics that will challenge you to your limits. You will need your full abilities and wits to meet those challenges. The boy will help his friend. The man will shape his own destiny."

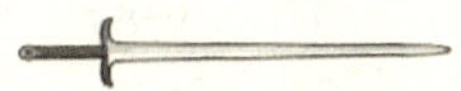

COUNCIL OF THE BLOOD SEA

Render added enchantments to the harbour at Viletri so that when the representatives arrived by sea for the inaugural Council meeting, they found the waters in the bay and harbour still and clear. Yet, strange currents moved their ships, guiding them into port. Where their vessels wake caused waves and ripples, the foam appeared like tiny dolphins skimming across the water before disappearing beneath the surface. The wizardry induced a mixed reception with some people impressed by the enchantment and others suspicious of any unnatural tinkering. Regardless, it was a message to take both Viletri and its wizard seriously.

Everybody was fascinated with the new Viletri. The city put on its 'best dress' for the occasion; the streets cleaned, people wore their finest clothes, and there was an atmosphere of celebration. In a short time, the ruined city had grown into a proud, diverse, and prosperous metropolis. Close inspection would reveal that areas of the town were still in ruins and unpopulated, but the visitors were amazed how something so grand had suddenly appeared on their doorstep. The Yanth enclave were resplendent in their full ceremonial dress. The other enclaves put on their best appearance as well, with flags and banners flying. Orchestrating the whole show was the Viletri Elder, Shepherd.

For Shepherd, the gathering represented eleven months of hard work to get delegates from the cities and nations of the Blood Sea to attend. Only Freman remained absent. In place of the Freman leaders, Shepherd invited representation from the three mercenary guilds that were based there. They readily agreed.

Ahead of the meeting, Mannace commissioned an artist to paint a wall of the restored grand council chamber with a map of the region. It included the nations of the Blood Sea and their cities, plus the continent known as The Land with the Rhalec, Fogmir Elves, and Tarash Gormoth. Also represented was what they now knew of the Great Continent as far north as the Icesleepers, including the nation of the Grey Dwarves, the Iron Jaw Orcs, and The Fallen. Alsaborg had helped him to add the detail of the regions near Arenland that included Two-Faces, the Madlands, Mecelay, and his Daglari homeland, commonly known as The Pillars.

Amongst the nations of the Blood Sea, there were two distinct factions, those allied to Yanth and those allied to Arenland. Yanth had long term alliances with Karanthos, Loryan, Cavastock, and the Isle of Malanos. Because of their proximity, they also enjoyed a history of collaboration with the Alani Elves. Arenland fostered close ties with Lapthos, Rummond, and Sylos, and they shared a long-standing military pact with Mecelay.

Hindas was a fiercely independent City-State, as was Freman, while The Pillars maintained a neutrality. The Grey Dwarves could be considered an ally of the Viletri but were otherwise neutral. Two-Faces, the Madlands, the Iron Jaw Orcs, and The Fallen were all considered hostile nations.

The three nations of The Land all acted independently of one another. The assault on their continent by the enemy referred to as 'The Collective', gave them a common interest.

Only those nations considered hostile did not have representation at the Council of the Blood Sea.

Two days were set aside for talks. Shepherd was to facilitate the sessions while Render and his apprentices were tasked with security and keeping the peace.

Shepherd arranged tables around the walls of the large Council chamber with the central area set aside for whoever was addressing the group. As the Council representatives settled in their allocated seats, two tables were noticeably empty. To fill those tables, Shepherd ushered in some unexpected participants who caused the Arenlanders to leap up from their chairs and shout their objections. The Daglari Chieftain went as far as to pick up his chair and break it across the table. With a chair leg still in his hand, he waved it like a weapon at the new arrivals. Some Councillors, deeply offended, chattered fervently amongst themselves, and were making their way towards the exits. Mannace, with help from Render, manoeuvred them back to their seats and Mannace promised them an explanation. The Overlord of Arenland looked at Mannace severely, as if his actions were a betrayal. However, it was a Minister from Yanth who yelled above the din in the room.

"Why do you bring these monsters here?"

He referred to the contingent of Orcs; four chieftains of the Iron Jaw. One was particularly old, his skin sagged over his arms and his white hair fell loosely over hunched shoulders. He had a presence about him though, like many old wise men. The other Orcs were large and mightily built, and they did their best to intimidate the crowd with savage snarls and stares. The hostility wasn't helping Mannace and Render to keep control.

Leading the second group was an ordinary-looking man flanked by two women in dark robes: the Mad King and his wives. The King was in his middle to late years, presented a pleasant smile despite his reception, and wore simple garments compared to many of those present. Arenland were in conflict with the Mad King over an area known as the Borderlands. It had been a battleground on and off for two decades. Lord Ravenborn of Ostoik stood on his chair, pointing down at the Mad King but looking accusingly at Mannace.

"You bring darkness to this hall. Put that head on a plate and end this debacle."

From the same table, the Overlord of Arenland continued to stare at Mannace as if this were some cruel jest. Mannace knew that if the Overlord were to react further, to oppose his surprise guests openly, it would irrevocably undo Shepherd's work to unite the Blood Sea leaders.

"WE WILL BE GREAT!"

Mannace's voice boomed out above all others.

"I have seen it in a vision", he lied. "We, gathered here, will rise to greatness above all others, and this is how it begins. Be seated at your tables. Listen to what I have to say."

Mannace waited for silence, grateful when those standing returned to their seats, though their hostility still radiated from them. He had naively hoped for a much better reaction, but now he at least held their attention and could start with his prepared speech.

"We are twenty nations, one Council. What does it mean to be a part of this Council? It means putting aside differences of race and beliefs, for the one belief that we all together can be stronger and better than our nations apart. It means that the actions of the past require forgiveness so we can focus on the actions of the future. Look around you now and see your neighbours; see your allies in trade, see your allies in defence of your lands, allies in forging a strong future for your people, your children, and their children."

There was grumbling all around, and the Overlords' unyielding stare assaulted Mannace. His mouth was dry, but he continued without pausing – raising his voice to keep his audience's attention.

"To be a member of this council means meeting the threat of the North, head-on and with ferocity. In Tarash Gormoth, the threat is upon us. Be sure that this is but a forerunner of the conflict to come. A taste of the threat that we must overcome if we are to survive and triumph and not become the victims or vassals of a Northern master."

As he scanned the room, Mannace observed that not all present were as antagonistic as the Arenlanders and their allies. The threat of the North or from other unknown enemies was real, reminding people why they were here - because divided they were vulnerable to foreign invasion.

Seeing a glimmer of support bolstered Mannace to continue.

"As a Council member, you will not tolerate aggression against your fellow members. Twenty nations, one Council, an attack on one, is an attack on all. A strong Blood Sea is a mighty bastion against the North and a colossal fist to smite our would-be oppressors."

The Orcs banged the table at the mention of smiting. They sneered and jeered at those around them as if the Council meeting were a game. By contrast, the Mad King and his family seemed dispassionate, unaffected by the speech or politicking around them. The Mad King whispered in a partner's ear, earning him a thin smile from her as if it were something mildly amusing.

Mannace was determined to make his point.

"What it means to be part of this Council. We will be giants in trade, titans in our craft, and the world will know that all that is good comes and goes through the Blood Sea. It means that our people will know pride and prosperity, and those here today, we magnificent leaders, will be heralded as the defenders of the lands and bringers of a golden age."

Shylo was Mannace's secret eyes and ears. As he circulated amongst the councillors after the speech, he sensed continued antagonism towards the surprise guests. Some hadn't focused at all on Mannace's words. Of those that listened, Shylo got the immediate impression that none had considered such a high degree of collaboration. Some of the leaders of smaller nations seemed puffed up by the speech. In contrast, the representatives from Yanth and Arenland were very quiet, giving nothing away of what they would do next. Most importantly, after the heat of the moment passed, nobody stormed away.

Part Three:

A Time For War

ANGRY MAN

Mannace greeted the envoy from the Empire of Bracadia. Their ambassador, a short woman named Delaria Trecatus, carried herself with great dignity and spoke with a high accent. She was somebody of importance. Like her entourage of lesser officers, Delaria dressed in a red waistcoat with a white puffy shirt, plus pants, leather belt, polished boots, and buttons all in black. The officials had rapiers at their sides. Delaria's auburn hair was long but rolled up in a top-knot, with a silver pin that held it in place.

On a mission of exploration and trade, the envoy travelled a great distance from the northwest. Their ship in the harbour was of unfamiliar design, a magnificent sailing vessel taller than any other ship in port, with three towering masts and two smaller ones at the bow and stern. Its crew of sailors and marines seemed well drilled and disciplined; all wore their red and white uniforms with pride. There appeared to be weapons or freight of some description stored on the main deck of the ship, concealed with cloth sheets. Jaal was suspicious, and as Mannace entertained the Bracadians onshore, the Dark Elf made it his business to investigate the ship and its secret cargo. When Jaal went to board the vessel, marines with their rapiers drawn came down the gangway to block his ascent.

"Move away. You are boarding a Bracadian vessel."

"Step aside, sailor. I am Jaal, Enforcer to the Lord of Viletri. I have authority here."

A Bracadian officer hurried to join his men. Leaning over the deck rail, he looked down and addressed Jaal with a firm tone.

"Nobody will board this vessel without the Ambassador's permission. Your authority does not extend past that dock," he pointed behind Jaal to make his point clear, an indication for him to retreat.

As the officer moved to the top of the gangway, Jaal could see his other hand around the hilt of a rapier, although the blade remained in its scabbard. Other crew could be heard hurrying to positions on the deck.

"My authority extends where I see fit."

The marines and officer in front of him showed no intention of moving. After a tense few moments, Jaal turned and returned to the dock. He heard a snigger from one of the marines behind him, but it was not enough for him to put reason aside. Instead, it fired his determination not only to see their secrets revealed but for those secrets to be their undoing.

It was the thirteenth anniversary of the re-founding of Viletri, and the Bracadian visitors observed the city at its finest. A vibrant mix of races and cultures arrived from the outlying towns and villages to participate in the celebrations.

Delaria did not look up as she passed the Temple of War. The great battle hall and shrine had been in use for some time, while the extended barracks and training grounds were still under construction. As a structure, it was not as grand as the temple in Ostoik, but the twenty colossal statues of heroic warriors that stood vigil about its perimeter made the war god's presence felt. Grey Dwarves worked hard to complete their projects, even during that week of celebrations.

Delaria asked about the God of War and the purpose of the temple. She had questions about everything and pushed Mannace for more detail. Mannace, normally eager to talk about the particulars on any subject and ask his questions in return, was reticent to do so with the Bracadian. He normally liked inquisitive people, but he felt that Delaria had a condescending tone. She seemed unimpressed by what she saw, making him question his achievements.

During the celebrations, Mannace encouraged the Bracadians to try the local delicacies available at the food stalls along the main streets. He pointed out some of the foods that were typical of different cities and cultures around the region. They tried most things but seemed to have a taste for the sweets. Mannace insisted that the Bracadians join him for dinner and promised them a feast to remember.

The envoy was free to investigate the city further by themselves. Mannace instructed Jayne and his spy Shylo to watch them. Jayne returned with news that some of their numbers spent the remainder of the day scouting the city end to end, including the barracks and military docks. Shylo learned that they purchased maps of the Blood Sea from the Merchants quarter. He was also surprised at what they didn't do, which was to discuss trade or other opportunities. When the three men reviewed the findings, they agreed that the Bracadians were taking their measure in preparation for an attack, be it soon or sometime in the future. It annoyed Mannace that they did so little to hide their intent as if he were too ignorant to notice.

The dinner was a grand affair held in the Council Chamber. The enormous room was decorated with tapestries and magnificent displays of flowers. The aroma of the blooms mixed with the smell of roasted meats and vegetables was reminiscent of a rural festival. Kakos arranged for entertainers, that journeyed to the city for the celebrations, to amuse the guests throughout the evening. The elite of Viletri and envoy from Bracadia ate, drank, and laughed late into the night.

Mannace was watching a troop of acrobats from Alani when Jayne appeared at the door and looked at him questioningly. Mannace nodded and, moments later, the room filled with soldiers that appeared through the main entrance and side doors. They pushed past other guests to subdue the Bracadians and roughly escorted the foreigners back out the main entrance.

Delaria, who was seated at the main table next to Mannace, quickly got to her feet but Mannace grabbed her arm with one hand and with his other he thumped her so hard in the face that her mind spun, and her vision blurred. Mannace led her by the hair as he exited the hall, moving down a corridor and entering another room before closing the door behind him. Anger consumed him. His hate fuelled another blow, this time he winded his captive and bashed her against a wall. He would show this superior bitch the consequences of looking down at him.

Jaal and Render met after the guests were all departed. Render was concerned.

"Did you see the look on Mannace when he hauled the woman away?"

"*Angry Man*".

Angry Man was the nickname they had given Mannace during times when his temper took hold. They had not seen Angry Man since coming to the Blood Sea, and both were worried about what might happen next. Mannace was a force of nature, and when he was fuming, he was the cyclone that rolled off the sea, unstoppable and destroying everything in its path.

"It's likely been building for a long time. We should have seen the signs."

"Light save us all." Jaal shook his head.

Jaal did not sleep that night. In addition to Mannace's rage, he was taken aback at not being involved in securing the Bracadian ship. Normally Mannace would come to him for such a mission, but this time Jayne Azaryn had been trusted with the harbour task.

FROM PEACE COMES WAR

The Council of the Blood Sea met on the last day of the celebrations. In addition to the membership at the inaugural meeting, there were three additional tables. The first, occupied by the Two-Face Orcs. They were mean-looking warriors with tattoos over half their face and most of their bodies. Ironically, they had larger jaws than the Iron Jaw Orcs and were wider at the shoulder. The Two-Face joined the council under an agreement to be paid as enforcers for the Councils plans of unity and expansion. It proved to be a good arrangement so far, peace was brought to the borders with Arenland as well as providing the Orc warriors with useful occupation.

At the second table sat a warrior and a slender man. Both were dressed in fur-lined studded leather jackets, leather trousers and knee-high boots. Like the Orcs, they had tattoos on their hands and faces. The slender man kept one of his eyes sewn shut, with the image of an eye inked over it. Long metal pins pierced his ears, cheeks, and nose - making the Councillors grimace. The Fallen were a recent addition to the council, given the opportunity to be part of the gathering after their defeat by the Blood Seas combined armies. They were a nomadic society who occupied the lands north of Hindas and north-west of Viletri. The two representatives had dour moods and sat with their arms folded. For some reason, being seated next to the Rhalec aggravated their discomfort, and they seemed ill-disposed towards the reptilians.

The Fesadi filled the third new table. They were an old nation that shared a mountain range with the Alani Elves, although it was only in the last five years that Fesadi merchants undertook the arduous journey through the mountain passes to commence trading with the Alani. The Fesadi knew special techniques for preserving foods that intensified their flavours, with their product already popular in communities across the blood sea. Their young king, his wife, and advisors were present.

Noticeably absent were the Freman. Angry Man took this as a personal insult, fuelling his temper to such an extent that he cast aside the agenda he planned with Shepherd. Instead, Mannace let rage consume him. He felt strengthened by it, fortified to take the hard steps that must be taken – steps that had waited too long to become actions. He stormed over to the table left vacant by the Freman Lord and with a great heave, he overturned it. Those nearby scrambled. All eyes were on him, and lips fell silent. He glared at everybody present, seemingly possessed.

"We have met here each year, and our people have come together to achieve great things. Yet one nation of the Blood Sea chooses to set itself apart."

Mannace's scowl could carve rock. Nobody in the room dared move.

"They insult us with their absence, and they harbour the pirates that attack our trade."

Mannace's eyes seemed to narrow and darken. He scanned the room. The wife of a Yanth official let out a small gasp and she had to look away to avoid Mannace's glare. The Lord of Viletri had hatred on his tongue and he spoke from the dark pit of his soul.

"It is time for the independence of the Freman to end."

After an uncomfortable period of silence, the Guildmaster of Swords, whose headquarters was based in Freman, stepped into the centre of the room as was the custom for those wanting to speak. He was not a man to be easily intimidated, but even he had an appeasing tone to his voice, not wanting to incur Mannace's wrath.

"The guilds have arrangements with the Freman. We have been based in that city for more than two hundred years and it is as much our home as the Freman. The Lord of Freman, Junis, is a donkey's arse. You'll never see him at this Council table. He likes to do things his own way. Wants everybody to know that he's the boss."

The Guildmaster looked over to the other mercenary leaders and they gave him the nod to continue.

"Mercenaries are often employed to do the hard, dirty jobs; make the noble pay his debts, move the settlers off their land, eliminate an enemy. It can make us unpopular, and it puts targets on our backs. Freman is a refuge when needed, a place to rest between assignments."

Mannace moved and stood alongside the Guildmaster. He used his height to look down at the man, at first dominating him, then gradually relaxing as if his anger were released upon a deep breath. The Lord of Viletri reached out a hand and he put it on the Guildmaster's shoulder. They looked at each other in the eye. Mannace's voice was much softer when he next spoke.

"What if you did not need to hide? What if the Guild Masters were generals? What if the mercenaries were the backbone of the war host of the Blood Sea? The Battalion of Swords. The Battalion of Ravens. The Battalion of the Crescent Moon. I offer you this and you will have no need for loyalty to Freman. Their time has come, I will see to it personally."

The Guildmaster of Ravens rose and responded without stepping forth.

"We'll see to it personally. Freman is our business. You just worry about how ya gonna pay for a mercenary army. The Ravens, and t' others have no love or loyalty for the White Shirts or their boss. Well carve 'em up and we'll keep the city. Speaking for the Ravens, you'll have your Battalion."

"And the Swords."

"And the Crescents."

All three Guildmasters gathered now in the centre of the room, exchanged glances and nods. The Guildmaster of the Crescent Moon continued to speak.

"But we'll not be sittin' on our arses like some bloody

garrison wankers. If ya want an army you're gonna need to use the army. Nobody got rich sittin' on a wall."

Mannace seemed satisfied with the response so Shepherd brought the stunned Council back to its agenda and they eased into discussions of industry and trade, taxes, and tariffs, as well as the regions security.

As he had done every year for the last nine years, Captain Veroff Odari, the representative for Tarash Gormoth became frustrated with proceedings and they all knew his intent as he took the centre floor. It was the stain on what had otherwise been a highly successful decade.

"By the four hells, how can you waste time on this trivia when the threat of the North is sitting on your doorstep, growing in strength and audacity? Tarash Gormoth, one of the twenty members of this council, is under foreign dominion, yet you sit back and watch."

Admiral Ithius Sartis of Hindas was quick to take the floor next to the Captain, facing him.

"The Collective still have over twenty thousand warriors in the region. They hold the three cities and their migrants have occupied much of the land for long enough that they might fairly call it home. Tarash is prosperous and it trades vigorously with its allies to the West, not the North. They have shown no interest in moving further south."

Veroff threw his hands in the air, but Ithius went on.

"What are we of the Blood Sea if we are not also a collective? A group of nations come together for a common purpose. Do not confuse this Collective that is our rival in Tarash Gormoth with the greater enemy of the North. When that enemy comes there will be no doubt of its intent and there will be no hesitation in its purpose. Time has moved on. We should reach out to the Collective in Tarash Gormoth, make our peace."

Veroff was incensed but before he could speak, Mannace stepped into the middle of the room. His mood was such that it commanded attention and when he addressed the

Council he presented a fierce demeanour that nobody would dare have challenged.

"Let me say it for you, Veroff, we have left it too late. We have pissed about for ten years, and we have let the Collective have its way. If we were now to raise our hand against Tarash Gormoth we will seem the invader, not the liberator. Well, so be it. The Council of the Blood Sea will not be taken seriously until we can command a fleet and army that strikes terror into the hearts of our enemies."

Mannace looked around the room. Staring at the leaders until he had their full attention.

"Let each nation make a commitment, one that they will have to work hard to meet; that they will make their ships and soldiers available to form a great southern host that will move west into Tarash Gormoth, then into the heart of the Collective. Veroff will have his revenge and we will show that we are here and that we are united and that we are a perilous and persistent foe. In one year, we meet here again, with our ships and our armies, and the assault shall begin."

Unsurprisingly, Mannace got a cheer from the mercenary Guildmasters and from the Orcs a savage "raaagh". Most leaders were more reserved. The War Priest Demmal who sat at Mannace's table stepped forth.

"We have enjoyed a time of peace. A time where nations have united, and we have become stronger. Through peace, we have set the foundation to raise a great host, one that will honour the God of War and bring him victories. Do not skimp in this military preparation; let the God of War rejoice at your industry in this endeavour."

Those in the centre returned to their tables. Though there was a mixed reaction amongst the nations to the proposal, none came forth to openly oppose it. During the ensuing discussion, the elderly Lord Bisan of Sylos made a suggestion.

"We possess amongst us the tools and technology of war, things of inventiveness and magic. The iron ships of

Arenland. The rapid crossbows of the Dwarves. The statues of the Viletri. The Shroud of the Iron Jaw. The Thog of Two-Faces. With these things shared we would be truly formidable, a host to sweep aside all opposition."

Bisan's suggestion brought an uneasy silence. The truth of it was undeniable, but for nations that went to great lengths to protect their secrets, it would be a radical turn around to share such artefacts. The fact that they were considering it at all was testament to how far the Council had come. The discussion around it took most of the day and some agreements were reached between allies, but it was an enterprise that would take considerable time to reach its full potential.

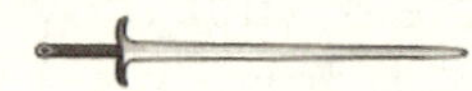

FREMEN BY SEA

Jaal and his troop were considered an elite unit. They numbered more than three hundred and had proven themselves in the clash with the Fallen and in many smaller skirmishes fought across the Blood Sea. While Mannace referred to them as Peacekeepers, they were more popularly known as the Blood Legion. It was not easy to gain a place in the infamous 'Legion'. Khing, Urgar, and Casteel were responsible for judging potential recruits, and they set a high benchmark. It became common for the leaders of nations and high-ups to want to place their sons into the legion, but the same scrutiny applied, and only the most capable were permitted entry. The force was a representation of most races in the region, bringing together many cultures, but also fostering their own notable ethos of comradery and loyalty. Because their foundation was as a group of mercenaries, the Blood Legion joined the attack on Freman.

After the announcement, the mercenary guilds abandoned their lodgings in Freman and temporarily based themselves in Yanth. They filled up the inns and taverns in the city and surrounds, with others living on troop ships or in a barracks leased to them by the city. More than six thousand sell-swords gathered; some come out of retirement for this historic battle and others newly recruited.

As anticipated, the Freman drew all their allies to themselves; every pirate, slaver and rogue that could be mustered. Agents in Freman reported as many as thirty ships in port, plus a garrison of two thousand made up of regular White Shirts and militia. Although they were outnumbered, behind their fortress walls they were formidable.

On a fine day, with a light breeze at their backs, the attack on Freman by the Mercenaries and their allies commenced. More than one hundred ships converged on the Freman harbour: mercenary troop carriers, the tall sailing ships of Yanth, galleys from Hindas, and the fleet of Arenland with its three mighty iron warships. As they approached the port, Khing joined Jaal at the bow of the Celestial.

"I've never seen the like of it. So many ships together. These pirates will piss themselves."

As Khing predicted, panic ensued within the harbour. The pirate ships quickly realised how badly they were outnumbered and, scrambling to escape the approaching fleet, they hurried for open waters, yet only one was fast enough to evade the allies' net. The lone vessel made its way east along the coast with two fast Yanth vessels on its tail.

"That's Kraken," said Khing to Jaal, "They'll never catch that wily old bastard."

The other pirate ships were backed into the harbour. While some put up a desperate defence it was quickly overcome, and most captains surrendered their vessels without a fight. Several Freman and pirate crews scampered to land and scattered themselves or hid amongst the buildings.

One enemy ship was enveloped in a shield of magic. When Jaal looked more closely it was akin to staring through warped glass. He could determine the shape of the vessel and see movement about its decks, but he couldn't make out what the crew was doing. Three Hindas war galleys boxed the ship in and for now, it seemed a standoff.

At the port and along the coast, the mercenaries, plus Jaal and his Legion disembarked the ships. Many of the mercenaries had travelled through this city numerous times and some were just as at home here as the White Shirts they came to fight. With their intimate knowledge, securing the port and city was an easy task, but not so simple was the fortress and walled compounds that contained the White Shirts' barracks and training grounds.

Khing joined some of the mercenary captains who scouted

the enemy position, then returned to Jaal at dusk with his report. They were joined by Casteel and Urgar. Khing had a concerned tone to his voice.

"The White Shirts are well prepared. The defenders are armed with crossbows, that's gonna hurt when we storm the walls. The captains weren't too happy about that. There were ballistae in the towers too. It's all new since we were here last."

Jaal was curious, "What news of the city?"

"Most loyal to the White Shirts are in the fortress. Their families as well. Those remaining in the city are staying indoors. Some of the locals are wives and children of mercenaries. Many know their invaders. A few may be sympathetic to Junis and his garrison."

Jaal shrugged his shoulders, "Are they a danger then?"

"We should be watchful, but the officers seem unconcerned."

Casteel slammed her hand on the table they were sitting at. She hated everything about this place. In her mind, it should all be burned to the ground. Not liking what she was hearing, Casteel got up and without meeting the gaze of her companions, returned to her accommodation. The Blood Legion were fortunate enough to secure an Inn and nearby warehouse so that those seated at the table would all have comfortable beds. When Casteel departed, Khing turned to the others.

"The White Shirts have been bastards to the people that live here. Many will want to see them gutted and thrown in a ditch."

After his long afternoon exploring the fortress perimeter and city, Khing was thirsty, and he gulped the ale delivered by a serving wench. He shared one last piece of information.

"The Mercenaries have divided into three shifts of two thousand soldiers. They have commenced the siege. We are to patrol the business district and port, three shifts of one hundred."

Urgar, smiling, also shared what he learned.

"The spell casters boat be at the dock. He's under guard with the other brigands. The Masters know the bastard captains well. T'will be a time of reckoning."

Urgar was a pirate himself when honest work was hard to come by. It was the way of the sea.

The next day, the fleets of Hindas, Yanth, and Arenland departed. As they did so, parts of the city came back to life and some businesses reopened. In the rural areas, farmers were already getting about their business and fishermen went back to their trade – with so many mouths to feed their skills and wares would be in high demand. Unsurprisingly it was not long before the brothels were also enjoying an excellent trade.

A sea fog drifted in and settled over the city and fortress, it cooled the air and gave Freman a dreary demeanour. It was a common phenomenon that they would get used to in the months ahead of them.

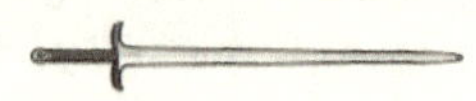

WILD ELVES

Chamaryylha, also known as Rylla to those close to her, was relieved that her child was white-skinned, not black-skinned like his father. Although Rylla was esteemed amongst the warrior caste, her judgement would be questioned if she birthed a Dark Elf child. The baby was born with some of the looks of his father and certainly had his piercing eyes, but he also possessed her resilience and intuition. She named him Athose.

When Athose was two years of age Rylla went to his nest one morning and found a second child: a girl perhaps slightly older, with very similar looks and attributes, but with dark skin. At first, Rylla was enraged, and she cursed the father for his audacity to place this burden upon her, but she could not abandon the youngster and she raised the two together. Rylla named the girl Roanna.

Athose and Roanna were inseparable. Being fast learners and naturally talented; they were superior to their peers when they raced, climbed, or fought. In their tenth year, on the first day of summer, as was the custom of the Fogmir Elves, they were tested by the Gathering. The senior lawmakers, druids, shapers, makers, wardens, carvers, hunters, growers, and runners all came together to help the young ones determine their life path. All Elves in their tenth year from throughout the Fogmir, gathered to be assessed.

Athose, like his mother, was tagged as a Warden. His training would begin immediately.

Roanna was selected by the Druids. They were very few and it was expected that Roanna would travel with one of them to a distant part of the forest to commence her apprenticeship. The children were distraught at being apart, but they were excited by the prospect of their training.

The Wild Elves of the Fogmir were nomadic. It was traditional that mothers would come together in small communities while they were nesting to raise their children to the age where they could attend the Gathering. Once the youngsters were assigned their apprenticeships, their well-being became the responsibility of professional mentors and ultimately themselves. Rylla said goodbye to her children as she left to search out and re-join her Warden tribe, sad to leave her offspring but relieved to be free of the nest.

Despite her mother's fears, Roanna was never treated differently for her dark skin, in fact, other children seemed to gravitate to her because of her striking appearance. The path of the druid did far more to set her apart and even adults acted differently in her presence – already as apprentice, other Elves looked to her for guidance and wisdom. It was much for her to take in, but a role she was well suited to.

Roanna's mentor was a female Elf named Ulalyyarwherri, or Ula to the young ones. Ula did nothing to teach Roanna, but they travelled together and even within the first months Roanna learned many things through observation about the forest, its animals, and different communities amongst the Elves. Sometimes they would encounter a tree suffering from rot or sickness and Ula would lay her hands upon it to draw out the disease. The task was tiring for Ula, therefore, Roanna started to help. The activity aided the youngster to connect with the forest and she began to see it differently, to feel it differently, and to better appreciate its wild splendour.

Athose joined a group of forty Wardens, and as part of his initiation, one of them gifted him a bow with arrows. Athose was told that the tribe travelled a regular path through the woodland, and over those first days, they made their way to several way-points before coming close to the forest's edge. He had never seen beyond the forest, and it was strange to observe land uncovered by trees. It looked and felt as if the life had been peeled from the earth which left it exposed and disfigured. After a day of travelling the border, they changed direction to a way-point deeper within the forest.

The young Warden was expected to do his part in the scouting, foraging, and hunting. He found life with the troop was physically demanding, particularly when they journeyed through the canopy high above the forest floor. Even with his natural strength and agility, Athose worked hard to keep up with the others. Eager to prove himself, Athose took to learning the basics of the bow and occasionally one of the Wardens would give him pointers, not only on shooting but also how to use a bow in close quarters in conjunction with other techniques of unarmed combat. He enjoyed the simplicity of his new role and appeared to be naturally suited to it.

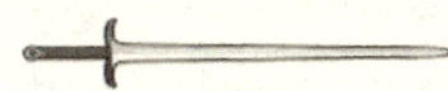

UNDER THE MOUNTAIN

Rollo was escorted into the depth of the mountain by the Grey Dwarven soldiers. He had travelled here many times and, on this occasion, he came with a troop of men carrying gear taken from the captured Bracadian vessel. He knew the route to the engineers' quarter and as he drew close some of the Dwarves hailed him.

Mannace and the Dwarf, Logthar, were collaborating on many projects. It started with the complex devices recovered from the Monastery but extended to include oddities and inventions from across the Blood Sea. Now the extraordinary weapons of the Bracadians would be added to the mix. Rollo expected that the engineers and clockmakers, as they always did, would take these things and seek to understand, replicate, improve and produce them. Render sometimes came with Rollo, and he helped to decipher those items touched by magic. In some cases, the wizard provided energy to things that needed it, although the Dwarves preferred to rely on their clockwork as a power source.

Rollo visited the military division. At their experimental facilities, he met with the Dwarven specialists working on Mannace's designs. The jovial engineers were enthusiastic to discuss and demonstrate their progress. A senior Dwarf named Thorbid held a suit of armour to show the visitor, juggling it up and down to demonstrate its lightness. He explained the basics to Rollo.

"She be a revelation boy-o, light yet strong enough to stop a bolt at point-blank."

The Dwarf turned the armour around to show a breast and backplate. Then he held up the left sleeve and shook it about to demonstrate its movement at the joints. The attached gauntlet was intricate, and the Dwarf revealed a small shield disk inlaid in the palm. Rollo had seen the magical disks in action before.

The smiling engineer took longer to extend the right arm, laying it out on a table so that he could better explain the parts.

"This is the mechanical arm. See 'ere, it's joined at the shoulder, elbow, and wrist with these alloy frames and clockwork enhancers. Still allows sideways movements. Revolutionary design."

The Dwarf twisted the arm back and forth to show how it mimicked the movements of its wearer. Finally, he lifted the gauntlet, which was oversized, and banged it on the table to demonstrate the significant weight it carried.

"She's got a tight grip and a powerful fist. 'Tis the clockwork boy-o that gives her strength. Turns a flick into a punch. Bammo."

A young Dwarf who donned a similar suit came forward and Thorbid stepped back.

To assist with the demonstration a group of engineers gathered and started throwing things at the armoured Dwarf who raised his left hand and shielded or battered the makeshift missiles out of the air with an invisible barrier.

When the missiles stopped he walked across to an empty bench and with a big wind-up slammed his right fist onto the tabletop. The table broke in half, both pieces slid dramatically across the floor. The engineers cheered and the armoured Dwarf gave a sly grin and acknowledged them with a nod. Not finished his demonstration, the Dwarf grabbed an axe in his right hand and cleaved a second table, not splitting it - but instead, the axe head chopped through the thick wood, embedded to its wooden shaft. The Dwarf attempted to pull the axe free, and the table lifted slightly but was of too much weight for the Dwarf to lever. The engineers cheered and laughed. The Dwarf pulled harder, applied pressures at differing angles until the axe handle snapped under the strain and he lost his balance, landing clumsily on the floor. His comrades were in fits and they applauded him in good humour. The embarrassed Dwarf stood up and took a theatrical bow.

Rollo would have spent more time with the Dwarves had a messenger not arrived to take him to Logthar. His escorts travelled at a fast walk through many corridors until they came to a large room with desks and clerks moving between them. Logthar was there and he came over to welcome Rollo. While Rollo enjoyed the engineers' company, being in front of the leader of the Grey Halls made him anxious. He wasted no time in relaying Mannace's request.

"Lord Mannace requests equipment for one thousand warriors to be delivered within the next six months."

"What equipment specifically?"

"The armour, shields, helmets, belts ... the weapons"

"Any specific weapons?"

"No, but after today, hammers would be best, with metal shafts."

Logthar was thoughtful and he took time to summon and consult with the chief of engineers.

"Rollo, I understand that Mannace will want to have his soldiers ready before the next council, but we will be hard-pressed to equip two hundred in that time-frame. We have our own preparations to make as well."

"Lord Mannace has an arrangement with a guild master in Ostoik who can supply engineers, or they can be commissioned to make parts."

"It won't be Dwarven quality you're getting if you follow that tunnel my lad, but if you can arrange a meeting with this guild master and get some engineers here to assist, we'll see what can be done. There's some magic in the shield and helm so we'll be needing one of the wizards too."

As a parting statement, Logthar added, "We're doing some amazing stuff here lad, tell Mannace he needs to come to the Grey Mountain for a visit, he'll be wanting to see the progress in person."

Rather than take the highway back to Viletri, Rollo followed a well-travelled road which wound its way through the hills and mountains east to the valleys of the Iron Jaw. He passed merchants with wagons as well as groups of Orcs and Humans who travelled between communities. It was a safe route and Rollo relaxed and enjoyed the walk. He stayed overnight at an Orc village before arriving at the City of Hagbesh the following day. Unlike human cities, Hagbesh had no symmetry to it. Whatever needed to be built was constructed on the next available piece of land, without thought of access or consequence. Additionally, things were built without any standards for design or construction, and the Orcs seemed to do a bit of everything themselves rather than have experts in a trade.

A handful of modern buildings commissioned by merchants or guildsman from other nations stood out amongst the chaos.

Rollo journeyed to the Orc cities many times and he had learned much about their culture. He understood that Orcs collected in tribal groups. They showed loyalty to both family and tribe, and they would defend both to the death, without question or reason. They were tough and aggressive, although fights seldom broke out. When they did, it was all on and there were no rules or limits. Orcs looked at other races as weak but respected any individual that could give as good as they got.

Mannace once explained to Rollo that underpinning Orc society was a warrior spirit, and to maintain the peace between the tribes they needed a common enemy. In this regard, Mannace called on the Iron Jaw to spearhead the war with the Fallen and had since asked for their assistance in securing border regions or clearing out monster hot spots in the wildlands surrounding Viletri, Sylos, and Hindas.

The thing Rollo found hardest to get used to was the public sex, which was typically rough, uninhibited, and sometimes involved multiple participants. He also found it challenging that Orcs would crap and piss wherever they happened to be, with little regard for others. In Hagbesh, there were Orcs that cleared away the mess. These cleaners were often the runts, born smaller, dim-witted, or physically deformed, and rather than kill them as was the practice in some cities, the Orcs of Hagbesh put them to the tasks that proud Orcs would never stoop to do. The city stank of faeces, piss, and sweat, and there was nowhere to hide from it.

Rollo made a delivery to an Orc Chieftain, a package from Mannace that made the Chief happy. He then found his way to a hut he had visited before. Degura answered his call and she invited him inside. Degura like other Orc females was smaller than the male Orcs and generally more human in appearance, but still big-boned, strong and with tusks that protruded from her jaw. Like the dwelling, the furniture was basic and poorly crafted. Rollo put a handful of small coins on a table. Without exchanging words, Degura lifted her skirt and leaned forward over the table to give Rollo a good look at what he was paying for. Rollo didn't require further direction.

ALSABORG

Alsaborg was visited by Arta, his journey companion of many years. Arta was a large woman, tall and broad. Big-boned and muscular but with a good layer of fat to keep out the cold. Freelance mercenary contracts were becoming harder to come by since the foundation of the Council and the reduction in disagreements between the nations, so Arta hoped to secure employment at Viletri. Her only possessions, a large two-handed maul and a knapsack, were on her back.

When Alsaborg was not at the barracks, he spent time at his kennels outside of the city, which had become a thriving business supplying guard dogs and working dogs to the local populace. He maintained his own pack of twenty hounds that he took with him on patrols. Arta joined Alsaborg on such a patrol, to catch up and share old stories as they moved about. The hounds scouted ahead so that Alsaborg did not have to be so alert. It was hardly frontier land anymore and Viletri had not been menaced by troubles on its borders for many years. The old friends spent two nights travelling the well-worn paths before they returned to the city.

A week later Arta was still unemployed. Although she was very experienced, most recruiters were reluctant to hire a woman amongst a male crew. It did not help that she was often brash and ill-tempered.

Knowing that Mannace often saw the qualities in people that others missed, Alsaborg thought he may have an interest in Arta for the Rangers or as a bodyguard for one of the many Viletri officials. The informal meeting took place in Mannace's private quarters, and the Lord asked Arta about her experience. His initial impression was good; her size and confidence gave her a commanding presence that he liked. In fact, he felt an attraction.

Behind him, through an open door to Mannace's bedroom, Arta could see a woman move about the Lord's quarters, tidying and making up a bed. She wore a metal collar about her neck, with a long thin chain that allowed her to move about the room. The chain was secured at the other end to a ring set into the floor. The woman showed bruises on her face and arms. She limped as if movement caused her pain.

Arta, who as a young woman had suffered at the hand of a brutal man herself, was immediately incensed and spoke without considering the circumstances or consequences.

"That is no way to treat a woman".

Angry Man revealed himself instantly, and the blatant accusation infuriated him.

"Mind your mouth! How I put an enemy to a task is my own business."

"I won't abide a man that takes a slave for sex or beats a woman, why would a man who can have any woman choose to force himself on another? What is wrong with you?"

Mannace was ready to strike. His face was red, and he screamed at Arta.

"GET OUT OF MY HOUSE. GET OUT OF MY CITY!"

Arta was not bothered by Mannace's temper, and she was not one to back away from anything. She took a step forward. Before either could act or speak further, Alsaborg interceded. He snarled through clenched teeth, holding Arta by her arms so that she could not reach for her maul, and pulled her to the side before he escorted her forcibly out to the street.

Alsaborg removed the distinguishing green Ranger cloak that he wore and dropped it unceremoniously onto the busy thoroughfare. He had served Mannace loyally but his tie to Arta was older and stronger. It was an action certain to incur the Lord's wrath. Worried for the safety of himself and his companion they hurried to the enclave of the Blood Legion, and to the residence of Jaal, where Alsaborg hoped to find a sympathetic ear.

While Jaal fought the Freman, Saska oversaw his holdings. She and Mannace shared little affection and it seemed to her an opportunity to poke the beast. Saska offered Alsaborg and Arta sanctuary and employment as her protectors, which they gratefully accepted.

Saska employed two other protectors; animated stone gargoyles that she called Tumas and Harvor. They were named after two young men of the Blood Legion who had been crushed when a ruin in the city collapsed. The gargoyles were ever vigilant and excellent climbers, seeming to move around the walls and ceiling easily, able to come and go through the windows. When they settled in the shadows, they were almost invisible. Saska treated them like pets and would pat them on their heads and backs when they settled beside her for attention.

The other people in Saska's employ were all women. Each was attractive and previously worked in the whorehouses in the city before joining her. While in her employ they enjoyed some special benefits that nobody else could give them and in return they performed whatever tasks were required.

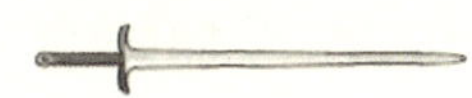

FREMEN SIEGE

At Freman, deals were being struck with the captive pirate captains and their crews. Generally, there wasn't a lot of difference between pirates and mercenaries, other than who paid the wages. Both groups were on hard times and the unification of the Blood Sea nations put the squeeze on their endeavours. With Mannace's commitment to fund a mercenary army, most of the pirate captains were satisfied to include their ships into the mercenaries' expanding flotilla. Those that the Guildmasters considered untrustworthy were quietly dispatched, left under the docks to feed the boltheads and crabs. There was nobody to mourn the loss of such crooked scoundrels, except perhaps the few backstreet whores across the Blood Sea who would have fewer coins in their purses.

It was a lazy siege of the Freman fortress with no casualties yet on either side. The mercenaries deployed enough numbers to ensure nothing came in or out of the stronghold. They were reluctant however to assault the defences, expecting heavy casualties if they were to make a direct attack. It was unknown how many months of supplies the garrison and the civilians kept, but after three months the defenders still appeared healthy and staunch.

At a meeting of the commanders, one of the mercenary captains that once served in Arenland made a suggestion.

"We should have been better prepared. Junis was never gonna let this be easy – it's not like he'd just leave the gate wide open."

The captain looked up at Jaal and gave him a wink. They all knew the story of Jaal's prior raid on the fortress. A few of the other commanders present sniggered. The man continued with his idea.

"It's gonna need proper siege equipment to take the rock. We should get to Ostoik and buy war machines. Nothing fancy, something basic to take down that gate and soften up the defences.”

There was a lot of nodding. Jaal was quick to offer his support.

“I’ll take you to Ostoik. This waiting is ridiculous, we have achieved nothing since coming here.”

Jaal was relieved to have an excuse to be away from the island and they left aboard the Celestial that same day.

It was always easy to get what you needed in Ostoik. Ten trebuchets and projectiles were ordered and by nightfall factories were already working to the designs. The war machines would be ready in eleven days. As part of the deal, an experienced engineer was commissioned to travel to Freman and train the mercenaries in their use.

During the construction, Jaal took leave of the others to visit the Temple of War where he was granted an audience with the High Priestess. He had a question for Ahmeda.

“How is our daughter?”

“She is learning magic and the ways of the forest.”

When Jaal gave over to the darkness, the price he paid was both his soul and seed. It was formalised in a ceremony where they were first joined in spirit, then in body. In Dark Elf society there was no greater commitment and it meant that their paths were forever intertwined. It did not prevent the priestess from returning to her human husband or Jaal from returning to his demon woman. It elevated Jaal in the Order and he was no longer compelled to obey the High Priestess’ command. It put him in high standing with other Dark Elves too. Importantly, Deckon Ruel and Jayne Azaren were now his peers. It was important to Jaal that Jayne, who was so close to Mannace, could no longer command his actions.

Jaal shared news from Viletri and Freman. Ahmeda talked about the politics of Arenland. Neither had much capacity or patience for small talk, but before Jaal left, Ahmeda added a final piece of advice.

"Jaal, you must investigate the third seed shared. I cannot see into the spider woman's domain, she skulks beneath the shadow. You should go to her and learn what has transpired."

Jaal was dubious, but still used to taking orders, he nodded.

Eleven days later the trebuchets were delivered as promised. It took another two days to get them into position near the fortress, under the cover of sea fog and far enough back to be concealed by the city's buildings. Instruction on their use were given and, when preparations were finalised, the assault commenced.

Junis, Lord of Freman and commander of the White Shirts, looked out from a fortress tower across the city. As he watched, a shape came suddenly out of the mass of houses and flew towards the fortress, it smashed against the wall. More missiles appeared from multiple locations and now that they were active, he could see the tall arms of the trebuchets as they arched above the rooftops before being winched back into position. At first, some of the missiles fell short, but as they continued the attack, they became more accurate and pounded the walls, the gatehouse, and some smashed into buildings within the defence. Junis could see the White Shirts and militia come to life, they mounted the walls and manned ballista in readiness for a full out attack.

Inevitably one of the huge missiles struck the gate to the barracks and it crashed inwards. Mercenaries swarmed from the city towards the opening. In response, crossbow bolts rained down on them and the first soldiers to the gatehouse earned a bath of oil, that was set alight with thrown torches. It halted the attack long enough for the White Shirts to ready themselves in the barracks courtyard. The hand-to-hand fighting was engaged. Junis could already see that his men would put up a brave defence, but their numbers were too few to hold the barracks quarter. His primary defence was always going to be the main fortress and he ordered the outer defences to be abandoned. Unfortunately, as he weighed up his options, those who fought in the barracks courtyard seemed already lost.

The mercenaries were merciless in killing the White Shirts, even those who pleaded for mercy, while some militias were taken as prisoners. There was little in the barracks to be looted and the mercenaries were instructed not to start fires. The inner fortress was built in a way that the gates between the barracks and the main defence could not be targeted by the trebuchets. Instead, the siege engines were aimed at the towers and parts of the wall that seemed most vulnerable. The assault again became a waiting game as the trebuchet crews went about their business.

Jaal and his men enjoyed their time in the brothels and bars in between assignments. One of the Blood Legion joked with his commander.

"This is not like any war I ever imagined!"

Jaal could only agree, and he smiled at the man, who continued his line of thinking.

"The inns and brothels have never had it so busy. Any woman willing to open her legs is making a fortune. They'll be far richer than the mercs when this is over."

It was true and Jaal added his own observation.

"The whores are some of the ugliest on the Blood Sea."

The legionnaire laughed but was nodding.

"And the beer's got lumps in it, no better than cows piss."

In saying that he pulled a silver from his pocket, and he gave Jaal a wink as he eyed the brothel across the road from where the two men stood. Jaal laughed, but he could not deny the man his pleasures.

In the fourth month, the ship carrying their wages from Viletri did not arrive. At first, they feared that Kraken might have made his move, but a week later a message came that there was a problem with finances. The guildmasters were not unused to having to deal with such issues but on this scale, it was a serious problem that they could not cover with their contingency fund. It meant they needed to act, a fact that was likely not lost on their sponsor, Mannace.

The trebuchets did tremendous damage, but a major breach of the wall had not been achieved. When the purchased ammunition ran out, the mercenaries used rocks from nearby bays, and stones from buildings in the city. Their opportunity for assault would get no better than now. Plans were made and the next day, in the early hours of the morning, they were put into effect.

Starting from the cover of buildings the mercenaries charged the open ground to the fortress walls. This time their preparations did not go unnoticed, and crossbowmen appeared quickly on the battlements. Fortunately, few of the ballistae were operational and some of the towers were too damaged to accommodate a full complement of bowmen. Mercenary units joined the attack from other directions and soon all six thousand warriors were involved in the assault. The walls were thick with ladders being raised, and in the spaces where the walls were damaged, there was nobody to push the ladders away. Heavy rocks were heaved over the battlements and crossbow bolts rained down on the attackers. The White Shirts deployed more crossbowmen in the fortress' large courtyard, ready to counter attackers that got past the first line of defence. Today the mercenaries would earn their pay.

Junis looked down from the central keep. He wanted to be more optimistic, but he knew he was going to lose the fortress. His troops fought fiercely but the enemy would eventually break through, and the numbers of experienced White Shirts would not be enough. The prospect of being dragged through his own city in chains, then paraded through Viletri to receive Mannace's justice was an unbearable thought. He looked behind him. His wife and son lay on the stone, their throats cut. Without ceremony, he leaned forward and closed his eyes. The breeze turned into a fierce wind that whipped about him as he tumbled through the air before smashing into the ground. Jaal turned around when he heard the sickening crunch of bones, in time to see a pool of blood quickly forming around the dead Lord.

Jaal and the Blood Legion were at the forefront of the fighting in the courtyard. They were the second troop to clamber through a partial breach. In front of them, the first mercenaries to break the defence had met the full wrath of the waiting crossbowmen and the courtyard was littered with allied dead and wounded. With the sudden demise of their leader, Jaal was close enough to see the hesitation and uncertainty in the faces of the White Shirts. In that moment he and his men charged, with Jaal summoning his unnatural speed to launch himself into the first rank of troops. Some of his comrades went down to enemy fire but the rest swarmed into the crossbowmen and once engaged the Legionnaires quickly had the upper hand. Casteel relished the opportunity to kill White Shirts and she fought at Jaal's side with extraordinary ferocity.

On the walls of the central fortress, mercenaries secured large sections of the battlements. From there it was a combat of attrition as both sides jostled for advantage. One group of fighters managed to capture the inner gatehouse and they used a winch to open the gate to the barracks area that was already secured. Reinforcements piled through.

The White Shirts expected no mercy and they fought like desperate men. However, many of their allied militia dropped their weapons and placed themselves at the mercy of their assailants. Once the militia gave up the fight, it did not take long to fully secure the walls and courtyards, then the rest of that day to take the central keep. No White Shirts remained alive, while several hundred men of the militia were prisoners in the barracks. The families of the militia and White Shirts were also in the custody of the mercenaries, uncertain of their fate. Standard pillage rules did not apply to this combat and a careful inventory was taken of supplies and loot in the battle's wake.

It took another day to fully assess the outcome and bounty. The mercenaries suffered almost four hundred casualties in the assault compared to fifteen hundred White Shirts and militia killed. The garrison had been very well supplied and there was still enough food in storage to support the mercenary army for several months. Most importantly, the treasury beneath the keep was a rich reward, enough to pay a good bonus as well as wages for the mercenaries through to the next Council meeting.

Finally, Freman was under the rule of the Mercenary Guild Masters. Five hundred captured militia were given their freedom but each with a debt owed, as was the same for their family members. The families of the White Shirts were kept under guard in the extensive caverns beneath the keep until arrangements could be made to sell them. There had always been a demand for slaves, although it was some time since there had been a flesh market open on the Freman docks. It would take time to move an inventory of six hundred woman and children. The Swords, Ravens, and Crescents were back in business.

Jaal lost over thirty of his troop in the attack, which irked him. While he was generally carefree with his personal safety, he liked to avoid unnecessary risks when it came to those he felt responsible for. Thirty was too many. As some compensation, Jaal convinced the Guildmasters to allow him to take the Magic-User from the ship back to Viletri. The Mage was a young Arenlander named Maresh. He previously served as an Acolyte of War for several years but was deemed unfit to rise within the priesthood. It was three years since he journeyed to Freman with the intent of joining the Ravens, but was lured to piracy by the promise of adventure and riches. As a wizard he was, at best, a hack, but with potential. Jaal tested his skill with the war hammer and found him to be competent, as you would expect from somebody temple trained. Maresh used a hammer in each hand which was a style Jaal hadn't encountered before.

SORCERER

Render became increasingly troubled. He could see the technology of the Dwarves and Arenland and he had a sense of what powers the artefacts from the Monastery might've provided. As a master of magic, he was concerned about the value of his craft, his personal relevance in a technologically advanced future. This drove him in many directions.

Unknown to Mannace, Render allied himself with the cult of The Fallen. It was prior to their defeat by the armies of the Blood Sea. Render maintained that the preservation of magic was above politics and after their defeat, he protected the Fallen priests and cultists from those that would have them destroyed. He also secured a residence in their territories, a secluded tower, and caves where he felt greater freedom to explore his magical potential. Many cultists gathered there, and he enlisted them as his apprentices or servants. Three displayed true magical potential, while the others proved useful in other ways.

The Fallen's attitude towards necromancy and demonology was refreshing. They called it *a purpose to an end*. Within the lands of the Fallen, near Render's secluded tower, was a place known as the Valley of Pain. It was once a battleground and the original litter of bones was added to over the years. The Fallen considered it a holy place and would bring their dead and dying there so that, over a decade which included the war, the valley was heaped with decaying bodies and skeletons. The Valley of Pain was named for the dark statues - sculpted in agonising poses - lining its sides.

Render could sense spirits amongst the bones and in the statues. It was one of those special places where the dead were trapped from passing on. Being in this place made Render feel very relevant and he conceived a plan which he tested by animating one of the dark forms. It took time to find the right statue; it was of a woman bent over and with a visage of intense agony. Render was now an expert in animation, and it was a short time before the statue was mobile and compliant with his commands. He prepared further spells and used them to draw forth souls from those trapped in the gorge, storing them using the statue's innate magic. They were life, energy, and sentience that he could use for other purposes. The statue of the woman followed him as he made the half-day trek back to his tower.

As another part to his plan, Render constructed a dimensional portal that allowed him to travel and transport people or things between his residence at Viletri and his tower in the lands of the Fallen. Once it was proven and stable, he extended the gateway so that he also had access to his tower and larger holdings near Vlustoven, where he once resided before coming to the Blood Sea. The dimensional portals were small tears in the fabric that separated the world of the living from the domain of the dead. Because the domain of the dead had no sense of distance or time, Render could navigate between the tears with little effort. The key to it was not drawing the attention of those that occupied that domain or revealing the tears to beings that might use them for another purpose. Render decided this was best kept a secret, even from Jaal and Mannace.

Central to his ambition, Render recruited and trained apprentices. As well as the three Fallen, he collected thirteen other women and men with magical potential. Amnicles was by far the most competent and he progressed considerably in aptitude over the last decade. Disappointingly, the healer, Jesephine, left his service and now worked for Saska. He thought his fantasies come true to bed both Jesephine and Saska together, all for the price of his assistance to animate the two gargoyles. It ended with the healer falling under the bitch's spell and his bed left cold. Truthfully, it was a price he would pay again if the opportunity were to arise. In recent times, the cultists were very accommodating of his needs.

Because of that experience, Render put measures in place so that loyalty of his apprentices would not be a problem again. It was something he learned from Saska, how to make others dependent on you. In magical terms, only he knew the arcane encryption that unlocked the apprentice's powers and maintained the enchantments that extended their lives. To leave his service, they would have to forsake their wizardry and immortality. If he were to die, the magic of his apprentices would die with him. It was possible that some would rise to a level where they would decipher his encryption and if so, earn the right to walk their own path. One night he gathered them together at his Viletri home, to celebrate what he called their *graduation*. During the evening he addressed them as a group.

"For the last decade, I have invested in your development. You know more than you ever imagined possible, and you each understand that there is far more yet to be learned."

Render enjoyed teaching, but it took up much of his precious time. He had more pressing priorities.

"Now you must attend to your own education, find your unique path, define who you are as a caster. I will check on your progress and sometimes I will set you challenges, but your experiments, your study, your elevation to higher levels, will be your own business."

Render did not want his apprentices to think that this was complete independence. He still had need of them.

"There are commitments I have made to the defence of Viletri, duties you must continue to perform. I will not be absent from your lives and never forget that I will always be *The Master*."

It was over a hundred years since Render completed his own apprenticeship in the necromantic arts. There were a lot of things that he found distasteful about necromancy, but he enjoyed aspects of the craft and formulated ideas that would evolve necromancy to be a contemporary discipline. Render never enjoyed spending time with corpses, but he was increasingly interested in the manipulation of life forces. The souls he secured from the valley allowed him to experiment; he wondered how he might shape the souls to his will? Program them to perform specific functions? Make use of the knowledge they had in life? Reuse the life force? Bind them to things or creatures? Ensure their loyalty?

Unfortunately, there was still some corpse work that needed his attention. At Viletri he achieved some small success in changing the attitudes towards the undeath arts. Through the relentless efforts of Kakos, it was realised that zombies made excellent public servants. Render, with permission from the deceased men's families, brought six others back from the dead. Like Kakos, they would work tirelessly day and night, for a minimal wage. Render thought of Kakos as one of his apprentices and he gave the zombie clear instructions.

"Kakos, ensure the money is passed onto the families of the deceased. It will encourage them and others to support this endeavour. I will be back in a few days to check this is done."

Kakos ran the city and its finances with great precision. Viletri continued to grow and was a hub for trade and commerce. However, as quickly as money came in, it was redirected to fund the Assembly's plans for expansion and militarisation. There were forty-three thousand Viletri citizens and perhaps as many as five thousand others living in the city or nearby. After an initial influx of eager colonists, at the time when there was an abundance of housing within the city and good cropland in the surrounds, migration to the city was now reduced to a steady flow.

While predominantly human, the city also boasted an Orc quarter as well as a Dwarven sector, with individual Orcs and Dwarves integrating into all aspects of city life. Viletri was too busy for Elves and very few of the Alani or Fogmir lived amongst the population.

Surprisingly, Kakos developed a passion for music. While nothing else seemed to raise any feeling within him, music consumed his mind with emotion. Elven melodies were particularly poignant. Because he could, Kakos invested city funds in a school for music and in sponsorship of a choir. The choir was made up of young boys and Kakos found inspiration in the haunting pitch of their voices, a view shared by the Temple of War who commissioned them to sing on holy days.

THE CHILDREN

After returning from Freman, Jaal spent his first night back at Viletri with Saska. They continually made the time to put all else aside to enjoy each other's company. Jaal always came away from their coupling with a clear mind so that he could focus on his next important task. This time he was headed to the webbed forest and knew that he would need all his wits about him. The journey was made simple by the road to the Dwarven and Orc territories that was respectfully constructed to go wide of the forest as had the trail before it. Unnervingly, although not surprisingly, when Jaal arrived at the forest there was a gap in the web that beckoned him. As he had done over a decade ago, Jaal stepped through the entrance and followed the dark path to that familiar clearing. Waiting there for him was the same woman, naked and radiant as before, stunning, and unashamedly feminine.

"Are you so afraid of me that you wait ten cycles to pass again by my forest, while every day your folk go back and forth?"

In truth, he did not use the road for that exact reason. But he was there now.

"We are both immortals and it has been but a morsel of time for ones long-lived."

"Hmmmmn, the father must show a greater interest in his children. They need his guidance."

This again felt like a trap.

"I am a servant of the Order, and my time is not my own."

"These children will be your boon or peril. Choose your course wisely."

He was reluctant to show an interest as it might commit him to more, although if they were Dark Elves he would at some stage need to pass on an understanding of the Order and their place in it. Jaal came to a decision.

"Let me see my children".

The woman looked toward the forest. There was movement in the darkness beyond the clearing and many forms shifted among the trees and webs. Of the mysterious shapes, two came forward, parted the web, and stepped into the light. Naked, he could see they were a male and the other female. They were part Dark Elf, and he expected the other part was inherited from their mother. From the waist their bodies morphed into an arachnid shape that extended back, complete with eight long, spider-like legs. They were hairless like their mother, and jet black like both parents. The spiderlings had Jaal's blue eyes. He liked that they seemed confident and inquisitive. A third suddenly appeared, another female, she seemed to come out of nowhere to appear at his side and examine him closely. Jaal was surprised.

"How did she do that?"

"She can slow time, like her father."

Jaal was about to respond that he couldn't slow time, but he considered it further and realised he may not have fully thought through the nature of his speed. It irked him that Jayne, so many years ago, may have been right that he still had much to learn and refine.

"How many children?" It was important that he knew.

"More than two hundred, most are beneath the ground. You might be surprised at the extent of my domain."

"Will they follow the Order?"

"They will follow the Order, as do I."

His path seemed clearer, "I will journey here more often."

"I am ready again for your seed." She could see uncertainty on his face. "It is the way it will be. I have a hunger that must be met. The Order has elected that you will satisfy that hunger."

Life seemed determined to be complicated. Jaal was wise enough not to fight but to traverse it, although the simple life he once enjoyed was now well behind him. The strangest thing was that this instilled a sense of family, something he never expected to experience. He felt somehow connected, even though he knew little about the mother, and the children might be considered monstrous. In that moment, Jaal thought of his children in the Fogmir. It was his nature to guard those he considered within his inner circle.

ARTA

Mannace strode with purpose through the streets to the harbour quarter set aside for Jaal and his mercenaries. Four of his Rangers scampered to keep up. Shylo, who was Mannace's eyes and ears within the city had reported back the rumours of him keeping the Bracadian as a sex slave in his private quarters. Mannace was enraged and the time it took to walk to the docks did nothing to calm him down. Jaal was not present but many of the Blood Legion gathered to observe. At the front of Jaal and Saska's residence, Mannace called for Alsaborg and Arta to present themselves. He knew from Shylo that they took refuge here.

The residence was a large three-storied building made of stone, with balconies supported by wide pillars that surrounded the second and third levels. On the second level balcony, Saska appeared, "Lord Mannace."

"Send out Alsaborg and Arta now!"

Saska paused for a moment. She could see Mannace standing alone, obviously enraged. His bodyguards were standing back. They seemed apprehensive, probably nervous to have barged into the enclave of the Blood Legion with Mannace in such an aggressive mood. Saska's blood raced in anticipation of a confrontation - Mannace was rash to have come here looking for a fight.

"Not when there is murder in your eyes".

"I am your Lord. I will not be denied".

Two of the Blood Legion moved to block him. They were both solid men and experienced fighters, not easily intimidated. Mannace stepped up to them and as they grabbed for their weapons he seized their heads. He smashed their skulls together so hard that they both dropped to the ground unconscious and bleeding. Several crossbows appeared, loaded and pointed. Nobody dared to come close. The door to Jaal's residence opened and Arta stepped out. She was almost as tall as Mannace and had a similar bulk. She left her maul at the door.

"Are you going to strike me down too?"

He wanted to. He wanted to strike them all down. He had no words and there was a period of silence. Mannace took a deep breath.

Arta broke the quiet, "Give the Bracadian woman to me."

"Why would I do that?"

"Because you have put yourself in a snare and you need help to be free of it."

Surprisingly the anger left him, as quickly as it had arrived. With his mind cleared of the rage, he could instantly see that he was making a mess of the situation. He turned to one of the men with a crossbow pointed directly at him and spoke in a tone that was much calmer but still firm, "Put that down or I'll break your head with it." The man complied. Mannace took another deep breath, then turned and walked away.

Even with their history, there was something he respected about Arta, a fearlessness. Mannace wanted to be free of Delaria but he did not want to be seen to have her blood on his hands. Strangely, he trusted Arta with this problem. The following night, Jayne of the Rangers delivered the Bracadian to Alsaborg, who in turn took her in secret to Arta. Delaria was full of gratitude, and she promised Arta great treasures for her rescue. Greater treasures for help to return to Bracadia. Even after her harsh treatment, Delaria still had arrogance in her voice and an expectation that Arta would serve her need. For Arta, who prided herself on doing the right thing, it presented her with a tough but clear choice. She would not sacrifice the Blood Sea for the sake of an individual. This woman, with her ill-conceived words, was an enemy. But it was not enough reason for murder. Arta would need to find another way to keep this pretty bird from singing.

GOD OF WAR

Nial and Aaron traded blows. To either side, other young men practised thrust and parry, counter thrust and dodge. Every day that they were not at the wall or on patrol, they would spend half their time training and the other half doing whatever tasks the Captain or quartermaster gave them. Nial struck high then thrust forward. Aaron parried the thrust aside and returned a quick thrust of his own. Nial brought his blade up but was too slow. He felt a pain in his gut where the practice sword snuck under his breastplate and pierced his abdomen. Aaron looked shocked, he stepped back while other young men ran to their comrade's aid and called for help. Training injuries were common although fatalities were rare. Nial's friends struggled to stop the bleeding and now the young man coughed up splatters of blood.

At the front of the Temple of War one of the mighty statues stirred. It shifted slightly in its position and its head bowed before returning to an immobile state. The small movements did not go unnoticed by two War Priests who were sitting on the steps at the temple entrance. Several of the Dwarves working on the temple construction also pointed and called to their kinsmen. The first of the Temple Guardians was given life. Nial knew that he had died, but he had no feelings on the matter. Now he took his place as a guardian as had been arranged. Again, this was just a fact, and he had no intent or instinct to do anything except wait and watch. He had a good view of the central square and out to the main city gate. He would know or he would be guided when action was needed.

The Grey Dwarves and the Orcs of the Iron Jaw had no organised religion of their own. It was a great opportunity for the Priests of War to increase their influence and young

Orcs embraced the doctrine. More than one hundred acolytes and ten priests resided in the temple quarter. Four Dwarves and twenty-six Orcs were amongst that number, with the first Orc rising to the rank of priest during the last year. To progress was not only the requirement to be a great warrior, but also a conduit for the War Gods divine might. Priests could bless others for battle, wield destructive powers, and perform miraculous feats. They were a rallying point for any defence and the hammer at the fore of any attack.

Warriors were always welcome at the Temple of War and could seek aid or guidance from the priests. It was common for warriors to donate to the temple when they came to Viletri, and many of the soldiers who served in the city bequeathed a part of their wage each week. When your life and afterlife both depended on it, having a god on your side seemed a wise investment.

Mannace would frequently visit with Demmal Fulstorm at the temple. The War Priest was pragmatic and wise about many things. Today, Mannace sought Demmal's thoughts regarding the war with the Collective. Demmal was confident that a great host would be raised and that Tarash Gormoth would be retaken.

"After that, it would seem up to chance. If you like to rely on your luck then you are on the right path. If strategy is your prerogative then perhaps information needs to be gathered and longer-term plans made."

Demmal paused to give himself time to find the right words that would guide Mannace.

"Your generals can execute your orders in Tarash Gormoth. What is your job as war leader, as a general of generals?"

"It is hard to look ahead when there are so many things needing to be done."

"Let those things be a subordinate's problem. If your vision is one of war, of a great battle, then focus on that vision. Forging peace has brought the nations of the Blood Sea together. The furnace of war will bind them to your purpose. Peace may not come again until the world is at your feet."

The priest was reflective before he made a final comment.

"Perhaps your council of peace is not the same council that is needed for war?"

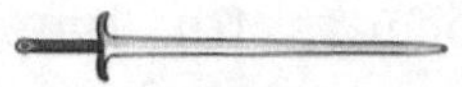

CONGRESS OF WAR

Demmal's words struck home with Mannace. He didn't need to sit and wait for the next Council of the Blood Sea - his time would be better spent on making strategic preparations for the war to come. Not the small preparations of his troops or strengthening alliances as he was doing, but planning the larger campaign. It was so obvious now that he was on this path and much of his tension and worry was replaced with enthusiasm.

It took a month to gather the right people. This time the congress was at Freman, away from prying eyes and other distractions. The table was a small one with Ithius, Demmal, the Mad King, and a trader named Milan Tash. Ithius was renowned as an admiral and strategist, somebody who always came out on the right side of a conflict. The Mad King possessed a genius intellect, was ruthless, and also had a winning knack. Demmal asked the right questions. Milan Tash owned a fleet of trading vessels that crisscrossed many seas and touched many nations. Over the last year, he established bases in Viletri, Yanth, Sylos, and Ostoik. Milan was smart, rich, and influential. The price for his cooperation was yet to be determined.

Milan led the first day of discussions. He knew the territories of the Collective well - the twelve nations, their people, cities, culture, and armies, and he knew much about their commerce. The merchant had knowledge of their alliances and enemies. He possessed maps and charts and texts. The Collective governed a larger territory than the Blood Sea and by Milan's account, their population was perhaps three times that of the Council nations. They had vulnerabilities though, such as their weak navy. The group gained a much better understanding of the enemy they faced. Ideas for a campaign started to formulate and come together.

On the second and third days, Mannace's Congress planned out the invasion of Tarash Gormoth. It was decided that the Mad King would oversee the attack on land and Ithius would command the fleet.

During the proceedings, Mannace was fascinated by the Mad King, who in person was nothing like his reputation. To Mannace, he looked more like a cobbler than a leader of men. His mind, however, was extraordinary and he absorbed and stored every word. The way he processed information and turned it into ideas or questions was remarkable. What he lacked though was charisma, compassion, and wit, which gave him an air of madness.

Before he invited the Mad King to the Congress, Mannace had covertly gathered information to better understand the odd leader. The Madlands spanned a great wasteland, with settlements restricted to isolated pockets of arable land. The largest communities were underground and the people that dwelled in such habitats seldom ventured far from their caves and tunnels. The Borderlands was a region claimed by both the Mad King and Arenland. It was a long-range of hills and valleys that were lush and bountiful. People of both nations would often settle there, but inevitably raiders from the wastes or soldiers from Arenland swept through the territory killing or driving settlers out.

A fact not known to many was that the Mad King once had another neighbour, a nation known as Urso Akeal. The Urso underestimated the Mad King when their warriors boldly attacked and ransacked one of his communities. The Mad King responded by summoning a host that overwhelmed their capital city, swept across their desert territory, and enslaved their people.

On the last day, Ithius approached the King who took a break on a balcony near the top of the fortress keep. He looked over the sea as he sipped from a cup of water.

"It's not easy talking to a man for three days and not know his name. We can't keep calling you Mad King."

"Why not?"

"I understand that it might make an enemy think twice before crossing your path, but here amongst peers it's odd."

The Mad King considered. He looked serious when he replied.

"You may call me General".

Ithius, who was a very serious man himself, laughed.

"As you wish, General."

RETIREMENT

Rollo stood in the shadows of the alleyway. Mannace had just arrived by ship and was returning along his usual route to his city residence. As always, four Rangers who kept vigil scouted his path. As they neared, Jayne spotted Rollo and nodded. Rollo nodded in return. It was a professional courtesy - neither had comradery for the other, in-fact Rollo had come to despise the Dark Elf for his insufferable arrogance. But that was a grudge that must wait for another day. When the Rangers eyes were diverted, he notched his bow, aimed, and tracked Mannace until just the right moment... then fired.

Mannace felt a breeze on his neck and a hand on his shoulder. A knife fell from that hand and bounced off his chest before clattering against the cobbles of the road. As Mannace turned, a figure slumped against him and toppled to the ground. It was a man like any other in the street, but with an arrow through his neck. Mannace could see Rollo in the alleyway beyond with bow in hand. When Rollo approached, Mannace thanked him for his fine shooting.

"I was aiming for his head".

Jayne and the other Rangers quickly surrounded their leader with weapons drawn. When it became obvious that the action was already over, Jayne examined the dead man. On quick inspection, he seemed no different from other city dwellers.

"We'll hang him up at the square and see if anybody recognises him," suggested Jayne.

One of the other rangers was staring at Rollo with a puzzled look. He asked the obvious question.

"Why were you here Rollo? How did you know that man was an assassin?"

"My vision at the monastery," Rollo answered directly to

Mannace. "I wasn't sure, but it felt like the right time, and when I saw you and the others on the street just as you were, I knew it had to be that moment."

As the others discussed the body and the attempt on Mannace's life in more detail, Rollo unpinned his Rangers cloak and folded it. He passed it to Mannace.

"What are your plans, Rollo?"

Rollo shrugged. He had never been much of a planner.

"I might spend some time in Hagbesh,"

There was a nagging thought, an intangible and unsubstantiated sensation connected to his original vision, that Rollo decided to share before departing.

"I don't know if it's helpful, but my gut tells me this assassin is tied to the Collective. And that he has a partner, a watcher".

"A watcher makes sense", added Jayne. "If the assassin doesn't survive, his partner can report back the outcome."

"Or get the job done," added another Ranger. "This one might look ordinary in these clothes, but he's fit and toned like a fighter. We got lucky."

Rollo left them to it and headed back to the barracks where he collected his gear. His next stop was the Healer's Guild where he met with Althea Kane. He helped with many errands for the healer over the years. This time she gave him a sack of salves to take to her agent in Hagbesh.

"Good luck to you Rollo, you are a good man".

Althea was saddened to see Rollo go. As well as errands, he spent time with the sick or wounded, talking to them, and selflessly doing them small favours. The Healer's Guild witnessed some busy times when sickness plagued the city or during the war with the Fallen. The Guild had grown to over two hundred practising members, including some who travelled with the military and others in remote locations like Hagbesh. Rollo volunteered his services since the very beginning.

Althea and her husband Titus lived in a large home that overlooked the harbour and out to sea. She was grateful to be out from under the mountain and appreciative that Viletri was once again a thriving metropolis. It was still a shadow of what it once was; when it stood a centre for culture, art, philosophy, and craftsmanship. Some of her kin, the immortal Viletri, re-established their trade and it gave the city some sense of culture and refinement, but the great artists like Porcheney, or the wisdom of a man such as Dogusta, could not be replaced. If she closed her eyes and let her memories fill her mind, she could still smell and taste the exquisite foods of the legendary chef Del Lamagao. Althea sighed. She felt that Mannace demonstrated the potential to be a great leader, but he was still a boy - full of enthusiasm but not yet appreciating the finer things.

Her husband liked the boy. Titus enjoyed his role as garrison commander. He arose early in the mornings, energised by his day's agenda, and returned home at night tired but satisfied. Titus' garrison troop consisted of eight hundred soldiers. They were responsible for the peace in the city and patrolled as far as the Viletri border. They also organised the militia and helped with the training of soldiers for the standing army. The living statues were a part of the garrison's responsibility, and late at night on rotation, they would check the statues to ensure they were in a functioning state.

ARMIES

Rowman was helping Mannace to prepare for the war with the Collective. He and his battalion from Sylos patrolled the long road from the east that wound its way across Arenland, to arrive at Viletri. It was his mission to get the Madlands and Two-Face armies safely to the staging grounds just north of the city.

The Overlord specified the route that the Mad King and Two-Face Orcs were to travel through Arenland. The ruler mobilised his army and he made it clear to Rowman that he would not tolerate any deviation from his instructions.

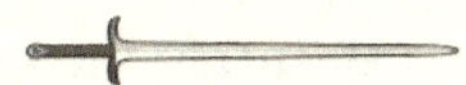

The Mad King brought every troop he could muster. Rowman met the Kings army in the Borderlands, and he travelled alongside the leader as they walked towards Arenland. The border region was lush and beautiful so that Rowman could see why it was coveted by the nations surrounding it. The host passed a small settlement of Arenlanders, perhaps thirty families brave enough to stake their claim in this neutral zone. Rowman was apprehensive. He turned to the Mad King who walked alongside him.

"We don't want any trouble here."

"Let them have the borderlands. I will not be coming back."

"Ever?"

"Ever is a long time Rowman. Look around you, the world is in a state of flux. The cogs are moving. All the pieces are shifting into place."

"Yes, sir."

Rowman didn't have time to indulge the Mad Kings ramblings. Instead, he moved to the side of the road where a unit of his soldiers stood between the settlers and the

Madlands hoard. They watched the army as it sauntered down the narrow dirt road. Five thousand waste hardened warriors and a similar number of slaves.

The warriors were mean-looking men and woman with a vast array of cruel weapons and spiked shields and armour. Some rode beasts captured or bred in the Wastes. A few of the beasts seemed intelligent and walked alongside the other troops on two or four legs. A tall weasel-like creature stared back at Rowman and hissed at him through its metal helmet. Groups of emaciated slaves, chained together at the neck, marched amongst the warriors. Strangely, they held clubs, and some had knives tucked into their belts. Rowman had never seen armed slaves before – it seemed a contradiction. The army's baggage was piled on their backs.

Near the rear of the force, more slaves pulled and pushed thirty covered troop wagons. Rowman called up to one of the wain drivers.

"What's in there?"

At first, the driver ignored him but when Rowman persisted and looked like he might climb up next to him, the driver relented.

"Mollies. Molemen. Get off there, piz off."

Rowman, not fully satisfied with the answer, reluctantly backed up to the side of the road. The final group of slaves heaved and chanted as they strained to move a wheeled platform upon which sat a gigantic metal bell.

When Rowman caught up with the Mad King later, as the army stopped to set up camp for the evening, he was inquisitive.

"What is the bell for?"

"I like the bell. I didn't want to leave it behind."

As usual, the Mad King was lean with his words. He didn't see the need for further explanation.

That night, news reached Rowman that the Two-Face Orcs

approached from the south. Trusting the King more than the Two-Face to keep the peace, Rowman took half his men and hurried quickly to intercept the new arrivals.

When he caught up with them, the Orcs paid Rowman and his men little respect and rather than provide escort, Rowman's troops kept ahead of the Two-Face army to ensure their path was clear. The Two-Face bullied anybody who got too close, and they jeered at the Arenlander units that arrived to shadow them. As they moved down the highway, they broke road signs and defecated against statues or buildings.

Rowman was grateful at the Overlords restraint, and it was a relief when the Two-Face had passed through Arenland and then Sylos without a major altercation. At last, they arrived at the plains north of Viletri and Rowman could take better stock of their numbers for his report to Mannace.

There were three and a half thousand Two-Face fighters divided into clans set apart by differences in their tattoos. The burly Orcs carried meaty weapons crafted from hardwood and stone in the form of clubs, hammers, and mauls. The shafts and heads of the weapons were intricately carved. Many of the Orcs wore hardened leather armour and most had an item that was crimson about them, such as a headband or weapon grip. They seemed ready for a scrap.

At their side each of the Orcs had a flask of Thog, the legendary potion that in small doses over time added to their bulk and size, and when quaffed in larger quantities in battle it gave them extreme strength and constitution - with the common side effect of uncontrollable rage, that was occasionally and unfortunately followed by agonising pain or death.

Ships from Rummond, Lapthos, and the Isle of Malanos arrived at Viletri. It was intended that these smaller nations would contribute supplies for the armies rather than troops, and the first shipment was chickens and cows, with herdsmen to tend to them. After that, salted fish, dried meats, preserved fruits, grains, and nuts were delivered and put into storage.

Fesadi Menders arrived at the Guild of Healers in Viletri. They brought with them medicines and techniques not seen before at the guild. Some of their healing was based on faith and crystal magic, which came under the scrutiny of the Temple of War. After much debate and intervention from Mannace, the War Priests cautiously agreed that healing was aligned to the War Gods purpose.

Mecelay, Daglari, and Arenland forces arrived together. The soldiers of Mecelay were uniformed and ordered. Each had a long spear, a large round shield, and a short sword. They wore metal breastplates and conical helmets. In total there were eight units of two hundred spears. Different units had different emblems on their shields, often the head of an animal etched in a stylised form. The commanders wore capes to set themselves apart and each carried a bronze whistle, high pitched so that it could be heard over the noise of battle and with it they gave commands as they travelled; to march or halt, keep formation, or move at a more leisurely pace, to stop for a break or to regroup. After a month of marching, they finally blew the command to make camp and set defences.

The Daglari sent three hundred and twenty warriors. Lofty dog soldiers like Alsaborg, each equipped in their own fashion. They were amiable and mixed freely with the other forces.

Of the nations to the east, Arenland boasted the largest contingent. Their field army marched in neat formation and took pride in their exceptional discipline. When Rowman came to assess their numbers, they were ready with documents that detailed all he needed to know.

The eight thousand Arenlanders were divided into four sections. First were the light skirmishers. Adorned with studded leather armour, they carried a variety of hand weapons, and some wore crossbows on their backs. Most had vials at their side containing the liquid that turned into choke gas when the ceramic casings were broken, and they all had the treated cloths around their necks that could be pulled up to provide an effective gas mask. Some of the skirmishers sported other equipment such as bags of caltrops, poisons, traps, or bolas.

The regular troops that made up the bulk of the Arenlanders were divided into units of three hundred men. Each unit donned metal armour and dark grey clothing, but their weapons varied so that there was a unit of halberdiers, another of axemen, some with swords and shields, several that carried hammers and shields, and others with repeating crossbows. The design for the crossbows was acquired in trade with the Grey Dwarves in return for the choke gas recipe.

The final unit were five hundred warriors on horseback carrying spears, axes, and shields. The nobles of Arenland travelled with them and stood out from the other soldiers by the variety of colours in their clothing and elaborate designs of their armour and weapons.

Amongst the Arenland infantry, the priests and Initiates of War would be the heart and spine of the army on the field. The High Priestess, Ahmeda Ravenborn, travelled with the force. Now camped on the plains near Viletri, she felt drawn to the two other women that were intertwined in Jaal's life. She touched upon them in her visions and sensed something of their capabilities and motivations. Ahmeda believed they had more than Jaal in common. She called for Dekon and set the War Priest to arrange a meeting.

HINDAS

The Mad King inspected his new ships. He completed the journey from Viletri to Hindas with eight hundred handpicked warriors and seventeen hundred slaves. They boarded the ships he had commissioned and dutifully took up their positions at the oar or on deck. Part of the arrangement was that for the first twelve months a captain and small crew would be provided for all ten vessels. The King would have liked more ships, but the boat builders were already busy constructing troop carriers and warships for Ithius. The dimensions of the triremes were impressive with their double deck of oars and colossal ram. They did lack character though and the King already had plans to commission carvers to give at least the foredeck and ram the visage of dread they deserved.

At first, the borrowed captains were concerned that the slaves looked too emaciated to have any strength at the oar, but they soon proved to have unnatural endurance and could sustain top speeds for long periods. It also troubled the Hindassians that each bench of slaves was chained together at the neck, but not to the oar. Many carried clubs or knives tucked into their belts. The Mad King explained they were augmented for hard labour and their loyalty was absolute. One captain's curiosity was peaked.

"Then why chain them?"

"They're slaves," replied the Mad King matter-of-factly.

While the ships trained in the harbour, the King took time to familiarise himself with Hindas. It was a military city with a large naval port, extensive barracks, and every type of industry to support a war effort. Even the civilians seemed to march rather than walk. In many ways, it was the opposite of the Wasteland. Here the men and women of the city trained vigorously, although only the men would travel to war. In the Wasteland, you learned by fighting and if you were a poor fighter you either didn't survive or you would become the lackey of a better warrior. In the Wastes, a woman had the same rights as a man to pick up a weapon and make a name for themselves.

It also surprised the Mad King that there was none of the invention and enterprise that impressed him in the neighbouring city of Viletri. By contrast, the Hindasians clung to their traditions and seemed determined in their way of life.

Hindas was to be the gathering point for the naval effort and while the Mad King was there, the iron ships of Arenland arrived in port. There were now six of the magnificent vessels. They were the same length as the triremes although wider and they sat lower in the water. The ships had a means of propulsion that allowed them to come into the harbour and dock, even though their sails were still furled. Their decks were protected by a metal cordon, behind which ballistae pointed out through small portals. Feeling envious, the Mad King reminded himself that he and the Arenlanders were on the same side in this conflict, at least for now.

The Mad King found talking with Ithius laborious. The man was very clever and an exceptional seaman, but listening to him was as exciting as reading the military manuals he held so much belief in. Ithius put great faith in the tried and true. By comparison, the Mad King was a book of blank pages. His strength as a commander was the ability to quickly sum up a situation and take the best course of action, whatever that needed to be. If he not had larger motivations, the King could see in his mind's eye his hoard sweeping through the streets of Hindas as the city burned. It was a task for another day.

TRINITY

Saska, accompanied by Alsaborg and Arta, travelled to the specified location. It was late into the night, and they met Dekon Ruel who stood at the side of the road and pointed to a light emanating from the webbed forest. Saska walked there alone. Ahmeda was waiting, a lantern on the ground gave minimal light. Before they could talk the lantern sputtered. In the resulting darkness, another shape lurked that seemed large and monstrous but, when it ventured closer, it had a woman's appearance, naked. As their night vision adjusted the three women drew close so that their faces were within reach, and they studied one another.

Ahmeda, who arranged the meeting, started proceedings.

"In darkness made, in darkness met."

It was an old welcome, but they were each long-lived and it had meaning to them.

"I am Ahmeda of the Shade Born, Second in Order, Disciple of the Second Tier."

"I am Saska."

"I am Eya, Mother of Spiders, First in Order, Disciple of the Third Tier".

Ahmeda was taken aback; First in Order meant that Eya was one of the ancients that existed before the Dark Elves. In the Order, it meant that for the first time in many centuries, she stood before somebody of superior rank. As a small consolation, Ahmeda ranked higher with her talent in magic.

The women took turns to talk about their past and their present.

Eya was one of the ancients who inhabited the world during the infancy of man. The ancients were the ones to establish the Order that was the foundation for rising civilisations over many thousands of years. As the nation's became stronger and bolder, they rebelled against the Order and its hierarchy. During that time most of the ancients perished or fled and the young races took charge of their own destinies. The Dark Elves alone remained fiercely loyal to the old ways. Eya had fought alongside the other ancients during the rebellion and in defeat, she escaped to this place. Countless years passed with little contact with the world outside of her lair. She did not explain her powers or capabilities, but she did tell Ahmeda and Saska that she was able to watch and track a great many things so that she knew the world intimately without traversing it.

Ahmeda had been left as a baby outside the doors to the Temple of War. She grew up in Ostoik under the guidance of the War Priests, and over the centuries had risen through the ranks to lead that order. Ahmeda could connect directly to the God of War, and she understood his will and purpose. She met her birth mother once at the age of thirty when the Dark Elf came to Ahmeda and educated her as to her heritage and her place in the order. Since then, Ahmeda held an affinity for other Dark Elves and together they established a society based around the Blood Sea that honoured the Order and the old ways. Ahmeda kept track of all the Dark Elves in the region and she was committed to supporting each of them. It became her personal crusade.

When it was Saska's turn, the seductress explained that she was summoned into this world by a sorcerer who kept her as a concubine for a great length of time. She possessed no memory of her life before. Once she developed a greater sense of her abilities and when the time was right, she took the life from the magus and for a time gained her independence. Saska lived like a predator; travelling and killing until she was lured into a trap near Rummond and captured by Syprus and other agents of the Oracle. Again, she existed there for a very long time. They took steps to educate and prepare her, although she did not know their purpose. In her new life at Viletri, Saska felt in control. For the first time, she shared her capability with magic and her ambition.

"I natural magic and learned magic. I grow practice. I have much magic cannot yet do. One day they will say, 'Saska is great Sorcerer'."

Again, Ahmeda was taken aback.

Each woman was fascinated by the lives of the others and felt a closeness and respect for one another. They asked questions and laughed about Jaal, each bonded to him in a different yet permanent way. There was a natural comradery between the three.

Eya made use of her authority.

"Saska, I name you Third in Order."

It was not something she did without proper consideration. The third tier would put her on equal terms with Jaal and Jayne.

"I name you Disciple of the Fifth Tier".

Ahmeda saw great potential in Saska and by assigning her an order in magic she made a commitment to help with her development. Eya spoke the final words.

"I place this meeting under the shadow, that none may share what they have learned here".

With that said they departed.

ZOMBIFICATION

Ahead of the monthly assembly when Kakos knew Render would be in town, he went to the wizards' home and requested an audience. Render made time and they sat and talked. Render was fascinated by the impact that music had on the zombie, and it raised several possibilities that he would experiment with when he had time. Kakos made a request.

"Render, I am not satisfied with this undead form, I want more."

"More of what?"

"More control, more power, more life, more!"

"I have an idea. You have the brain for it but not the magic. Magic is not in you except for what I have already put there. I have a way to give you the power of magic, then how you manipulate it, bend it to your will is upon you to conceive. This is more Kakos. Possibly more than you can handle."

Render used the black statue to draw forth a soul, which he passed over to Kakos, adding it to the necromancy that gave him life. Kakos could feel the spirit within him, and he was quick to control it and put it to rest in a place where he could recall it when needed.

"I understand, give me more Render.".

Render was hesitant, he thought that one would be a good start and perhaps others could be added later. However, he added another soul and then another four at Kakos' insistence. Render had no idea what would happen next but enjoyed the prospect of his discovery. Kakos quickly demonstrated that he had the knack. Render liked talented people and anticipated some robust conversations with Kakos in the future.

Kakos thanked the wizard and went back to his normal

business of running the city. His major crisis was raising enough funds to pay for the mercenary battalions. It helped that the allied armies started to arrive and the reality of war with The Collective was upon them. He increased the taxes upon business and trade and placed a levy on all citizens' earnings. It would be enough if Mannace didn't commit to new ventures. Managing the detail of the taxes consumed his time.

When he found some spare moments, often at night when the city slept, Kakos practised using his mind to direct and control the souls. The first success was using them to move things. With his mind, he could send a soul out to an object and have it move across the floor. He could close a door and even lock it. A failure was his attempt to see the souls as the people they once were, to access their memories and knowledge. It was as if the memories were wiped clean or possibly hidden from him. He decided to take what worked and improve on it. He started by moving two objects at the same time.

THE ROAD TO WAR

At Viletri, mercenaries were arriving from Freman every day, ferried by their fleet of troop carriers and other vessels. The Battalions of the Crescent Moon, Swords, and Ravens were forming up in and around Viletri; five thousand strong.

Next to arrive were the Grey Dwarves and Iron Jaw Orcs. It was a bizarre sight to see them sharing the same road, but their rivalry over past decades was a thing of location and circumstance, rather than a systemic hatred of one another. Both nations were committed to the Council and its endeavours.

Sixteen thousand Iron Jaw warriors marched to the beat of stretched hide on wooden drums. They carried a mix of primitive hand weapons and bows. Most dropped what they were doing in their normal occupations, picked up their weapons and whatever food was to hand, and joined the march south. As many as three thousand of the Orcs were full-time warriors. These professionals were better equipped with iron or steel weapons and leather or metal armour. The formidable command unit was nine hundred strong and comprised of the largest, most muscular specimens, hand-picked at an early age for their physical attributes and trained in the Rage, an aggressive style of movement and combat. These Orcs carried spears and shields, with swords, hammers, or axes at their side. They wore fur-lined, studded leather or metal armour. Each sported a wolf's head helmet and wolf skin cloak. Finding and killing one of the giant wolves was an initiation rite of the unit, that marked the completion of their training. Accompanying the command unit were warriors mounted on winged bulls, the showpiece of the army. Some of the riders were counted amongst the First Orcs and revered by the warrior caste.

Shamans walked amongst the troops, often tinkling bones or chanting as they walked. As keepers of the Rage and the Shadow Cloak, they possessed great spirituality and responsibility. Some were old and often long-lived for Orcs. Also on the pilgrimage were a few young bulls that were only recently gifted their talents during the sacred Spirit Ceremony. Even these fledgling Shamans were treated with great reverence.

The Grey Dwarves committed three thousand warriors to the campaign. They were uniformly dressed in long grey coats worn over armour and each carried the formidable repeating crossbow with combat blade attached. The Dwarves slung either a two-handed mallet, pick, or shovel over their backs. Simple, practical helmets were worn. Some carried vials of Choke Gas and all of them had goggles and a mask that sat on their chest but could be pulled up to protect them from gas or smoke. Interspersed amongst the units was a new weapon designed to cast flame in a wide arc. The fire tube was similar to a spear and connected to a backpack filled with liquid that burst into flame when it made contact with air. Under the cloaks, some of the Dwarves donned the enhanced clockwork arm and each unit leader wielded a shielding disc, much larger in size than the ones they had prepared for Mannace's troops.

The last troops to arrive at Viletri were from Sylos. Two thousand regular trained infantry, all equipped with spear, shield, and longbow, and wearing chainmail armour. Following them was a long train of horse-drawn wagons full of supplies and ten animated statues that were a gift from Mannace. Lord Bisan had been motivated to have his men trained in the longbow, thinking that it would give the armies of the Blood Sea some needed versatility.

Mannace's own standing army of one thousand soldiers was finely equipped with war hammers and modern armour supplied by the Dwarves. Each wore a surcoat and cloak of blue, with a golden hammer embroidered on the chest. On closer inspection one in twenty of the soldiers was an animated statue, equipped similarly but without need for gadgets. One in twenty was a priest or Acolyte of War. The Blood Legion, back to three hundred strong, accompanied them.

The combined armies marched North-East through the territories of the Fallen where they were joined by mounted warriors that were remnants of that nation's military. When the host eventually came to the coast there were ships waiting for them. The navy had already completed transport of the Alani, Yanth, Karanthos, Loryan, and Cavastock troops who were camped within the Fogmir under the protection of the Wild Elves. Now they began to ferry the waiting host to that same location.

NEW PLAYERS

The Collective knew of the Blood Sea's intentions and were making their own preparations. A great host was collecting in Tarash Gormoth as it had before. The Congress of War gave thought to bypassing Tarash Gormoth and attacking the capitals of the Collective, but the effort to transport troops was prohibitive and they decided that a triumph in Tarash Gormoth was still the best start to their campaign.

The military build-up was observed by others too. An envoy from Roundhome and Galandar arrived at Viletri, in time to speak to Mannace before he departed to be with the military forces. Milan Tash and Shepherd joined them.

In the Council Chamber, Mannace talked to the envoy about the Council of the Blood Sea and their intent to reclaim Tarash Gormoth.

The Galandar ambassador, Faso Timlar, outlined the dimensions of Galandar and Roundhome in the context of Mannace's map, and also marked out the nations of the Horseclans and Remman. He talked about their size and resources, which at face value seemed vast. Galandar's attention was focused northwards, on the defence of the Rift, and they hadn't considered the disparate nations of the Blood Sea region to be a relevant factor. A united Blood Sea was something of interest particularly if it was an ally prepared to join the war against the North. The envoy was unconcerned about the sideline conflict with the Collective.

Faso Timlar invited the Council of the Blood Sea to send representatives to Galandar to discuss alliance at their convenience. After the envoy departed the city, Mannace asked Shepherd to pursue more contact and opportunities with these nations.

When Mannace set sail for the Fogmir it was aboard the captured Bracadian vessel, re-purposed as his flagship. Its large sails were half white and half red, each boldly displayed the golden hammer emblem. Sixty sailors manned the deck and rigging. One hundred marines equipped with the same modern weaponry as his land troops stood to attention on deck as the vessel pulled away from the port to the cheers of the city folk that gathered.

On the voyage, when rounding the Cape of Knives, they were hailed by another vessel. Under a flag of parley, the ship approached and drew alongside. A broad plank was placed between the vessels and a man in his older years, dressed in simple clothes and with a blade at his side crossed the bridge to Mannace's ship.

"Beyjorn Remiss, but you can call me Kraken."

He extended his hand and the Flagship Captain clasped it in a seaman's grip. The Captain introduced Lord Mannace, and Kraken looked the leader up and down.

"Well met, Lord of Viletri".

Kraken smiled. He had good teeth for an old man and Mannace saw some other traits that he was becoming more familiar with.

"Well met, Kraken of the Viletri."

Kraken laughed.

"I stopped being Viletri a long time ago. Now I'm a man on a ship and no more. I have information. The Blood Sea is being scouted by tall ships like this one you have here. I have seen three groups of two ships. They have some tricks to stayin' out of sight, but we have a few tricks of our own."

Mannace appreciated the information and it reinforced what he already knew in his gut, that the Bracadians were going to be a problem.

"Thank you, Kraken. There are few Viletri, you would be welcome in the city."

Kraken laughed again, then he appeared thoughtful.

"You look like an old friend. Do you know Vertov?"

"That was my father's name."

"Huh. Well, those scouts mean business. Expect they'd be excited to see you in this ship, eh? Good travels, son of Vertov".

Kraken turned abruptly and he headed back across the planks. It seemed odd to Mannace that Kraken did not seek more information about his father, and he was forming some questions of his own. He wanted to follow Kraken but because he hesitated, the planks were already being withdrawn. Mannace watched the old man and his ship as it departed. When it was a short way off, the flag of parley came down and the plain white flag indicating an independent ship was raised. A few of the men on-board knew who Kraken was by reputation, but none were bold enough to raise it with their Lord.

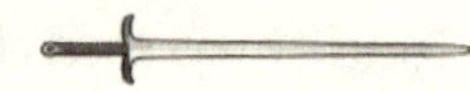

BATTLE ON THE PLAINS

The Mad King finished inspecting the Blood Sea army to get a full appreciation of their numbers and capabilities. The contingent from Yanth impressed him. They were four thousand strong, very confident and well armoured, about a quarter with crossbow and sword, while the others were armed with halberds. They seemed likely to be disciplined and dependable in the heavy fighting.

He was less sure about the soldiers from Karanthos and Loryan, about twelve hundred light infantry in total. A sneeze would blow them over.

Cavastock provided five hundred heavy cavalry. They were cocky and had a confident swagger that the Mad King liked. They were likely to pack a punch.

As much as he disliked the Alani Elves, he was impressed with their warriors. There were two regiments of one thousand troopers each. They wore chainmail coats that fell to their boots, polished breast-and-back plates, and glistening helms. Each was equipped with a bow, sword, spear, and shield of the finest quality. The men and women were experienced fighters and in the last year, they trained as a unit in preparation for the coming battles.

Amongst the Alani units, champions were dressed and equipped differently, and some were magic users. They drew attention with the bold colours of their cloaks or robes and allowed themselves a flamboyance not permitted of the line troops. As much as the champions stood apart in the line-up, they were also expected to stand apart in battle as masters of blade and spell.

The Wild Elves were a frustration for the Mad King. In the forest, he had no idea how numerous they were, and he was aware that many would not leave the woodland. It was obvious that in the forest they would be a formidable force, but elsewhere their usefulness was yet to be determined.

Almost four thousand Rhalec journeyed to the edge of the Fogmir to join the other forces. They were large, experienced warriors, though poorly equipped with perhaps a tenth of their number having metal weapons. The others used clubs, crude spears, and shields crafted from stretched hide. Like the Wild Elves, the Mad King saw great potential in them but only if used wisely.

By his calculations, gathered in the Fogmir were just over fifty thousand infantry, around ten thousand bowmen and thirteen hundred mounted troops. The lack of cavalry did not concern the King, he had never liked horses.

With the information gleaned from scouts and agents active in Tarash Gormoth, it was time to summon the war leaders and generals to share his plan.

The Fogmir Elves prepared a glade for the meeting. All the senior war leaders gathered, and the Mad King started by explaining to them the enemies' disposition. With help from elven scouts and under the guidance of Captain Veroff Odari, he marked out a large map of Tarash Gormoth with sticks and pebbles on the ground. Coloured rocks were used to show the locations of the cities Tarash, Gormoth, and Sarcross, plus a scattering of strategic points such as encampments or towns.

Palm-sized wooden tokens, each with an identifying symbol of a unit in the army were placed in a pile at the location of their camp in the Fogmir. Tokens, painted white with the number of the estimated enemy forces, were placed on the map. As they were positioned, scouts were asked to describe the enemy. There were several large concentrations of hostile forces at each city, and in the territory between the cities of Tarash and Gormoth.

The Mad King instructed each war leader to pick up their token or tokens. As he allocated troops to the campaign he directed the war leaders to place their tokens on the map. There were fewer tokens than expected placed against the main field army that occupied the territory between Tarash and Gormoth. This was the key to the Mad Kings strategy, and he took the time to explain his reasoning.

"We need to draw the forces in Tarash and Gormoth out of their defences and onto the plains. They will only do this if they think they will have a decisive victory. The more time they spend fighting us on the plains, the less time they will have to counter our other actions. The outcome of this war will be decided by the battle there."

The Mad King spoke with such confidence that many of the commanders were nodding.

"The troops that will fight on the plains have been carefully selected."

The Orcs made up a large portion of that contingent and their chieftains gave a bellowing "Raaaaghh" in response. The war cries raised the blood and spirit of all present and the Daglari commander added his own howling to the racket.

At dawn, the liberation of Tarash Gormoth commenced. Leaving the other commanders to get on with their assignments, the Mad King personally led his select force out of the forest and toward the field army of the enemy. In the sky, the Orcs on the flying bulls guided the Kings progress and kept him updated when anything of interest was observed.

On the ground, the force took what roads or routes they could to make the best time. It was clear now that the soldiers had been selected for their constitution and they continued to march hard through the night.

Mid-morning of the next day they arrived at the wide plain where the enemy was camped and immediately quickened their pace while forming a long front as they had been instructed by the Mad King. At the centre of the line were the Grey Dwarves. To their left and right were the Two-Face Orcs. Further right the Daglari kept pace with the Madlands' fighters and beasts. Further left, veteran Iron Jaw warriors jogged to the beat of their drummers. On each flank, a host of Fogmir Elves picked up their tempo and began to outpace the others. Behind the force was the heavy cavalry of Cavastock having to canter to keep up - now swinging left at the Mad Kings signal to join that flank. The Blood Sea host of fifteen thousand quickened their pace and soon they were close enough to see the enemy faces. On both sides soldiers jeered at their adversaries, snarling, yelling, and brandishing their weapons. Blood boiling as the roar of war rolled like the war gods thunder across the field. The army of the Blood Sea charged.

The Mad King sat behind one of his fighters on the back of a large reptilian beast. It gave him a good view of the battle. Two of the flying bulls kept pace with the reptilian in case they were needed for protection or to relay the general's orders.

As the Mad King had intended, the enemy was taken by surprise at the appearance of the Blood Sea host but not enough that they were completely unprepared. When the force had emerged on the plains the Collective soldiers had scrambled into action and quickly formed a coherent line. It was not in the order they would have chosen had they more time to consider best options, but they outnumbered the Blood Sea fighters by as many as two to one. Some of the best troops in the Collective were here; taking their place at the centre were the monstrous Belg and alongside them the renowned Kessian Pikemen. Other infantry of various nationalities and armament formed into their units. Behind them, cavalry gathered in reserve; more than six thousand light and medium horsemen. Units of archers were making their way to the flanks, though possibly too slow to take up their normal positions before the battle commenced.

The Fogmir Elves launched their arrows as they charged. They weren't afraid to get close to their enemies and shoot them point-blank or tease them in hand-to-hand combat. The enemy they faced had no answer, it was like fighting bowmen and infantry at the same time and they struggled to counter the unorthodox style of attack.

The Grey Dwarves confronted the Belg and the Kessians. The Belg were human-like but almost twice the height and broad-shouldered. Each were well armoured and armed, sluggish, but immensely strong. Next to them the Kessian pikemen worked in close formation and could use their long spears from four ranks deep. Pikemen in the first rank braced their tall shields to ready against the Dwarves assault.

They were all easy pickings for the Dwarves who tossed choke gas as they charged, turning the enemies order into chaos. Like the Fogmir Elves, they relished close combat, taking a heavy toll with clockwork crossbows that could each fire eight powerful shots. When the Dwarves were pushed into fighting hand-to-hand they used the bladed bows to thrust and parry. Where the enemy regrouped or had success, more choke gas or flamers would be employed to drive them back.

The Two-Face quaffed their Thog as they approached the enemy. By the time they engaged, they were mad with fury. The infantry they fought were overwhelmed by the brutes. On their flanks, the experienced Orcs of the Iron Jaw fought ferociously. Not to be outdone by their brethren, the Rage style of mass combat practised by the Iron Jaw was all-out aggression and placed primary importance on reaching the next enemy – to bully and bash past your current foe, to hack and slash at the next, and so on. In the heat of the Rage, the lead Orcs relied on other Iron Jaw to clean up behind them. The Shaman gave fuel to the Rage through their chanting so that the Orcs could more easily reach the pinnacle of frenzy.

The Daglari and Madlands fighters were tough and mean. When they charged the enemy, they hooted and yelled their battle cries, and left nothing behind in their ferocity and bloody resolve. The enemy infantry they faced stood firm and combat was joined.

In support of the Elves on the left flank, the Cavastock heavy horse charged into a group of enemy horsemen. The Mad King heard the thunderous crash of their impact from where he rode at the centre of the line. He raised himself from the saddle for a better view.

The King could see it was not going to be a battle of back

and forth. The charge of the Blood Sea host broke the lines of the Collective forces in the first moments of contact, and not long after the sheer weight and ferociousness of the attack pushed enemy units back, and in some cases, they broke and ran. The Collective bowmen and cavalry behind looked to plug the holes in the defence, but as the panic turned to rout they were hampered by their own fleeing troops. With their formations broken, the cavalry became prey to Orcs, Elves, and other fighters of the Blood Sea who continued to push forward and engage. Horns of retreat sounded and those enemies not already in flight, turned to flee. The Orcs had no plans to give the Collective an easy withdrawal and the Fogmir Elves were efficient and merciless in picking off the enemy as they ran. When the Mad King cast his eye across the carnage, he estimated a quarter of the enemy had perished. It was a pleasingly decisive start to the campaign.

Wasting no time, the Dwarves took command of constructing a defence. They grabbed their picks and shovels and mallets and created the outline of a wide trench. While the Elves set about collecting their arrows, the Orcs and humans rounded up horses and pulled loot from fallen bodies. The Mad King instructed them to move the dead away from the area they chose to occupy, and because they travelled without their own baggage – he ordered the soldiers to repurpose what useful items they could from the enemy camp. It wasn't until night that some of the Two-Face Orcs calmed down enough from their drugged state that they returned to the main host. The Shaman walked about the battlefield and rattled their trinkets and bones, while the Orcs on the winged bulls scouted and protected the skies.

Before it became light and under the cover of a concealing shroud provided by the Shaman; the Orcs of the Iron Jaw and Two-Faces, Madlands fighters with their beasts, and the mounted warriors of Cavastock travelled to the edge of the plains to hide and wait.

With dawn, enemy troops reappeared at a distance and

gathered their strength. The flying bulls were forced to abandon the skies for the superior number of enemy flyers – winged creatures that were half-man, half-demon, armed with long two-handed spears. The Mad King watched them take stock of his forces within the camp, to then fly away and report back to their commanders.

The temporary defences were impressive for the time they took to prepare them. The Dwarves had dug a trench deep and wide enough to accommodate themselves, the Elves, Daglari, and a token number of Orcs and Madlands infantry. The trench protected a square of land that gave all the appearances of a camp. During the night, the Orcs and humans used the thousands of discarded pikes collected from the battlefield to shape stakes that they wedged in front of the trenches to be a defence against charging cavalry and to break up the formations of attacking infantry. Behind the trenches, the displaced earth was piled up, and with more time it might have been used to form further barricades.

After the quick march, battle, and night of digging, the Dwarves reached their stamina limits. As morning approached, the Two-Face in the trenches shared sips of their Thog with the army to renew their strength and endurance. It was accompanied by a breakfast of food stolen from the enemy camp.

While others ate, the Mad King walked the length of the trench, ensuring the right placement of the flamers and Dwarven captains who carried the shield devices. There was only enough of the choking gas left to counter one assault, so the king issued clear instruction to the Dwarven commander to be passed on.

"Throw the gas wide so it won't come back to affect the Elves."

The commander gave nothing away with his expression or tone.

"We know our business, King."

The Mad King continued with his instruction.

"Let your soldiers know that nothing less than a heroic effort is expected of them. They must understand that not just their fate, but the success of the whole invasion depends on the determination of this defence."

Again, the Dwarf was expressionless and his tone flat. He was making no visible effort to move and convey the message to others.

"The Dwarves will hold."

The Mad King held the Dwarf's stare, and after an uncomfortably long period, the commander finally turned and made his way down the line of defenders. As he did so he slapped his warriors on the back, and he made it clear to them that the Dwarves would hold this defence this day. No retreat and no surrender. He nodded at the small groups of Daglari too, who returned the nod and bared their teeth to acknowledge that they were bound by the same expectation.

At midday, the anticipated counterattack came. Troops from the cities of Tarash and Gormoth merged with the regrouped field army. Fifty thousand enemy soldiers manoeuvred into place, intent on overwhelming the Blood Sea position.

The Generals of The Collective arranged their units so that bowmen walked ahead of the infantry, with cavalry gathered behind. The Collective fielded sufficient numbers that they attacked all four sides of the encampment, hoping they would expose a weakness. Once in position, the enemy archers let loose their volleys - wave after wave of arrows that might have had terrible impact had the Dwarven Captains not easily defended using the invisible barrier created by the shield discs.

When the arrows stopped, the defenders looked up over the lip of the trench to watch the archers fall back through gaps left by infantry units that were soon running towards them, charging once they were close. The infantry included barbaric warriors that hooted and roared as they came at full pace. Other units were more ordered, keeping their ranks and holding their shields up for protection as they ran.

Nobody had warned the Collective about attacking Dwarves in a hole. Firstly, the vials of choke gas were thrown, followed by the combatant Dwarves who raised their heads and crossbows above the trenches and gave the approaching forces everything they had.

At the same time, Elves leapt up to the ground behind the dugouts to let loose devastating volleys of their own before jumping back down to safety. It was just in time, as enemy archers fired over the Collective infantry to protect the survivors as they limped back to safety and regrouped. Thousands had died in the botched assault.

With a moment bought, the Dwarven Captains redeployed the invisible shields and crossbows were reloaded. They need not have hurried; for now, the shaken Collective army held its ground.

Late in the afternoon and upwind of the trenches, bails of cut grass, bushes and tree branches were soaked in oil and set ablaze. A cloud of thick smoke filled the air, and on the soft breeze, it drifted across the trenches, causing discomfort to the Elves and Daglari who did not have masks like the Dwarves, and obscuring the vision of the defenders. Under the cover of the smoke, they could hear the enemy as they manoeuvred forward. Arrows rained down intermittently through the haze and there was little choice but to wait for soldiers to appear through the smoky cloud. When they revealed themselves, the Dwarven flamers let loose their chaos and close combat began in earnest. While the Dwarves and fierce Daglari were happy to defend from the dugouts, many of the Elves again leapt up behind the trenches where they could fire their bows with more freedom.

The Mad King stood behind one of the flamers who was clearing the battlefield in front of him. In the chaos, screaming men set alight were running in all directions. The King grabbed a gas mask from a dead Dwarf and stood on the body of the unlucky warrior so that the extra elevation allowed him to see further down the defensive line. As the smoke from the fires started to dissipate, it appeared to him that the defence held strong. The Mad King hadn't slept since the meeting at the forest and now he tried to stifle his yawns behind the mask as he stretched his arms to keep himself awake. At times like this, he could feel his age, but at the same time, he felt keenly alive.

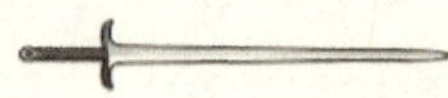

THE LIBERATION OF TARASH GORMOTH

The city of Tarash was well protected from land but poorly defended by sea. As the Mad King had anticipated, the standing army at Tarash rushed to help with the battle on the plains and the Garrison left behind was inadequate to mount a worthy defence. When thousands of warriors appeared near the fortress on the peninsula and a flotilla of ships assaulted its harbour, including those that flew the colours of the old Tarash Gormoth, the Collective Garrison commander raised the flag to parley. After a brief negotiation, Mannace accepted the commander's surrender. Three thousand garrison troops were taken prisoner and ferried away to Viletri and Hindas for processing and detention.

Gormoth was a much tougher nut to crack. It was a massive fortress in the mountains that protected a secluded valley. It had taken the Collective eight years to complete their siege of Gormoth and claim the capital for their own.

Like Tarash, the standing army rushed to the defence on the plains, but more than five thousand troops remained in defence, which the Collective commander expected was more than needed.

Jaal and the Blood Legion moved up the mountain road ahead of the main force of Viletri soldiers and Battalion of Ravens. Behind them marched the remainder of the Madlands' troops; fighters, beasts, Molemen in their covered wagons, and slave soldiers who persisted in lugging the giant bell.

Jaal was impressed at the magnificence of the fortress as it came into view. It appeared to be carved out of the mountain and then added to so that its walls were high above the road and its towers higher still. It hugged the side of the steep slopes, roughly following the line of the road until it disappeared out of sight around a distant bend. He expected from the general lay of the terrain, that beyond the fortress, the road would descend into the valley and city of Gormoth. The road they were on became a tunnel passing through the fortress. It was blocked by a large portcullis and Jaal could see that siege engines and archers placed in the towers would make easy pickings of anybody who approached.

The Mad King's slave soldiers were ushered to the front as the Mad King had instructed. It took almost half a day as they lugged the massive iron bell with them. More than three thousand slaves gathered, with a thousand Madlands' warriors and beasts to back them up. The slaves began a low chant as they heaved the bell closer to the gates. Arrows and boulders rained down on them killing hundreds, but the remainder ignored the carnage and continued forward. As they neared the gates the chanting intensified as did the slaughter.

One of the slaves raised an iron rod and struck the bell. The ground shook and a crack appeared in the rock above the gatehouse. A splintering noise rose out of the deep bedrock itself as if the mountain were awakened and wounded. Jaal and his Blood Legion moved back as stones rolled down the mountain onto the road nearby. The bell struck a second time and there was again a great rumble within the mountain, deafening for Jaal and his soldiers. More cracks appeared across the foundations of the fortress and one tower buckled before it finally toppled. Jaal could see archers tumble through the air and their screams echoed about the chasm. Terrified men on the fortress walls and below on the road scrambled desperately for what might be a safe area. As the slave prepared for a third strike he was suddenly swept off his feet as the road before the gatehouse slipped suddenly away from the mountainside taking the bell and most of the surviving slaves with it. Jaal was dumbstruck - it was madness and terror.

There came a thunderous crack, the shock of which threw any man still standing to the earth. In a slow, unimaginable motion, most of the fortress, attached to a single great piece of rock, slid away from the mountain and plummeted like a giant boulder into the gorge below. Surrounding it, bodies of defenders glided through the air, limbs waving as if they were attempting to fly – horrific but insignificant against the larger calamity that played out around them. The screams of the dying were consumed by the greater noise of the mountain shrieking in agony.

Gradually, the rumbling abated and the worst of the cataclysm seemed over. Survivors, awe-struck and in shock, were slowly regaining their senses, some still clambering for what they considered more stable ground.

One of the Blood Legion was crushed by a large rock from above, causing those close-by to scatter. Jaal could see other casualties amongst his troop, but at least the road where they stood held firm.

In place of the fortress was a long fissure cut into the mountainside that revealed corridors and underground rooms. The Madlands' fighters and what slaves were left climbed and crawled their way along the crevice and entered the closest tunnels. They reappeared and waved items of loot at others on the road. It wasn't until darkness came, and the Molemen were let out of the wagons, that the exploration of the corridors was properly undertaken. The Molemen were humanish but hunched over, appearing deformed. They possessed unusually powerful chests, and arms with long metal claws attached to their hands that Jaal imagined they used for digging, equally useful as weapons. They scuttled across the exposed mountain face and quickly disappeared into the tunnels like rats.

About midnight, the Molemen returned with news of discovery of a passage to the valley of Gormoth. With caution, the army navigated the fissure single file and were led in a long procession through the mountain to caves that exited into the fertile valley as promised. By early morning they formed into units and scouts returned with directions to the capital city.

When the Collective commanders discovered an enemy at their back, they marshalled their forces from the city and what was left of the fortress garrison. Both armies soon faced each other across the verdant fields. Sheep and cattle wandered the gap between them, casually eating grass and ignorant of what would soon follow. Jaal was amused.

"Beef and lamb stew tonight," he bantered to the legionnaires.

They laughed and were right to be confident. The Collective was hard hit when the fortress was destroyed, and three and a half thousand fighters were arrayed – Fifteen hundred swordsman in the centre with twelve hundred bare-chested fighters on their right flank and eight hundred archers to the far left.

The Blood Sea centre was made up of the Viletri infantry and Blood Legion. The Battalion of Ravens was to their left and about seventeen hundred Madlands' fighters and Slave soldiers to their right. Jaal could see that the enemy was outclassed, but it would be a good initiation for the men of Viletri, and a chance for them to prove their worth. When the two forces clashed, he was not disappointed – with the modern equipment, powerful statue warriors, and War Priests, the Viletri soldiers were a potent force, and the enemy swordsmen were utterly crushed by their attack. He couldn't see what was happening elsewhere, but it was not long before the enemy were in rout and with their defences and troops in disarray, Jaal knew they would soon be seeking terms.

Far away, near the coastal city of Sarcross, a great host of Blood Sea forces gathered. The Arenlanders and Alani were the first to arrive. There were as many as twenty thousand enemy troops based there and the numbers increased daily. In addition to the troopships coming and going, scouts reported up to fifty other ships in the harbour or just off the coast. It was a major staging ground for the Collective war effort.

Elsewhere, the infantry of Yanth, Loryan, and Karanthos

worked together to secure the smaller towns and villages. They fought many minor skirmishes and at one town they were surprised to find a camp of more than five thousand soldiers. It took half a day to collect their forces and call on the Rhalec for support, but once they arrived, the Blood Sea army outnumbered the enemy who were quickly surrounded and defeated. When the survivors surrendered, the infantry of Loryan were set to guard them while others resumed the task of securing other outposts.

MAD KING'S GENIUS

On the plains, the Dwarves and Fogmir Elves continued to mount an impenetrable defence. The Collective suffered terrible casualties and reluctantly withdrew a short distance to regroup and consider their options.

To the south, more units of Iron Jaw Orcs appeared on the plains. In total, twelve thousand reinforcements arrived, eager to join the battle. In response, the enemy cavalry and archers left their positions and lined up to face the oncoming threat. The Collective forces again outnumbered and outclassed the new arrivals.

Unexpectedly, at the Mad King's command, the Dwarves and Elves erupted out of the trenches and charged the surprised Collective infantry that were left to guard them. Without the archers to harass them, nor cavalry to counter their charge, the Blood Sea troops covered the ground and engaged the startled enemy. Although less in numbers, the Dwarves and Elves were crack troops and made easy work of the demoralised Collective men. Amongst the enemy soldiers, only the few veteran units offered worthy resistance, and there was one unit of champion swordsmen who gave as good as they got.

After waiting patiently for this moment, the elite Iron Jaw and Two-Face Orcs erupted from the cloaking shroud, appearing suddenly behind the enemy horsemen and charging into them. The Two-Face had shared their Thog with the elite Iron Jaw and together their berserk assault was unstoppable. Seeing their comrades in combat, the horde of approaching Orc reinforcements quickened their pace across the plain to join the attack, charging when they were finally close.

The Cavastock Heavy Cavalry chose that moment to appear from the cover of the shroud at full charge, descending upon the shocked Collective archers as they manoeuvred to get a clear line of fire at the Orcs. The heavily armoured horsemen slaughtered the bowmen in close quarters, and when they were joined by the Madlands troops, attacking with surprise on another flank, it was predictable that the archers were the first to panic and break. Those that could, took flight for open ground.

The Collective cavalry was more resilient. After the initial shock of the ambush, they rallied, and some units counter charged to drive the Orcs back. The fighting became fierce and there were heavy losses to both sides.

Broken, the cavalry unit that was smashed by the Two-Face and elite Iron Jaw, fought desperately as they were pushed back, many forced to turn and flee. Others, witnessing their withdrawal, also pulled back, and knowing that the archers were already in disarray, the Collective commanders shouted for the remaining horsemen to gallop for open ground.

While some Orcs gave pursuit, most joined the Cavastock and Madlands' fighters who hurried to the aid of the Elves and Dwarves. With their added numbers, the fight there became another massacre, and the enemy units that could also fled the battle. Those trapped were shown no mercy by the crazed Orcs and merciless Elves.

The battle on the plains was won and the enemy forces scattered. In the wake of the conflict, the Mad King would have liked to pursue his foe to prevent them from regrouping, but the Blood Sea army was too exhausted to give chase. It was enough to claim the battlefield and tend to their many wounded.

The next day, Ithius and the Blood Sea fleet arrived off the coast at the city of Sarcross. Two hundred vessels cast a wide net around the city and tightened it to ensure no enemy ships escaped. The Fifty ships in harbour made a wedge to break free, choosing the battleground in an area near the shore where they knew the depths and currents better than the Blood Sea sailors. Battle was joined and quickly became a crush of ships, with marines, archers, and crews trading savage blows. The enemy fleet was predominantly sailing vessels with fewer troops and were less useful in close quarters than the triremes and galleys which made up much of the Blood Sea navy. Regardless, the fighting was fierce and raged for half a day, before the last of the Collective sailors holed their craft onto the rocks near the shore and scrambled for the safety of land.

Ithius ordered survivors be dragged from the sea and prisoners detained. Few Blood Sea ships had been lost to the rocks or via clashes with other vessels, although casualties seemed numerous. Healers busied themselves with the many wounded.

Some of the Blood Sea ships did not engage in the fighting and they ensured the blockade of the harbour was maintained. Two daring Yanth warships, with archers in their towers, were making sweeping attacks along the port and harbour to test the defences, doing their best to avoid return fire.

With the harbour under his control, Ithius approached the city in his flagship and flew the flag of parley. He was met on the docks by the Mayor of Sarcross and the General of the Collective armies based there. Ithius demanded unconditional surrender. The General received updates from the winged scouts, so as well as the armies on his doorstep, he also understood the poor outcomes in other cities and in the field. He proposed to Ithius that his army would return home. The Mayor said nothing. Ithius tested the waters.

"A single sailing ship filled with whomever you choose may pass the blockade and return to your homelands".

The General and the Mayor moved aside and discussed the terms. They countered.

"Three ships."

Ithius was dumbfounded at their lack of honour.

"Agreed. I will have three ships brought to this place with a full complement of sailors, returned from those captured. In return, all Collective troops must surrender their arms."

The General acted as he had promised, and the surrender commenced. However, in one area of the city, the Collective units refused to conform and several thousand barbarians and large groups of Belg began to construct barricades in the streets. For now, they were left to their own devices.

As other Collective units gave over their weapons, Ithius had their senior officers brought to the docks. Together they watched the General and the Mayor, with their families and favoured others, board the three vessels and set sail. Ithius addressed the leaders.

"Your full surrender bought so cheaply. Never have I seen such cowardice and disregard for the code of arms and honour. An agreement was made that all Collective troops would surrender, but that agreement has not been fully met."

As they watched the three ships take the path made for them through the Blood Sea fleet, fire arrows and vials of oil arching from the Blood Sea ships struck the Collective ships against their sides and on their decks. Flames could be seen quickly taking hold. Ithius turned his back on the scene, and he gave his terms to the Collective officers.

"Tarash Gormoth is under the control of the Blood Sea. This is the last city to fall and there are only small pockets of resistance. I have accepted the surrender of your army. I invite each of you to negotiate terms for your warriors. Talk to your men and return before sunset if parley is an option. I encourage you to speak plainly."

After that, Ithius gathered his elite Merthos and he made his way to the part of the city that was barricaded. He called for the leader. A woman with red hair and tattoos on her naked chest and arms stood defiantly on an upturned cart.

"Ya can come an get it if ya got the balls for it."

Some of her comrades sniggered and a few jeered at Ithius'

men.

"I can," Ithius replied mater-of-factly. "Or I could let you go free".

"Ya could do that."

"Or I could hire you as mercenaries."

The woman jumped off the cart and walked towards him. The Merthos closest to Ithius tensed but the Admiral stayed relaxed. The woman looked him up and down.

"Ya could do that too."

"I will leave you with Namol to agree to terms."

The man named Namol came forward and the woman looked him up and down as well. Ithius walked away and the Merthos followed him. Ithius had already requested the Battalions of Swords and Crescents to enter the city to help manage the surrender and negotiations.

The Mad King hurried from the plains to Sarcross with his fighters, expecting to take charge of the land attack. He was surprised and impressed that Ithius so cleverly negotiated terms. The King privately set himself a target to liberate Tarash Gormoth within ten days and he was gratified to be ahead of schedule.

RESTORATION

Ithius stayed in Sarcross long enough to see to the surrender and to reorganise the fleet. It was his task now to control the seas and blockade enemy movement. To help with scouting and communication, the Winged Bulls then became his to command.

Thirteen thousand Collective soldiers at Sarcross reached terms with Ithius; that they would serve in the army of the Blood Sea for a period of five years, then have their freedom or continue with wages. Three thousand Barbarians and Belg were taken on as mercenaries, significantly bolstering the battalions of Swords, Ravens, and Crescents. Four thousand troops, mostly from the region known as Attica, chose loyalty to the Collective over self-interest – possibly under the belief that rescue would be forthcoming. Their pride earned them passage to Hindas and Ostoik, fated to life at the oar or in the mines.

Captain Veroff Odari worked with the Mad King to track down and kill or enslave any surviving Collective soldiers still rampant across Tarash Gormoth. It was an impossible task to keep the dispersed enemy cavalry from reforming and, regardless of their efforts to isolate and eliminate the threat, a significant force of five thousand horsemen assembled in the south under the cover of the forest's edge. It was a disastrous choice of location for the Collective troops, and when the Fogmir Elves gathered their full strength and attacked, the Cavalry was utterly overwhelmed and massacred. Never one to miss an opportunity, the Mad King ordered the horses to be collected and they were led to Sarcross to help feed the army and prisoners based there.

The cleansing of Collective migrants was a task well suited to the Orcs and Madlands' troops who rounded up the tens of thousands of foreign settlers that had claimed lands or property. They put them in chains and took from them everything of value. Any captured soldiers were taken away on ships to become galley slaves, labourers, or slave soldiers. Civilian prisoners were transported to Gormoth and confined in the extensive catacombs within the mountain, to be watched over by the Molemen.

The ancient Molemen were experts at human repurposing and reprogramming. The challenge would be how to feed such large numbers, but the Molemen also knew how to weed out the inferior slaves and did not let anything go to waste. Part of the slave conditioning would be to adjust their intake to be minimal without compromising their usefulness.

The Mad King was impressed with the Two-Face Orcs and many of the surviving warriors agreed to stay in Gormoth for pay. As an experiment, the Mad King gave them access to female slaves – at least the ones not already claimed by the Molemen.

When the army finished its business, the Mad King reached an agreement with Veroff that he and the Admiral would restore and administer Tarash Gormoth until a proper government could be re-established.

The Congress of War convened at Sarcross; Mannace, Ithius, Milan, Demmal, and the Mad King talked briefly about the success of the campaign and then focused their discussions on the homelands of the Collective nations. Ithius drew their attention to Attica as the ringleader, and Demmal raised Dunedain as another potential target. Dunedain was home to the Fa'al Barbarians and winged men. Demmal suggested that if the winged men could be defeated or turned, the enemy communications would be crippled. Milan was considered the best person to discuss terms with the Fa'al as he already maintained trade agreements with them. He would take Ya, the barbarian leader whose warriors were from that region. As a final consideration, Milan suggested that the shipyards at the Coral Isles were important to capture or destroy.

In the wake of the fighting, the Fogmir Elves held their own congress, which was attended by Jaal and Casteel. Casteel often talked to the Fogmir Elves through spirit meetings, and it was good to see them in person. She had helped the Elves to refresh their knowledge of the world outside of the Fogmir and to re-establish ties with the Alani. Jaal had come as her guest.

After the campaign at Tarash Gormoth had been discussed, anybody was able to raise questions or make proposals. Jaal made a request to see his children and he explained the circumstance. He was instructed to wait at the gathering place and if after twenty nights nobody came, he was to leave.

After just a day of waiting, a figure entered the clearing. It was a boy Elf, of an age Jaal would expect. The boy walked to stand before him, and he stood up from his seat on a log.

"I am Jaal, your father, third in Order".

The boy stared at him for a long time before speaking.

"We have your eyes, and my sister has your skin. My name is Athose, son of Chamaryylha". He added more tentatively, "Son of Jaal. I am a Warden and I have counted two with my bow in the war with the Collective."

Without other formality, Jaal gave Athose the required instruction in the Order and he made Athose repeat it to him, so he knew it had been understood.

"You are eighth in order."

"Should I come with you?"

"No. You must find your own path. You may come to me if you have need."

After the boy left, Jaal waited until the twentieth night passed and on the following dawn, he departed. As he left the forest he felt a presence amidst the trees as if there were a breeze that kept pace with him, rustling leaves and putting a chill in the air. He stopped at the forest edge and when he glanced back there was a female child lurking.

Dark-skinned so that in this place she was unmistakably his kin. She stepped behind a bush and disappeared, blended seamlessly into the surrounds.

"I am Jaal, third in Order. Your mother is Ahmeda Ravenborn, Second in Order. When you are ready or in need, come to me."

ATTICA

Attica was on the south-eastern tip of a large continent known as Varghonia. Milan's agents detailed two coastal cities in the region and many inland towns. They also noted that the nation bordered with the lands of Kogath, famous for its horsemen. From his past dealings with the Collective, Milan suggested that both Attican cities were large and prosperous, about the size of Yanth. He had not traded directly with Kogath.

Varghonia presented a gentle southern coastline and the host of the Blood Sea made easy landfall. Mannace's choice of troops were those he was most familiar with; the soldiers of Viletri, the Blood Legion led by Khing in Jaal's absence, the Grey Dwarves, the reinforced Mercenary battalions, and the infantry of Sylos with their longbows. The Iron Jaw Shaman and some of their warriors were also there to assist with their shadow cloaks, key to Mannace's plans for covert attack.

Mannace ordered his troops towards Dos Neran, the closest of the two Attican cities. As they marched, enemy Brula were observed scouting his forces and Mannace made no effort to hide his movements. However, on the second night, he ordered the shaman to cast a shroud over his army and they departed camp before midnight. As the first rays of sun touched the verdant landscape, the army arrived at the city of Dos Neran unseen.

The three gates that allowed entry to Dos Neran were of black wood, ominous and towering, with sentries dutifully patrolling the high city walls. Mannace focused his forces at one of the mighty portals. With the Sylos longbowmen deployed to surprise the defenders on the walls, the shroud was lifted, and the archers commenced their assault. At the same time, the War Priests and stonemen ran forward. With their magic and might the great gates were broken asunder, allowing the Blood Sea host to pour into the city before the stunned defenders could properly react.

The commercial district close to the gate was quickly overrun and pockets of fighting ensued as garrison troops arrived in numbers to defend the wide streets and buildings leading into the city's centre. Mannace was methodical and merciless as his soldiers moved through the metropolis, fighting the garrison and militia, securing it piece by piece. Because Mannace did not know if reinforcements might arrive from the neighbouring regions, he pushed hard to have the business done quickly so that the assault continued throughout the day and into the night. By dawn, the blood-stained streets, military posts, government buildings, and inner citadel were fully under his control.

Dos Neran was to be made an example and Mannace allowed the Viletri soldiers and mercenaries to loot and pillage. Away from the chaos, the Sylos infantry secured the city walls, and they patrolled the surrounding territory to warn of any counterattack. The Dwarves, also wanting no part in the bloody aftermath, retreated to set up their camp near the city entrance.

The supporting fleet were positioned a little off the coast. Now they came unopposed into the harbour to participate in the spoils. Mannace watched the chaos from a balcony, high atop the captured citadel. He had expected much tougher resistance, but again, the Collective military proved no match for the might of the Blood Sea.

Further along the Varghonian coast, Milan and the Barbarian, Ya, arrived in Dunedain, at the coastal settlement of Cha'Se. Milan knew that the native Fa'al lived in small communities throughout the hills and valleys. Intending to parley, he also knew it was not as simple as negotiating with one leader. Ideally, a council of Tribal Chiefs would be called so that an alliance could be discussed. In Dunedain, there were at least eighty Fa'al chiefs and it would take many days to summon them together.

The Chief of Cha'Se considered the words of Milan and Ya before agreeing that a council was needed. He suggested that the neighbouring Belg would also attend and Brula were sent to issue the summons. Milan observed the winged creatures for the first time; they were mannish in form, tanned and with a reddish tinge to their skin that was exaggerated with deep crimson paint on their faces and chests. Their bat-like wings were compact when folded against their backs and expansive when unfolded. The Brula faces were human with angular features and an unpleasant permanent scowl. Most wore leather pants and boots and carried long spears.

The Fa'al barbarians that were with Ya at Sarcross and those that occupied the settlement here at Cha'Se seemed a tough lot. They went about many trades but all the men and some of the women looked as if killing might be their primary occupation. When Milan asked for her opinion, Ya was confident that the chiefs would be angry at the treachery of the commander at Sarcross and that their allegiance would sway to the Blood Sea who acted with honour towards her people.

Even further along the coast, Ithius already secured the Coral Isles and the Collective's main port was under his control.

In Attica, Mannace left his ships and marines to hold Dos Neran while he moved the army to the next large city of Dos Elmere. The defence at Dos Elmere was well prepared and the possibility of a surprise attack was cleverly negated by units of Kogath cavalry that patrolled the plains, wiser after the conflict at Dos Neran and looking for signs of troops that might be cloaked. Scouts reported as many as seven thousand Kogath cavalries. The horsemen were a mix of lightly and heavily armoured troops, some with bows but most with spear and shield. More were arriving all the time.

With a determination to see the campaign in Attica concluded quickly, Mannace boldly marched his forces up to the main city gate and arrayed his troops for both an assault and a defence - units back-to-back so one faced the city and their pairing faced back to the plains. It was designed to force the defender's hand. He sent stone men to batter down the city gates. Progress this time was slow but the enemies' attempts to counter the animated statues with arrows and burning oil were futile. When the gates began to buckle under the relentless attack, Demmal, with two of the Viletri soldiers to shield him, ran at the doors, and with a mighty smite of his hammer, broke them asunder. He and the stone men charged through the gap, with units of Viletri infantry and mercenaries close on their heels. A strong defence was prepared beyond the portal and the shield discs were vital to weather the storm of bolts and arrows. The Blood Sea soldiers sprinted forward to engage hand-to-hand.

Outside the city, Kogath cavalry picked that time to launch their attack. They rallied quickly into a great mass and cantered forward, looking to overrun the Blood Sea position with the strength of their horses and momentum of their charge. The men of Sylos took a toll on them at a distance with their longbows, then at the last moment dropped the bows and set their spears to take the impact of the charge. The enemy did not anticipate that these archers might also be capable infantry, and the spears set into the ground blunted the attack; horses and men impaled or pushed back in the ensuing mayhem. They hadn't encountered the choke gas or repeating crossbows of the dwarves either, the combination of which brought down the closest horsemen and created chaos for the ranks behind.

Mannace strutted amongst the men of Sylos. He had not lifted his blade against an opponent for over a decade but today he fought with the spearmen and had planted a spear like the others to break the impact of the charge. Drawing his broad two-handed blade, he used it to bash and slash a path through the enemy warriors. It was invigorating to be involved at the bloody end of the war. Khing and the Blood Legion ran past the Sylos spearmen to fight near Mannace and protect the Lord. Khing was similar in size and prowess to Mannace and when the two warriors fought side by side, grotesque heaps of dying or maimed horses and men, were piled around them. Mannace was impaled by an arrow in his shoulder, deep enough to draw blood but not to hamper his fighting. It was a reminder of his own mortality, and the vulnerability made him feel alive.

The Kogath cavalry fought bravely but they were outclassed and when Khing cut their leader from shoulder to hip, almost slicing his victim in half, the Kogath warriors broke off the combat and galloped for open ground. With the combat outside the city won, the Dwarves redeployed to reinforce the troops fighting in Dos Elmere, leaving the Sylos troops to guard the rear.

In the city, the fighting was fierce but with the superior weaponry of the Viletri troops and the experience of the mercenaries, the streets and buildings were slowly being won. It was not long after the arrival of the Dwarves that the garrison and militia were scattered, and the defence became a rout.

Before the fighting ended, the mercenaries were already looting and raping. After Dos Neran they had renewed their appetite for it. In some places, fires started burning and a sector of Dos Elmere was in flames. Mannace looked on at the anarchy. As always, he considered his broader goals of unity and his vision at the monastery. While it was satisfying to take the city by force, the conflict was becoming tedious and predictable. Mannace had witnessed what the future looked like, and he just needed others to get on board. He knew there must be a better way to finish this war with the Collective.

Part Four:

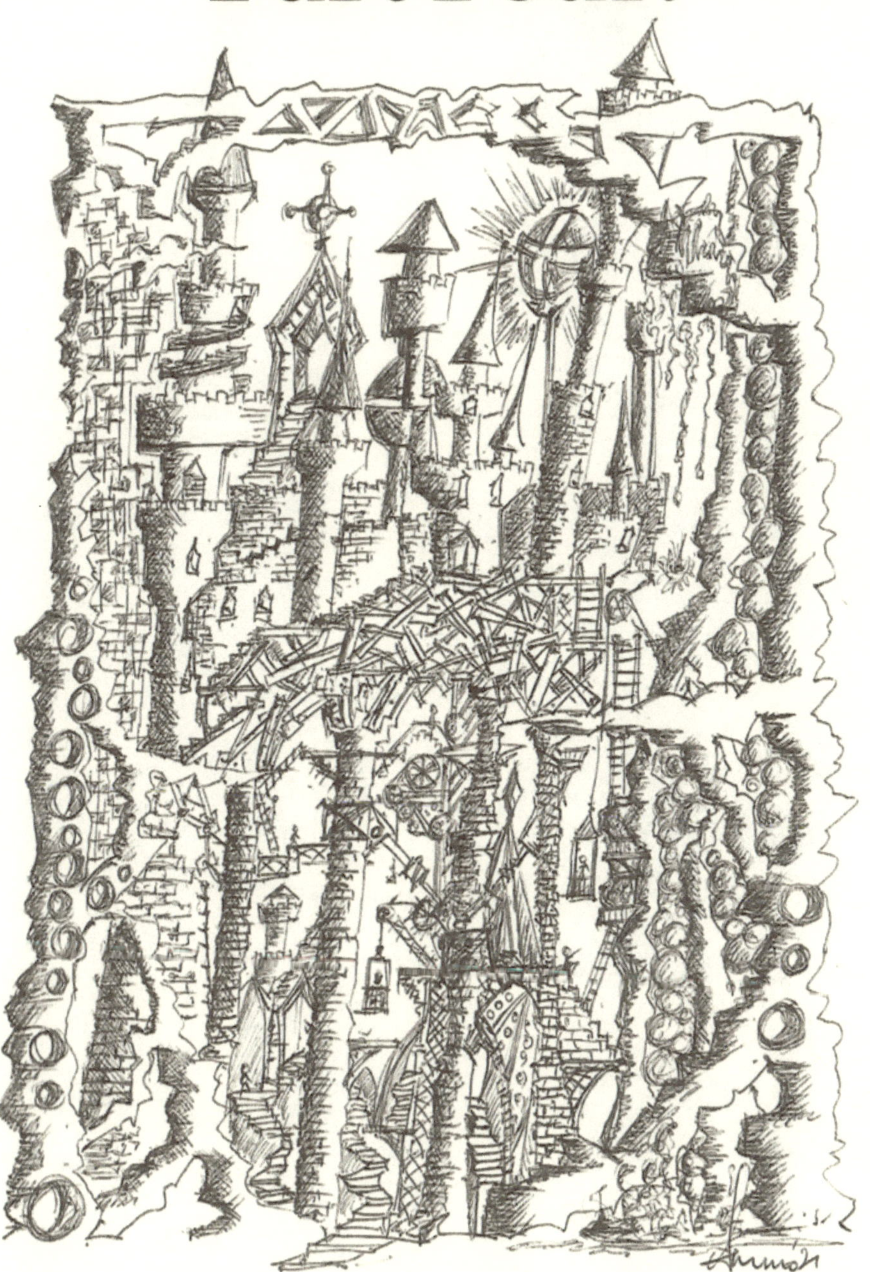

Wrath of the North

THE BLOOD SEA COALITION

It was ten years since the Council of the Blood Sea conquered the lands to the west and became the Blood Sea Coalition. Mannace looked back at his achievements with pride, although it required all his wits to keep the brittle alliance from splintering into its many pieces. Even though they won the war in the west, Mannace retained the position of *Lord General*, and he used the escalating conflict against the North to further unify the Coalition's forces. Through military alliance with Roundhome and Galandar, the Blood Sea Coalition regularly dispatched troops to the northern Rift. For those soldiers fighting at the Rift, it was confronting and overwhelming, yet, for those not directly involved, the North often seemed a distant and intangible enemy.

It appeared to many leaders that the young men who sailed north to Roundhome and from there marched to the battlefront were full of fire and bravado, but the soldiers that returned home were often crippled or broken, their flame extinguished. It was an unpopular war, and support for continued involvement rapidly diminished. Mannace did not have the time to visit the northern allies or the Rift. Instead, he was dependent on Shepherd to be his ambassador and Demmal Fulstrom to be his field general.

The war with the Collective had ended with the conditional surrender of fifteen nations. Attica, Kogath, Indana, Mogos, Jerusso, Ingola, and the Coral Isles were territories on the continent of Varghonia. Arackland, Valthar, and Chance bordered the boundless Barren lands. Danatu Salu and The Choore shared a majestic arboreal island. Macetown was a thriving port on the Great Tundra. Further inland was the Silver Valley, a young nation risen out of a mining boom.

Farther south, the Kessik dominated a long stretch of the

bleak tundra. They were the last nation of the Collective to succumb, and terms were not reached until the Blood Sea defeated their field army and arrayed its full might before the gates of their capital. During the furious fighting, Mannace was inspired by the masterful discipline of the Kessik soldiers and the rampaging elephant cavalry that fronted their defence. Some of his finest officers and advisors were now of Kessik descent.

The surrender terms imposed upon the defeated nations emptied their treasuries and compelled their soldiers to fight in Mannace's army – many were sent north to Demmal to reinforce the fighting at the Rift. While the nations kept their independence, each was allocated a place at the Council table, and like other Council members, they pledged commitment to unity, openness in commerce and trade, as well as military collaboration in defence of Coalition territories. Some uttered the oaths through embittered lips, while others buried their past animosity and took full advantage of the new arrangements.

The tribal leaders of Dunedain had ceremonially mixed blood and spirit with Milan and aligned themselves with the Blood Sea before the Collective's surrender, thereby avoiding the admission of defeat and a punitive treaty. Their warriors, including the Belg and Brula, filled their purses from mercenary contracts managed through the Guild of Swords. Many generals coveted the versatile Brula as scouts or messengers. The Belg, with their massive stature and stoic natures, commanded a high price for their services and enjoyed their pick of lucrative assignments.

Attica was another exception. Although they were the first to submit, the Attican nobles proved defiant and incited mutiny among the Collective nations. Left unchecked their incessant plotting would surely provoke rebellion. In response Mannace bound the nobles in chains and ordered them dragged to Gormoth to be the Mole Men's playthings. This was a period that saw the Angry Man surface in all his fury. It was not only the Atticans that suffered. Anybody that crossed Mannace felt his wrath. Mannace appointed

Khing as Lord of Attica. He recognised that Khing was of Viletri stock, having at least one immortal parent. Khing himself doubted such heritage but Mannace liked and trusted the man.

AGE OF INVENTION

The metropolis of Viletri flourished as a centre of commerce and a diplomatic hub for the Blood Sea Coalition. Migrants from as far as Galandar were attracted there. Residents crammed themselves into every nook and cranny within the city proper, while city districts overflowed its walls and crept north and east alongside the busy highways. As part of the city's spectacular rebirth, old government buildings were demolished and replaced with Dwarven constructed masterworks.

One such edifice was the Institute of Technology, which included a magnificent clock tower that chimed over the city every hour. To the people of Viletri, the timepiece was symbolic of their invention and innovation. It was also a vexation on those nights when it relentlessly carved their slumber into hourly chunks. The institute was Mannace's passion, and his legacy, and he spent what time he could there with the Dwarves and men of science. He and the Grey Dwarf, Logthar, collaborated on a multitude of projects and they argued the point about many things. Mannace was frustrated with Logthar's persistent reluctance to incorporate magic into his designs.

"Be pragmatic, Logthar, if magic will do the job, then use it. What point is there in wasting months on this clockwork, when it will never do the job as well.".

"You're missing the point, lad. We must push the limits, improve on what we know, always be looking for new ways."

The Dwarf knew that to mention Mannace's rivals would fire his blood, but it needed to be said.

"The Arenlanders understand - they won't touch magic - it stonewalls real progress."

Mannace was shaking his head, clearly exasperated by the

Dwarf's stubbornness.

"You are wrong to think magic has no place in invention. Mage-Tech, Technomancy, they're contemporary disciplines, they push boundaries. Look at what we have achieved."

Mannace could see that the Dwarf, standing with his arms folded and a steely look in his eyes, was immovable on his position. Reason was not going to penetrate that armour.

"You are blinded, Logthar, by your cogs and spinners. You have springs in your eyes. Magic, Logthar, there is no greater source of power."

The Dwarf scoffed, and he leaned in and whispered to Mannace.

"The Core, Mannace, magic is nothing compared to The Core."

"What is The Core, Logthar?"

The Dwarf seemed agitated and looked about him as if he were terrified that someone might overhear.

"I have said too much. For the sake of our friendship, don't repeat what you have heard, Mannace, but know that there are forces much deeper than *magic*."

Mannace did as Logthar asked and let the conversation go, but he would claim the last word.

"Whatever achieves the end, my friend. Progress is nothing if not outcomes."

As the institute's centrepiece, Mannace commissioned a hefty cube of black marble that Render imbued with potent enchantments. Using his prowess in necromancy, the wizard conjured forth the spirit of *The Architect* from his place of eternal rest and bound his essence to the stone. Before his death, the Architect lived at the Monastery and crafted many devices based around his futuristic visions – artefacts that started Mannace's obsession with science. *Students of the Architect*, a name that a group of enthusiastic engineers had dubbed themselves – would arrive each day and lay their hands upon the stone. This peculiar contact enabled them to link minds with their spirit mentor and continue to work on his designs. Their present undertaking was to fathom and manipulate the inscrutable forces of up and down.

When the Architect was summoned, another spirit returned with him, one that attached himself to the other, knowing that this time would come. That spirit was not bound to the stone and escaped into the city. With determination that was almost obsession, it sought out Mannace. Once found, the spirit of Syprus whispered in Mannace's ear. The Lord was taken aback, but he recognised the voice and was oddly grateful to have an old ally resurrected, even if it was not in his physical form.

Mannace knew Jaal would be incensed. However, he asked Render for help, and the Sorcerer employed a full-length mirror in Mannace's house to bind the spirit so that Syprus could use it as a physical medium. Mannace could see the ghostly outline of Syprus in the reflection, and if he touched the glass, he could better hear the older man's voice. In the evenings after his busy day, Mannace would update Syprus on events. The spectre would listen and give Mannace his insights. Often, he reinforced to Mannace the importance of following the Oracle's vision and purpose.

"Mannace, remember that you are at the centre, chosen by the Light to lead us all into a new age. Look at what you have already accomplished. You are above law and reason. You must do whatever is needed. Take what is needed. Let no obstacle block your way."

Often Mannace was mentally exhausted at the end of a day, and in such a state he found that doubt was a tenacious enemy. He drew great comfort from Syprus' affirmation.

Work on a Manufactory was almost complete. Dwarven craftsmen were adding blast plates, extractor fans and other finishing touches to the east wing. In the meantime, equipment was moved into the massive western hall – forges and clockwork machines for smelting, refining, and shaping all types of metal. At the command of human overseers, a tireless workforce of stone men positioned complex contraptions or devices. Larger steel men, thin but extending to three storeys in height, helped with the heavy lifting - their clockworks whirred at a high pitch as they strained to install the heavy metal chimneys. The ventilation would guide smoke from the boilers and forges out through the roof, and high into the sky above the city. The Dwarves prepared to add filters, and a mage placed enchantments on the smokestacks to reduce their foul pollution.

Next to the completed Temple of War, a Temple of Healing was under construction. Althea Kane was overseeing the project, which took its inspiration from a Fesadi design. Joining the five separate buildings were paths that led to courtyards and private sanctums. It was a place where people in search of healing of the body or spirit could find accommodation and care. Fesadi crystals, some as large as a fist, hung in windows to entice the healing power of colour and light into the multi-story buildings. In the courtyards and its magnificent central atrium, rare plants sourced from Alani, Fesadi, The Chore, and the Isle of Malanos were placed in pots or hung about the courtyards, their blooms providing vivid decoration and aromas. As well as their stunning beauty, most contained healing properties.

Althea liked to stand outside of the temple on the street leading up to its entrance. She adored the clean lines of the construction, the whiteness of its stonework flecked with colour as the crystals reflected out toward the city. Even at that distance, she caught the scent of the flora and could sense the structures intrinsic life-enriching properties. It made her chortle to glance over at her neighbour, the imposing Temple of War, and its ridiculous homage to the male ego. She reflected on the cycle of war and the horror and damage it caused. "If only we started with healing," she thought.

Another enormous building in the city was the residence of the undead. It was a large, windowless dormitory with a central feeding area and another shared space for upkeep and repairs. Vines were encouraged to creep across the towering outer walls, and there were flower beds about its perimeter, skirted with a knee-high, white picket fence.

The Assembly rejected the practice of zombification, and there were sections of the community that vehemently opposed it. Kakos persisted regardless, and he benefited from both Mannace's and Render's backing which seemed sufficient to trump the naysayers. Viletri was filled with migrants who were more tolerant, embracing the city's many strange quirks. Supported or not, the undead became another subculture amongst Viletri's diverse mix of residents, beliefs, and lifestyles.

Zombies maintained and cleaned the city and were an essential part of keeping the intricate cogs of government process turning. They were Kakos' menial and clerical army. Two Necromancers operated the *Return Services*. They reported to Render for their continuing development, and to Kakos for their assignments.

As well as the zombies, Kakos controlled many spirits. As he moved about, he used them almost subconsciously to open and close doors, dispense orders to employees who were accustomed to hearing the voices in their heads, and artfully filter noises or conversations to distinguish anything important. His expertise was omnipresent, and all treated him with dutiful, sometimes fearful, respect. He did have his haters, but none brazen or foolish enough to openly challenge him, yet.

Kakos and Mannace worked together to showcase the best use of technology within the city. Steam-cranes towered over the docks and were always busy loading and offloading ships. The metal towers were loftier than the original design from Ostoik and incorporated complex gears and Dwarven clockwork that improved their strength and efficiency. Mannace would sometimes stand on the city walls that overlooked the harbour to watch the cranes unload freight from heavily laden ships. The clockwork was mesmerising, with tiny cogs that moved faster than the eye could catch, while the largest gearwheels turned at a leisurely but constant pace. Other mechanisms slid back and forth as the crew of engineers operated their pedals and levers. When the long arms strained to lift a heavy load, steam billowed from the main shaft, and dark clouds puffed up from the nearby boilers. It peeved Mannace to see the dirty smoke that blew across the docks. It reminded him of his arguments with Logthar, knowing there were better alternatives. Still, like Logthar, he didn't want to be wholly reliant on wizards for the future.

Clockwork carriages travelled in a loop around the city, frequently stopping so that citizens could jump on and off. They were the latest mechanical marvel, generating much of their own energy as they moved, with a small power stone supplied by Render's apprentices to augment their self-propulsion. The zombie drivers operated a series of levers to move the carriages forward and to veer right or left. As they leapt from gear to gear, it seemed a desperate process to keep the carriages on a straight path. Bells on the front of the carriage warned others to scamper out of the way.

The Arenlanders were innovating too. Rail carriages arrived at Viletri every day from Ostoik. Another mechanical wonder, although in typical Arenland fashion they were horrendously noisy and generated copious amounts of filthy black smoke. The train of gloomy carriages, fuelled by coal-fire and water, could make the journey to Arenland in a day and night. The wagons mostly carried coal, ore, or grain, but some transported people. The train rode on two sets of rails that stretched the long distance to Ostoik and facilitated passage in both directions. Mannace was not the only one to consider the railroad and carriages a blight against the pristine landscape, but he could not deny the Arenlanders astounding feats of engineering. The Viletri Lord enjoyed the rivalry with Ostoik and its industry Guild Masters.

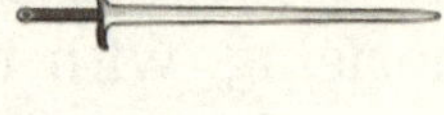

HOUSE OF MIRRORS

Saska and her household were famous in the city. The locals called her abode the *House of Mirrors* as the female residents there held a shining, immortal beauty and appeal. Even Arta seemed more youthful. Wealthy merchants or prominent diplomats that were guests at the residence spoke highly of their hostess and her employees.

One guest that frequented regularly was the High Priestess Ahmeda; at least two or three times a year. She would spend time with Saska teaching her the ways of the disciple. Saska continued to demonstrate a natural affinity for magic and some aspects such as Fire Elements and Control came naturally to her. During the visits, they made time to travel to the Spider Wood and meet with Eya. Their bond of sisterhood continuing to strengthen.

Both Eya and Ahmeda possessed some ability to observe the future. It was a surprisingly common trait amongst women, although few knew how to recognise and interpret such visions. Ahmeda's talent derived from a keen self-awareness and uncanny intuition about others. Eya was able to see through the eyes of her offspring. Every spider in existence linked back to her. The innate magical abilities of both matriarchs amplified their awareness.

When they were alone, Eya and Ahmeda often shared their experiences to help one another understand what they had felt or perceived. Ahmeda experienced a recurring sense of foreboding.

"I have in my care a Bracadian; a spy we found in Ostoik. He has been a great source of particulars about that nation, their capability, and their Emperor.".

Ahmeda considered her next words carefully.

"I sense a connection to this Emperor, an alignment of vision and purpose."

"Is it because he is powerful, this Emperor?"

"No. It is because he is not powerful."

Ahmeda knew that what she had said to Eya did not make sense, and when the Ancient did not respond, the conversation quickly moved on.

"The Bracadian's are far away. We are at the very edge of their Emperor's vision, but they will come. They are a greater threat than even the North and they will seek to conquer us. My prisoner says they will quickly overwhelm the Coalition with their mastery and numbers. But I do not fear them. Rather I have a sense of destiny.".

"Perhaps if these Bracadians overcome the Coalition, some leaders may fall, and others will rise within a new regime?"

"Perhaps."

Eya was unaware of Bracadia and its ambition. Her intuition drew her north.

"Everything I can see and sense tells me that we build toward a great event in the north. A cataclysm, although I cannot tell its nature. It all began in the north and perhaps it will end there too."

"Mannace has said that. He speaks of a final battle.".

"His vision is born of Light. What does the Light gain in this final battle, Ahmeda? What is of benefit to the Light may not serve other masters. We of the Darkness might desire an alternate path, a different outcome."

 "What will you do, Eya?"

That was a question Eya had considered for some time. Ahmeda was the first person she trusted to share her plans.

"I will travel north."

"Now?"

"Not yet. There is time still to prepare and watch. And we must help Saska to grow. She is important to the future."

Ahmeda nodded. She shared a strong sense of Saska's

potential. Eya smiled, which Ahmeda hadn't witnessed before.

"Ahmeda, if you and Saska were unimportant to the future, we would never have met. I do not waste my time. You are much like Saska, a child. What you have achieved so far in your short life is just the first step of a long journey."

When Ahmeda seemed agitated, Eya added, "If you see what you have accomplished as the pinnacle of your life, your vision and actions will be limited to what you know. If you accept you are at the beginning, then you will look forward and achieve greater things."

Jaal spent an increasing amount of his time in the company of Eya and the Spiderlings. He found great purpose in aiding his offspring to learn to fight and harness their natural talents. The spiderlings aptitude and ability to slow time made them formidable warriors. As servants of the Order, the spiderlings were disciplined and followed instructions implicitly.

Jaal became familiar with sections of the underground domain that was home to Eya and her spawn. The caves and catacombs were vast and formerly occupied by other creatures who had shaped crude rooms within the subterranean habitat. There were still some occupants that dwelled within the depths where the Spiders and Spiderlings hunted for food; often rodent-like or monstrous. The other thing that astounded Jaal was the eerie underground lakes of which he discovered a dozen in his time there. Fish and sometimes larger denizens populated these soundless grottos. It was a welcome sanctuary.

Although on different paths and spending long periods apart, he and Saska upheld their passion and need for one another.

CULT OF THE FALLEN

The cultists chanted, some thrashing from side to side in their zeal. Hundreds of men and women sat in a full circle - a pentagram at its centre. Render was nestled amongst them like a king peacock surrounded by his flock. He was able to sense, almost taste, the palpable psychic energy from the chant and the remarkable power generated for the summoning.

Bit by bit, as if unfolding out of the flickering torchlight and shadow - a contorted, malevolent shape manifested within the pentagram; a disfigured woman, twice the height of any cultist - had she not been hunched over. There was a putrid green tinge to her rubbery skin, and old stains down her legs suggested she was not always in control of her functions. Render knew this was Ruu, Demoness of Pain. Her pitiless eyes were yellow and razor-sharp, much like her pointed teeth. She scanned her audience and took visible note of Render who wore the token of cult leader against his chest. Ruu's forked tongues flicked at him, and despite his calm demeanour, Render felt a surge of heat across his body, using his sleeve to wipe away the sweat that quickly formed on his brow.

A wave of force abruptly emanated from the demoness and all in the circle except Render writhed in agony, some screaming, while others collapsed. Render watched Ruu stretch up to her full height with arms raised into the air, her gross form reverberated and at one point seemed to shift a fraction to the right, out of sync with the mortal world. When the demoness relaxed back to her hunched state, the forces subsided, and those cultists still able returned to their seated positions. Many sobbed or moaned.

Render walked to stand in front of the Demoness.

"Ruu, would you walk again upon this land?"

The demoness took her time to ponder the question. Again,

forked tongues flickered at Render, she tasted his scent, hunted for signs of his fear.

"Yesss".

"You will have what freedom I give. You will obey my commands."

"Yesss".

"For now, you must remain at this temple during the day. You may roam at night".

The demoness seemed pleased with that.

Render waved his hand, brushing the pentagram away. The demoness leaned over and grabbed up a dazed cultist, her long talons slashing the man's abdomen and neck, so that blood and innards gushed onto the floor. The demoness buried her face in the dying cultist's gut and gorged herself. Grotesquely, Ruu twisted the body in her powerful grip to squeeze the remaining juices from it. Finally quenched, the demoness settled back on her haunches. She gave the torso a final lick and set it aside.

Render turned and exited the gathering. He was not familiar with demons and their behaviours, so relied heavily on the cultists to manage the summoning and bidden creatures. He remained uncertain if demons would be a help or hindrance. Extra time was needed to fully comprehend the cult, their customs, and their dark rituals.

A focus for Render was his adaption of necromancy, which he referred to as *Technomancy*. He defined it as, "The harnessing, containment and manipulation of life force and sentience to give life, movement, and intelligence to non-living entities."

His experiment with Kakos proved that magical talent was not a prerequisite for involvement in the discipline. Instead, an exceptional mind was essential. He took on fifteen such students that he called *Animators*.

There was a hierarchical progression to Animation. Firstly,

each Animator controlled and manipulated the life essence of a creature, which Render referred to as a *Life Familiar*. It was possible to do simple things with the familiar, like move an object or create a breeze. When a student could demonstrate mastery of the Life Familiar, they were given a human life force, called the *Gia*. What could be done with such a gift was limited only by imagination and mental discipline. The Gia could learn or be programmed. The animators used their Gia to power the steel men, run machines in the Manufactory, or to give life to their inventions. The best of the animators might have several Gia under their control. The final stage, which none of the Animators had yet achieved and might well be beyond their capability, was the harvesting of life. Render toyed with the name Technomancer for this advanced level. In Render's vision for the future, Technomancers would create additional Gia for themselves and produce Familiars and Gia for new students.

Over the last decade, Render attracted six new apprentices, bringing their number to twenty-one. In addition to the two Necromancers assigned to help Kakos, Render had three cultists amongst the Fallen, six Battle Wizards under the instruction of Amnicles, two Creation Mavens that specialised in living statues and supported the work of the Animators, one Sea Mage who took care of the harbour and waters around Viletri, and seven junior apprentices that were still to choose a speciality. It was a magnificent collection of casters to rival the revered spell weavers of the Alani, and Viletri held its magicians in high esteem. The apprentices referred to Render as *The Sorcerer*, while many citizens in Viletri revered him as *The Protector*.

Render kept one life force in his possession that demanded special attention. Morgan Cain's tormented soul was amongst those he unearthed at the Valley of Pain, and the Sorcerer brought it and the obsidian statue of the man to his holdings at Viletri. The soul subsisted in a tortured state for over twenty years, and it was not as simple as wiping it clean as he did with the others. To restore Morgan to the statue, and animate it in a way that would be recognisable as the explorer, required Render to patiently massage the spirit of the Captain back to good health.

SLAVE LANDS

The Mad King reshaped Tarash Gormoth. The enterprise was entirely self-indulgent – a game he conceived to pass the time, and test how far he could push humanity beyond its reasonable limits. In the ravaged, post-war environment, he leveraged the population's lingering hatred of the Collective to fuel a brutal order. As part of his malevolent design, each family was allotted one or two slaves as labourers for their farms or businesses. The slaves were amongst those Collective immigrants that once occupied their lands, imprisoned after the Collective's defeat, and processed within the dank catacombs beneath Gormoth. Cruel conditioning by the Mole Men left the prisoners emaciated and void of conventional thought. The slaves were hardy, obeyed instructions explicitly, and worked harder when berated or lashed. Most were kept outdoors and often used at night to guard property or livestock. Under this new order, there were no laws nor honourable constraints to protect them.

The Mad King gained morbid satisfaction in turning people inside out to see them with their guts exposed – metaphorically – their true, ugly, bloody selves revealed. Although the King appeared benevolent in public, his private reflections held little respect or compassion for the common man.

How the Tarash Gormoth citizens treated their slaves strongly influenced how they dealt with their neighbours and foreigners. They were fast becoming hard, unpleasant people.

Similarly, the ferocious Madlands and Two-Face warriors that formed the post-war police and garrison forces, set the tone for the military. Justice was delivered with a heavy fist and soldiers earned rank by being strict and dominating. Impressed with the Iron Jaw warriors during the battle on the plains, the Mad King arranged training of his fighters in The Rage, which further spurred their violent and uncompromising natures.

Surprisingly, the Mad King did nothing to rebuild the defences of Gormoth. He held the belief that walls encouraged cowardice and complacency. Instead, he widened some of the passageways through the mountain to provide access to the secluded valley and city.

After a decade, there remained no national government in the Capital. In its place, when decisions were needed; nobles, officials, guildsmen, merchants, and others would all go to the Mad King. Despite his busy schedule, he always made time to help them with their problems, and he guided them with pragmatic solutions.

Admiral Veroff Odari commanded the fleet of Madlands ships and Tarash Gormoth vessels. The flotilla progressively expanded and undertook constant action. They travelled North, raiding coastal towns and provincial areas of the Great Continent for slaves. Recently they discovered a region infested with goblins. The goblins were orcish yet smaller in stature and less aggressive. Goblin slaves proved as useful as humans for menial tasks once they were trained and conditioned. Since the war with the Collective, slaves were an essential commodity in the larger cities of the Blood Sea, and flesh markets were common in most ports.

Far away and forgotten by the Mad King, the Madlands fell to chaos in his absence. Warlords divided the nation into factions that were in constant conflict with one another. The Council of the Blood Sea Coalition decided not to interfere. Instead, they waited to see if a new leader would ascend to unite the region. In the meantime, the opportunistic Arenlanders laid a strong claim to the Borderlands, fortifying and garrisoning the fertile territory.

GALANDAR

Shepherd had not been back to Viletri for more than two years. As the representative for the Blood Sea Coalition, he undertook the vital role of maintaining diplomatic alliances with both Galandar and Roundhome. At his residence in the Galandar capital of Rotherdan, he possessed all the comforts he might have needed and more. Servants that fed him, others that cleaned, and those that attended to his pleasures. When he was required to travel, a carriage would be waiting at his door.

At the centre of a vast plain and considered by its residents to be the hub of the civilised world, Rotherdan was a gigantic metropolis and home to almost one million people. Shepherd imagined that through a birds-eye, the city would appear as a giant wheel with the Empress' immense palace at the hub, from which the city's main thoroughfares spanned like carriage spokes in many directions. They ended at a towering wall that encircled the inner city. Other districts existed beyond the wall, but they were not organised and pristine like those inside. Instead, they were the poorer districts, and some were little more than tent towns or slums.

The citizens of Rotherdan were proud and industrious. Their industry was impressive in its scale, although Shepherd felt that he had seen superior engineering in the factories at Ostoik, and more significant innovation in the works of the Grey Dwarves. After observing the dynamic enterprise of Mannace, it also appeared to Shepherd that the Roth's were stagnant, perhaps a little bit too satisfied and set in their ways. What he gave them great credit for was their organisation. For its size, the inner city ticked like Dwarven clockwork, and everything and everybody knew its place and purpose. The garrison was highly visible on the streets and walls, stepping in time as they moved about, and every twenty steps ceremoniously clashing their spears into their shields to make their presence felt. It gave the city a resolute, comforting beat. The districts outside the city were left mostly to their own devices, some maintained their factions or soldiers, others fostered violent gangs. Twice, Shepherd observed the army sweep through the outer districts where they would pressgang any man not employed and send them to training camps to fight in the conflict at the Rift.

The army of Galandar was over one million strong; every man needed for the defence against the North. The forty thousand troops of the Blood Sea Coalition were a welcome addition, and their involvement was enough to get Shepherd a place at the Empress' War Council, along with Galandar's other close allies: Roundhome, Cavalere, and the Holy Lands. Interestingly, the Nations of the Horseclans and Remman were also part of the defence at the rift, but they held separate assemblies.

The war against the North was more than a thousand years old, but it intensified in recent centuries and more again in the last three decades. Shepherd did not travel to the rift but met with soldiers as they journeyed to and from there. He knew little about warfare, but enough to have an impression of its futility and waste. After so many generations of fighting, the Galandarian's hatred of the northerners and dedication to the conflict seemed obsessive and unhinged. It warped the entire shape of their civilization. This was an opinion he was careful to keep to himself.

Shepherd had met the General, Demmal Fulstrom, when the War Priest attended a meeting at Rotherdan with the other generals. He recalled their first conversation.

"Demmal, how goes it at the Rift?"

"As well as can be expected in a war where the beginning cannot be remembered, and nobody expects there to be an end."

The general smiled, and he was more philosophical than Shepherd expected.

"Demmal, how do our armies fare?"

"They serve the War God admirably. We do our part, and we hold our line. The Bull and Brula flyers have been a revelation; we control the skies, which means the South is well informed of northern movements. It is a titanic duel, a scale of war unlike anything ever seen in the Blood Sea."

Demmal had smiled again, surprising Shepherd once more with his choice of words, "The War God is laughing at us … at these games of war that we play."

Much of the discussion at that meeting was about the logistics needed to transport soldiers, garrison and feed them. For soldiers of the Blood Sea Coalition to journey back to their homelands was a month's travel by road to the western coast of Roundhome, then a sea passage of days or weeks depending on the destination.

Shepherd brokered trade deals on behalf of merchants and guilds. There were massive profits to be made by anybody willing to travel the long distance between the Coalition lands and Galandar. He was in current discussions with the Wain Lords for access to lucrative markets further east. The Wain were nomadic traders who travelled in covered wagons between the cities of the Southern Alliance. It was not uncommon to see large groups of Wain journeying together, often with armed riders or Remman mercenaries for protection. Shepherd heard accounts of a secret army; one of shadow, that did whatever the Wain needed to protect their interests and remove obstacles. He was not game to see if the legend was true.

BLOOD LEGION

The Blood Legion relocated their base to Dos Neran in Attica, although a small contingent remained in Viletri to garrison their holdings there. When the war against the Collective ended, many armies became inactive, and part-time soldiers returned to their ordinary occupations. Some of the best warriors, unimpressed by the notion of turning their hand to farming, baking, building, labouring, or such like, instead joined the Blood Legion. Jaal set the size limit for the Legion at one thousand active troops, with up to four hundred inactive. The inactive forces often remained based at Viletri or Dos Neran, going about their own business.

For the last decade, the Blood Legion secured frontier regions, settled disputes, and fought alongside other troops against northern raiders. While Jaal spent some time with them, Casteel was now their regular commander. She was ferocious and hard when needed, but like Jaal, she also enjoyed the camaraderie of the troop. The Legionnaires routinely sparred against each other for practice or sheer bravado, and Casteel could foot it with the best of them.

The Blood Legion comprised of many races, all sworn to a brotherhood. The barbarian, Ya, was amongst them, now strongly bonded with Casteel. Also, from the province of Dunedain, were a veteran Belg named Rey and two Brula who the Legionnaires referred to as Hammy and Spit. Rey took responsibility for the Legion's youngest member; a Wild Elf named Athose. Athose joined the unit soon after the war with the Collective and consequently never underwent the same hard tests the other recruits had. However, because he was affable and did his part with the bow in battle, he nonetheless become fully one of them. Casteel would take a likeable boy over a seasoned champion if they were a better fit for the legion – the Legion relied on teamwork and had no tolerance for egomaniacs, braggarts, or bullies.

The Blood Legion responded to a raid reported in the territory of Jerusso, an attack on the small port of Holsted. Leaving Dos Neran, their journey followed a road that was at first broad and well kept, passing through farmland and busy villages. When they crossed the Attican border into Kogath, the highway turned into a rough trail that wound through the hills and into the Jerusso highlands. Casteel enjoyed the scenic trek. She hadn't visited this place before, and the ancestral traveller in her heightened her senses so that when the legion approached the windy Jerusso coast, she relished the briny tang of the ocean and lonely cries of circling gulls. Only the messy business she must now deal with dampened her excellent mood; it was time to get to work.

From his high vantage, Hammy discovered the distressed Holsted garrison who awaited them in a wind-swept valley near the coast. The earth where the soldiers camped was sandy, and the Legion descended a steep dune to reach them. Casteel could feel unwanted grit collecting in her boots as she sidled down the slope. She had never liked sand; it was the worst kind of parasite, wrangling its way into your gear and about your body, travelling uninvited for days or even weeks. The smell of it reminded her of rotting fish bones. It was one thing to smell the tang of the ocean and quite another to carry it with you as an unwanted sandy guest.

The garrison commander, a young man, dressed in simple leather armour and with a sword at his belt, reported to Casteel that they abandoned Holsted. He sent the civilians scampering east towards the capital and dispatched a messenger to Dos Neran - seeking out the Blood Legion because of the unusual nature of the invaders.

"They're an uncanny lot, pretty boys all dressed up in their fine uniforms, no armour, and thin blades like that one."

The officer pointed at Casteel's Rapier. Before he

continued, he cleared his throat with a small cough.

"They have long bow sticks, that they point and shoot. The weapons are noisy and bellow fire and smoke. They fire metal balls. Can't see 'em coming, and they pack a wallop."

The man pointed out some of the soldiers that sported wounds from the weapons, and one presented a small metal sphere that he held between forefinger and thumb. Meanwhile, Spit returned from scouting and reported four ships and a contingent of the enemy still in possession of the coastal town. The officer concluded his account.

"They fired at us from their ships, and when we pulled back, they unloaded at the pier. We didn't hang around, nor did they chase us. Too many of 'em for us to take on. You lot though, you'll outnumber the bastards and push them back to the sea."

Casteel was unsure what to make of the so-called bow sticks, but she was confident in her troops' ability to adapt to any situation. Casteel ordered the Blood Legion to advance toward Holsted. They did so in small groups and made use of ridges or trees for cover, then once they were close - darted across open ground to the outskirts of the town itself. In the face of the Legions superior numbers, the enemy pulled back from the buildings and formed into a long line, three ranks deep, at the pier. Four enemy warships pulled closer to the docks so that their marines, armed with bow sticks, provided additional support to those onshore. Casteel recognised the type of ship from the one taken a decade ago at Viletri. Now was the first time since then that the Bracadians were engaged.

Under the cover of buildings, the Legionnaires moved as close as they could to the pier and those with ranged weapons took up positions in windows or behind cargo crates. When everyone was in place, Casteel wasted no time shouting "FIRE!". Numerous enemies went down, but unperturbed by their losses, the Bracaidians levelled their weapons and returned fire. Metal balls whizzed through the air and easily pierced the wooden cover sheltering the Legion fighters . One of the missiles buzzed past Casteel's ear, close enough that it blew back her hair and twanged her nerves. Some legionnaires were thrown backwards by the impact of the enemy weapons, dead or dying, while the survivors with bows or crossbows continued to shoot.

Casteel could see that the Bracadians were professionals; confident and steadfast. They fired their bow sticks again and once more Legionnaires were killed or wounded. In the time it took for the enemy to reload their weapons, Casteel shouted "CHARGE!" over the noise of the combat and from their places of hiding the Blood Legion burst from cover to sprint at the enemy. Legionnaires roared and hooted as they came in a great wave, some fired their last bow shot or threw axes as they ran. In response, the Bracadians drew swords from their belts and in an organised line, made ready to defend. Casteel knew that in close combat the Legion would make short work of these invaders.

The ship's portals opened on the vessel's sides and metal tubes appeared at these apertures. With a great ear-shattering series of booms and clouds of fire and smoke, much larger metal balls were hurled at the legion, delivering shocking carnage and death. Limbs and heads were blown off in a cascade of blood and gore. Horrified, Casteel immediately screamed "RETREAT!". She was amongst those that charged. But now she stopped to pull frantically at the backs of those who hesitated. It was not in the legionnaires' nature to withdraw but all Casteel's instincts shouted at her to escape this bloodbath. She yelled again "RETREAT, MOVE YOU BASTARDS!"

The Legionnaires dragged their wounded with them and made what desperate haste they could. A second volley of the large balls chased them, claiming more lives. Casteel watched Athose nimbly duck under a shot that narrowly missed another warrior, before ricocheting off a stone wall and then disappearing in a slow arch over the roof of a nearby structure. Around the Legionnaires, less sturdy buildings collapsed, flinging debris far and wide. The fleeing fighters did not slow their pace until well clear of the docks. There was no pursuit.

As they limped back to the foothills, Casteel moved frantically amongst the legion to take stock of the casualties. She estimated that as many as a hundred warriors had perished and a similar number carried wounds. Casteel was relieved to see that some she knew well were amongst the survivors - Ya, Rey, and Athose were together - but she was horrified to think who might have fallen, all comrades under her care. It was a terrible price to pay for her error in judgement.

While comrades cared for the wounded, Hammy and Spit scouted further along the coast. Three other towns on the Jerusso shoreline were untouched. However, the Brula observed a fleet of sixty ships arrive and wait off the coast. They were mostly the same type of Bracadian vessels, although a handful were of a different design – with two wide hulls joined by a broad platform and with banks of oars.

Hammy continued to observe the enemy while Spit scurried south to raise the alarm in Attica. The Holsted garrison troops hurried to take further warning to their countrymen.

FIRST RESPONSE

Ithius worked hard to build the capability of the Blood Sea Coalition fleet. The Council agreed that the navy would be the first and best line of defence against invasion. When news of the Bracadian attack reached the leaders of the Blood Sea Coalition, they looked to Ithius to deal with the threat. Possibly, the attack against Jerusso did not herald an invasion, but Ithius' senses told him otherwise. While messages were sent for the Coalition navy to gather at Hindas, the first standing fleet based at Sarcross was immediately deployed.

The first fleet was comprised of ten squadrons of five ships each. Three squadrons were of the latest Ironship design and included the flagship Harmsway. Harmsway was the first vessel to have steel incorporated into the construction of its monolithic hull. It was also the War God's temple on the sea and the souls of the valiant coursed through its divine frame.

Four of the ten squadrons were Triremes, while squadrons eight and nine were mostly large sailing vessels including one ship of Rhalec construction. The Rhalec warship was broad, with a canopy that covered it giving it the semblance of an enormous turtle. There was a stone obelisk on the turtle ship's prow, tilted forward and carved with inscrutable symbols.

Urgar the Gull commanded the tenth squadron, also known as the *Flying Devils*. Two of the vessels were of Yanth make; three-masted sailing ships with raised towers at the bow and stern. Flying Brula based on these ships were critical to the fleet's scouting and communication. In addition to being elite scouts, Urgar had seen the Brula fight. They were ferocious warriors, and although their wings looked like they might be fragile, they used them as weapons to beat and hold down their foe.

Two of the other Flying Devils were Silver Blades – sleek Alani ships of white wood with silver railings and trim. A glistening silver blade started below the waterline and extended out and up from the ship's bow, like a great scythe. The vessels raised a single sail, low and triangular that added to the sleekness of the design and seemed to catch both the breeze and sunlight in its shining canvas, propelling it along at a fantastic pace when needed. The crews of heavily armoured Elven warriors and spell weavers were formidable opponents.

The fifth ship in the squadron was the Celestial. Often used as a scout ship, the Celestial was smaller than most of the more modern vessels but was considered a quick and lucky craft. Twenty Blood Legion were amongst the forty marines aboard the ship and the sea mage, Maresh, added to their capability. Since swearing allegiance to Jaal, Maresh served an apprenticeship with the Alani Spell Weavers and for several years he worked alongside the Sea Mage at Viletri. Now he helped to keep the fleet safe, and when needed, he was a formidable offensive force.

Also travelling on the Celestial was an apprentice Shaman of the Iron Jaw, who helped Urgar to interpret the omens and predict the weather. He could also hide the squadron under a mystical shroud – now more commonly known as a cloak of shadow. He was one of ten Shamans travelling with the fleet and their ability to cloak the squadrons was crucial to their effectiveness.

In total, eight thousand sailors and marines crewed the oars and decks. It was a modern navy by Blood Sea standards, equipped with the best armaments available to them. To an unknowing spectator, the fleet might appear a mishmash, but they trained tirelessly to operate as a cohesive and formidable force.

Just three days sail from Sarcross, and still less than halfway to Jerusso, the Brula were already returning with reports of large numbers of enemy ships ahead, just beyond the horizon. As the First Fleet practised many times, all but one of the Ironship squadrons hid themselves under the cloak of shadow. Soon just four iron ships and the mighty Harmsway were visible as they moved directly towards the enemy armada.

Meanwhile, reports came from Jerusso that the coastal towns Metris, Orun, and Fedock were captured by the Bracadians. They were unloading troops and establishing a firm foothold in that land. The Brula described Orcs and Belg warriors disembarking alongside human soldiers. Casteel knew that the small standing army at the Jerusso capital of Thun would be no match for the host they faced.

After their defeat at Holsted, Casteel and the Blood Legion retreated through Jerusso and the southern tundra of Kogath. They intended to regroup in Attica at their base in Dos Neran. Casteel hoped that Khing might have some ideas and resources to help. The Guild of Ravens also maintained a barracks in Dos Neran with several hundred mercenaries stationed there.

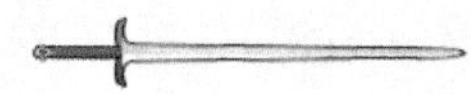

TO BE FEARED

The Blood Legion never deserted an ally and Casteel felt a great responsibility to return to Jerusso and assist against the Bracadians. Khing promised to make what preparations he could, but it would take time to call on allies as well as gather mercenaries. Regrettably, most standing armies based in the neighbouring regions were already active in the distant Northern conflict. The Bracadians had chosen their moment well.

In desperation, Casteel sought the Wisdom of the Elves. She removed from her pocket the small device she was given so many years ago by the Fogmir Elves and had since become proficient in using. It was a tiny knot of wood with a bright gem held firmly by three wooden fingers. Without hesitating, Casteel closed her eyes and envisioned herself in a dull room still holding the device, then projected three words that were the key to unlock it. Another elf appeared instantly in the imagined space, then three more. Together they waited silently until two others joined. Now, as their thoughts collected together, a spell weaver amongst them conjured some suitable furniture. They all took a seat, facing one another. Seamlessly the room continued to evolve - a warm fire set in a brick hearth and windows that appeared to let in natural light. The scene helped Casteel to relax. She could hear distant bird noises, both tuneful and squawking.

Having instigated the emergency meeting, Casteel cleared her mind of its pervading anxiety, and with a calm, steady voice addressed those present.

"The allied nation of Jerusso is under attack from the nation we know as Bracadia. In just a few short days they have already taken all the coastal towns by the sea. They will soon march on the capital."

As she recalled the event, Casteel could not quickly put

aside the grief she felt at the loss of so many legionnaires, but it was important not to show emotion in front of the Alani elders. They prided themselves in their clarity of thought and pragmatism.

"The Blood Legion engaged the Bracadians at the town of Holstead but were defeated. The enemy has weapons that we have never encountered before."

Casteel went on to describe the details of the battle. An Alani Elf interrupted her.

"The First Fleet are intercepting Bracadian ships as we speak. It has the look of an invading force."

Casteel was honest.

"I do not know how to respond to this invasion. The enemy is unlike any we have faced before."

There was a hint of fear in her voice that didn't go unnoticed by her audience. The other Elves glanced at one-another, and Casteel felt as if they were judging her. An elder Alani leaned forward. His voice carried emotion too; menacing and powerful.

"The Alani will be like nothing these Bracadians have faced before. Remember child that *we* are an ancient warrior race. In times past, we lived by sword and spell, and we were the hand and fist of Light upon this earth."

After shifting slightly in his seat, the Elf smoothed a crease out of his robe, then continued, emotion now gone from his speech.

"The Spell Weavers and the Battle Lords are returning; one by one they are responding to the Light Lord's summons and journeying to the land of their origin. The Alani are ready for war."

A druid of the Fogmir spoke next.

"We will gather what forces we can. The Fogmir will stand with the Alani."

Ahmeda of the Dark Elves was not to be left out.

"If I can reach you in time, I will walk with the Alani."

The Alani were quiet and gave nothing away in their expressions. Instead, the Fogmir Druid responded.

"I will show you how to take the path."

Two doors appeared. The Druid explained, "Let this path remain open so that the Fogmir Elves and Dark Elves may pass through this place to join with Casteel. The Alani will travel their own path."

The Alani Elves nodded. Casteel was perplexed but relayed her thanks. When the impromptu meeting ended, the device remained active, and as expected, if she closed her eyes and concentrated, she was brought back into the room with the two doors. Ahmeda appeared through one of the doors and exited through the other. When Casteel opened her eyes, the Dark Elf priestess was standing in front of her.

"That's incredible".

"It is. I did not know such a thing was possible."

Then, as Casteel watched, the priestess stepped behind an invisible wall and disappeared.

Casteel gathered together the small number of Elves that were part of the Blood Legion and travelled with them on foot back to Jerusso. On the way, Fogmir Elves started to appear and join them. Casteel understood they were using the pathway left by the Druid. Ahmeda also returned.

Athose, who was amongst the Blood Legion Elves, was approached by two women, one he recognised immediately as his sister, the other one puzzled him. After more careful examination, he suspected this was Roanna's birth mother - the resemblance of colour, shape and facial features was striking. Athose was grateful that his mother, Rylla, did not appear with the other Wardens as he was sure that would put a wind beneath the leaves. He held his sister's hand and touched her forehead with his. The young Elf felt a gentle warmth through his body that he had not experienced since leaving the Fogmir.

"Earth and Water, sister".

"Water and Earth, brother".

It was ten years since the siblings were last together, and for Roanna, Ahmeda was the mother imagined but never beheld. Ahmeda was uncomfortable with the apparent bond between the two youngsters, not for a sense of jealousy, but because emotions always made her uncomfortable. When she was able to, she got to the business of explaining the Order to Roanna. Athose nodded as she spoke so that Ahmeda knew he had already received his education in Elvish lore. The siblings understood the concepts but seemed dubious. Ahmeda knew that deeper comprehension would come with experience. Task accomplished, she excused herself to allow the young Elves time together.

On the second morning of travel, the group arrived in sight of Bracadian troops. Casteel ordered her force to stop their march and to spread out along a ridge overlooking their foe. At a quick estimate, the enemy force was over three thousand strong and followed the road between the town of Holsted and the Jerusso capital of Thun.

Feeling a presence behind her, Casteel looked around. Although expecting it, she was still amazed when approximately four thousand Alani Elves stood with them. They stepped into their regular formations of four battalions, four ranks deep. With uncanny timing, the Alani simultaneously nocked arrows to their bows. Each kinsman held a tall spear in the same hand as the bow. The weapons were cleverly intertwined so that they could be gripped together, and by grounding the spear, it helped to steady the bow. The wood used in both weapons was light, yet tough as steel. Like everything about the Elven warriors, the armament gleamed in the sunlight and the metal spearheads sparkled as they captured the sun's rays. Their chainmail coats and glistening helmets were of a light metal that allowed them freedom of movement as well as excellent protection. It was an army that took great pride in its appearance.

The enemy was also hurrying into formation, still well out of bow range, and once in place, the Bracadian units in front aimed their bow sticks and fired. Mostly the metal balls hit the ground or whizzed overhead, but some struck their targets, and several elves collapsed. Others were hit but saved by their armour. A few clutched at minor wounds. Being hit by one of the balls packed a much harder punch than being shot by an arrow. The Bracadians that fired were reloading while others moved closer to be within better range. Behind them, Orc Pikemen were taking up position and a unit of Belg, armed with large metal tubes like the ones Casteel had seen on the ships, readied themselves.

One Spell Weaver was quick to react, and a mist swirled up from the ground, rapidly obscuring the vision of both sides. Other Weavers and the Fogmir Druids added to the fog that billowed out to cover the valley. The enemy fired again, but this time nobody was injured. In freakish unison, the Elves swapped bows for the shields on their backs. Several Weavers stepped forward and lightning, ice, and fire blasted from their fingertips towards the enemies in the mist. The Fogmir and Blood Legion Elves ran ahead and from what cover they could find, launched volleys of arrows toward the enemy position. Like the Bracadian fire, at long range and in poor visibility, it was unlikely to have much effect.

Athose and Roanna moved ahead of the others, their youth emboldening them to get close to their enemy. As they came off the slope, to their left there was a clatter of movement; Orcs, jogging in formation with their pikes lowered. Instinctively Roanna reached forward and let her senses feel out the wood of the pikes. The timber was dry and lifeless. With a flick of her mind, the pikes twisted around arms and torsos, before becoming solid forms once again. The Orcs called out in shock and frustration, attracting the attention of other figures who now emerged from the mist. Some were men with bow sticks that pointed at the young Elves and one of them fired, the shot grazing Athose's arm.

Ahmeda, sensing the danger, grabbed Casteel and they dashed to aid the siblings. As they arrived, Casteel avoided the balls from two bowsticks by diving to her left. Ahmeda stood side-on to her aggressors, making herself a smaller target, and pointed at them with one hand. The other hand reached skyward, and then she used that arm to throw a powerful invocation. A wall of force swept before her and rumbled across the battlefield. At the forefront of the thunderous magic ghostly shapes of warriors charged, their eerie cries matched those of the enemy who were swept off their feet and thrown about like ants in a hot tin. Ahmeda accompanied the magic with a scream of rage that in itself held remarkable power and reached into the hearts of the enemy close by; terror pulsated throughout their bodies. The fog that filled the valley was blown asunder by the priestess' spell. Many of the scattered enemy were slowly rising to their feet. A breeze whipped about the priestess as she brought the remnant of magic under control.

Elven warriors descended from the ridge, taking advantage of their shocked adversaries to engage with spear and shield. Among them were the greatest fighters of the Elves, flamboyant and elegant, artists of combat who moved with speed and grace across the battlefield. They killed effortlessly as if the battle were a dance and murder were a game.

Casteel watched one of the Belg point his metal tube at the combat and fire. Chains and bits of metal exploded from the chamber in a broad arch, shredding Elf and man alike. Sickened by the indiscriminate carnage, a cluster of Druids reacted with wild magic that assaulted the unit of Belg, blinding and weakening them. Some of the Belg tumbled to the ground paralysed, and where they fell the earth shifted to consume them so that in moments only mounds of dirt remained. Roanna rushed to join the attack, copying what she saw and moving the ground in time with the others. When the job seemed done, the young apprentice hurried forward to stand on one such mound. Looking about her, Roanna could see that the battle was coming to an end and warriors were quickly finishing the battered enemy that remained.

Showing mercy to the last few survivors, the Elves stood back and watched in silence as the Bracadians ran past them and back the way they had come. The Light Lord knew these spared few would carry the message to their generals that the Elves are to be feared.

In the wake of the fighting, Alani healers appeared on the battlefield and tended to those with injuries, while the Fogmir Elves slew the dazed enemy who were too stunned or wounded to flee. Impressed by the range and impact of the Bracadian weapons, an Elven officer ordered the firesticks and their ammunition to be collected.

FIRST LINE OF DEFENCE

Urgar kept his cloaked squadron close to the steel flagship group. Ahead of them forty enemy sailing ships disengaged from a more massive fleet and were headed on a course to intercept them. The captains were briefed on the tall Bracadian vessels, though Urgar could see that some sailors were intimidated by their size and in such large numbers.

"Into it, lads. Jobs to do."

Had the whole Bracadian fleet come at once, Urgar was sure that the flagship would signal a withdrawal. Still, now they were only minutes from contact, and the enemy contingent were spread out in a wide arc to ensnare the five uncloaked ships that were visible to them.

As the hidden vessels closed with the enemy ships, some of the enemy sailors pointed at their wake, but their captains did not have time to react. Two squadrons of triremes uncloaked as they smashed into the Bracadian flank. There was a crunch of splintering planks and shouting sailors. That noise was instantly lost against the thunderous boom of return fire from the Bracadians.

Moments later, two more squadrons of sailing ships uncloaked as they came alongside the larger Bracadian vessels. Their marines tossed choke gas over the Bracadian decks and toward the open portals on their sides. Others threw grappling hooks, while crossbowmen on the forward and stern towers fired their hail of bolts into the surprised enemy crews.

The choke-gas only partly disrupted the enemy from firing. Soon, smoke billowed out from the portals, and large iron balls ripped holes through wood and sails. On one of the Yanth sailing ships, the mainmast came crashing down, creating chaos amongst those on deck. Where the balls targeted the Blood Sea crews, they carved a bloody path that killed many and left the survivors stunned. The unholy noise was deafening. Everywhere, marines scrambled between the ships to fight at close quarters.

As the Bracadian vessels swung about to aim at the revealed ships, the remaining squadrons of cloaked iron ships and galleys struck them by surprise. Only the Rhalec turtle ship hung back as their priests activated the obelisk at its prow. Bolts of magical force erupted from the glowing stone, arching across the water to strike like chain lightning across the deck of their target, sweeping it clear of sailors and marines, and setting the sails aflame.

Meanwhile, the flagship squadron that led the attack was taking heavy fire. Metal balls launched from the Bracadian ships whizzed overhead as they ricocheted off invisible barriers. The Dwarves contribution to the fleet was four large shield discs, which against the Bracadians were proving invaluable. It was the first mate's responsibility to lower and raise the shields as needed. Occasionally a metal ball pierced the defence and clanged into the metal hulls.

The Bracadians were expert seamen and those not engaged at close quarters cleverly manoeuvred out of the iron ships path, swinging around to appear from behind as they fired more volleys.

The Harmsway was the only vessel that towered over the Bracadian ships and even amongst the ensuing chaos, the flagship held its commanding presence. Warrior-priests fired ballistae and crossbows at any enemy that came within range. While they did not have a Dwarven shield to protect them, the steel plating on the hull proved effective, and where there was damage to the sides of the ship, ghostly hands appeared to heal the wounds.

Urgar's squadron was the last to uncloak. The two Elven blades both slammed into the same enemy, cruelly breaking it apart and sending it to the depths. The other ships joined the fighting already in progress.

Urgar commanded from the bow of the Celestial, standing on the deck rail, balancing himself by holding onto a rope that hung down from the forward mast. He had no fear of the balls from the firesticks that whizzed past him as he looked up at the Bracadian ship they drew alongside.

"Stay in her shadow, clear those bloody shooters from the decks. Get some choke gas up there. Hurry to it lads."

The Celestial was too small to be more than a nuisance, but it played that role well, and it supported the efforts of the larger ships in its squadron.

It was the superior weaponry of the Blood Sea Coalition at close range that gave them the advantage; the choking gas rendered crews incapable and repeating crossbows were as devastating at sea as they were on land.

The greater danger now was the rest of the Bracadian fleet that was racing to reinforce their comrades. To counter them, the Celestial moved around the combat and placed itself between the fighting and the Bracadian reinforcements. From the deck of the ship, Maresh manipulated the winds to slow the main Bracadian fleet so that they laboured to gain any ground and were careful not to collide.

The First Fleet was close to victory, and while the combat continued to rage across the decks of several ships, elsewhere, the Blood Sea vessels were regrouping.

After overcoming the last enemy crew, the sailors quickly searched for comrades stranded amongst the wreckage. The Iron ships fared well, as did the Rhalec and Elven vessels. Two Triremes and four Sailing Ships were lost, either sunk or too severely damaged to escape the approaching Bracadian fleet. The victors used flame tubes and oil to set alight the vessels that were no longer seaworthy. Maresh's magic kept the enemy at bay, though they were close enough now that some were angling to fire.

The First Fleet manoeuvred away, drawing the shadow cloaks over themselves, and making haste for the Coral Isles. The Elven Spellweavers aboard the Blades summoned a thick sea fog that they fed with their enchantments until it covered a vast expanse of ocean around and behind them, further concealing their departure.

Urgar called out to them.

"Set the Sea Dragons upon them, lads. Let the Kraken feast."

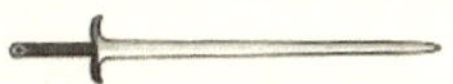

INVASION

Veroff Odari and his fleet of slavers returned from the Northern Sea to Tarash with news of an enemy fleet hot on their heels. After a week of successful raiding against Northern settlements, circumstances took a dark turn. They had dumped their cargo overboard in a desperate attempt to increase their speed and fled south. When Veroff went to the Mad King, he was dramatic in his description.

"It is an invasion from the North. A blackness of ships that filled the horizon."

When the Mad King seemed unperturbed, Veroff misguidedly thought he was not clearly understood. He made the mistake of repeating himself.

"A blackness of ships, that filled the horizon from east to west."

The King moved to be very close to the Admiral, and he slowly walked a circle about him as he talked.

"Veroff, blackness is not a very specific number, though I can imagine it is a lot. Have our seamen lost the ability to count, Veroff? Should we make a school for them to teach them numbers? There are a lot of ships also coming from the West, a Bracadian Armada."

Veroff was confused. The King's movements were off-putting, and he was not one to use or understand sarcasm. He had hurried here to give warning.

"They were only a day behind us. It took me half a day's hard ride by horse to come to Gormoth. The Northerners will be in Tarash by nightfall. I have dispatched messengers to Sarcross, Viletri, and Yanth."

The Mad King paused to stand in front of Veroff, giving the seaman a small smile.

"Well then, it seems we are at the pointy end of a two-pronged invasion that will soon overwhelm us. Thank you Veroff, I appreciate your sense of urgency. We must make good use of the time that you have gifted us."

The armada from the North passed the coast of Roundhome, then through the Ice Flow and around the Cape of Knives, arriving at the Blood Sea. A part of the fleet peeled off to attack Tarash which they quickly overwhelmed with their numbers, and the Northerners established a forward base there.

Once at the Blood Sea, the fleet divided again, half headed for Hindas and Viletri, the other half attacking territories to the south-west. In the first day of the assault, the city of Loryan was overrun and put to the torch. Northmen hunted the fleeing Loryans who made haste into the hills or towards Yanth.

Karanthos was another city to fall quickly, and its people scattered like panicked ants.

To the surprise of the invaders, Alani Renai Del and Alani Ruhen Efaari were not to be found. Where the Northern Generals expected to discover the Elven town and city, an ancient forest grew, and there was no sign of civilisation.

At Freman, the mercenaries and people of the city retreated to the fortress and made ready to stand against a swarming assault. Already their port and city were engulfed in flames.

At Yanth a brutal stand would be made. A chain was set across the harbour mouth, and the well-trained Yanth militia scurried to join garrison soldiers on the seawall and the forts. Some of the militia from the towns near the city were renowned for their marksmanship with the longbow and would be a formidable check to the invaders. Likewise, Hindas and Viletri would not be taken easily, although the forces arrayed against them seemed overwhelming.

Mannace liked to know the numbers and odds.

Unfortunately, in the face of this sudden and devastating assault, the only reports he received were vague at best, and then the trickle of information became nothing. Viletri was isolated. Mannace called for reinforcements from his neighbours, the Grey Dwarves and Iron Jaw. He did not expect aid from Sylos or Arenland, who were also likely under attack by sea, or soon to be. In some ways, this made his job more straightforward. He had a foe at his door that he must defeat.

Mannace called for Amnicles, who was soon ushered into his office by Jayne of the Rangers. Mannace wasted no time in asking his questions.

"Amnicles, are the wizards organised for the defence?"

Amnicles stood with his spine straight, his hands clasped behind his back, and his feet shoulder width apart. Despite more than a decade in Viletri, he was still every bit the proud Hindasian.

"They are my Lord. Each knows their duty. We are prepared."

That wasn't the primary reason Mannace summoned Amnicles here; what he wanted at this desperate time were the two people he trusted most at his side.

"Summon your Master. Do it now. Render is required for the defence."

The wizard gave a short bow, turned, and departed. Before Jayne could escort him out, Mannace called the Dark Elf to him.

"Jayne, go to Saska, ask for her help to bring Jaal back to the city. Go now; there is little time."

When Jayne left, Mannace kicked over a wooden chair. It clattered across the floor but did nothing to improve his mood. He despised asking for the bitch's help.

Viletri had enough warning of the approaching Northern forces that their harbour was already empty of ships when the enemy fleet arrived. The desperate craft fled to the safety of the open sea and then possibly on to Ostoik or Rummond. Workers transferred everything of value at the docks and warehouses into the safety of the walled city. Citizens that were not part of the militia, nor useful to the defence were encouraged to move north to the plateau where they would camp and if needed, take sanctuary in the mountain with the Grey Dwarves. Mannace now understood what the fall of old Viletri must have looked like, and he was determined not to let history repeat itself.

Mannace's scouts informed him of three hundred ships gathered off Viletri. At a guess, they might land thirty to ninety thousand troops. The Viletri garrison was fifteen hundred well-equipped soldiers, with seven thousand citizen militia equipped with single-shot crossbows. Counted amongst the defenders were six hundred and thirty animated statues about the city, ninety stone workers and eighty steel workers. Eight of the colossal temple guardians were alive. Prototype clockwork warriors that could aim and fire repeating bolt throwers waited at the main gate.

The forty towers along the city walls each had a new defence; stone statues, lowset and powerfully built, stood at each location. The animations were surrounded by large boulders that were stacked for them to use as missiles. Testing proved that the animated statues could launch a boulder as far as a catapult. The animators were still refining and enhancing them to increase their efficiency.

Unfortunately, the mercenaries and Viletri's standing army were fighting at the northern Rift. There were perhaps as many as one hundred and fifty Priests and Initiates at the Temple of War, and Render had his apprentices, which included the Battle Mages and Sea Mage. The Yanth, Arenland, Tarash Gormoth, and Sylos enclaves still maintained their garrisons, in total another five hundred trained soldiers.

The Dwarves would not commit troops to the Rift, and Mannace was confident they would arrive soon in force.

The Iron Jaw, however, deployed most of their army to foreign duties, although there would still be a great many Orcs in the cities that would answer a call to battle. He was right on both counts, and before the enemy attack, two thousand Dwarves passed through the city gates with the promise of more to come. Nobody knew how many Grey Dwarves lived under the mountain and what their full military capability was. As more units travelled the road south, the first bands of Iron Jaw Orcs were not far behind them.

The attack did not come on that first day. Instead, Rangers reported enemy troops disembarking in an eastern bay and at a fishing village to the West of Viletri. People on the coast and in the rural hinterland headed into the city or north to the Plateau.

On the second day, reports came to Mannace that there was looting and burning of farms and villages. Dwarves coming down to the plains from the Mountains encountered resistance and were digging themselves in along the road just south of the great swamp to protect the civilians who fled north. Iron Jaw Orcs also gathered there in large numbers and formed into bands to counter the enemy raiders who ransacked the countryside.

Saska sent word that Jaal was also at the border and involved with the defence there.

Render returned. With him, he brought a collection of obsidian statues. Strangely he'd requested Kakos to join him in his preparations. Many in the city would be looking to Render and his magic as their saviour. Mannace hoped they were right.

At night, the attack came.

LESSON IN CHAOS

Soon after the army of the North overwhelmed Tarash, gigantic troopships arrived at the port to unload many thousands of reinforcements. Tarash Gormoth was to be the staging ground for the invasion. The Northern troops were expanding out from Tarash to secure the region and scout the other cities.

They did not account on the tenacity of the Mad King. As soon as the invasion started, the Mad King ordered all soldiers, slaves, and civilians to the foothills of Gormoth where he gathered them into a vast horde. Beasts from the Madlands tromped amongst them, howling and screeching, giving the mass a menacing presence. As the troops and civilians waited, they recited chants taught to them over the years by the Mad King's agents. Weapons were passed around the makeshift horde, while slaves shared a variant of Thog - small vials suitable for a single swallow. The concoction instilled the same battle effects as normal Thog but lasted longer and had a much higher chance of generating berserk frenzy, followed by imminent death.

Over the last decade, the Molemen blended the Thog with some of their potions for conditioning the slaves, resulting in enhanced slave size and muscular growth. Other slave augmentations were proving successful, including incorporating or replacing body parts with either animal parts, weapons, or mechanical objects. Amongst the horde, there were many examples of oversized or mutated bodies. Some with an extra arm or tentacle. Others with a hammer or blade in place of the forearm. A large specimen from the mines, with whirling clockwork drills in place of his forearms stood on a crest and bellowed at the sky like an enraged bull. Chains still connected many of the slaves arriving from the Tarash catacombs, and every slave bore a neck ring. Most of the female slaves were pregnant as part of the Mad King's aggressive breeding program.

On the flat land before the hills, an enemy multitude gathered. The host of the North was a varied mix of regular and irregular troops, infantry and archers, cavalry and giants, magicians, and champions, mostly humans with a scattering of other races. This time the Mad King was not intent on analysing his foe. His simple tactic was to lure them close and unleash his horde. The repeated mantra chants were those used by the ancients to prepare themselves for battle, and when the time came to charge, the Mad King's horde was clear of purpose and filled with energy. When they quaffed their Thog, they felt unstoppable.

As the horde descended, arrows rained upon them, and magic exploded about them. Orcs and humans on horses charged at them and in places drove them back. However, the combination of the chanting, Thog, and conditioning, made the horde resilient and tough to kill. Few that were shot or knocked down stayed down for long. With unnatural fury, they threw themselves upon the enemy and for those that had the Rage training, they launched themselves forward to hack, rend, and break the enemy lines.

The Mad King walked down the hill. He was not one to stand back and watch the bloody combat. He found it much more useful to be amongst the melee where he could direct his troops to where they were of most use. Even the ones at the peak of their frenzy rallied to him and followed his lead.

The Mad King learned a lot about his enemy by studying their faces as they fought. Today he saw a fierceness and confidence, but under the weight of an attack that was fanatical and unyielding, he saw that they valued life much more than death. He knew this would be their undoing.

Around him, tens of thousands of combatants hacked, stabbed, hammered, and slashed at one another. Their roars and cries were a symphony of chaos and he, at the centre, directed the violent concerto. Where he saw men at the end of their endurance, he gave them gentle encouragement and sent them back into the fray. Where warriors stood confused, he directed them at new targets. For those that were stymied by determined defence he spurred them to greater efforts, and they responded with fanaticism.

At one point, the Mad King stepped ahead of his troops and found himself surrounded by enemies, but in the chaos, his calmness drew little attention and within moments allies threw themselves upon the enemy, and he was safe to move on. Eventually, the King made his way to where some of his loyal Madlands fighters battled. He liked the familiarity of being amongst these veterans, and they gloried in his presence.

It was not easy to overcome some of the enemy, but the Thog was relentless and the stamina of the horde uncompromising. Eventually, the throng of melee gave way to the pursuit of the remaining Northerners, a chase that would be equally relentless and ruthless. With the enemy in retreat and his horde hard on their heels, those of the horde that lingered had fought beyond mortal endurance. They were succumbing to their wounds. Soon the Mad King was the only one left standing and all about him for a considerable distance lay the dead and dying; friend and foe, men and women, butchered and blood-drenched, ghastly in death or moaning in the agony of their wounds, gasping their dying breaths. It was a rare joy to be in this place at just the right time, where the euphoria of victory collided savagely with the agony of the price paid. He breathed it all in, then breathed out to allow the moment to pass. He used everything in this endeavour, and a new plan was already taking shape. The Mad King turned and strode purposefully back towards Gormoth.

COMPROMISE

At Jurusso, Casteel and the Elves drove the Bracadians back to the sea, but the foreigners seemed determined to make a stand at the coastal towns. There were perhaps a thousand enemy troops fortified in each of the four towns, supported by thirty to fifty Bracadian ships.

The Brula brought reports of fighting on the ocean, as well as Bracadian assaults on the coastal cities of Valthar. The mountain men of Valthar were fearless warriors, but Casteel understood they were no match for the firepower of the Bracadian ships and troops. She suspected their defences would not hold against a determined naval bombardment.

Other news of the regions neighbouring Valthar suggested that, at the City of Chance and the coastal villages of Aracland, the civilians chose to abandon their communities and fled inland. It seemed a sensible strategy to Casteel, leaving the Bracadians as conquerors of nothing.

Word also reached Casteel and the Alani Elves of the attack of the Northern men against the nations of the Blood Sea. Was that just a coincidence? Casteel tried to imagine what Mannace would do in such desperate circumstances. She suspected the answer - he was forever pragmatic and always took the best from a situation - reshaped challenges to be opportunities.

As Mannace's agent, Casteel approached the town of Holsted under the banner of truce. The commander met her outside of the defence, arranging a conference in two days. It was a risk to wait for so long and not to attack the Bracadians before they could reinforce. However, as commander of the Blood Legion, Casteel felt a responsibility not just to protect Jurusso, but to stop the invasion.

Ahmeda agreed to help Casteel in the negotiations, coaching the younger Elf on what to expect. After two long days, a grand flagship arrived at the docks of Holsted with a small fleet of other vessels in tow. In a tent raised at the town boundary, Casteel and Ahmeda met with Admiral Mangello D'Austini of the Bracadian armada. He looked to be a man of great status and was treated as such by the other Bracadians. Two staff officers joined him, ready with pen and paper to record what was said.

Casteel did her best to appear and sound confident.

"I am Casteel of the Alani, commander of the Blood Legion, speaker for the Blood Sea Coalition."

"Then speak".

The Admiral's voice was impatient and arrogant, but Ahmeda prepared her for this, and Casteel let it slide.

"I will speak plainly. In Jerusso, we have defeated a force of your countrymen. We could easily retake the four towns on the coast, but where land meets sea, neither side can hold these positions for long. We know that you besiege Valthar and that the people of Chance and Aracland have eluded you. At sea, there has been fighting. You have a taste then for our navy and our armies, so know that we will not fall easily to an invasion. You have watched us for many years so understand that the war to follow will be bloody for both sides. Why have you come here, Admiral? What is it that you want to achieve?"

"What I want is not relevant. What the Empire of Bracadia wants it will take."

"You would not be here talking with us if it were that simple."

The Admiral gave nothing away with his expression.

"I too, will speak plainly. The Empire of Bracadia has tasked me to return a conqueror, with its territory expanded and ships laden with bounty. The Empire is immense, and its resources vast. Bracadia will be victorious here. These lands will be its vassal."

"At what cost? We are not to be underestimated. You will limp back to Bracadia with less than you came with."

"Do not underestimate me. This is not my first outing. It is too early to demand your surrender, but that conversation will come."

Ahmeda interjected.

"Is it surrender that you need or alliance?"

"Who are you to ask?"

"Ahmeda Ravenborn, High Priestess and voice of the God of War. You are not the only enemy we face. On another front, we fight the armies of the North, who, if you remain here, will also become your foe. Aid us against this enemy, and we will be indebted to Bracadia. You may win what you want as a hero and saviour rather than foe."

"It is too late for that!"

"It will only be too late if you waste your time with these minor factions. What do you gain from taking Valthar or Jurusso? You will never conquer and hold these distant shores through the strength of arms. You will do so through alliance and mutual need."

"I come to conquer, and you ask me to save you?"

Both women nodded and replied.

"Yes."

HORDE OF THE NORTH

The night attack at Viletri came from both sea and land. The forces that disembarked gathered at the outskirts of the city within the abandoned districts outside the walls. While they moved among the buildings, it was hard to judge their make-up or numbers. At the Viletri harbour, enemy warships made haste for the docks or to position themselves to use their catapults against the port gate and towers.

Render placed himself at the city wall overlooking the port. The Sea Mage and several other apprentices accompanied him. Kakos watched on, with the obsidian statues also in attendance. They shared a wall tower with one of the stone-throwers, and along the walls near them, militia with their crossbows took up their positions. Twenty years of preparation went into the harbour's magical defences, and these Northern men were about to discover what that meant. Render waited for the enemy ships to disembark their first troops.

Large sailing ships were the first to pull up to the docks. With archers to give them cover, infantry equipped with metal armour, shields, and curved swords disembarked. They moved quickly to the shelter of the harbour buildings and started winding their way between cover to get closer to the city wall. In support, the ships with catapults on their decks launched their boulders at the wall and beyond. The first shots were mostly range finders with little effect as they bounced off the fortification. The men and stone-throwers of Viletri returned fire.

At Render's signal, the Sea Mage began his incantations. Around him, other apprentices formed an enchanter's-circle to lend him their talent and strength. In response, the latent magic imbued into the harbours waters was awakening. Enemy ships near the docks were the first to begin rocking - gently from side to side. Then those further back were pulled to an involuntary stop. Slowly, all the trapped ships, by Render's calculation perhaps as many as sixty, began to rotate. At first, it was a gentle motion, but as the magic tightened its grip, the movement gained momentum, spinning hapless vessels faster and faster until their decks leaned into the swirling water. Desperate crewmen scrambled to control their ships, but there was no counter to the magical battering and no safety to be found. On many ships, masts were snapping. Some of the out-of-control vessels collided, their timbers shattered, and water poured into their hulls.

On the city walls overlooking the chaotic scene, most of the militia looked away from the dizzying display, with many kneeling behind the crenulations. The noise of the carnage was terrifying, and the splintering of great timbers assaulted not just the ears but clawed at the soldier's bones. Some inexperienced militia were bent over, their heads between their knees vomiting, rocking from the shock and horror of it.

With the magic at its peak, many ships were now on their sides, while the bows of others pointed skyward, with sterns fully submerged. At the Sea Mages urging, more vessels were drawn to one another, still spinning, and smashing apart as they contacted. Where sailors and soldiers plunged into the briny water, slimy, tendrils of seaweed seized them and dragged them down into the depths. Eventually, nothing remained in the harbour but whirlpools and swirling wreckage. Beyond that, other enemy ships, fortunate to be outside of the effect of the spell, hastily retreated.

On the walls, the defenders rose from crouched positions, dazed, although a few shouted their war cries. Soon this jubilant handful were joined by many more in celebrating the power of their mages. Below on the piers, shocked Northern infantry now left unsupported by their navy, frantically sought out places to hide and regroup.

Render was vigilant for signs of enemy magic, but there

were none. It was something of an anticlimax for him. He waited long enough to be sure the Bracadians would not resume their naval attack, then left the mages to stand guard and made his way to the other side of the city. As he passed a group of armed civilians, he could see that the port gate was open, and militia poured out to take care of the enemy there.

Away from the harbour, the Viletri Garrison and Dwarves guarded the battlements. From where Mannace stood, he could see that the defence was thin in places, although there were militia and animated statues ready to reinforce as needed. The priests of war and the temple guardians were his most trusted reserve.

For now, the expected assault did not come. Perhaps it was because the Northerner's plans were thwarted at the harbour, or conceivably because the enemy was waiting to gather their full strength. Mannace was not sure if time was his foe or friend. He ordered extra ammunition to the walls for the stone-throwers and crossbowmen. When Render arrived from the harbour, Mannace summoned Titus Kane to join them, and they talked through their tactics. That night and through the next day, the forces of Viletri waited and took what rest they could.

North of Viletri, on the south side of the swamp, the Dwarves and Orcs were well entrenched. When Jaal first joined them, the enemy came in small groups that were easily defeated, but now they were numerous and organised. For the first time, the Northerners braved the swamp to surround them, which meant they were defending on multiple fronts. At Jaal's instruction, Rangers scouted the rugged terrain behind their position to warn of any enemy that might go the long route around the swamp and try to come at them through the hills. Jaal felt that such a ploy was only a matter of time. For now, the main assault came from the front as if the enemy expected to overwhelm them. The fighting was relentless and desperate.

Jaal estimated as many as three thousand Dwarves and a similar number of Orcs were dug in. Perhaps three times that number of enemies confronted them, and many more were joining each hour. Most were heavily bearded, wiry, tough men. They carried shields and hand weapons, some with throwing spears or axes. Their armour was a mix of leather and chainmail. Among them were Orcs similarly equipped, except that they were a particularly short breed and had an odd walk, shuffling sideways rather than striding forward. There wasn't much here that would cause the Dwarves problems, but Eya, who saw everything, warned Jaal that there was much more to come.

Jaal talked with the Dwarven captain who followed orders from the Grey General to hold for as long as they could and then to retreat. Jaal confirmed his plans for the Spiders, which met the old warrior's approval. With that done, Jaal grabbed a face mask and vials of choke gas from a Dwarf who no longer needed them and headed back down the road and into the Spider Woods. From there he navigated familiar tunnels to a place above the forest and valley where he had vantage of the road. Several spiderlings joined him as he waited. Like him, they were patient and did not feel the need to talk to pass the time. Instead, they enjoyed the warmth of the sun and sounds of nature rising from the valley below.

After another night passed at Viletri, Render felt an alarming shift in the energies around the city. He knew instinctively that the magic at the harbour was extinguished. Only a mighty magician could achieve such a feat. It reminded Render how much Viletri depended on other magical things for its defence. He hurried towards the harbour and as he did so apprentices, alerted by his summons, ran from where they were in the city to join him. The mind link Render maintained with his underlings was short-ranged, and he could only communicate simple thoughts. But it was proving very useful. Kakos and his entourage of tortured statues followed close behind.

At the harbour wall, the Sea Mage remained vigilant. On seeing Render, he immediately pointed out to sea, amongst the enemy vessels, to where he thought the powerful counter-magic originated. He did not look confident. It was insufficient detail for Render to act. He dared not strike and reveal himself unless he was sure that he could eliminate the rival mage. Unsurprisingly, enemy ships off the coast were now moving closer.

At the other side of the city, Mannace was called back to the walls and could see enemy units collecting. There was a killing ground in front of the defence covered in grass and flowerbeds. In the buildings beyond, faces appeared in windows and weapons poked above low walls. Mannace and the defenders of Viletri continued to watch and wait.

Another evening passed before Jaal saw the Iron Jaw Orcs beat a hasty retreat, passing the webbed forest. It was dark when the first of the Dwarves, carrying their gravely wounded, travelled the same path, followed closely by the walking wounded. Lastly, the remaining Dwarves made a fighting retreat in the dark of night. The choke gas kept the enemy at bay, and occasionally there was a blast of flame in the dark. Even with his night vision, it was hard to tell who or what the Dwarves were fighting. Jaal could hear horses and the roars of things bigger than men, possibly giants or some huge beasts.

As the last Dwarves passed the webbed forest, a mass of shapes emerged from the trees and swarmed over their pursuers. It caused a panic amongst the enemy and allowed the Dwarves to gain some much-needed distance from their pursuers. Hundreds of giant spiders cast webs and bound their prey, dragging them back to the forest. When the spiders withdrew and the mess of webs was burnt away with torches, the Northern troops continued their trek along the highway to the Plateau. A large contingent of heavily armoured riders pushed past the others in pursuit of the Dwarves.

As well as infantry and cavalry, there were also much

larger creatures amongst the enemy ranks, and some Jaal considered of gigantic stature, lumbering warriors four or five times the height of a man. Their procession toward the plateau continued throughout the night. Twice more, spiders launched attacks from the forest, overwhelming their prey and dragging them off to stock their ghastly pantry. Each time, the spiders retreated before the Northmen could organise an effective counterattack.

As Jaal continued to watch, a carriage pulled off the road, away from the main force. Three robed figures disembarked in the light of the carriage lanterns. One of the figures pointed a staff and released a great wave of sorcerous flame that enveloped the southern tip of the forest. The three mages focused their energies to feed and fan the flames, consuming the trees and shroud of webs.

In the light from the fire, Jaal was rewarded with a better view of the Northern host; well-organised units of heavily armed men and archers, marching at a quick pace. When Jaal glanced back at the mages, a shape extended out of the ground behind them, unfolded its many legs and pounced. The giant size of the spider was enough to knock the mages off their feet, and they were pinned instantly by webbing and powerful legs. The arachnid injected poison into each of its victims so that they went limp and quiet, appearing lifeless. Too late, terrified soldiers ran to help, throwing spears that missed or bounced off the spider's hard carapace. It was enough to drive the magnificent creature backwards, and in a blur of speed, it turned, disappearing into the night. Another wave of spiders emerged out of the darkness and overwhelmed the soldiers on the road, dragging more victims back to their lairs. The southern end of the webbed forest, damp as it was, continued to burn.

As morning approached, the procession of soldiers did not ease. It was not until later in the day that the last unit of light cavalry appeared. They set guard along the road beside the torched forest. Messengers on horseback appeared intermittently, galloping up and down the road with great urgency. During a period of quiet, the sleek spider that had attacked the mages returned to where they still lay and took the bodies, one by one, back into the ground. Seeing the creature more clearly in daylight, Jaal felt it was different from the other spiders; much larger, with a unique shine to its carapace, and a strange grace to its complex movements.

Although they might have done more to harass the enemy on the road, the intent was to let the bulk of the Northmen pass through the valley and gather into one large force at the plateau. The trap agreed with their allies was set. Jaal ended his vigil and travelled with the spiderlings down many paths and tunnels, then through a long passageway that rose steeply to a lookout. From here he could see across the plateau and into the mountain range beyond. In a semicircle encompassing most of the wide plateau, the Dwarves made a great defence; trenches and bunkers and barricades of dirt, behind which many thousands of their kin made their stand.

It was hard to miss the orange puffs of flamers or the blue sparks that lit up the trench line where enemies came close. As Jaal watched, a heavily armoured group of giants led a charge of infantry and cavalry against the Dwarves' extreme left flank. The giants seemed unstoppable, kicking obstacles out of the way, stepping across ditches, and scattering the dwarves with sweeping cuts of their massive swords. Cavalry jumped the trenches too and spread-out, causing mayhem, while infantry took hold of the position and secured it.

Dwarven reserves were scrambling to fill the breach, while teams of engineers wheeled their war machines into position to shoot at the giants. There were all kinds of mechanical contraptions, with whirring clockwork and bursts of steam, shooting massive metal bolts and missiles of acid and fire. They were the only thing that could hold back the giants. With the help of the war machines the breach in the Dwarf lines was repaired and the handful of Northern survivors driven out. Jaal observed dead giants scattered across the battlefield but others were still alive, yet to be committed to the fighting.

Jaal needed to have confidence in the Grey General and his army. Nobody outside of the Grey Halls had met the Grey General. He was something of a legend, residing deep beneath the mountain where he resided for many Dwarven generations. The general was rumoured to be one of the True Dwarves, left behind when the Icesleepers were sealed off from the outside world. He spoke only the old tongue of his kin, so Logthar was his spokesman. This Grey General sounded a bit like a show pony to Jaal, only brought out on special occasions.

From his high vantage, Jaal could see that behind the Dwarven lines at the eastern end of the valley, a host of Iron Jaw Orcs was gathering. He counted the war banners of the allied chiefs and expected that everything they could muster would come down that road. Jaal had his preparations to complete.

At Viletri, a Northern warrior walked up to the front gates. He wore heavy black metal armour from head to toe. Its design was unadorned except for two elaborate horns that curled up from the helmet. Despite the heavy armour and a grisly burden, the warrior's movements were fluid and lithe. He hurled his burden at the gate: a large bundle of severed heads tied by the hair. From their black, curly locks and sun-hardened faces, they were Hindasians. It was a message that Hindas had fallen. While staring up at those on the wall, the warrior reached back to draw his two-handed sword. The defenders on the wall were silent. If Mannace was standing there, it may have been a challenge, but after he waited a short while, the warrior turned and walked back to join his troops.

Outside the city, the defenders were alerted by the roar of many warriors, and the enemy charged forward. They flooded down the streets and into the main thoroughfare that led to the closed gatehouse. Groups of infantry ran with tall ladders, and others with bows pushed forward wooden shields on wheels to give themselves cover. Behind the troops, giants appeared over the rooftops. They were well armoured, and tall enough to strike at defenders on the walls. For now, they hung back, not prepared to take the concentrated fire from the stone-lobbers and crossbowmen that were waiting for them.

Behind the troops, slinking down the main thoroughfare, was a great beast, scaled and lizard-like, with a knot of bone on its forehead that curved back into horns. It was big enough that it might have clambered over the gatehouse, but instead, it lowered its head and charged. Enemy troops scrambled to get out of its way before it crashed against the gates. When it impacted, the stone around the gatehouse shook, and the doors buckled but did not cave. As the beast retreated to charge again, the steel bolts securing the gate were pulled aside, and the massive doors swung outwards. Mannace with his bodyguard of Rangers and three massive Temple Guardians emerged, followed closely by the Priests and Acolytes of War.

The guardians were so massive that they crouched as they exited through the gatehouse. Outside the wall, they strode towards the lizard creature, forcing it further back, then used their incredible strength to grab its legs and throw it on its side. Two of the guardians grappled the beast around the neck while another thrust his giant metal blade repeatedly into the lizard's exposed belly. In its death throes the lizard thrashed about, rolling over its allies; crushing those not quick enough to scamper away.

From his vantage outside the gate, Mannace took a moment to survey the scene. Looking left and right he saw ladders leaning against the wall and the killing ground in front of the wall filling with adversaries. Missiles were flying in both directions, and for the first time, the stone-throwers on the walls launched rocks into the mass of attacking troops. A Giant charged across the killing ground and assaulted one of the towers. It raised a massive shield that the creature used to knock aside a tossed boulder and with its heavy mace, smashed down on the stone thrower, knocking it back but not toppling it from its perch.

In the chaos around him, an enemy slipped past Mannace's Ranger guards and thrust his sword at their leaders' neck. Mannace instinctively raised his weapon to knock the blade aside. Intuitively, he attacked, slashing his opponent across the chest, then running him through with a powerful two-handed thrust. Next to him, Jayne was a blur of blades, fast and clinical against the advancing foe. Mannace stepped past the Dark Elf and swung his two-handed sword at others who approached, cutting one swordsman severely on the arm and slicing deeply into another's side. He wrenched his sword free and moved to finish the one whose arm was hanging limp. It was an easy kill. Around him, the War Priests were joining the fray, and the Temple Guardians were inflicting terrible casualties.

The War Priests spread out and pushed back whole units of the enemy with their incarnate might and magic, using waves of spiritual force to clear space. In the furnace of battle, the priests drew power from the death and carnage they created, using it to forge prayers that fuelled their wrath and gave them the strength to continue their onslaught and smite down the toughest of foes.

Behind them, the Animators and steel men, including those with repeating bolt throwers, came through the gates to keep the path back to the defences secure.

Render and Kakos stood together on a tower that overlooked the harbour. Behind them, the obsidian statues stood in their agonised poses. This time Render deployed his apprentices amongst other defenders along the city wall overlooking the docks. He could see Saska and her bodyguards nearby. Even in this time of worry, Render took a moment to appreciate her sensual shape. It pleased him that he had felt her skin close to his, tasted and survived her poisoned fruits. An unintentional, sarcastic snigger issued from his lips. It amused him that even the bitch played her part in the city's defence.

The enemy fleet, having been reinforced, resumed their attack on the port facilities and walls. With the harbour magic dispelled, they were willing to get close and unload their troops again. In response, the stone-throwers tossed boulders, crippling several ships, and punching holes in others. Courageously, the Sea Mage created chaos as he smashed ships together and turned sailing vessels back with summoned winds.

Amidst the enemy ships, an enormous fireball lifted into the skies and arced towards the wall where the Sea Mage worked his spells. The brightness of the magic made many avert their eyes and Render felt its intense heat even though he was not close to its path. This moment was the opportunity Render was anticipating, and he immediately gestured with outstretched arms, summoning a great spell. A sudden wave appeared amongst the enemy fleet, fifty boat lengths wide and quickly rising just as high. It sucked the sea from around it so that ships in the shallows ran aground, while others took what measures they could to survive the turmoil. With a massive crash, the wave broke over the top of the Northern ships where the enemy spell had originated, crushing them, and sending the wrecks tumbling to the ocean floor. The aftershock threw other ships about, and many were damaged as they rolled or collided.

When Render looked back at the city wall, there was an enormous hole in the defences where the Sea Mage made his stand, and nearby buildings were aflame. Enemy marines on the docks were running towards the breach. Render was disappointed to lose such a capable apprentice, but fighting wizards was a risky business, and it was a lesser price than his own life. He was extremely pleased with the execution of his magic and satisfied that the spell had found its target. It was a shame that he might never know who he defeated. Regardless, a spectacle like this would put his name on many lips as a Sorcerer to be feared.

Even with his vast reserves of energy, executing the massive invocation left Render exhausted. He touched the obsidian statues, drawing energy he had stored within them. It rejuvenated him enough to join the other spell casters and crossbowmen on the walls, who rained fireballs and arrows onto the enemy as they gathered below. The winnowed enemy still swarmed closer, raising ladders against the walls.

Render whispered to Kakos, "Take what you need and do not let the enemy enter the city".

The zombie wasted no time in placing his hands on the statues, hungrily drawing out the captive souls, greedily consuming them. Bursting and afire with the life forces of so many, he made his way purposefully down the tower steps and entered the city streets.

Kakos' mind was abuzz with energy and thoughts, not all his own. It took every morsel of his self-control to catalogue and store the souls as he walked. He mercilessly dominated their sentience with his own. Feeling elevated and elated as he approached the Port Gates, Kakos ordered them opened. When there was no response from the soldiers, he used spirits to snap the steel mechanisms and throw the doors wide himself.

On the other side of the gate, a group of enemy archers traded shots with those above but turned their attention towards Kakos as he approached. Opportunist swordsmen that sheltered in pier-side buildings rushed towards him and the open portal.

As he so often practised, Kakos compartmentalised his thinking; he took direct control over critical decisions such as the direction walked, but he let his deeper consciousness react to other events that unfolded around him. Arrows were deflected, enemy soldiers were tossed aside, while others stopped dead in their tracks and fell, lifeless, to the ground. Some were confused and struck at their comrades. Around Kakos buildings collapsed, fire took on human shapes as it spread mayhem to port facilities and ships alike, a frenzied captain stabbed at an imaginary spider on his neck. Where Kakos walked, pandemonium played, and chaos danced.

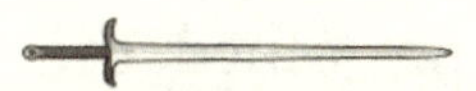

On the other side of the city, Mannace and his companions made short work of the first wave of enemy fighters before a second more experienced wave approached. These veterans were heavily armoured with thick metal plates that covered their whole body and most carried shields. They matched blows with the War Priests, and like them, they possessed inhuman strength.

Of Mannace's Ranger guards, only Jayne still fought at his Lord's side. The others perished when they were set upon by demonic dogs. Mannace, who was the hounds' target, although bloodied, was not ready to die.

Now Mannace looked up from combat to witness a Temple Guardian crash to the ground. He wouldn't have thought it possible, but an armoured giant knocked the stone head off its shoulders with a mighty sweep of a two-handed hammer. The triumphant creature roared, and the enemy around it, invigorated by the victory, cheered, and charged towards the walls. To replace the fallen protector, two more Temple Guardians bent over as they appeared through the gate from the city. It meant that on the wall, two of the chosen were defeated and their souls transitioned.

At sea, behind the enemy fleet, more vessels appeared, but they were of a different type, and as they neared, Render recognised them as Bracadian. He didn't know what to make of that, but when he saw them open fire on the Northern fleet, he grinned. The rolling thunder and flashes of the Bracadian weapons were breathtaking to behold. Render thought that up close the Bracadians must appear a terrifying foe.

Mannace battled in the outer districts for most of the day, and with the help of the animators and Steel Men, he directed the battered remnants of the War Priests and Temple Guardians back into the city. It was a relief that his troops still held the walls, at least as far as he could see. To regroup, he and Jayne joined the War Priests at their temple where they quickly ate, sipped Thog, and then returned to the walls to help the defence.

When the day turned to dusk, the attack intensified. Mannace and Jayne hurried with the war priests to the aid of a desperate Militia who struggled to hold the battlements. Touching Mannace's shoulder to get his attention, Jayne pointed across the killing ground to units of defeated enemies that were returning with reinforcements. The revitalised troops hurried to pick up ladders and raise them against the walls. Ominously, large shapes in the background signalled that more giants had also arrived. Pointing further along the wall, Jayne indicated where the defences were breached. In places, small groups of Northerners broke into the city but were now trapped in a handful of buildings. Animated statues entered the structures, while other stone men, backed by armed civilians, were climbing the steps to help on the walls. Viletri was leaving nothing behind in the brawling defence.

COUNTERSTRIKE

When night descended, Jaal moved closer to the action, to a new vantage point at the top of the valley. The battle on the plateau still raged, and in the night, even with his Elven vision, he could not get a feel for how the Dwarves fared. The fact that the fighting still seemed widespread was a good sign. The Allies' plan was for the enemy to break themselves against the Dwarves, then bring everything to bear upon them in a decisive counterattack. Jaal received confirmation from his watchers that the Iron Jaw were in place.

It was time. He gave the signal and immediately the valley behind him came to life. Thousands of giant spiders spilt forth onto the plateau from hidden mountain tunnels. Amongst them were his children, the Spiderlings. Like them, Jaal also leapt from his sanctuary and ran as best as he could to keep up, but the arachnids quickly scuttled ahead. In front of Jaal was a tangled mess of webbed bodies, dead or paralysed. At the east end of the valley, he could hear the loud "raaaahhh" of the Orcs who were also entering the fray. The staunch Northmen were not panicked by the surprise assault but knowing his allies, and on seeing the spiders in action, Jaal was confident about the outcome.

At Viletri, Mannace walked the walls to rally his troops. The Dwarves needed no reminder of their purpose. Still, the Viletri fighters and militia grew in confidence as Mannace moved amongst them, and they appreciated his help when he came with the War Priests to strengthen the defence. In places, it was not enough and more enemy over-ran the walls so that the fighting continued in the streets. Some districts were entirely in enemy hands. The animated statues and metal workers fought relentlessly to gain back lost ground, but where they faced the giants, even they were battered about and broken. The Temple Guardians were the last bastion in preventing the wave of enemy crossing the walls from turning into an unstoppable flood. Mannace wanted to do more than swing his sword to help, but the battle line stretched far beyond his reach, and the most he could accomplish was to be where he was most needed. Jayne continued to be invaluable by his side, aided by Rangers that replaced those fallen. A group of War Priests also made it their responsibility to keep Mannace safe, and their unwavering confidence and strength did much to inspire those they fought alongside.

Whatever catastrophes were occurring in the city, Mannace kept his back to it. Not far from him, heavily armoured enemy fighters made their way up ladders and engaged the Dwarves and militia. The Dwarves who ran out of ammunition were fighting with either their bladed crossbows or two-handed tools. Mannace watched one of the Viletri soldiers smash down at a heavily armoured fighter who scrambled to come over the battlements. With the soldier's strength, given him from his clockwork armour, the enemies helmeted head snapped back, and he tumbled downward. Further along the battlements, other Northern warriors successfully clambered over the crenulations. Mannace manoeuvred in that direction to help. Unexpectedly there were loud cracking noises, and several of the enemy went down. Below in the street, Bracadian soldiers were appearing out of a narrow lane and collecting into a unit. They pointed their bow sticks at the walls and waited for other targets to appear. Now that Mannace focused he could hear the same sharp pops elsewhere in the city. At this desperate time, he was thankful for the aid but was immediately concerned about having his city overrun with more foreign troops.

AFTERMATH

In the aftermath of the victorious defence, Mannace, Jaal, and Render met at Mannace's residence. They each described their experiences, and now as they sat and supped their wine and ale, the companions discussed the broader saga. It seemed to Mannace that they had survived the Northern storm. On the plateau, the enemy were utterly defeated. At Viletri, the Northmen had been crushed at sea, pushed back on land, and their surviving army was retreating west.

The Bracadians controlled the Blood and Middle Seas. Mannace was expecting the Bracadian Admiral to arrive at Viletri soon and messengers would gather Council members. If the latest reports were to be trusted, the only place where fighting continued was Tarash Gormoth.

Mannace looked at his friends. He seemed serious.

"Are we still in this?"

Jaal shrugged his shoulders. He was a pragmatist, to the point where the question made little sense to him. When he could see that Mannace needed more, Jaal stated what he thought was already evident.

"We can't go back. Thirty years ago, things were simple, and the world was small. Now we know the world is vast. I have commitments here and offspring."

They all smiled at the last point.

Render contributed, "I am happy with the progress made. I have everything I need here."

"It's harder than I imagined ... and endless. I thought we would be fighting deep in the North by now."

Mannace seemed frustrated and in that moment of misgiving, maybe even defeated. Jaal was intolerant of self-doubt, and it irritated him to see such weakness in his friend. His tone was accusing.

"Do something about it! What would the Angry Man do?"

Mannace's dour demeanour was replaced with a wry grin. He knew they had that nickname for him, and even though he was unable to control Angry Man, he understood his temper, at least while he was good-humoured.

"Jaal, my friend, you are right. I have been too patient. I spend all my time convincing people of the right course. I am weary, Jaal, of these bloody politics. Perhaps we need a tyrant, somebody to tell people what to do and if they rebel, then ... " He thumped his fist on the table with such a force it made everyone jump.

As much as Mannace's words made Jaal uncomfortable, he would rather see his friend in a rage than indecisive and weak.

"Then tell them what to do! Be the leader you need to be! Take what you want, Mannace, we will help you do that." Jaal raised his voice, "Act on your gut instincts! Let passion take you forward!"

Render usually liked to keep to his own business, but he saw personal opportunity if Mannace were to take a firmer hand.

"Don't let anything get in the road of getting what you want."

As Mannace deliberated, Jaal raised something that had irked him.

"Isn't it interesting that the Bracadians didn't know of the war against the North? Is the war with the North so important? Is it the cataclysm that will decide the fate of the world?" He glanced sideways at Mannace.

Mannace didn't like to be challenged about his vision and knew such thinking was venomous. It seemed to him typical of Jaal to say one thing, then immediately contradict it.

"It is what it is Jaal! It is the challenge put in front of us; to defeat the North. We have each seen the scale of what will come!"

Jaal saw more than a glint of Angry Man in Mannace's eye and rather than poke the beast further he changed the subject to avoid further angst.

"You need a good woman, Mannace. To put steel in your blade and give you perspective."

Mannace snorted his disdain, but Render was quick to quip, "For Hell's sake, Jaal, you must have enough perspective for us all."

They all laughed, and the atmosphere did indeed lighten.

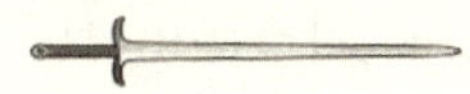

THE EASTERN COLONIES

Admiral Mangello D'Austini arrived at the port and made his way immediately into the city to meet with Mannace in the council building. Casteel and Ahmeda were at the Admiral's side. Once introductions were made, Ahmeda outlined what occurred in the west, the agreement made, and the role Bracadia played in driving the North out of the region. It filled in some of the essential missing pieces for Mannace who did not know of the battles at Yanth and Freman. Mannace needed time to think and therefore suggested Casteel give the Admiral a tour of the city.

Once alone, Mannace first attended the Temple of War to give his thanks to the War God. Then he went to the south wall where he looked out over the harbour and at the armada of Bracadian vessels gathered there. The ships were an impressive sight with their tall masts and finely dressed crews.

The Bracadians had easily handled the Northerners, and there was no doubt that they could just as quickly cripple the Blood Sea Coalition. Mannace did not want to share the North's humiliation, nor did he want to be usurped of his position. Ahmeda and Casteel acted with wisdom, embracing the future, and he must do the same. Mannace now knew what he wanted, and when the Admiral returned, they met alone.

"What do *you* want, Mangello?"

"I am a servant of the Empire. I want what is best for the Empire."

"I want the Armada."

It was a rash and inflammatory thing to say, a deliberate attempt to turn the inescapable negotiation on its head. Mannace watched for the Admiral's reaction, but he was stony-faced, and he stuck to his agenda.

"This is an interesting piece of the world, Mannace. A true frontier. Before we talk further, I must know that you will honour the arrangement made by your agents, that the Blood Sea Coalition will recognise the sovereignty of the Emperor of Bracadia. That the Emperor will have his war prize, and that you will pay his annual tribute. Doubled I think, for what you ask, and with access for the Emperor's auditors to all places and records. I will leave an officer to Govern until the Emperor appoints somebody more experienced."

Before Mannace could answer, the Admiral who typically prided himself on being unflappable, suddenly had a greater passion in his voice as if he were weary of being reasonable.

"You are beyond bold to ask for such a gift - arrogant to assume that the world will fall at your feet. Here you are saved from ruin and confronted by a superior adversary, yet you request more. I can take what I want!"

"Then take it! It would be a mistake to think that I am ignorant, Admiral. I know what it means to meet your demands - it will leave us in ruins anyway. You would *politely* pillage us and escape to leave us as prey for the North's return. How easy for you. There is always a better way."

Mangello gained back some of his demeanour, although he remained agitated. He was turning over Mannace's words, deciding his best course.

"Will you agree to my terms?"

Up to this point, Mannace wasn't at all comfortable with that arrangement, and surprised himself when he confided "Yes". He would have preferred an alliance rather than becoming a vassal, but he knew, without a doubt, that would not be enough for the Admiral and his Emperor. He didn't have a choice; the Coalition would bleed gold, but that was a wound that would heal.

"The Empire will protect its interests."

Both men needed more time for thought. Therefore, Mannace ordered food and drink brought to the courtyard at his home. During the afternoon, under a warm sun, the two men talked about many things and gained a better understanding of each other. When the Admiral left, Mannace realised that the fate of the Blood Sea Coalition would depend on the Admiral's next act - if he would honour their conversation or if he played Mannace for what he needed to know and would now finish the job started by the North.

Three days later, when the Blood Sea Coalition met in Council, the Admiral also attended. Nobody was in the mood for a motivational speech. They already talked about the war and the outcomes before the session started. Leaders, such as Ithius Sartis had died, and there were new representatives in their place. Mannace sensed the Council looked for decisive leadership.

"Welcome. We have waged war on two fronts, and there have been victories and defeats. Our enemy is now our friend. The war in the North has leaked war into the South. You can be proud of the defence made here at the Blood Sea. We have lost friends; Lord Ithius and the city of Hindas were amongst the casualties. Karanthos was sacked, with many people butchered. Loryan is in utter ruins. Much of Yanth lies in ashes. Freman too. But our true enemy, the North, have fled. We will work together to heal and rebuild. Let us honour the fallen by looking towards the future."

Mannace moved to stand next to the Admiral who rose from his chair so that they stood together.

"This is Admiral Mangello D'Austini of the Empire of Bracadia. He came here to be conqueror, and in Valthar and Jurusso blood *was* spilt. We must look past this, for when the North came to overwhelm us, Bracadia was our protector. Without the intervention of Bracadia, we would be the vassals of the Northern Lords or destroyed. Without Bracadia, we will not have the time to rebuild and recover before the North returns. At the time of crisis, an agreement was reached. You have all benefitted from it and are all bound by it. There is no negotiation."

He paused to ensure all eyes were on him and that he had their full attention.

"The Blood Sea Coalition is now a part of the Empire of Bracadia."

Mannace let the group have their moment to react; many shouting and throwing their hands in the air. A few appeared confused, while others sat back watching the reaction, amused. Mannace mentally blocked out all the noise, then when the outcry died down, he continued.

"We are to be known as the Eastern Colonies. I have accepted the role of Colonial Governor."

That set off a raucous debate. Mannace tried to ignore the noise and yelling, but this time he couldn't. When a Two-Face chief stood, shook his fists, and denounced the Council, Mannace let Angry Man emerge to take centre stage. He stormed over to the large Orc and leaned so that their noses were almost touching. With no room left for doubt, he made clear his position. His voice was so loud and full of menace that the crowd fell silent, and all heads turned to watch him.

"THERE WILL BE NO TALK OF INDEPENDENCE. There is no room in this new world for any nation to stand aside. Are you so stupid to think you have a choice!"

Leaving the stunned Orc and returning to the centre of the room he looked for other dissidents, but nobody would take him on. In the same commanding voice, Mannace reiterated the blunt truth to all present, "Do not think you have a choice!"

The Overlord from Arenland stood. It was an effort for him to do so, with legs that were too old and frail to walk. He was one of the few not intimidated by Mannace's fierce disposition.

"We all have choices, Mannace."

Admiral Mangello D'Austini stepped forward to support

his new Governor. He held a commanding presence, and people quickly stopped their chatter to hear what the Bracadian had to say.

"Governor Mannace may run the colony as he chooses."

He put a hand on Mannace's shoulder and smiled warmly at those gathered. It was a skill he had practised for such occasions.

"The Emperor requires that all citizens act in the Empire's best interest. The Governor must ensure he meets that condition."

His grip on Mannace's shoulder tightened, conveying solidarity.

"As the Empire's agent, I recognise your war with the North and acknowledge the immediate and ongoing threat. To that purpose, I leave one hundred and fifty Galleons at the Governor's command and two Charikon divisions. The Charikon are like your Belg and your Orcs, fierce warriors that serve at the front of the Empire's armies."

Most of his audience was dumbfounded. To those that understood politics, it was apparent now that these terms were already agreed outside of the Council. They were unsure if they were happy or not with the outcome. It seemed to some that Mannace elevated himself.

"When I return to the Empire, you will fill twenty ships with gold and bounty so that the Emperor can rejoice in his victory against the Northmen and celebrate the expansion of his territories. I leave it to the Governor to outline other responsibilities."

The Admiral finished what he needed to say, but for good graces, he added more.

"I give my appreciation to the Elves for their wisdom and guidance in these matters."

The Two-Face Orcs eyed the Elves suspiciously. This time nobody intervened when the Councillors continued conversations amongst themselves. There was much to absorb and discuss.

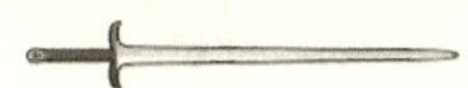

The Mad King was not aware of the Council meeting. At Tarash Gormoth he was still fighting Northmen, and his depleted armies withstood the second wave of assault. It was not until the Wild Elves and Rhalec came from the Fogmir in large numbers that they purged Tarash Gormoth of the invaders.

When the port city of Tarash was retaken, amongst the spoils was an enormous troop carrier. Crafted by giants, the gargantuan ship accommodated all sizes of passengers. It inspired the Mad King to collect the heads of all those killed and store them aboard the vessel. It was a grim harvest, but as with everything they did, the surviving slaves set about the work without question or complaint.

Once the dark trophies were collected and stowed, the Mad King and his most devout followers departed Tarash Gormoth. He left one of his longest-serving slaves in charge. The elderly slave was ancient even by Elven standards. He possessed no race or name, so the Mad King adorned him with the title of Slave King and gifted him Tarash Gormoth. With the nation in ruins and much of the population perished, nobody opposed the appointment. The Mad King wanted somebody who would stay true to his vision, to care for his progeny, his beautiful babies beneath the mountain.

Part Five:

Rebirth

THE GOVERNOR'S BLADE

Jayne was no longer on bodyguard rotation with the other Rangers. Now he went everywhere with Mannace, and everyone knew him as The Governor's Blade. He fought with two swords and seemed equally dexterous using either hand. At *The Pit*, where fighters honed their skills against one another, Jayne was a regular participant until there was nobody left in Viletri who would face him. Occasionally he got the call that a champion from out of town journeyed here to challenge him. But he defeated them all, even the big Belg, with few scars to show for it.

Jayne had placed himself in an ideal position at Viletri to execute any order that might come, yet none had. He was incredibly patient, but after decades of waiting, restlessness was settling in. Jayne decided that if his sponsor was not clear about his purpose, an interim plan was needed. Typically, he prided himself as a person who followed orders, ruthlessly and exceptionally well, so shaping his agenda was a challenge. Until now, he never gave much thought about what he might personally desire.

Mannace was planning a day at his residence, meaning that Jayne would have little to do, so the Dark Elf made his excuses and visited the markets near the docks. He browsed through fresh food stalls and tasted a variety of herbs and spices before buying a select few. Other things he liked, he bought: a soft blue cheese from Rummond, dried fruits from Fesadi, and a haunch of beef produced by a local farmer. He was less familiar with fish but purchased some heart-shaped shellfish and a fresh Silver Flatback. He took them back to the Ranger's barracks where he made use of the large kitchen. The head cook there let him go about his business and answered his occasional questions.

Recently, the barracks were renovated, including a modern kitchen outfitted with the best technology the city had to offer; coal-fired boilers that provided hot water and steam to drive the slicers and meat saw. A cold-room to store meat and vegetables. Huge fans hummed overhead, drawing the heated air through vents to warm other areas of the building and often tormenting its inhabitants with the sweet smell of roasting meat and fried onions.

All-day Jayne cooked and tried flavours. He shared some titbits with the kitchen staff who came and went. Most of the cooked food was well received. Jayne ate little himself, but he enjoyed the scents and flavours and the sound of cooking on the massive grill. At the day's end, he went back to Mannace's residence and resumed his duties there. A sip of Thog helped to take away his fatigue. It was a pleasing tiredness though, as he had enjoyed his day. For the first time, Jayne let his own motivations lead him; it was empowering. It ignited a spark in his mind, and that small flicker provided the faintest of light - a speck of sanity in the boundless darkness of his mind.

THE ARK

Casteel, Athose, Rey, and Ya looked up to the sky and followed the directions of Hammy and Spit. The two Brula discovered something in the Varghonian interior, and Casteel wanted to understand firsthand precisely what the Brula scouts were so excited about.

Before leaving Dos Neran, Casteel let Khing know her mission. The expedition took them across the familiar lands of Attica, Kogath, and Indana, and now they trekked their way through wildlands towards the high mountain range known to locals as *The Giants*. There were still independent tribes of men and Brula in these wild regions. While they were mostly peaceful, Hammy and Spit were careful not to enter their territories and risk trouble. It meant detouring through some rugged terrain.

After days of climbing rocky hills and navigating deep gorges, they could finally see *The Giants* poking above the skyline. After another day, they came to a place high on a knoll that overlooked a broad river valley. The base of the valley was a rubble of stones and boulders, with patches of hardy trees that seemed like tiny green islands in the sea of grey. Several streams meandered their way along the valley, joined and split, then gathered at the end of the valley into a single tumbling river. On the other side of the basin, a tall mountain rose, steep and craggy. The Brula didn't need to point at the thing that had brought them there. A chunk of the mountainside was collapsed away, revealing a human-shaped impression. It looked as if something humanoid and of enormous size had stepped out of it. In front of the hollow, partially covered by rubble, was a mammoth mound of bones. On closer inspection, tens of thousands of skulls – too many to count.

It was an often-told tale that after the war with the North, the Mad King had mysteriously left Tarash Gormoth, taking with him the many heads of the fallen. It seemed inevitable to Casteel that this mysterious heap had the King's shadow cast over it. She could see that the mound was there for some time, long enough to have weeds grow amongst it, but not long enough for the skulls to be washed away when the river valley flooded. There permeated a feeling of dread from being so close to these severed heads. It made Casteel's spine shiver and the hairs stand up on her neck. She visited many places of death, and they all resonated a sense of unnatural energy and foreboding. Unfazed, Athose clambered to the top of the mound, upsetting many of the heads that slid about like scree. It seemed to him that something large and heavy had been placed atop the skulls but was since removed. He called down his discovery to the others.

The barbarian, Ya, wouldn't go near the horrific mound. Instead, she and Rey investigated the mountainside. They confirmed that something massive trapped within the mountain had been set free. Casteel estimated it to be large enough to dwarf the Temple Guardians at Viletri.

Following a trail south, they distanced themselves from the mountain and were soon back amongst rugged hills and ravines, continually mirroring the course of the river. Eventually, they could see the ocean on the horizon.

Ahead a man stood on open ground, and as they cautiously approached, Casteel recognised the Mad King. He smiled at the surprised faces.

"My Brula gave me warning of your approach. I wanted to welcome you personally. Come this way".

Without further conversation, the Mad King led the party away from the river valley and through an open forest. Near the coast, and still within the woodland, was a community of men and Brula. They constructed shelters and huts as well as functional buildings for drying furs, hanging meat, cooking, and such like. As the party moved further into the forest community, they could see a massive ship wedged upright between trees, its deck well above the tall canopy. Casteel caught a glimpse of a Moleman sitting in the shadows beneath the vessel, Orcs too provided a lazy guard, and slaves went about various activities.

"Welcome to the Ark".

The Mad King seemed pleased with himself. Four ramps were lowered to the ground from wide portals in the massive ship's side, giving access to its upper decks. However, the King continued past the Ark and led them to a large pond. Sitting in a prone position on the other side of the pool was the mountain creature. Even as it sat cross-legged, it was almost tree height. Jet black, with a lean human form widening at the torso to support powerful arms that shaped up into a strange faceless head. Casteel imagined that it would be smooth and glasslike to touch. Athose darted to the right of the pond and reappeared soon after on a tree limb close to the creature's head. As he leaned forward, the smooth face turned towards him. Rather than leap back as Casteel expected, the young Elf reached out and touched the creature. Athose could feel warmth, possibly from the sun that beamed through the trees.

"I like that boy. He has a rare courage."

The Mad King was not usually one to compliment. Casteel was immediately irritated – the King seemed smug, and it appeared to her that he was showing off his new acquisition. His interest in Athose made the hairs on her neck stand on end. Her words were abrupt.

"What are you doing here?"

"Going about my own business."

The Mad King knew more explanation would be needed to satisfy the Elf.

"I am collecting Colossi. As you can see, I have found one, and I will find others."

"Why?"

"Why not?"

Casteel hated talking to the Mad King. It was always

impossible to know if and when he was literal in his peculiar fashion, or if he were entertaining himself with wordplay at her expense. She wanted to avoid any mind-games and get to the point.

"I need to know that what you do here is in the interests of the Eastern Colonies. You know my job."

There was an uncomfortable silence, and the king gave nothing away with his flinty expression. Eventually, he sighed and gave another of his incredulous smiles.

"As you wish. I will tell you a story that has never been told."

The Mad King took more time to choose his words carefully.

"I was once the servant of a powerful man. I brought him food and tended to his other simple needs. When the rebellion came, and my master met his end, I was fortunate to walk away. Who was I to warrant any attention?"

The King quickly captivated his audience. Even Ya stopped her usual fidgeting – and bent closer to catch his next words.

"Other servants of other masters were not so fortunate. Most were slain, but some that were not so easily killed were imprisoned, in place and time. My friend here was a servant to a master, imprisoned for the crime of loyalty, but now he too is free. What we do next, my friend and I, is our business."

Casteel read between the lines.

"You were a servant to an Ancient One. Who?"

"Enough!"

The Mad King was abrupt, his sharp manner leaving no room for doubt. He turned to Athose who returned to them.

"Boy, stay here with me. You have the freedom of this camp."

 Athose nodded.

His companions were shocked. Casteel and Rey had grown

very fond of the boy and felt a jolt to their souls. Athose already leapt back to the trees to explore. When he returned to the pond, it was again to check the face of the Colossus. There was a strength there that was more than just rock, a firmness of jaw and a gaze with a sense of purpose. Athose looked where it might be staring, but it was just into the trees.

The Mad King addressed Casteel.

"I know his nature. He will be loyal to you, yet to evolve, he must move on."

Casteel understood Athose well enough to know his mind would not be changed. Now she could claim further reason to despise the Mad King, a cruel master manipulator. One day he would finally exceed beyond the limits indulged of a "Mad" king, and she would catch … no … crush him like a mouse within her fist. Casteel was not vindictive by nature, and she didn't like that the King brought out her latent darkness. Seeking a distraction, she looked skyward, embracing the sun's light, and drawing calmness from it. Casteel breathed deeply. Still, with her eyes closed, she whispered to the Mad King. Her steely manner carried a promise of menace.

"Protect him. I will hold you accountable."

"He will have the freedom to decide his fate."

"Why the skulls?" Ya was still intrigued by the Mad King's tale and her intervention relieved the building tension. There was a pause as both the Mad King and Casteel let their posture relax, turning to face the barbarian.

"Good question," the Mad King replied amiably. "Because things, sometimes ordinary things, have magic if you know how to find it. I needed magic to release my friend. Now he is all the magic I need."

The next day, Athose accompanied his Blood Legion companions as far as the river. He did not understand their emotions. His friends seemed distressed to leave him in the

Mad King's care – the potential that this might be a final farewell. For him, distance changed nothing; they would always be with him. He would always be of the Blood Legion.

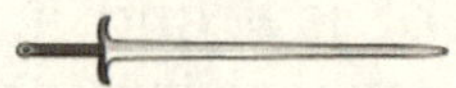

A MODERN SOLDIER

Command of the Bracadian ships and the Charikon regiments gave Mannace the authority and military might to not only secure the territories already part of the collective but also bully the few independent lands in the region to recognise Bracadia as its sovereign power. Amongst those were the Wanderers of Furi and the gentle people of the Footsteps. The Black Valley Orcs were resistant, with just one of four clans now part of the colony. The Belg and Orc fighters of the Charikon would continue to work with the allied tribes to bash and bully the others into the fold.

Mannace transitioned quickly into the role of Governor. It seemed to him that his position was much the same as it was in the past. He learned a lot from Admiral Mangelo D'Augustini who took the time to work with the leaders of each nation so that they understood what it meant to be part of the colony. Though his manner was authoritative, the Admiral still showed a knack of making others feel important and involved.

Accepting what it meant to be Governor helped Mannace to see the politics of the collective population with fresh eyes. He better understood that the differences between nations were both a strength and a weakness. Strong in that it sparked competition and innovation. Weak because each government followed its own priorities and agendas.

To encourage unity, he decided that a National Soldier was needed, of a military design that was the same for all nations and the best that they could offer. It would need to be like the Bracadian design yet with colonial differences. Mannace started with those smaller nations that did not have a strong sense of their military, commissioning the First Colonial Battalion with just eight hundred young recruits sourced from Lapthos, Rummond, Malanos,

Arackland, and the Footsteps. They dubbed themselves *The Young Bloods*. Muskets were being made for them by the Dwarven gunsmiths, who received training from the Bracadians. The Dwarves were already crafting clockwork improvements to the firing mechanism and barrel to enable faster loading, plus they attached a combat blade to the barrel so that it could be more useful for in-close fighting. These were ideas they were playing with since they first looked at the Bracadian weapons fifteen years ago. It was the secret of gunpowder that had eluded them, and while the Dwarves were lean in contributing to the Emperor's war prize – they joined Yanth and Arenland to fund the acquisition of this vital technology. Logthar invested extra to have smiths and alchemists trained.

For Mannace's battalion, the Dwarves collaborated with men from Silos to manufacture a version of their military long-coats that were Bracadian red. The coats were a thick blend of wool and metal fibres strong enough to turn a blade or arrow and blunt the impact of a musket bullet. A tall collar protected the neck and the large hood was deep enough to cover the head and helmet when pulled forward. For this reason, helmets were of a simple, open-face design. Rather than a full gas mask, the Arenland cloth filters were worn about the neck and only unit Captains were equipped with vials of choke gas. Easy access to Thog was becoming a problem in some communities. For that reason, again only the captains were provided a flask of the substance, with a cleverly designed metal stopper that delivered small doses to help with endurance. The battalion was assigned a Combat Wizard, Combat Healer, War Priest, Shaman, two Warden Trackers, and Brula Scouts, as well as an animator with four large steel workers.

Mannace involved himself in the training of the soldiers to gain a sense of, not only their equipment, but also their capabilities. Caring for and using a musket was far more complicated than owning a sword and for all his prowess with melee weapons, Mannace found the gun frustrating. He didn't have the eye for aiming, and it seemed to him that these new recruits relied on mass effect to compensate for their inaccuracy. He hoped that would improve with time. Alfar, an Alani officer, helped with unit formations and tactics. After watching the Elf in action, Mannace spoke to him in private.

"Alfar, you truly have the knack for this."

The Elf gave a wry smile.

"These weapons, Mannace, they will change war as we know it."

Alfar looked down the side of a barrel, stroked it with his hand, and admired the Dwarven craftsmanship.

"It's not Elven craftsmanship, but they do well with what they have."

Mannace chuckled. He couldn't tell if Alfar was serious or joking.

"Stay as leader of this Battalion, Alfar. Help me build a new army, one to conquer the North. We can do it, Alfar. The North will be defeated. I have seen it."

"War is not so simple, Mannace. It is fought as much off the field as on it."

Alfar seemed like he wanted to share more and Mannace encouraged him with a curious look and nod of his head. Alfar's demeanour was serious as he spoke.

"When your way forward is uncertain, the Light will always be your guide, Mannace. Never lose sight of it. When you follow the Light, you are walking the same path as the Alani. Stay with the Light, Mannace, and I will prepare this Battalion, and I will see them fight on the field. The fire and thunder of muskets in the North will herald a new dawn."

At sea, Mannace commanded the forces he needed for now. The Bracadian galleons in combination with the Iron Ships and First Fleet were sufficient to secure the local sea routes and ports, then push into the North Sea. In the warm months, they worked with the Tarash Slavers to raid the Northern coastline, destroying shipyards, and looting their settlements.

At the insistence of the Council, now called the Colonial Council, Mannace reduced the military commitment at the rift. For the moment, less than twenty thousand fighters assisted on that front. The spirit of Syprus was agitated at the news. He and Mannace argued, ending with Syprus and the mirror being shut away in a closet. It was two years before Mannace felt the need to talk with the spectre again.

"I am sorry to have banished you for so long, my friend."

"I have only ever wanted the best for you, Mannace."

Mannace didn't want to dwell on past events, and in truth, he felt no remorse for what he did. He finally retrieved the mirror because he felt the need again to have Syprus as a supporter.

"I am tired, Syprus. I feel like we are always at the beginning."

"You are strong, Mannace. When I met you, that *was* the beginning. Look at where you are now, a leader of nations, marshal to a vast host, a decisive step closer to your vision. Have faith in what you have achieved and acknowledge your accomplishments."

Mannace brought Syprus up to date with events and asked his advice on topics he was pondering. He felt calmer after their discussion. When they finished, he arranged for the mirror to be hung on the wall in his study, where Syprus enjoyed a view out the window and over the city.

RAVENBORN

Lord Ravenborn of Ostoik died in his sleep. His death did not come as a surprise as he was an older man with failing health. Ahmeda Ravenborn was at his side at the end. In his prime, Lord Ravenborn was a potent, powerful man, and during his rule, Ostoik had become a hub of innovation and industry. With Ahmeda as his wife, Lord Ravenborn advocated and sponsored the Temple of War. As such, it was apt that he received a Warrior's send-off.

Saska travelled by rail carriage to attend the ceremony. Arta and Alsaborg were there as her bodyguards. Mannace planned to sail to Ostoik for the funeral but was delayed by a visit from the Galandar Ambassador. Therefore, he also travelled by rail to arrive on time. Jayne and three other Rangers accompanied him. When he saw Saska and her entourage, he was not pleased with the choice of company. Against his better judgement he sat close to them.

The bitch, the mouth, and the traitor. As he looked over his three unwelcome travel companions, Mannace mused at how much Saska had changed over the years; evolved from the wild predatory beast that she was, into something much more complicated and dangerous. He did not like nor trust her.

"How is Jaal?"

"He is with the Spider kin. He spends most of his time there."

Mannace couldn't help but prod at the obvious, his tone self-satisfied.

"He has made his choices then. He was always one to take his pleasures and move on. I am sure you have no troubles keeping your bed warm."

Like any predator, Saska struck out when baited.

"And your bed empty? I know your secret, Mannace!"

With sudden anger, Mannace stood, and the others followed. Reacting instinctively, Jayne grasped his sword hilts and drew the blades a hands width out of their scabbards. It was his habit to do this as a threat. The few people that failed to heed this threat had met a swift end. Arta, though, stepped closer and grabbed his arms at the elbow. Her big mitts were strong, and she was blessed with great balance to go with her size. Jayne was unable to move. The anger on his face at being so easily handled made everyone except Arta and Mannace take a step back and ready themselves for a fight.

"ENOUGH!"

Mannace's booming voice was intimidating enough that Arta let go of Jayne's arms, and Jayne pushed his blades back into their scabbards with a huff. He and Arta continued to stare each other down. There was an awkward shuffle of bodies to accommodate Mannace and his followers as they moved to other seats. The mood remained sour for the rest of the journey, so it was a relief to arrive in Ostoik after a day confined in the rocking, often smoke-filled carriage.

Mannace rarely travelled to Ostoik, but each time he did, he was amazed at the city's growth. The port facilities were colossal, and in dry-dock there were another two steel ships in different stages of construction. Manufactories dominated a large district with their looming presence and cacophony of noises. The daunting buildings and the black smoke they billowed into the air obscured the rest of the city from view.

As the passengers disembarked, they passed cargo carriages laden with coal being joined together in a long train for the trip to Sylos and Viletri. Coal, replacing wood and charcoal, was becoming essential to the industries in those cities too.

This was Saska's first visit to Ostoik. Her first impression was that the city lacked magic; it was unnecessarily dirty and needed a wizard's hand to clear the air and give it some shine. Everything seemed coated in smog and drabness. The Dwarves who loaded the coal carriages were an excellent example. Saska had never seen such dirty and depressed looking creatures. As the party moved through the main thoroughfares and away from the industrial district, the city came to life with streetlamps that cast a yellowish light into the gloom, and with crowds of citizens going purposefully about their business. Dressed in fine clothes and talking energetically amongst themselves, they were a stark contrast to the dreary dockworkers.

The funeral was at the Temple of War, and crowds of mourners crammed into the great hall. Mannace joined the Overlord, who waited with Ahmeda and the other Ravenborns. While they mingled, a noble named Fitius Angelcry, whom the Overlord already appointed as Lord Ravenborn's successor, introduced himself. He seemed capable and business-like; the Arenlanders would term him a modern gentleman. The Lord Angelcry was full of ideas that he enthusiastically shared with Mannace. Mannace nodded, but in truth, some of the concepts were beyond his reckoning.

The ceremony was lengthy and formal. It culminated with Lord Ravenborn being placed on a stone dais. As the War Priests and acolytes chanted, the dais became a bright light, so brilliant that Mannace looked away. When the light faded, he glanced back, and the body was gone. Mannace placed the back of his right hand against his forehead to salute the past leader. Before the proceedings, the presiding priest instructed him on the words to end the ritual.

"In service and valour, we pave the way to the Light".

The words seemed contradictory in this temple to the God of War who was of the Darkness, but Mannace understood that Darkness and Light were intertwined. He knew too, that he bore that same contradiction.

Following the ceremony, Saska remained at Ostoik to support Ahmeda and receive her tuition in magic. She learned that magic was forbidden in Arenland outside of the priesthood. The Overlord strongly felt that 'witchery' was a barrier to progress and invention.

Ahmeda faced the challenge of preserving the Code of War and the celestial magic that underpinned it - keeping the old traditions relatable in a society that stepped into a new era of industrialisation. To help with the challenge, she gathered together senior War Priests and Industry Guild Masters and tasked them with creating a new blueprint for the Doctrine of War.

OLD FRIEND

While leading the Colonial forces at the Rift, Demmal Fulstrom was mortally wounded, his body dragged away by the Northern troops as a trophy. The news hit Mannace hard; not only was Demmal the General of his armies, but a mentor and friend. He dispatched orders to Khing that he take reinforcements from Attica and travel to the Northern Rift to assume command of the Colonial forces there.

Sympathetic to his friend's loss, Render decided it was time to reacquaint Mannace with Morgan Cain. He had been working with the obsidian statue of Morgan since recovering him from the Valley of Pain. It proved challenging to repair the damage that so many years of agony inflicted. The treatment that made the most significant difference was to transfer his soul to another medium. Render organised a bronze statue to be created that mirrored Morgan's current obsidian form, with a less tortured visage. It was not difficult for him to complete the soul transfer and animation. With additional enchantments, Render's magic allowed Morgan to hear and speak. The wizard was delighted with the outcome.

Mannace was astounded to be reacquainted with the explorer and shocked by Morgan's story and years of suffering. Mannace remembered his promise to Morgan, that they would build a nation together, and honoured that by making the bronze man an advisor. Morgan was honest with Mannace and confessed that he was not entirely in his proper wits, and prone to abnormal thinking.

Mannace consulted with Morgan about the Syprus mirror and the plans they were making to retrieve the Oracle from the ruined monastery.

"Morgan, the Oracle is an area of earth beneath the Monastery, we have discussed it before. I expect you will find something if you excavate the foundations, something miraculous that has enabled the visions and guided the lives of so many.”

Mannace could see that the adventurer was intrigued – immediately lured by the prospect of discovery.

“Excavate and retrieve the ‘Oracle’, Morgan. Escort it in secret to Viletri.”

“What if transportation is not possible, Mannace? What if the Oracle is the earth and not a thing hidden within it? It could have defences. There are many things not accounted for.”

Mannace simply shrugged. He knew Morgan well enough, even in this new bronze form, to see his friend was thinking aloud. These were not questions to be resolved today.

“I have made a troopship and twenty animated workers available to you. A clerk is waiting outside the door who will give you the details and whatever other resources you need. Thank you, Morgan.”

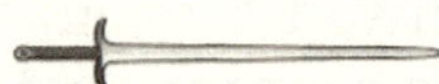

As Governor, Mannace needed to focus on the meeting of the Colonial Council, with the third gathering of colony leaders only a month away. As always, Kakos was helping him to organise it. Like Mannace, the administrator understood the benefits of being the Eastern Colony of Bracadia. From his desk of power, Kakos controlled the policy and financial framework governing forty-four nations. It was an enormous enterprise requiring a small army of administrators and envoys to maintain. He estimated the region to have a total population between three and four million. United and secure, the Eastern Colony was becoming a significant power.

COLONIAL COUNCIL

"Friends, we are in a time of prosperity and growth. Of innovation and invention. Of collaboration and unification. I welcome you to the third gathering of the Colonial Council."

At this Council, there was to be no talk of war. The previous decade revealed to Mannace the might of the North, and he knew that, for now, he could but only scratch it. To strike and break the North would require patience, preparation, and alliance. Mannace felt as if he had been a student before, and only now, as Governor of the Bracadian Eastern Colonies, was he becoming the leader he always strived to be.

The extended Council Hall included raised tiers so that all the colonial leaders and officials could view the central podium. The council meeting took just a day. It started with the Governor's Speech, then updates from leaders or experts and concluded with a dedication to the God of War. Negotiations and more detailed discussions would take place throughout the week. The city of Viletri was at its most alive during this time with joyous festivities and gatherings.

Mannace's itinerary gave him no leeway to relax, but it was not all tedium. He enjoyed his time with the Grey Dwarves and Arenlanders. Both groups shared his passion for Technology, and they each learned that working together was much more productive than the pursuit of rival projects. That didn't mean that they all held the same vision or objectives, but that friction and competition further fuelled their motivation to achieve wondrous things. Mannace gave ambassadors from Arenland and Yanth a tour of the Institute of Technology and the Manufactory. The students of the Architect and Animators explained things as they went. Most impressive was the floating platform the officials rode on that manoeuvred them about the buildings. Attached to the underside of the platform were magic-imbued plates like the Dwarven shield discs that provided the force to keep it elevated. By manipulating the magical powers, the students were able to move the platform horizontally and vertically. One of the young men, named Symin, was appointed their spokesperson. He seemed anxious as his amused colleagues pushed him toward Mannace and his guests.

"It's a union of Technomancy and science," he blurted.

When he could see his audience expected more of an explanation, the student fumbled at first for words, but on closing his eyes to avoid the spectator's stares, he was able to forget them and focus on his speech. Once he started, he became unstoppable.

"Technomancy is giving things life so that you can give them commands. So, the disk knows when to move. Up, down, forward. Programming. Stopping too. Science by comparison is inanimate innovation, while Technomancy is animated. Technomancy and science, like eggs with bacon. Four shields positioned underneath, but angled just right, with only the right amount of weight in the disk. Four-point-eight cubits. Levitation. It's the architect who designed it, but the Dwarves who built it. They're smart with reproduction, Dwarves. It's adjusted for up and down. The Technomancers do that. The Architect, though, he can explain it best. Attraction and repulsion. Using the natural properties of things. Amplified. It's the amplification that's key, at the molecular level. Sixteen density, that's the other key. Repulsion."

Symin opened his eyes briefly. His audience moved away with their backs to him. It was an immense relief, and for the first time since starting to speak, he drew a deep breath. The student shuffled sideways and sat on a nearby stool, putting his face between his knees, and as Althea taught him, Symin focused his full attention on a thin crack in the floor.

During the week of the Council, something extraordinary happened. Runners from the Grey Mountain passed a message to the Dwarves at Viletri, then departed the city by ship to share their communication further afield. By the way the Dwarves reacted, it was a missive of great importance, though the Dwarves were closed-lipped regarding its detail. The Leaders of the Grey Dwarves departed Viletri immediately. Other Dwarves were leaving their homes at Viletri and returning to their old residences beneath the Grey Mountain. In the weeks that followed, a migration of Dwarves from other lands passed through the city, and it became clear that they were answering a summons. Even the Dwarves at the Temple of War put aside their oath of loyalty to the War God to honour some ancient promise that led them to their Dwarven hold. Without explanation, the Grey Dwarves ceased communication and closed the entrances to their domain. Soon, the only Dwarves to be seen were those stragglers that travelled the furthest to return to their ancestral home. Within a year, the Dwarves were gone from lands that saw the sun, even the dour miners from Arenland had departed, and the entrances to their underground holds were sealed up completely.

Mannace was frustrated. As well as the Dwarves, the Alani Elves were also absent. Since the attack from the North, their communities remained hidden from the world. Mannace summoned Render to his home.

"It makes no bloody sense, Render. Where have the bloody Alani gone, nothing's simple with goddamned Elves."

Render could see Mannace was agitated but he wasn't in the mood for being summoned, nor for games, therefore, to keep the encounter as short as possible he simply shared the facts.

"They are in Nearspace, Mannace. In another dimension - they have not moved - everything is as it was. The Alani can shift between the dimensions. Tomorrow their cities may reappear."

"What does that bloody mean?"

Render lost his patience.

"It means bloody nothing, Mannace." There was a heat to his voice that could melt steel, "The Elves are still loyal, they are still on your Council. They haven't abandoned the land like the Dwarves. Let it be!"

Mannace was shocked that Render would speak to him in such a blunt way.

"You are my advisor, Render. I need your advice."

"I am busy, Mannace. I have priorities of my own. I am not here to babysit the bloody Elves."

Mannace laughed, which allowed Render to relax.

"I am sorry, my friend, for dragging you away from your business. You can go back to your devilry and conjuring."

In truth, Render's matters were not so pressing that they would prevent him from spending a few hours in Mannace's company, and it was apparent that Mannace was reaching out to him. Render remained a little annoyed at the pretence for the summons if all Mannace wanted was company.

"Of course, I can bloody go. I can come and go as I please – I'm the bloody Sorcerer – the Four Hells can't stop me. I'd sacrifice my best apprentice for a bottle of wine, though. Where is the goddamned wine, Mannace? You need better servants."

Mannace laughed again and called for one of his retainers. Unlike the Dwarves and Alani, his household and cellar were something he could fully control.

A NEW ORDER

The towns and cities of Tarash Gormoth were governed by Mayors, appointed from the oldest of the slaves. These high officials passed new laws that prevented simple things like travel between communities, trade agreements, and marriage. Any infringement was dealt with harshly, with offenders dragged off to the catacombs for re-purposing. Only the soldiers seemed exempt, and their authority appeared to have no boundaries. It was not long before commerce and trade ground to a standstill and the citizens, where they could gather in large enough numbers, were in open rebellion.

The citizens' representative, Admiral Veroff Odari, confronted the Slave King. Between them stood a line of slave soldiers connected at the neck by chains, veterans by appearance, who silently watched the Admiral as he paced back and forth, stating his case to the King who remained silent and blank-faced. The free citizens of Tarash Gormoth, as the civilians started to call themselves, persuaded Veroff to make the journey they wouldn't, to the catacombs at Gormoth, to convince the Slave King to change his path.

Veroff was livid.

"When the Mad King returns, he will not be pleased that these lands are in chaos."

The Slave King seemed impervious to Veroff's dark mood and ignored the threat. Instead, he gave a thin smile and laid praise upon the Admiral.

"The Mad King will not be returning. As Admiral, you have served your nation well, and through your industry, the depths beneath the mountain are filled with northern captives. I appreciate your loyal service."

"Will you listen to the people? Will you consider what I

ask?" implored Veroff.

"No."

There was no emotion or empathy in the response. The Slave King wore a metal collar around his neck that was no different from the other slaves. There was nothing about the man that defined him as anything but a servant, but here his authority was absolute.

"Then I must resign my post as Admiral. I will leave immediately. Governor Mannace knows of this meeting, and I am under his protection."

The Slave King looked to a Moleman standing to his left. The creature extended a claw from the sleeve of its hessian robe and made a subtle gesture. Slaves standing near the lamps on the walls reached up and extinguished the small flames, plunging the underground room into utter darkness.

LEGACY

Bollo, son of Rollo and Degura, was more Orc than human, fortunately for him – enough that he was not put to work cleaning shit off the streets in Hagbesh as soon as he could crawl. His mother taught him how to survive life in the city, while his father trained him to be skilful with the bow and club. Already he could easily overpower the old man. Bollo was robust, sturdy, and quick – suited to the warrior caste but not able to take up duty as a warrior in Hagbesh because he was not purebred. Instead, he travelled now with a note from his father to seek employment in the garrison at Viletri.

Because of his young age, the letter was not sufficient to secure him a position as a soldier, but it was enough to put him within the employ of Morgan Cain, advisor to the Governor himself. Bollo was one of sixty men and mechanical workers helping Morgan to build and fit-out an estate east of Viletri. The large mansion overlooked the sea, and its grounds and outer buildings were extensive. Before they started the construction, there was already an earthwork marking the centre of the estate. Something of importance was entombed. Bollo was to stay on with some of the others as estate guardians.

Bollo was fascinated by his bronze employer, always imagining how he might vanquish him as an opponent. The Half-Orc watched how Morgan moved, maintained his balance, how his weight left deep footprints in the earth, how he reacted to noises and other stimulation, the way he easily lifted weights that the mightiest Orc would struggle to carry. At night, Bollo's imaginings started to manifest in his dreams. They evolved quickly into vivid scenes of brawls, duels, and battle. In the mornings, he would awaken invigorated and confident – feeling superior to those around him. Only Morgan seemed to provide a potential challenge.

Morgan agreed to help Bollo in his training, and during breaks from the construction, he sparred with the young warrior. Even with Morgan's experience and other advantages, he found the Half-Orc a capable and persistent opponent – physically gifted and skilled beyond his years. As well as helping Bollo, it also assisted Morgan to get used to his new body, with all its advantages and challenges. Bollo couldn't hurt Morgan, so it was really just pride that spurred Morgan to be at his best and keep an upper hand. Bollo revelled in the opportunity to try anything without having to hold back for fear of hurting his opponent. He still used blunted and padded practise weapons though, because hitting a bronze opponent would damage his proper weapons, and the jarring that came from a full-blooded strike on a bronze body was appalling. Despite the time they spent together, no friendship formed between the two. Bollo inherited none of his father's easy-going ways. Instead, he was aggressive and increasingly cocky, demonstrating no camaraderie or empathy for others. After a time, Morgan declined to make himself available to train further with the Half-Orc. He wanted no part in fostering the bully that Bollo was rapidly becoming.

The recovery of the Oracle and construction of the estate was a time of healing for Morgan. His mind felt clear, and he was becoming himself again – albeit a new self.

Oddly, people arrived at the estate before it was completed, pilgrims drawn to the location through visions and dreams. They helped with the construction and then took up roles that maintained the residence and grounds, even growing and preparing the food. It seemed to Morgan that his task was complete.

CITY OF THE ARK

Athose travelled with two Colossi and several Brula. He balanced himself on the shoulder of a colossus he named Hu. The other he called Sandman. The Mad King explained that the servants of the Ancient Ones did not have names and that it was not up to a boy to bestow names where they served no purpose. The Mad King made Athose responsible for finding more Colossi and entrusted him with the bell. The young Elf diligently explored the mountain range for signs.

Sandman had been easy to find. The native people of the region marked out the valley as a sacred place with totems and rock drawings. When he investigated, Athose felt the spirit of the Colossus fill the air, it called to him on the wind. Hu struck the bell. One great clang was enough to crumble the side of the mountain and reveal a second Colossus. Since then, Hu sounded the bell a further three times, but those locations proved to be false leads. The landscape was left scarred and rubble-strewn in their wake.

Now Athose was in a valley between two towering mountains and the sense of spirit in the air felt palpable. With signs all about him – an abundance of fish in the river, deer hiding in the shadows of the valley walls, clumps of mountain flowers with their vivid colours – it was all drawn from power exuding from the earth around them. This time when Sandman struck the bell, a thunderous crack sounded, followed by a great rumble and a sudden shake of the earth. Along the valley on both sides, massive chunks of stone and rubble avalanched downwards and filled the valley floor. Hu and Sandman strode quickly to the centre of the valley to avoid being buried or crushed. From his shoulder perch, Athose gasped, then laughed. The Mad King would be very pleased. It was a magnificent spectacle as six colossi flexed to break free of their rocky prison, then stretched like any humble human that had just awoken from a long sleep. Looking about, they appeared to share an understanding, although Athose could hear no words. After giving them a short time to reacquaint, the young Elf indicated to Hu and Sandman that it was time to continue west, traversing the range. They complied, and in their own time, the Colossi followed.

The Brula brought word of the discovery to the Mad King who was indeed pleased with Athose' progress. He was equally as satisfied with the advancement of the City of the Ark. It was probably premature to call it a city, but it was on its way to being a thriving community. Tribesmen from the region and migrants from elsewhere travelled to the Ark to trade and start businesses. It helped that the area was abundant with natural resources, with the discovery of gold in the local waterways the most notable. It was still an untamed habitat though, and the native tribesmen were not entirely agreeable to an influx of prospectors and claims on their lands. The Mad King left the people to work out these differences for themselves.

His focus was on the community within the Ark, which spilled out into residences around the great ship. Most of those leaving were female slaves with their babies and small children – part of the breeding program. About half of the children possessed Orcish features. One in thirteen of the children bore similarities to the Molemen. The resemblances varied from small characteristics such as pale skin or pink eyes, to children who were almost indistinguishable from their monstrous fathers. Through the slave conditioning, they were leaner and potentially tougher than their fathers. However, it wasn't what the Mad King hoped for, and as he grew bored, he called the experiment to an end. Thousands of pregnant slaves and their offspring were expelled from the Ark, leaving just his Molemen, wasteland soldiers, a handful of Two-Face Orcs, and the oar slaves that would again be required to power the majestic vessel. While he didn't give the slaves that departed the Ark their freedom, he did not set anybody in command of them either. He was curious to see how that evolved.

It wasn't surprising that, after living in the darkness of the Ark for such a long time, the freed slaves chose to dig their homes in the earth amongst the roots of the forest, and then much deeper until they encountered bedrock. Above them, the community also took shape, with areas of trees cleared by the migrants to make way for streets and buildings. Mostly the influx of local tribesmen made their homes in and around the tall trees as they had done for many generations. On the nearby coast, the Traders Guild were constructing a port and facilities. Guildsmen were taking control of the trade in gold which they knew would soon attract more wealth seekers to the region.

Ishnar, Head of the Trader's Guild, met with the Mad King in a clearing, with benches set about a small table. The King seemed distracted and stared past the forest and out to sea. Ishnar moved from his seat to stand before the man, to look him eye to eye. He reiterated his key points.

"This region needs stability. Under the guidance of the Guild, the mining, warehousing, and shipping would be regulated. Profits would be maximised and for your part, you will be a wealthy man. Let us establish a policing force, protect our investment, and to secure the outer regions we should extend through Drager Pass."

The Mad King looked through Ishnar as if he were a window, still staring at the ocean beyond. Abruptly, he changed his focus and met the Merchant's gaze.

"Nobody is stopping you, Ishnar."

The Guild Master appeared as if he were about to talk, then thought better of it. Instead, he wisely stepped away from the King, gave a short bow and headed back towards the port.

When Athose eventually returned, there were twenty-two Colossi with him. While they were all similar in appearance, Athose found some small physical differences that enabled him to tell them apart. Although they did not speak to him, he also recognised different personalities in the way they acted and reacted to situations. In response, they rallied to Athose. At the city of the Ark, they appeared to acknowledge the authority of the Mad King.

At the Mad King's direction, the Colossi assisted the slaves to manoeuvre the great Ark back to the coast and then set it upon the ocean. Designed to hold giants from the North, the Ark was not large enough to fit these Colossi from the mountains. Instead, as the Ark pulled away from land, Hu sat cross-legged on the main deck, as guardian to the bell, while the other Colossi walked into the sea, eventually dropping out of sight beneath the water's surface.

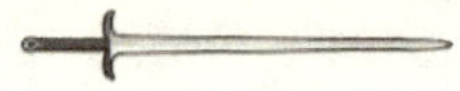

EXPEDITION

Morgan set sail from Viletri aboard his flagship. Three other Bracadian vessels followed, like sleek swordfish chasing a great shark. As he had done before, Morgan voyaged around the Cape of Knives and north along the coast of the Great Continent. When he passed the Icesleepers, he was surprised that the glaciers were thawing and sparkling with wetness. The occasional stream cascaded off their surface or through fissures in the ice - into the sea where mountain and ocean became one. It was a magnificent sight.

Against his better judgement, Morgan allowed the Half-Orc, Bollo, to travel with him - not that it was his choice. Bollo had taken the letter from his father to Mannace, who invited the young warrior to join the Viletri Rangers, both as a legacy and for a debt owed to Rollo. Now he and three other Rangers formed Morgan's bodyguard. Bollo was a hornet in a bee's nest, always causing problems and happiest when trouble boiled over into fights. Morgan would not be surprised if he awoke one morning to learn that the Half-Orc's throat was slit in his sleep. Perhaps that was just wishful thinking.

Morgan and his bodyguards disembarked at Landsborough. It was nothing like the town he visited decades ago. It was now a major port and hub for trade between the Bracadian Eastern Colonies and allied nations of the Great Continent. Like Viletri, Landsborough incorporated embassies and enclaves representing Galandar, Remman, Yanth, Arenland, the Rhalec, and many others. Morgan stayed only long enough to purchase horses for the rangers. He was too heavy himself for a horse but was able to maintain an easy run to keep pace.

An affluent port such as Landsborough was large enough to command a wizard patron who served as its protector. Morgan was wary of magic users since Render warned him that he would be vulnerable to sorcery and that his work to craft Morgan in this new form could be undone.

The trek to Galandar crossed a vast plain, sometimes crumpled into small hills and valleys, but mostly it was just long stretches of flat land. At one point they passed a cluster of mountains called The Prophets. The black granite forms jutted out of the landscape at odd angles and looked to Morgan as if enormous rocks fell from the sky, half burying themselves in the flat earth. Forest grew around the base of the formations, and it was the only piece of terrain Morgan passed in Roundhome that was not cleared for farms and crops.

When they crossed the border into Galandar, the highway became an endless chain of small towns busy with traders and markets. Soldiers patrolled the roads and kept the laws. In many locations along the way, there was new construction underway which came with the bustle of engineers, tradespeople, and labourers, and always long processions of carts and wagons carrying supplies up and down the highway.

Farms filled all the land around the towns. Only in the far distance on the horizon could be seen expanses of uncultivated wildlands.

It was several days before they reached communities with larger populations and more advanced infrastructure. Soon they were passing through cities as big as any Morgan had seen in his travels, and yet they were still many days from the capital. Here the land was cultivated, irrigated and alive with all colours of crops, orchards, and domesticated beasts. Soldiers continued to be ever-present, making the roads safe under their watchful eye. At times, Morgan and the Rangers would run into checkpoints where the soldiers questioned them, but they were easily satisfied with the explanation that they were travelling from the Blood Sea to the Capital.

The cities eagerly welcomed travellers and their money. At night when they rested, one Ranger would remain with Morgan, while the others were free to explore and enjoy the entertainment on offer. Bollo was as brash and intimidating as ever, but he was savvy enough not to get into serious trouble. The Half-Orc ran the fine line of the law, always intimidating or bullying, but not causing serious damage or harm, at least not where it might get him arrested or killed.

Finally, after weeks of travel, they arrived at the Galandar capital of Rotherdan. Taking their time to investigate places of interest, the travellers followed the directions given to the residence of Shepherd, who provided rooms for them and ordered his servants to prepare a feast. The Viletri ambassador seemed used to entertaining, and Morgan could see that he enjoyed an extravagant lifestyle.

Even though Shepherd was an attentive host, Morgan felt his mood darken. Something about the colossal size of Galandar and its capital made him uneasy. There was also a superiority to the way Shepherd handled himself that made Morgan think that he didn't measure up. However, he didn't know what measure that might be, and he had no tangible reason to believe the man was doing anything less than an excellent job. Morgan felt like drinking wine and possibly a tumble with a pretty wench, but that was just his mind taunting him. It all added to his frustration. He missed being human.

Over the next few days, many people came and went visiting Shepherd, and on one occasion a group of Remman stayed the night. The country of Remman shared a short border with Galandar, and they were allies in the war against the North. From what Morgan could tell, this was where the similarities ended. Like the Remman mercenaries he observed so long ago at Gormoth, these men were wiry and muscled as if bred and trained solely for war. As guests at Shepherd's mansion, they wore simple, plain clothes, but it seemed they would be more comfortable adorned in armour with weapons in hand. Morgan made sure to keep Bollo away from them. The leader of these men, a sharp-faced, dark-eyed man named Mendas, came to him as he stood in the courtyard one night.

He was direct.

"How did you become a man of bronze?"

Morgan relished the opportunity to tell his story and gave a colourful account of his time since meeting Mannace. He didn't see the need to hide any of the truth.

"Why do you ask?"

"There are many things that I don't know. Now there is one less. Why does the Colony of Bracadia send soldiers here to fight and die at the Rift?"

"Governor Mannace is committed to the war with the North."

"Ha! Remman is committed to the war with the North. For more generations than I know the Remman have trained and sent warriors to fight the North. Every boy trains, and when he comes of age, he joins the battle line. Governor Mannace sends a handful of men to die in a war he does not understand."

The Remman leader was forthright, and there was no malice in his tone. Morgan could appreciate the Remman's perspective, but he knew Mannace's motivations and felt more explanation was warranted.

"Mannace follows a vision that set him upon the task of strengthening the Blood Sea and Eastern Colonies to be ready for war with the North. Already we were victorious over their fleets and defeated their host in defence of our lands."

Morgan could see that Mendas was genuinely interested, so he continued.

"Mannace prepares the Colonies and their armies. In a vision of the future, Mannace commands the armies of the South in a great battle to defeat the North."

The Remman was quick to respond.

"Ha! the North will not be defeated in a single great battle. In the histories, there have been epic victories over the North and catastrophic defeats. Neither have ended the war. Still the war continues, and lines are constantly redrawn at the rift.”

“Do not underestimate Mannace. He will surprise you.”

“I will meet this Mannace one day. I am sure he is a great giant, with fists of steel and balls the size of barrels. You have not been to the Rift. I will show you the Rift, and you can tell your Governor what enemy he faces. Until you have seen the Rift, you cannot understand what the conflict is and why every man must join the fight.”

Now Mendas grinned at Morgan, and he puffed out his chest.

“You will see the Remman fight.”

Morgan liked the man, enough to agree to journey to the Rift to see firsthand what it meant to fight on that front. He had heard stories, but now they did not seem adequate. He asked Shepherd to send word to Mannace of his intent, and in the morning, he started the long march with his four Rangers, and the small band of Remman warriors.

ABSENT FATHER

Jaal shared a loaf of fresh bread, butter, and cherries with Casteel. They sat apart from the other Blood Legion and talked about the recent years as they ate. For much of that period, Jaal had lived with the Spider Mother and their swarm of children. He spoke freely about his role as lover, teacher, and peacekeeper. He talked with pride about the skill and abilities of the Spiderkin. Jaal confided in Casteel that his duty as a father to the Spiderkin, and as a friend to Mannace, was fulfilled. He was again, at least for the moment, a free Elf. For now, he chose to re-join the Legion, though Casteel remained in command.

Casteel and the Legion were paid from the colonial coffers and left mostly to their own devices. As commander of the renowned troop, Casteel was often approached directly by leaders and people in need, and she chose what assignments the legion would take or decline. Currently, the Blood Legion were deployed as peacekeepers at Karanthos. Since the sacking of that city by the Northmen, the Lordship of the region changed hands several times. Very recently, yet another of Mannace's appointed leaders met a messy end. Casteel travelled there to restore order and sort it out once and for all. The Blood Legion went about their work in a relaxed way and seemed able to blend into any community they visited. They were generally respected, liked, and trusted. Only the best warriors served in its ranks, a fact acknowledged by local soldiers who happily worked alongside them.

"What are your plans, Jaal?"

"What would you have me do?"

It wasn't what Jaal intended, but Casteel shared her concern.

"The Mad King worries me. The last time I saw him, he was collecting invincible giants. I observed one of the creatures, and it was ... formidable. I have heard that he set sail from his City of the Ark with them. He has so much power with these creatures. The Mad King can take anything he wants and defeat anything that stands against him.”

Jaal shrugged. When Casteel gave him a dirty look for his seeming disinterest, he added some context.

“He is just a man.”

“Do you truly believe that? The Alani has a term for such a man: a ‘Dark Light’. It is somebody not aligned to the path, somebody who shapes their own destiny and impacts those about them unpredictably. He is a risk to the future.”

“Like Mannace. He shapes the future.”

Casteel was a little annoyed that Jaal needed to have these things explained.

“No! Mannace follows his destiny. The Mad King is the opposite of Mannace. No Oracle nor sage can see the path of the Mad King because he moves against the current, chooses his direction. He goes out of his way to work against destiny and in doing that he may change all our fates.”

“Good for him. We should all be commanders of our destiny.”

Jaal appeared determined, making Casteel choose her next words carefully.

“There are those amongst the Alani that can see ahead in time, who comprehend the many paths. They foresee adversity, but ultimately the future is one of unity and peace. That is why they work with Mannace because he aligns with that future.”

Jaal was over Mannace and his bloody vision. Over Elves and their constant manipulation.

“Alani care only about their own destiny. A good future for the Alani may come at a cost for others. Everybody is in it for their own interests, however they may cloak themselves in fine words. I am a father. It is not my role to choose a path for my children. It is my role to prepare them and support them in shaping their path."

Casteel couldn't help but smile at Jaal's philosophy regarding fatherhood, which didn't go unnoticed. They ate quietly for a time. Despite his comments, Jaal was just as curious as Casteel to know what the Mad King was up to - tempted enough by the mystery that he made a snap decision.

"I will find the Mad King."

Vilera, Ya, and Rey joined them. Vilera was one of Jaal's Spiderkin offspring. She had a strikingly beautiful face, slim torso, and arms, with her abdomen and waist transforming into a sleek spider body. Eight long legs scuttled as she moved around the big Belg to stand before Jaal. She was naked except for a shoulder belt that held a curved blade, and a headband of silvervine that, amongst her kin, marked her as skilled in magic. Vilera learned the sword from Jaal and the basics of spell casting from the Northern mages captured by her mother. She was the first of her kin to seek experience outside of the Spider Mother's domain.

Jaal addressed his daughter.

"Tomorrow we move on."

MILAN TASH

Kakos Agamos was Lord over the city of Viletri. Mannace didn't think it through when he appointed Kakos. Unsurpassed as an administrator, Kakos no longer possessed much of the tact required for politics and negotiation. Having their city placed under the lordship of an undead threw the immortal Viletri into a foul temper that just dropped Mannace into a bad mood as well. They were constantly bickering, and the more outspoken Immortals went out of their way to sow discord amongst the populace. The whole city was infected with their darkness.

Viletri continued to grow and prosper despite political dissension. As the capital city of the Colony, it attracted people and trade from cities beyond any maps Mannace held in his possession. Milan Tash was spending more time at the port and Mannace formed a solid friendship with the man. He shared stories of far-off places with Mannace, but he refused to disclose the trade routes that made him incredibly wealthy. When Milan visited Viletri, he would always bring gifts that he knew would appeal to the Governor. This time Milan gave Mannace an enormous tusk recovered from some magnificent beast. The yellow tooth engraved with runes was hollowed out to contain a liquid. When Mannace pulled out the wooden stopper and poured a small amount on the table, it was white and viscous – at first, it oozed and spread out, but then contracted and expanded again as if taking a breath. Eventually, it lay still.

"The Mahoo call it the *Essence of Life.*"

Mannace laughed heartily, and Milan grinned as he realised why. He had not considered its resemblance to semen.

"I hadn't thought about it in such simple terms, but regardless of its potential source, it is something of a curiosity."

"Perhaps Render can make use of it."

Mannace saw an opportunity in everything, and he knew Render's passion for Life Magic. For now, he would add the tusk to the oddities displayed in his offices.

"I envy you, Milan. Your freedom to travel and do as you please, to explore these different lands."

"And I envy you, Mannace. There is a spark here that will ignite a new future for all lands, one of great industry, invention, and innovation."

Mannace felt that too.

"It is time to focus again on the war with the North. I have set myself a goal that in eight years, the march north will commence. Already in the last two years, preparations have begun. The priests take the message of war to the Eastern Colonies, and their voice will become the voice of the people. No force will be able to stand against our modern army, Milan. We will see in a new Age."

"I doubt not that you will bring a new Age, but you will need more than muskets when you move north. You enter a conflict that is many generations deep. It is a way of life for those involved."

"That is why I will need you with me."

Milan quickly changed the subject to trade, and they spoke at length about new opportunities. The two men drank mulled wine and ate fine foods brought to them by Jayne and his assistants. Nowadays, Jayne often blended his role of a bodyguard with that of a personal chef. Mannace's food taster found that a pleasant change, much to his surprise.

"How big is the world, Milan?"

"Bigger than I know, Mannace. The Guild of Merchants has been pursuing that very question. They have determined that the world is a sphere, like this apple." He picked up the fruit from a bowl on the table. "From what they can tell, the lands that we know cover but a small area.”

Milan took a small gold coin from his pocket and held it against the fruit.

“About this size. Often, new lands are discovered.”

“Where are the Eastern Colonies?”

“The Guild originated in Bracadia and is based there. Bracadia and all its colonies are within the area of the coin.”

Mannace typically took things at face value, but he was struggling to accept that the world might be so immense. That simple revelation, if true, challenged much of what he thought he knew.

“Knowledge is power, and I am sharing more than I am permitted with you, Mannace, but if we are to work together, it is important to understand our part in things. Knowing how big the world is now, does it change how you perceive the war with the North?”

“Yes, and no.”

It was much to comprehend, but one thought stayed clear with him.

“We must defeat the North. Are you immortal, Milan?”

The merchant smiled.

“We will see my friend, we will see.”

THE RIFT

Mendas took Morgan and the Rangers to the Rift. It was a deep crack in the earth, seemingly bottomless and perhaps the width of twenty ships laid end to end. Morgan was awestruck at its enormity.

"The width varies along its length so that in places it is like a valley, but in others the sides touch. The Northern side is mostly higher than the southern side".

From where he stood, Morgan could see the rift cut its way east and west, and indeed most of the northern land was obscured by the height of its bank. On the southern side, from what Morgan could tell, farms and communities were busy with everyday life and seemed mostly unaffected by the war on their doorstep. The group continued west, at times cutting back inland from the rift, then approaching it again to gain an appreciation for its immense size and variation of form. In one place, a host of Galandarian soldiers were encamped, thousands of infantry, archers, and horsemen. At Mendas' request, Galandarian Scouts escorted the travellers closer to the rift. The chasm's width near the camp was perhaps only ten ships laid end to end. It was still a wide space, but along it for a short distance, enormous roots cascaded down or protruded from the far bank and reached out across the divide to dig themselves into the earth on the southern side - a tangle of tree-trunk vines and man-sized thorns. There was bloody evidence of a recent battle, although whatever bodies had fallen had likely been thrown into the abyss, and any items of value taken back to the camp. A group of engineers were in deep conversation nearby. They seemed unperturbed as one of the vines moved, pushing deeper into the earth near them, then became motionless again.

Morgan looked at Mendas and back at the area.

"What is that?"

Mendas shrugged.

"They don't seem to know either."

He nodded at the engineers, then pointed west, and in the distance, Morgan could just make out another vine bridge.

A shape appeared in the sky above, then quickly descended and landed next to the engineers. It was a Brula, a soldier of the Eastern Colonies as clearly marked by its uniform. It took off after passing on a hurried message. The engineers turned and ran, signalling for them to do the same. As he fled, Morgan looked over his shoulder. Already the vine bridge was alive with insect-like figures that swarmed across then fanned out at an alarmingly fast pace. As Morgan and his troop followed closely behind the engineers, they passed by the Galandarians who already manoeuvred into formation to confront the attack. Arrows started to fill the sky above them. At Mendas' urging, they kept up their pace and left the sounds of the engagement behind.

Bollo came alongside Morgan.

"We should stay and fight."

Mendas replied from behind, "Not today".

When Bollo looked set to argue, the Remman added, "We have a message to deliver. Until that task is complete, the fighting must wait. Don't worry, Orc; there will be plenty of opportunity to dip your blade."

Bollo stopped and turned. Without any acknowledgement of his companions, he drew his sword and axe and ran back towards the conflict. Morgan simply shook his head, and the group continued away from the fight. Wordless, the other Rangers only exchanged glances.

Once well away from the skirmish, they cut inland for three days before moving back along a well-used road towards the rift. There were large camps, most of them with wooden barracks and some large enough to attract traders who constructed shops, taverns, smithies, and other buildings. Most of the troops here were Galandarian, but they also passed the Eastern Colonies encampment which was similarly expansive and impressive. At the Governor's insistence, the Colonial Council voted to renew their support of the conflict at the rift. From what Morgan could tell, the colonial troops in the region numbered in the tens of thousands, still modest numbers compared to the other nations' contingents.

The Remman camp at the Rift's edge was imposing, stretching along the southern cliffs for as far as Morgan could see in both directions. The chasm was much narrower here, and in places, the two sides rubbed up against one another. Where they touched, the northern bank was often much higher, forming cliffs, which were dotted with passages leading into the earth. In other places where the gap was wider, bridges angled upwards, some of them broken or burned. Remman soldiers guarded the connections, and their sentries could be seen on the distant cliffs as well. Warriors crossed back and forth, many of those returning from the northern side were injured themselves or helping wounded comrades. Mendas looked concerned.

"When I left, we had struck deep into the North and even lay siege to the cities of the Veldaan. It seems we have lost ground in the last few months. I have a message to deliver. Pitch your tents here."

As they set up their shelters, Morgan examined the camp about them. There were no permanent buildings, rather thick hide tents rounded like huts. Some were moss-laden at their base as if they had been there for many months. The Remman themselves were fierce in appearance, most bare-chested, although some wore breastplates, vambraces, or greaves. Those moving to and from the front carried round shields, spears, and swords. Like Mendas and his men, they all seemed bred for war. Morgan noted that there was not a lot of humour to their interactions with one another, but no friction either. He would best describe them as professional soldiers - disciplined. From what he observed looking about the camp, the Remman men took care of their own cooking and other basic needs. There were no camp followers. Morgan could not make out the leadership or unit structure.

Familiar soldiers from Cavastock passed nearby. There were perhaps three hundred of them, leading their horses through the Remman throng and up one of the less steep ramps to the Northern side of the rift. They were heavily armoured and carried long spears as well as swords and shields. Even their horses were donned in metal plates and chainmail to protect them. Along the rift, Morgan could see a mass of other units making their way into the cliff tunnels or across the bridges. There was a smattering of other Eastern Colonies forces; Two-Face Orcs, Archers from Sylos, and Yanth Pikemen. In the air were Brula scouts and he observed one of the Iron Jaw bull riders fly directly overhead. However, the colony forces were few compared to the massive movement of the Galandar troops who seemed to cover the land like endless trails of ants as the march across the rift intensified. Mendas returned.

"The Southern Generals are determined to keep their hold north of the Rift. News would have it that the enemy is digging in, which means they don't have the numbers to push their counterattack, or they're waiting for reinforcements. The Remman camped here will cross the rift tonight. In the morning, we join the attack."

THE MASTER

Render knew that he was losing his way, but what was the point of immortality if he couldn't take a little time to indulge? The Fallen called him *The Master* and, as such, all cultists and warriors paid him homage, did his bidding, and explicitly followed his directions. He helped them to restore their places of worship and power. His magic recalled the demon deities that underpinned their faith and controlled the nightmare creatures summoned from the depths of the Dark Dreaming. Render's influence with Mannace allowed the Fallen to restore their nation without unwanted interference. Exotic, uninhibited women competed for his attention. He once thought he might grow tired of that, but now he could not imagine going back to his life before becoming The Master.

Working with demons was like playing with fire. It took all Render's wits and too much of his precious time to keep them in check. There were perhaps as many as sixty demons, the Dreamers, living amongst the cultists, brought into existence through ritual summoning. They were from the third Hell and took on a variety of forms and minor abilities. The three that consumed most of his time were Ruu, Gax, and Fek. Ruu was the Demoness of Pain, and she had two forms that she freely moved between. The first was that of a misshapen, giant ghoul, and the second was human, beautiful, but also twisted and with eyes that were plain white like polished pebbles. Without Render's influence, her appetites for killing and sadistic pleasures were insatiable.

Gax was human-like and tall, skeletal to the point that his bones pressed hard against his skin. His face was elongated, almost equine, with two twisted horns that extended from his forehead. Orange eyes blazed like fires. Gax could summon and control flame and left to his own devices would set everything ablaze. Like Ruu, he liked to mix his sexual appetite with sadistic play.

Fek's shape appeared to have once been human, but his skin was grey and, like Gax, tightened to the point that he was deathly gaunt and hairless. Small eyes looked out from sunken sockets and both his teeth and nails were long and sharp. The cultists called him the Demon of Nightmares for his habit of ambushing men or woman as they slept, raping, and often maiming them. Fek was obsessed with the smell of blood, often covered in the gore of his victims. During daylight hours he slept in the basement below Render's tower residence, in a gruesome nest carefully constructed of skin and body parts.

The demons emanated power; raw magic that the cultists could draw on. The Followers of Fek lived in or around the tower and provided Render's personal servants and guards. Their ability to blend in and not be seen suited Render. The sorcerer benefited from his contact with the demons, and by reciprocating, the Demons in turn also grew in power. Like his other vassals, they became dependent on him. In establishing this bond, a partnership of sorts with Ruu, Gax, and Fek - he now had a real sense of what demonology and the cult were about. As well as access to their abilities, Render felt their consuming lust and hate, but was resilient enough not to let those things engulf him, at least for now.

Render spent very little time at his residence in Viletri. His apprentices and the animators took care of themselves, and in addition to the Animator's Guild, the wizards recently established their own Conclave. They all still took commands from Render and assisted in his arcane endeavours when needed.

The Animators powered the industry of Viletri. Most aspects of city life benefited from their influence, and to fuel their innovations, the slaughterhouses that processed food for the city now also collected the life essence of the slain beasts. Some farms bred livestock for the primary purpose of enabling the Animator's work.

At the centre of it all, Kakos felt intimately connected to the city, to all those parts powered by the life force he could feel and control. Not that the animators understood that, even Render seemed blinded to it. Controlling the life force was the only unique talent Kakos acquired, but he did it exceptionally well.

Everything Kakos achieved was through hard work and unwavering determination. He was proud of the city of Viletri. Proud of his zombie workforce that kept the city running. It would be so much easier if everybody were as simple to control as the undead. Kakos' loyalty to Mannace helped keep him focused, gave him a broader purpose, and reminded him that he was both a Lord and a servant.

Interestingly, Kakos further discovered that music helped him to remember passion, hope, intimacy, and ambition. Through music, he was re-exploring an old self that was mostly forgotten.

A MODERN SOCIETY

Saska established a residence in the City of Antigoth that was like the one she and Jaal possessed in Viletri. Here, in the capital of Arenland, Saska's mansion was famous for the beautiful woman who resided there and the wild parties they threw for the gentlemen elite. In a city that held little patience for magic, they turned a blind eye to the demoness living in their midst. Not that Saska resembled the wild creature she was when she first met Jaal. Now she dressed in elegant clothes and knew how to live in modern society, though everything about her was still hypnotic and seductive. It helped that Saska had the protection of the Temple Order of War. Ahmeda visited from Ostoik regularly to continue Saska's training and to solicit her assistance with Temple projects.

Saska trained her own apprentice, Jesephene, who since leaving Render's service to reside with her, proved herself not only useful as a healer but also eager and capable as a seductress. While in her employ, all Saska's followers emulated in a small way her ability to take a little of a lover's life, enough to keep them young and vivacious. Jesephene, though, could dominate a lover, a control that lasted well beyond the bedroom. It meant that Saska and her household maintained useful friends in both high and low places.

Lord Angelcry and the Overlord would sometimes visit Saska's establishment. The Overlord was old and bent and needed a stick to walk, or when he was at his worst, a servant to push him about in a wheeled chair. The ruler of Arenland was always sharply dressed in the finest tailored clothes topped with a tall, brimmed hat. While his outward manner was gentle and kind to strangers, he was mean and ruthless in the way he treated those closest to him, and he possessed some unusual tastes that required Saska to make special arrangements when the Overlord visited. By comparison, Lord Angelcry was handsome and a genuine gentleman. When he visited Saska's house, he was the only one she cared for personally. He was visiting Antigoth more regularly in recent months.

Deedee, a beautiful and intelligent young woman, ran Saska's household at Viletri. Saska and Jaal seldom visited. Therefore, the regular patrons had started calling the residence *Deedee's*. It became a refuge for retired Blood Legionnaires - often those maimed or severely wounded would use the old barracks that made up part of the estate. In return, they protected the girls who looked after them.

Deedee visited Antigoth. She travelled to Ostoik by rail and then shared a carriage to the capital with an obese merchant who, between short, laboured breaths, offered her coin to sit on his lap. She did more than that and, as well as a pocket full of silver; she also felt invigorated and alive. It was Deedee's first time in Antigoth, and it amazed her with its majesty and opulence. Near the city's centre, the streets were full of people and lit by glass globes hanging from poles. As well as the main thoroughfare for carriages, wagons and horses, there were separate paved paths for civilians, dressed in their fancy clothes. A welcome innovation that enabled pedestrians to avoid the plentiful horse dung. Deedee wished that Viletri would emulate it. Perhaps a word in the right ear after coitus would do the trick. Shops opened their doors onto the pavements, and some businesses fronted glass windows that showcased their wares. Deedee could see tailors, bakers, smiths, grocers, and shops full of the latest fashions and contraptions.

Alsaborg was there to welcome Deedee and see her to Saska's residence. He was looking older with patches of white fur around his snout and ears. He didn't enjoy the same benefits as Saska's female followers. She hugged him dearly.

"Hey, big dog. We've missed you back in Viletri. You should come and visit."

He gave a toothy grin.

Deedee was excited and nervous about meeting with Saska. Being near Saska made her blood pulse and breath quicken. The sensations were both primal and sexual, giving Saska complete domination over Deedee if she chose to use it. Alsaborg waited for Deedee to freshen up in a guest room before taking her to the top story balcony that overlooked Antigoth's central city square. Saska was there.

"Deedee, come and sit with me."

Deedee did as instructed. It gave her time to calm herself, although her mind was still too clouded to initiate any conversation. Saska continued with some small talk about the view. Once Deedee seemed more settled Saska started with her questions.

"Has Jaal been at house?"

"Only briefly, mistress, before leaving for Karanthos."

"No matter. I asked you keep track Mannace. What news you have for me?"

"He has travelled twice to Yanth, but mostly people come to visit him. There are new military bases near Viletri and at Dos Neran and he has told his officers that he wants two hundred thousand soldiers trained. He calls it a modern army."

Saska's tone was sharp. "Anything interesting?"

"The Governor has made several visits to an estate west of Viletri."

"Why he go there?"

"I don't know mistress."

"Who he see there?"

"I don't know who he meets with, mistress."

This time Saska's sharpness could cut steel.

"Is there any limit what you don't know, Deedee? Find out. Ask yourself questions I ask, and next time come with answers. I would thought, of everybody, you and I have most interest knowing that man's business. I want information I use, Deedee. Understand?”

Saska’s gaze was fire and Deedee felt trickles of sweat between her breasts that ran down across her stomach.

“Yes, mistress.”

“What else happened Viletri?”

Deedee was not sure what was of interest, but she tried her best to answer.

“Migrants from Bracadia have started arriving. They are mostly the families of sailors in the fleet. Some sailors weren’t expecting their kin, and wives arrived to find their husbands had died in the war with the North or had taken new mates.”

“What happens wives with dead husbands?”

“I don’t know.”

“Deedee, make sure wives looked after.”

“Yes, mistress”.

Again, the fiery gaze, scrutinising Deedee to take a measure of her composure. Not knowing what else to say, Deedee did her best to meet the demoness’ glare and repeated her answer.

“Yes, I will ensure the wives are taken care of, mistress. There is space at the barracks, and they will be fed and clothed. I will do what is needed.”

Deedee went on to describe other things she had made a note of, and Saska did not interrupt her again. When Deedee finished, she was allowed to return to her room, and in the morning, started her return journey back to Viletri. As she boarded her carriage, Alsaborg came and instructed her to return in two months and give another report. Deedee hugged the Daglari again, and they wished each other good fortune.

WAR AT THE RIFT

The war on the northern side of the rift was beyond anything Morgan imagined. It was of immense scale that was both spectacular and horrifying. The Remman soldiers he accompanied were not committed to the battle right away. Instead, they divided into three large forces and deployed behind the allied front. The contingent that he and Mendas were attached to waited on a slope that overlooked the central battle line. Like the Southern side of the rift, the land here was once farmland, orchards, and communities. Now the earth was a criss-cross of makeshift defences, trenches, and battlefields, for as far as Morgan could see, all littered with debris and death.

The battle line spread east and west for a great distance. From his high vantage point, Morgan saw reinforcements arrive for both sides, pressing the attack or rushing to the defence where needed. Occasionally there was a flash of magic, but so far no sorcery mighty enough to impact the shape of the battle.

Morgan, and the tens of thousands of Remman warriors on the slopes with him, did not have to wait long to be involved in the action. The order came to push forward. As the Remman moved down the hill and across the pastures and fields, the warriors gathered into formation, always five ranks deep. The most senior soldiers manoeuvred to the front. Mendas and Morgan were amongst those at the fore, while the three Rangers trailed behind.

With rehearsed precision, the Remman moved through the Galandar units that made up the front lines, and soon Morgan was rewarded with his first look at the enemy as they closed quarters.

The Northern troops they faced defended a low stone wall, marking the boundary of a neglected farm. There were a mix of Veldaan heavily armoured infantry in deep ranks as well as lighter armed forces with javelins and spears. The enemy soldiers appeared organised, clean-cut, and very similar in appearance to the Galandarians.

As the Remman came closer to the wall, Javelins filled the air. Morgan could sense the tension about him as the spears reached the top of their arch, but at the last second, the Remman warriors instinctively stopped and crouched, their large round shields raised to form an effective barrier against the missiles. Along the line, javelins clattered about as they ricocheted off the defence. One spear bounced off Morgan's shoulder. When the barrage ended a shout rose from the Remman warriors in the first rank, and like clockwork, shields were lowered, and the march continued forward.

The javelin throwers retreated as more heavily armoured soldiers replaced them. Morgan was expecting a charge, and it seemed an anti-climax when the Remman walked the gap towards their opponents. As they engaged, both sides kept tight formations, slashing, and stabbing at each other across the wall. The Remman were disciplined, well-practised, and patient. The Northmen were experienced too and bashed at the Remman shields searching for gaps in the metal wall. Morgan could see that the Veldaan troops had an advantage of heavy armour to protect them. Notwithstanding the measured approach to the engagement, there was still savagery in the attack, and soon men were dying on both sides, while others clambered to fill the front ranks.

Using his gift of magical strength, Morgan kicked over a section of the stone wall and waded into the enemy defenders, swinging his blade in wide arcs to clear himself a path. Behind him, a fresh warrior took his place in the Remman line.

Morgan's weight and strength allowed him to move about and be a great menace amongst the enemy ranks. He felt like a butcher: hacking off limbs and cutting deep into flesh. It was a practical but gruesome style, and Morgan was grateful for the practice with Bollo. It was around him that the enemy first started to fall back. To both sides of Morgan, the Remman became ascendant and keeping their line as best they could, they crossed the wall to press home the assault. It was not until the enemy started to panic and break that the Remman abandoned their formation to allow those in the deeper ranks to flow through and join the pursuit. The Remman were highly skilled and efficient killers, faster than the heavily armoured enemy. Merciless.

In the distance, behind the Northern lines, Morgan heard the loud blasts of horns, and riders appeared - a great host of them. The Remman warriors were quickly aware, and in an orderly fashion, they began to break combat and hurry back towards the other Southern troops. Morgan was impressed that even as they hastily retreated, they reassembled into units so that if need be, they could turn and be ready to defend an attack.

As the Remmans passed by them, units of Galandar pikemen, halberdiers, and archers were already marching into place. The Pikemen would be useful against cavalry and Morgan could see from the manoeuvring that the generals knew what they were about.

At a gallop, the enemy horsemen quickly covered ground to where the southerners defended. What seemed a decisive push-back of the enemy host only moments ago, swung about so that the Southerners were now scrambling to defend. Hundreds of thousands of enemy cavalries suddenly commanded the plains.

"They are magnificent, Mendas, like the tide sweeping across the sands. Mesmerising." Morgan approved.

The Remman, bemused, shook his head at Morgan's misdirected praise.

"It will not be so magnificent if they turn and charge. It will be a bloody day."

It was not to be, and the cavalry seemed satisfied for now to cover the Veldaan retreat. Some of the riders came close enough that Morgan sighted their faces; hard-looking men with long beards and moustaches. Most wore light armour, brandishing a variety of weapons. Although numerous, Morgan could see why the enemy might not charge against large numbers of halberds, pikes, and bows. It appeared that the battle was at an impasse.

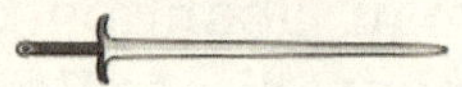

A GREAT DEFENCE

As the day progressed, Galandarian carts arrived at the front line, unloading palisades the height of a tall man. All along the front line, the sections of palisade quickly came together as a wall. Engineers, assisted by Galandarian troops, used the emptied carts to gather rocks and any other rubble they could find to place behind the barrier as reinforcement. Soldiers shovelled dirt to make a trench in front of the wall and a rampart behind it. In some areas, large caltrops were scattered as an obstacle to cavalry if they were to attack. Other carts with a ballista on them were next to arrive, parked at intervals behind the walls and tall enough to fire over them. By the afternoon of the next day, the barricade encompassed all territory north of the rift that was currently held by the southern forces.

The cavalry that confronted them yesterday were nowhere to be seen, though Morgan expected that the Brula were keeping a careful track of them. Other reinforcements joined the enemy ranks. Amongst them were the first non-human troops he had seen since the insects, goblins in large numbers and the occasional giant ambling along behind the main lines.

On the southern side, he knew the Eastern Colony forces were part of the defence, but they must have been on the distant flanks. Here at the centre, Galandar reinforcements continued to arrive. Morgan looked to Mendas to learn more.

"What happens next?"

"A new chapter. Remember this is not a war that will be won with a single battle or on a single field. Here a new line has been drawn, and both sides make their preparations. Raising a defence like this is a new strategy. We must trust that the generals know what they are doing."

"Why did the enemy horsemen not attack when they had

the element of surprise?"

"Because they are not so desperate to have a victory that they would risk a bloody defeat. The horsemen from the Ryde did what they needed to do. They come from the plains to the Northeast, and we have fought them many times. We will meet them on the field another day."

"Mendas, the Remman are excellent soldiers. Their discipline is extraordinary."

"The Remman are bred for war. We live and die by the spear and sword."

"There is a new kind of war coming. The army of the Eastern Colonies has new weapons and devices never seen before at the rift."

"We will adapt, and the enemy will adapt. You might be surprised at the things I have seen at the rift; when the sky is black with demons and the battlefield dead rise hungry for your flesh, then you will be tested. What you see now is a skirmish compared to battles past and battles that will come."

Morgan simply nodded. The scale of the warfare here was a shock to him. The thought that the battle he witnessed might be a minor conflict was beyond his comprehension.

THE AVATAR

At first, The Architect enjoyed the grounding and soulfulness he felt when his spirit form was bound to the grand marble block. The stone medium helped him to focus as he manoeuvred his consciousness through the passages of time, sifting through the myriad of data and searching for those bits of knowledge that would help to shape or influence the present world. But the stone also limited his communications to just those apprentices that placed their hands on the rock. Often the apprentices did not have the comprehension to understand, shape, and utilise the data he relayed to them. In addition, he could not see into their world except through their thoughts and words. It became increasingly unsatisfactory. To resolve the problem, The Architect instructed the apprentices to craft for him a human mask. He remembered liking silver, and he preferred a serious, unemotional expression. Such details were always paramount.

At first, he planned for one of his students to wear the mask, but they convinced him that a statue of the same marble he was encased in now could be made and animated, with the facemask fitted permanently. In fact, with the help of a Technomancer, the animators were also able to assist with vision and speech. While he preferred to develop his own unique solutions, The Architect was not above utilising other ideas if it added some value. He knew the major challenge would be creating a link between his consciousness in the stone and the silver mask. He told his students that the marble statue must be tall, at least a head taller than a normal man, and slim. It was important to him that the hands and fingers would allow him intricate movements. The Architect performed similar things in the past, or perhaps it was in the future.

What he needed next was a large amount of energy. Once ready, his apprentices transported the marble block and animated statue to the manufactory. A pit designed by the Dwarves produced the intense heat that was needed to shape the toughest alloys. Engineers helped to prepare the chemicals and other elements required. Then the fire was lit. The marble block that was The Architect was suspended above the intense blue flame. As the heat increased The Architect drew it to himself, focusing the energy on a point in the centre of the block. Using his mind, he minimised the focal point until the power was targeted at a single particle. He pulled at the particle until it expanded - remaining one particle but now in two parts. One of the parts he left where it was and the other he drew forth into the newly constructed statue, attaching it to the forehead of the mask. His mind relaxed. The Architect tested the link and was pleased that he could travel via the particle so that he could be in both the marble block and in the masked statue at the same time.

Through the statue, senses flooded back into his consciousness. Not complete human senses, but at least sight and sound. He could also feel that start of control of other mechanics such as voice and movement, although these would take some practice. He spoke through the new medium.

"Done."

The students, animators, and manufactory engineers set the marble block back on the earth, and they marvelled as the architect moved his new body, his avatar, for the first time. The Architect felt resistance from the particle, and it was soon apparent that the two parts resisted separation, so that the distance the statue could travel from the block was limited. Although it was satisfying to see the world again, it was time to get back to his work and continue the study of up-and-down. His success here gave him some critical insight, potentially a breakthrough as to how he might progress or even bypass that challenge.

THE NAVIGATORS

The Architect had no sense of time in the present world. However, since he split the particle, space-matter was becoming his domain, and the success in stretching the element between the block and statue exposed his spirit self to new sensations and possibilities. It was not long before The Architect was able to lift and move the marble block that held his essence. By manipulating that one particle in space-matter, he could affect all matter attached to it. This phenomenon went far beyond the levitation that was achieved with Technomancy to date. It had the potential for instantaneous movement across space. Now, with an inkling of what he was looking for, it helped when searching the passages of time for clues and insights. It became apparent to him that he needed two things, a device for containing a large amount of energy in a usable form, plus people with the mental dexterity to manipulate space-matter. Creating tools was his forte, and with the knowledge he gathered through his visions and access to the resources at Viletri, he was confident in his ability to solve that challenge. He remembered creating such a device before, although memory was less tangible in the conflux of time, and unfortunately, the equipment he had designed was now lost with the Dwarves.

Finding people that could navigate space-matter was a more significant trial, and the Students of the Architect, known now as SOTA, were assigned to solving it. Governor Mannace already put his support behind the work, so they were able to cast a wide net to find the right people.

It was almost two years before they discovered the first Navigator, and another year for the second. Once SOTA knew the characteristics common to the early Navigators, they uncovered six more. All candidates were simple of character except that each excelled in one small aspect of their lives – often exceptional with numbers, an ability to remember detail, or a penchant to see beyond the physical world into that of the dead. *Touched* in some way, so that their minds could extend beyond the norm.

Meanwhile, from his seat as Governor of the Eastern Colonies, it was obvious to Mannace that they were in a golden age of prosperity and collaboration. The flow of wealth and ideas between communities and even to distant shores, heralded a time when all nations of the Eastern Colonies enjoyed peace at home, growth of their economies, expansion in trade, and progress in many other areas. Even though they struggled to afford the annual Bracadian tribute, increased homeland security and prosperity was giving the people renewed confidence. It was a new world, very different from the past.

Mannace's plans for the military were progressing nicely. His two hundred thousand Colonial troops were in training, and the nations of the Colony were all making their preparations for war with the North. The activity created cohesion amongst the Eastern Colonies and motivated those nations or leaders that had a penchant for war. There were still ongoing skirmishes with the Northerners along the western shores of the Great Continent, and the Colonial fleet was determined not to allow the Northmen to rebuild their ports and fleets at those locations.

When Morgan returned after two years abroad, including more than a year at the front line, Mannace called an Assembly of War. It was sobering to hear from Morgan the scale and history of the Northern conflict at the rift. The Elven Congress, as they called the collaboration between the Alani, Fogmir, and Dark Elves, were tasked with collecting further information and maps of the Northern lands.

Internally, four hotspots within the colonies consumed Mannace's time. In the Madlands, there was now a dominant warlord simply known as "The One", confirmed to be a daughter of the Mad King. Her dominance restored some stability to the region, and Mannace gave her active support in return for her pledge to the Colonial Council. It was an uneasy peace that held the Madlands together, forged in steel and blood.

His most frustrating problem was that Tarash Gormoth was falling to financial and moral ruin under the heavy hand of the Slave King. The King broke the people and was remaking them in line with his dark vision. Kakos sent food and other supplies to help rebuild communities and sustain that nation's populace, but the ships returned with their holds full, turned back by the Slave King's agents. In all other respects, the King obeyed the rules and played his role as a member of the Colonial Council, enough to stay Mannace's hand as Governor.

The third hotspot was yet another legacy of the Mad King, left behind when he travelled North. The City of the Ark was a wealthy and rapidly growing community on the edge of the Colonial territory, and Mannace thought it would be easy to assimilate them into the Colony. The Merchant's guild, who controlled the region, were not of the same opinion and negotiations were not going well. Mannace waited for a visit from Milan to get his assistance or advice. In the meantime, the Ark remained independent.

The last hotspot was the Orcs of the Black Pass. The four Orc tribes agreed under duress to join the Colony. Still, they continued to fight amongst themselves, and they were also raiding southeast into Vlustoven, which would cause more significant problems if allowed to continue. Mannace was of a mind to use the Orcs as practice for his new military. Instead, after consultation with his advisors, The Governor sent Morgan and the Charikon divisions to bring the Orc tribes into line. As they prepared to depart, Mannace stood on the deck of the Celestial with Morgan and Urgar the Gull. The three men enjoyed talking while the crew prepared for departure. Mannace approached the plank to disembark but turned and addressed the other men.

"If you should encounter a sailor named Kraken on your travels, please tell him that the Governor seeks an audience.”

Morgan and Urgar exchanged a glance that didn’t go unnoticed by Mannace.

“I know he’s a bloody pirate. He knew my father, and I have questions.”

“Yes, Governor”.

Urgar waited for Mannace to depart then ordered the crew to push off and raise the mainsail. He turned to Morgan.

“And we’ll invite the bloody *Goddess of Death* for breakfast while we’re at it.”

BENEATH THE SEA

Jaal stood at the very front of the Ark. He pitched his tent on the deck, not keen to spend time in the massive ship's hold where the Molemen and slaves went about their business. Vilera, who travelled with him, was content to live below deck. Behind Jaal, the enormous colossus sat cross-legged, one hand reached out to steady the great bell that was beside it.

Weeks earlier, Jaal watched the Colossus lean out over the side of the ship and strike the bell, twice. There had been a great turmoil deep beneath the sea. On the surface, waves as tall as the Ark almost toppled the great ship, throwing some of the slaves gathered on the deck into the sea. Now, whatever the bell summoned followed the Ark. Sometimes when Jaal looked ahead of the ship, he could see the immense shadow of the monstrous creature beneath the surface. More than once it had knocked against the bottom of the Ark, causing a massive jolt to those on board.

They travelled North. Twice, Bracadian galleons of the Eastern Colonies came alongside them. The deck of the Ark was taller than the top of their sails and Jaal called down to them, stating his authority, and securing their passage. When he was talking to the first group of ships, he saw the shadow of the sea creature pass under them. If it surfaced, it would easily have smashed them to driftwood.

The Mad King was looking for a deep harbour, and he found it in a fjord where the water seemed as deep as the mountains were high at its edge. There was a ruined port, razed by the Eastern Colony fleet like others along this hostile coastline. The resident Orcs and Goblins hadn't tried to rebuild the harbour or coastal fortifications, but they came now in numbers to confront the Mad King and his ship. There were perhaps three thousand warriors, and knowing Goblins, more were likely skulking about in the shadows.

Rather than risk his slave soldiers that were needed to power and run the ship, the Mad King sent out the Colossus. The King was surprised at the organisation of the Orcs, who withdrew in good order when it became evident that nothing in their arsenal could harm the creature.

Over the next weeks, the Mad King established a camp and restored the port facilities enough to be useful under his control.

The other Colossi caught up with the Mad King's forces. They came out of the sea, climbing up from the depths and striding across the rocky shore. When the Orcs returned in greater numbers, perhaps as many as fifteen thousand, complete with siege engines and contraptions designed to test the strength of the Colossus, there were now twenty-two gargantuan hulks confronting them. Wisely their leader decided to parley rather than fight, agreeing that the Mad King would keep the Port but expand no further inland. In his typical fashion, the King opened his gates to the enemy, and after a time the Orcs and Goblins mingled and traded with the Mad King's contingent. Jaal enjoyed seeing the Mad King at work, watching the world bend to his will. Orcs were setting up huts about the perimeter of the port, and the community was expanding. Jaal frequently talked with the King, but regardless of many in-depth discussions, Jaal was no wiser to his ultimate plan. It was clear though that everything he did aligned to some higher purpose. Although the Mad King seemed content for the moment to put his time into building this new home, Jaal was certain there must be more.

"Why have you stopped here?"

"It all began in the North. It will all end here too. I don't know what the end looks like, Jaal, but I can feel it, can't you, the coming together of a great story - the final volume in an epic saga."

That told Jaal nothing useful.

"What is your part in this story?"

"I don't know, but we must all prepare. I am not the only one; others who were there at the beginning are gathering their strength too."

"So, you once controlled great power?"

"Not at all. I possessed the least power, I was a servant, like my friends here. There is nothing more to me than what you see."

"I see a man with great authority."

The Mad King smiled, amused. Jaal expounded on what it was that drew him to the King.

"What greater power and influence is there than to swim freely against the tide."

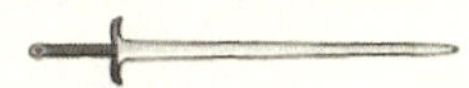

ATHOSE

Athose enjoyed the company of the Colossi, and in their way, they seemed to like having him around. He was also fond of Vilera and, like him, she didn't waste words. He was less sure about the company of his father. Jaal spent some time with Athose on the foredeck of the Ark, teaching him sword technique and sparring. Since his early apprenticeship in the Fogmir, Athose was not in the habit of practising, and it seemed both arduous and unnecessary. In essence, he already acquired the talents necessary for combat, preferring to grow his skill through experience. It also seemed to disappoint his father that Athose was unable to accelerate his movement as he could do. It wasn't that Athose didn't like his father, more the fact that he was relentless and expected much of the youngster. The Mad King, on the other hand, fascinated the young Elf.

The Mad King placed his confidence in Athose. Firstly, he trusted the young Elf with the task of finding the Colossi. Now in this Northern land, he tasked Athose with exploring the territory. The region was mountainous and forested in its lower valleys which gave Athose enough cover to move about unseen. He quickly learned that Orc and Goblin tribes lived about and under the mountains and in one area giant birds, crow-like, nested in a high vale. After a time, Athose found a mountain pass that was well travelled. Orcs patrolled the crossing, and Athose was wise enough not to risk exploring further alone.

Jaal and Vilera returned with Athose to the pass. With them were five hundred of the Mad King's slaves and ten of the indestructible Colossi. The pass wound between the mountains and at one point, where it was narrowest, they came upon fortifications. Orc warriors manned the defences, but it was no obstacle for the Colossi who smashed it apart and chased off the garrison. From this point forward, the pass was dotted with underground entrances, most fortified, yet again the Colossi easily cleared any defences. Jaal knew that there would be just as many entrances that they could not see, but he did not expect any force would be foolish enough to confront the Colossi. As the pass came to an end, it opened out to an expanse of wooded land. There was a more substantial fortress protecting the pass here, designed to be an obstacle to those entering the pass from the other side. Orc huts clustered in the valley behind the fortifications and more tunnels marked the mountainsides.

Perhaps as many as five thousand Orcs gathered at a distance to watch them pass, however, none stood in their way. The fort gates were open, but instead of passing through them, Jaal called the troop to a halt, taking up a defensive position.

An Orc Chief and his entourage of burly fighters approached Jaal. Like the Orcs of the colonies, these creatures were heavily muscled in their arms and upper body. Their jaws were unusually wide and protruding, with large tusks like those of a wild boar. They wore leather armour and furs, with a variety of iron forged weapons, mostly mauls and axes. The chief looked Jaal up and down and snorted. He spoke the common language. although his tusks slurred his words, and he drooled as he spoke.

"You can pass. Why you stop here?"

"This pass and road. We will travel it as we please."

"Do you want war with the Longjaw?"

The chief and his guards puffed out their chests. He pointed at one of the Colossi.

"The Longjaw have fought monsters before. The next time you enter lands of the Longjaw you will learn that Orcs are smart, not just strong."

"You will learn that the Men of the Ark make better allies than enemies."

Jaal called a slave over and drew the slave's sword from its sheath. He passed it to the Chief who accepted the steel blade and made a couple of cuts at the air. He seemed pleased, so Jaal ordered other slaves to hand over their weapons to the chieftain's entourage.

"Not enemies. Men of the Ark can pass through land of the Longjaw. Bring more weapons."

Jaal nodded. It was a beginning. He didn't have the patience to negotiate detail with Orcs - he would let the Mad King, or his lackeys do that. The King still employed some Two-Face he might set to the task. For now, Jaal was satisfied to move his troop out of the pass and skirt the woodland until he found an ideal place to make camp, still in sight of the Orcs fortifications. Jaal planned to make this a semi-permanent base, so he put the slaves and Colossi to work to clear and fortify a large area. It was audacious to establish a camp in the middle of hostile territory, but Jaal didn't feel part of the war, and having the Colossi to command made him feel untouchable. Regardless, in the mood he was in, he had no fear of the consequences.

While the others made themselves busy with the new camp, Athose and Vilera ventured into the woods to check the immediate surrounds. Athose was surprised that Vilera was as comfortable moving through the trees as he was, so it became something of a competition between them to lead the way. The forest was thick with trees but mostly void of animal life, likely the outcome of decades of foraging by the Orc tribes.

GATHERING

It was time to gather the armies of the Eastern Colonies for the march north. Mannace reached an agreement with the ambassador from Roundhome that the military would marshal on the plains north of Landsborough, and for a fair price, Roundhome would provide logistics and food for the force. He expected as many as three hundred and seventy thousand troops, which included his twenty divisions totalling two hundred thousand Colonial soldiers.

By his account, Yanth, Arenland, Iron Jaw, and the Rhalec each promised two divisions. He maintained his two Charikon divisions. Tarash Gormoth would provide a full division. The Blood Sea nations, Nations of the continent of Varghonia, Nations of the Barren Lands, and Nations bordering the Great Tundra would each provide a further division. Milan Tash promised ten thousand Charikon mercenaries, which matched his own Mercenary Division in number. Lastly, there was the Elven Congress who made up the final division and was already active as scouts across the North.

Most importantly, the great southern nations of Galandar, Roundhome, Remman, the Horseclans, and the Holy Lands all agreed on the timing of a major offensive. They would bring other nations of the Great Continent with them. In total the old alliances would put another million troops in the field, effectively doubling their current deployment. It was the most massive offensive in living memory, with energy and optimism evident in the preparations.

In support of the army, the combined fleet of the Eastern Colonies was almost six hundred vessels, an enormous armada that would both be a national defence and continue its work to harass the Northerner's western coast.

At last, it was time for Mannace to journey to the rift himself and meet with the other generals. Morgan and Milan would travel as his aides, while three hundred Rangers, commanded by Jayne, formed his bodyguard and messengers. First though, at the suggestion of Syprus, he spent a night at the Oracle.

Mannace visited the Oracle estate many times and slept the night there whenever he could spare the time. Strangely he experienced no further visions or explicit dreams. Rather, his mind would empty, and after a night of deep sleep, he always felt rejuvenated. After his final visit, he felt prepared to meet his destiny head-on.

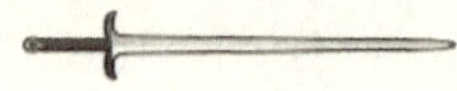

ROANNA

Elven scouts located the Mad King and Jaal deep in the Northern lands. As usual, the Mad King's motives were unclear, and the Elven Congress decided to keep a close vigil of his activities. By design, the Elves set Roanna the task, transporting her to the expanse of the forest surrounding the Mountains that were now the Mad King's domain. It was not long before Roanna discovered both Jaal, her father, and Athose, her beloved brother. She waited until Athose was exploring alone to reveal herself to him, appearing to step out of the forest shadow. She was as beautiful and graceful as she had always been, but now wild energy radiated about her, assaulting Athose' senses so that the hairs on his arms stood on end. Roanna's eyes were a deep mesmerising blue.

"Water and earth, brother."

"Earth and water, sister."

They held hands and placed their foreheads together so that their noses touched, and they could feel the other's breath on their face. Emotion flowed between them, and although each was used to walking their own path, both hearts eased with the reunion. Athose could feel the druidic power in his sibling, the sense of an impending storm or a flood. Roanna's energies ebbed, flowed, and sparked. As befitted a druid, she appeared a force of nature.

"You have become clumsy sister. I heard you coming a league away."

Roanna pushed him back.

"I didn't want to frighten you, brother. I remember how fragile you are."

Athose smiled.

"This is Vilera."

Roanna turned and was genuinely surprised. Vilera stood quietly behind her after descending from the trees on a thin web. Nothing escaped Roanna's notice in the forest, but this creature somehow eluded her.

"Blessings of the forest, Vilera".

The Spiderlings did not use pleasantries, and it was not a skill Vilera learned in her travels.

"We are sisters. I am of Jaal and Eya. You are of Jaal and Ahmeda."

Now that they were near, Roanna could sense the well of arcane power within her new sibling.

"You have magic."

"I am learning. I am fifth tier."

"We do not have tiers. We learn what we must learn. We do what we must do. In all things, nature is our source and guide."

There was an awkward silence. Athose finally spoke.

"I will take you to our father, then I will take you to the Mad King. I will show you the Colossi and the Ark."

"No, brother, my presence here is our secret". To include her sister, she added, "A secret between us. I will explore this forest and the lands surrounding it."

"This forest is at least fifteen days travel east and north. It is beautiful in the east – cliffs overlooking deep valleys, and in some places, there are trees three times the height of these."

He indicated the tallest of the trees around them. "I will join you."

Vilera added, "I will come too."

A NEW HOME

The forest in the East was as spectacular as Athose promised, even more so for Roanna who could sense the deep currents of power that flowed through the region – it fed and encouraged the giant trees and filled the woodland with life. Ancient rivers of an unknown source cut through the forest, leaving deep, cavernous ravines. It was a wild, beautiful land.

They stood atop a cliff gazing into one such gorge, made even more glorious by the giant trees on the opposite cliff whose colossal roots reached over the edge to hold tight to the rocky face and in places anchor themselves in wide cracks in the grey rock. Far below, a narrow but deep river poured over boulders and swirled as it moved quickly northward. Birds nested in the cliffs, and the trio enjoyed watching down on them as they glided and dived about the ravine chasing insects. Roanna reached out, and a bird landed on her wrist.

"Our people will journey here. It is a special place."

A very feminine voice came from behind them.

"Vilera."

They turned quickly, Athose with an arrow notched and his bow raised. In the shadow of the trees was a dark-skinned woman, naked and radiant. She took a step into the light.

"Mother."

Vilera was as surprised as the others. Lost for words, she repeated herself.

"Mother, how?"

"Ask your friend."

Eya gestured towards Roanna and acknowledged the Druid

with a slight tilt of her head.

"This is indeed a special place. You have done well Vilera."

Many other shapes appeared in the shadows and the trees near them. Athose counted eight Giant Spiders, ranging in body size from wolf to deer. While they were not part Dark Elf like Vilera, he could see a resemblance to his Spiderling sister in their body and legs.

Further along the ravine, a tide of black shapes cascaded over the side of the cliff and fanned out as many more of the spiders explored the landscape. Roanna was defiant.

"No! This will not be. I will not allow this."

In support of her words, the forest seemed to rise, becoming larger as if it was puffing its chest and there was a terrifying moaning from the earth itself as it answered the young Druid's call. A swirling wind swept through the trees and threatened to blow the whole party off the ledge. The spiders hunkered down.

Eya, the Mother of Spiders, raised her palm to face Roanna.

"Enough!"

It was as if Roanna's magic were never there. The spiders unfolded and were again their usual menacing shapes. All returned to normal, except the forest was now deathly quiet, and no animal or bird dared move. Eya looked across the chasm.

"This place will suit my purpose."

As the spiders did moments before, Fogmir Druids now manifested within the forest near the cliff, transported here by the same netherworld pathways. Instinctively, Athose moved in front of his sister to protect her from the spiders if fighting were to ensue, his arrow still aimed at Eya's chest. He saw several Druids crouched behind the foliage, but there were likely more that did not want to be seen. Two Druids revealed themselves to stand beside the youngsters. Both wore simple cloaks of forest colours. One clutched a tall staff in his right hand that glowed as if the sun reflected off it. The other possessed nothing that bespoke what magics she might have, but there was a look of wisdom in her face, and her eyes were sharp. She looked about, taking in the scene, then spoke softly.

"This is a place of power. A haven for nature and its creatures." Touching Roanna on the shoulder, she added, "You were right to summon us here."

Meanwhile, there were already webs crossing the lower reaches of the ravine, and giant spiders scaled the far cliff and scuttled up the broad trunks of the giant trees. Roanna felt the terror of the forest creatures as their haven was assaulted. It was like a plague that crawled across both the forest and her skin. From one of the big trees, a giant crow launched into the air. Athose recognised it as the same type of creature he saw in the mountains. It circled above the forest and squawked.

Summing up the situation, the female Druid spoke.

"We will negotiate. What do you want from this land?"

After a pause, and knowing the power of the Druids, especially in this place, Eya responded coolly. The reality now was that what she desired was no longer possible. She wanted a place in the North where she could prepare while remaining unnoticed. While this place was secluded and rich in food, there was already unwanted attention. She was irritated by the interruption to her plan.

"What I want is my business."

"Are we not allies, Eya of the Spiders? Are we not of the Eastern Colonies at war with the North? Are we not in the midst of the enemy lands? An enemy that is vast and relentless."

The ignorance of the Elves always surprised her. How much they thought they knew and how the truth of things so often eluded them. They saw themselves as puppeteers, but often they were marionettes themselves, oblivious that higher forces pulled at the strings. These Wild Elves though seemed more pragmatic than some of their kin, less arrogant and likely more pliable. She was also watching the boy, Athose. There was something about the boy that drew her in, made her pay attention, to the point where it influenced her decision.

"The Elves of the Fogmir and the Spiders. If it must be, let us arrange it."

AN OLD DEBT

Render was expected to join Mannace and his army as they travelled to the rift. There were still some weeks to prepare while the army slowly marshalled at Landsborough. In the meantime, there were troubling rumours from the Great continent of a political divide between Galandar and the Horseclans. The Clans withdrew their troops from the rift and made themselves unavailable for talks. At the same time, Render heard that the Remman King was seriously ill. If he were to die, the Remman might fall back from the northern front to choose a successor. It was hard to understand the politics of nations Render had never visited, but discord amongst the countries made him nervous. Mannace remained calm, assuring Render they were on track.

Render made his way to the Undead Dormitory where he expected to find Kakos Agamos. The Lord of Viletri was spending more time at the building. Surprisingly, it was the first time that Render entered the Dormitory, and he was astonished at how many zombies were housed there. He looked in several large rest chambers that all seemed full of the undead standing quietly, leaning against the walls or each other. Some greeted him, but he ignored them. They were all dressed in the uniform of the public servants and were clean so that the smell of death was barely noticeable. Eventually, he ran into one of the two Necromancers also resident there.

"Georgan, where will I find Kakos?".

Georgan was taken aback to see the Sorcerer but recovered his wits quickly. "This way, Master".

He turned Render around by walking in the opposite direction, and the apprentice seemed overly keen to get him away from the central chambers. Render pointed to the central area.

"What is that way, Georgan?"

"The Dining Room, Master".

Georgan seemed to have forgotten that Render served his apprenticeship to a Necromancer. There was little that would shock or surprise him. At least that's what Render thought until he allowed himself to be led to Kakos' chamber. Georgan knocked on Kakos' door, and when it swung slowly open, Render entered.

Kakos sat at a desk working on some papers. The office was in good order with things neatly arranged. Each wall was shelved floor to ceiling, and every shelf was full of papers. Along one wall in front of the shelves eight young boys stood, bare foot and bare chested. One of them was singing a haunting high-pitched melody. Render was not about to let himself be distracted, and he knew that with Kakos, it was best to get to the point.

"Quiet boy! Kakos, when we march to the Rift, you will join me. I need my most powerful servants at my side."

Kakos didn't look up. He remained focused on his work.

"I am a servant of Viletri. My place is here."

"You have four weeks to put arrangements in place. Then we leave by ship for Roundhome."

This time Kakos did raise his head to meet Render's stare. His eyes were dark, but there were swirling shapes moving across them. To a normal man, it would have seemed both mesmerising and frightening, but Render was not perturbed. Kakos was defiant.

"I am Lord of this City."

Render was not going to let this be a heated argument. The Sorcerer kept his voice firm but level.

"This is not a request Kakos. I have given you life and power, and now I am giving you an instruction. You will not be the only Lord leaving his city for the war with the North, so make what you will of it. We leave in four weeks."

When Render departed, Kakos ordered the boy to return to

his singing. He closed his eyes and reminded himself to be calm, but the boy's voice coalesced into anger inside his head and when he reopened his eyes the room was a whirlwind of papers flying about the air. The boys were nowhere to be seen, likely fled. Kakos was unsure how much time had passed. He was consumed with anger at being trapped in this zombie form and ensnared to serve a Necromancer. He was mostly annoyed that he hadn't prepared for this moment, not anticipated it. It did not align at all with his plans. The anger made him hungry … ravenous.

Part Six:

The Rift War

THE GENERALS

Mannace arrived at the Rift with his unit of elite Rangers well ahead of his army. Jayne led the Rangers, and Morgan and Milan travelled with them. He enjoyed their company, and the time to journey there passed quickly. The mood, as they came to the command camp, was dour by comparison, with few smiles on the faces of the allied soldiers as they went about their work. The military camp was not what Mannace expected. Buildings long ago replaced tents, and civilians operated shops and canteens. The Galandarians prepared a barracks for Mannace's troop, who took the afternoon to settle in. That night, Mannace attended his first meeting with his military peers.

Rakor, the King of Remman, was younger than Mannace expected, perhaps in his late thirties. He was muscled like a fighter and had a warrior's swagger. He didn't look dissimilar to other Remman he encountered on the journey, except for the rich red cloak that he wore and the quality of the blade at his belt. The sword boasted the largest ruby Mannace had ever seen on the pommel.

"So, this is the man who united the Blood Sea. Welcome to the Rift, Mannace of Bracadia."

An older man was seated. He acknowledged Mannace with a short wave of his hand and a soft smile but said nothing. Mannace assumed this to be Arathos of Kaste, Apostle of the Holy Lands. When Morgan briefed him on this group of leaders, he had warned Mannace not to push Arathos - he was vastly knowledgeable and a brilliant strategist. He was also a little mad and prone to losing his temper - although he gave every appearance of being harmless and fragile as if a fart could knock him over.

"The metal man has talked up your armies. Let's hope he is not prone to exaggeration. Welcome to the Rift."

The man who spoke was Callos Reylor, First General of the

armies of Galandar. He looked sharp and military, dressed like a common soldier with a leather hauberk and skirt. Like the Remman King, it was his trappings that set him apart - a blue cloak with gold trim, golden vambraces on his arms and an exceptional quality sword and scabbard at his belt.

Harold of Toth was the only man here whom Mannace had previously met. The Marshal of Roundhome nodded to acknowledge the newcomer but otherwise continued to eat what looked like meat and cheese wedged between two thick slices of bread. The juices from the meat ran down the man's chin. Mannace usually found the Marshal pleasant to deal with - pragmatic and accommodating like most of his kin.

Greygor, Prince of the Horseclans, came forth and put his hand on Mannace's shoulder as was the way of his people.

"Welcome, Mannace, welcome to the Rift."

He laughed and slapped Mannace on the forearm. "We will bash heads together."

He chuckled again. Greygor was dressed in a simple leather jacket and riding pants. He carried none of the trappings of a warrior, but he looked and moved like one. Mannace was curious.

"Well met, Prince. Rumours say that the Horseclans have withdrawn from the rift, that there is a fallout in alliances."

"Let's hope those same rumours are heard in the North."

Greygor locked eyes with Mannace, his tone becoming very serious.

"The Clans are gathered. The thunder of hooves will roll across the Veldaan, and we will make our ancestors proud."

He slapped Mannace on the other arm and laughed once more.

Otheygo, the Knight General of Cavalere, entered through the same entrance as Mannace. He seemed preoccupied and bustled past Mannace, acknowledging him and others with a nod of his head, seemingly a common custom here. The Knight General took a seat at the main table. Seeing his impatience, the others, including Mannace, all took seats at the table as well. Harold started the conversation.

"So, here we are, days away from launching the campaign of our generation. I don't know about the rest of you, but my cock is stone hard."

Greygor banged his hands on the table and laughed. Before he could speak though, Callos called them all to order, "Generals, to arms!" Even the distracted Otheygo seemed to sit up and become attentive. Mannace, unused to the formalities, did the same.

"We are all eager to get to business. Tonight, we will discuss our forces. Tomorrow, we start planning the campaign."

Each of the generals gave an account of their armies and the make-up of their allies. The Galandar general seemed to represent many allied nations. Like Mannace, they were incredibly organised, talking in terms of divisions, typically ten to twenty thousand soldiers in number and covered details such as their troop type and primary armaments. Sometimes they called out unique information such as a champion of renown, a wizard, or some other noteworthy characteristic. When it came to Mannace's turn, it was clear that his army comprised an astounding array of troop types and attributes. The others asked many questions to get a better understanding of the men he commanded and their capability. At the end of his account, they seemed pleased. Callos summed it up for the group.

"This war will be like nothing that has gone before."

Arathos added, "There is a prophecy that a man will come from the South that will unite all nations and herald a new age."

Greygor banged the table, "So be it!"

Arathos smiled slyly and elaborated: "It is a prophecy spoken of in the North."

Greygor banged the table again and laughed, "You sly old bastard."

Callos called the meeting to an end. In the morning, the Elves would give an account of their scouting of the North and then the generals would look at the current deployments at the Rift. Meanwhile, their combined armies continued to gather.

THE SORCERER'S CAVALCADE

Of all the troops marching to the rift, Render and his odd collection of vassals brought the most attention. As he passed through Roundhome and Galandar, word seemed to travel ahead of him so that people would line the streets to see him and his followers pass. He enjoyed the celebrity, and for the bigger crowds, he rewarded them with spectacular displays of pyrotechnics and apparitions.

Render himself rode on a levitation platform that was large enough to accommodate himself and up to ten other wizards. For now, it was just he and Kakos on the oval-shaped disc, seated on high backed chairs. Render intended to keep Kakos close – ever alert and a formidable defence if they were to attract the wrong kind of attention.

Behind the disc, cultists and demons walked together, including Ruu, Fek and Gax who were always close to the Master. The other demons came in all varieties of shape and horror. For now, they behaved as Render instructed them, although it was hard for some to curb their instincts. They eyed the onlookers hungrily.

Next in the procession were a group of animators and a workforce of the towering steel men. It would take the manufactory at Viletri a long time to recover from having their best animators and workers seconded. The animators brought with them the best of Technomancy, including the few shield discs they had managed to manufacture, as well as their unique inventions. Behind them, horseless wagons filled with the army's baggage followed.

To the rear of the force, the obsidian statues from the valley of pain ambled forward, still caught in visages of agony. For Render, they carried with them the most precious cargo, the souls that would power his magic in the battles to come.

His apprentices also walked or rode with the procession, some of them with their own entourage of followers. After careful consideration, Render decided to bring all the magicians, except for the Necromancers who were needed to keep Viletri's civil workforce in order. Amnicles was his Battlemage and General. He left the activity of managing the odd troop to him.

A small number of Fallen riders rounded out the force. They were Amnicles' scouts, messengers, and guards.

Amnicles was a potent magic-user in his own right, having progressed rapidly under Render's tutelage and then through his studies and experience with the army. As a battlemage, he had been preparing for the coming conflict since first raising a spark, and he felt ready for the fight. Amnicles commanded two apprentices who travelled with him now, always a few steps behind the Battlemage – watchful.

DOCTRINE OF WAR

The modernised Doctrine of War included the War God's scripture and promise. The nations of the Blood Sea embraced it; first in Arenland where the War God's influence was most prevalent, then at Viletri and amongst the Iron Jaw, then slowly amongst the warrior castes of the other allied nations. Followers of the Doctrine were to be found in most cities in the Eastern Colonies and even into Roundhome.

The Doctrine was a set of principles to guide a follower of the War God to his reward – the promise of life in death, be that in the physical world or the afterworld. In a word: Immortality. The primary principles were elementary: Loyalty to the War God, loyalty to country, loyalty to Lord or officer, loyalty to fellow soldiers, glory in battle. There were lesser principles to guide behaviour on and off the field of war.

The most devout of the War God's followers – his priests and champions, were further rewarded with control over the souls of the enemy slain in battle. Killing was the source of the priesthood's power, the ability to collect the life from those defeated to use as fuel to smite their foes and give themselves unnatural constitution and endurance.

Ahmeda convinced her Order to embrace the magic and industry that was flourishing around them, modernising the priesthood, and ultimately preparing it to play its part in the war with the North. The armour Deckon Ruel wore was a primary example. He was tall, even for a Dark Elf, but the rig he wore now made him another head taller and far broader. Alloy plates, thick enough to deflect any blow or bullet, interlocked into full body armour. Integrated Technomancy elements gave him the strength of limb to wield the God Hammer, a weapon more massive than even the strongest elf could otherwise lift. An under-robe enchanted with magic made the suit more comfortable and kept the body both clean and healthy. The souls of his defeated opponents moved through his body and armour, awaiting release. His helmet was enchanted, so it felt like he was not wearing headgear at all, yet Deckon's vision and hearing were both enhanced.

Deckon led a squad of War Priests, all equipped with similar rigs. Their task was to ensure the War God's Thunder made it safely to the Rift. The Thunder was a mighty mortar based on a Bracadian design but crafted in the factories of Ostoik on a massive scale more befitting the God of War. The mortar was constructed of steel and shaped like an enormous cauldron, designed to shoot missiles at a steep angle over fortifications. Two hundred and twenty slaves, strengthened in the catacombs of Tarash Gormoth, pulled and pushed the wheeled weapon, keeping a good pace. Another two hundred slaves followed behind, manoeuvring carts of ammunition and driving the wheeled cranes that were needed to prepare and load the mortar. The temple acolytes who would wield the Thunder in battle moved amongst the slaves, giving orders and keeping a constant watch over the precious cargo.

Ahmeda rode alongside Deckon. In his suit, his head was level with hers, and occasionally the High Priestess would pass a comment.

"The trees are beautiful, are they not Deckon. The leaves are broad and lush. It is a rich land."

The Dark Elf War Priest nodded but remained silent.

"Smell the air Deckon. There are scents I have never experienced. It is a rare joy."

This time the mighty warrior sniggered. He made a counter observation.

"I smell the sweat of an army that has not bathed in a month, and the shit of their mongrel horses."

The High Priestess laughed. Deckon was right, and it immediately ruined the experience for her. Now when she sniffed, her imagination was tainted by the War Priests blunt cynicism.

Ahmeda wore a light suit of alloy armour, lacquered red with an ornate silver headband on her simple helmet. Like Deckon's armour, Technomancy gave the suit its power, but the mechanics were subtler and the magic more attuned to her divine abilities. She felt the War God inside her, his anticipation growing as they marched north, his power hers to shape and channel.

The retinue travelled with the First Arenland Infantry Division. Modelled on the Dwarven units that were so successful in the war with the Collective, the infantry wore chemically hardened leather armour under thick grey coats. Completing the uniform were black boots and gloves, with a simple dark grey helmet made from a hardened resin. Some units employed an enhanced version of the repeating crossbow or new shard guns, while others hefted muskets. All carried the choke gas and gas masks to protect their breathing and eyes. Every man slung an entrenching tool over their backs, with sledgehammers and picks carried on wagons. Each unit included two artillery wagons, either with a steam-powered cannon or repeating ballista. They were mostly a defence against giants or other large creatures but might also be useful when attacking fortifications. Siege works would be the responsibility of the engineer units, equipped with all manner of engines for assaulting or undermining defences. This division was an offensive force that meant business, well-drilled and fuelled with religious fervour. The Priests and Acolytes of War moved amongst the troops to inspire them and to be their champions in battle.

VELDAAN

The Northern territory of Veldaan was like the Southern territory of Galandar with lush plains and gentle hills, ideal for farming and able to support a large population.

At the Rift, almost six hundred thousand Veldaan troops were fortified or dug in against a similar number of their Southern enemy. There were another two hundred thousand soldiers in reserve and allied nations to their east and west that would rally to their aid. Veldaan was always at the forefront of the Rift War. This gateway to the north was firmly under lock and key.

In living and recorded history, the Veldaan was always at war with the South. There had been the Generation of Legends where their armies struck so far south into Galandar that Rotherdan was sacked. Similarly, there were black years where the southerners decimated the northern holdings. In very recent times the war was fought on the Veldaanian side of the rift, and for the most part, Veldaan saw to its defence without assistance. Now though, messengers hurried in all directions with the call to the North to honour the ancient oaths of allegiance and answer the summons to battle.

Gathering behind the Southern defences was a vast host. Veldaan's spies suggested it would take the Southerners perhaps a week to collect their full strength before an attack. It seemed that the invaders benefited from both the numbers and initiative. Tyriah, High Commander of Veldaan, acted decisively. She called messengers who appeared straightaway at the door to her chamber.

"Order Generals Tevik and Yanoul to pull back from the front. Their armies will make haste to the cities of Astindul, Orroco, Aruselum, and Adash. Send word to General Isuman to muster at Palainth. Command all cities to raise the Chokra, every man and woman who has the training.

Tell the Usari that it is time. Bring me updates to the war room".

The messengers completed the task within the hour. Tyriah smiled; this generation of Southerners would soon learn that the Veldaan shines brightest in the darkest hours. She had held the position of High Commander for over twenty generations and been an observer long before that.

The War Room was a long hall with a massive table in its centre. The carved tabletop was a map of the Great Continent. Crafted silver figurines represented both allied and enemy forces deployed at the Rift. Figurines were being placed and moved as updated reports came in from the front. Tyriah watched the placement of the Chokra figurines, painted blue and carrying standards of their cities. There were eighty of these representing ten thousand soldiers each. The robed Usari each had its distinct ornament. Seven of these were placed at the table edge. One was placed on the Capital – Elderlin, the Protector and Librarian. It was Elderlin's apprentices that provided the messenger service.

Detailed maps lined the walls. Cabinets and drawers of figurines were also about the room. A man and a Dark Elf were seated in comfortable lounge chairs set back from the table. Jayne Azaryn stared at the Mad King. The Mad King was unfazed by the Elf's glower, and he spoke to Tyriah.

"Do you believe this is the time. That Mannace is the one?"

"Maybe." Tyriah hesitated. Her agents alerted her to Mannace when he first appeared at Yanth. "It seems likely."

"I do Tyriah. Others do too. They are making their preparations."

"How many can there be left from the beginning? Only Nordan of the Ancient Ones still lives."

The Mad King considered.

"Eya of the Spiders, Grengal of the Flies, Churgwarthos. They were minor amongst the Ancients, but they have survived, *they* will come from hiding to wait here in the

North. And there is us, once servants to the Ancient Ones, watching and waiting. I have the bell."

"What game are you playing? Do you still serve a master long past?"

"I serve nobody." The Mad King was uncharacteristically terse. "We were there in the beginning, Tyriah, we should be there at the end."

"We are old, you and me. Are you so keen to see the end? Why not leave the world to choose its course? Let these young races have their time; decide their future."

The Mad King was not used to being challenged. He didn't much care for it.

"My actions are my own. When the time comes, I will choose my path."

Tyriah moved across the room to stand before the Mad King.

"I was a servant too. Let it go. Until you do, you only continue to serve the ancient ones - let their prophecies die with them. That age has long gone, be free of it."

The Mad King folded his arms, his normally calm demeanour evaporated.

Jayne was also frustrated. He shared no interest in the conversation, and he had been waiting for some hours. After so many years of hearing nothing, he responded in haste to Tyriah's summons, travelling secret paths.

"Why am I summoned?"

Tyriah returned to the large table, watching the placement of more tiny statues.

"Tell me about Mannace. Leave out no detail."

Jayne did as he was asked. He answered other questions that followed about Jaal, Render, and Saska. Surprisingly, there were no questions about the Southern lands or their armies.

Tyriah surprised Jayne by asking, "Do you like the man? Is

he a leader you willingly follow?”

The interrogation was potentially a trap, and rather than answer, Jayne asked a question.

“My Lady, I am your blade, your soldier to command. What command do you give me?”

Tyriah, Jayne, and the Mad King were all tense. Eventually, Tyriah moved again to be in front of the chairs and the two men.

“Stay close to Mannace. Return here in two weeks.”

Jayne stood and left the war hall. It was time for the Mad King to depart as well and he exited the room and the citadel without farewells, as was his way. Tyriah let her mind empty of the drama of his visit, and she focused her attention back to the planning at hand. The presence of the Mad King reminded her of how tired she had become of being immortal.

ACROSS THE RIFT

During the night, the northern enemy abandoned their defences – hundreds of thousands of troops snuck away into the dark. In their place were empty earthworks, barricades with traps and caltrops spread to hamper cavalry. The traps and caltrops were a nuisance more than a threat. More concerning was that the Southern Generals expected the Northerners to hold their positions at all costs. It was not a favourable omen to be outmanoeuvred so early in the campaign. Now they would need to reconsider their strategy and wait to gather their full strength before marching northward.

A week later the Southern host finally advanced. Mannace marched his army to the city of Orroco to besiege it. The design of the city and its defences were known, and Mannace was confident that his army would be equal to any fortification encountered. Again though, the city was abandoned, with its inhabitants fled north.

Meanwhile, the Elves reported a great Veldaan host gathering in a region known as Palainth, and not wanting to play the enemies game any longer, Mannace left the ghost city untouched and made haste for Palainth ahead of his allies. He sent messengers, so the other generals knew his intent. He asked himself, "What would Demmal do? What would the Mad King do?" In his gut, Mannace knew they would seize the initiative. Milan was also a risk-taker, encouraging Mannace in this course. Morgan, however, was more conservative and his advice was to rely on the Southern Generals' experience, who led their armies at the Rift for so many years. But where did their tactics get them except generations of trading blows? It was a way of life for them. This campaign was a quest for Mannace.

Reports came to Mannace that the cities of Astindul and Aruselum were conquered without resistance. The citadel of Adash, renowned for its immense fortifications, was under siege by the Roundmen. Adash was a bastion that in all the years of conflict had never been taken. Galandarian engineers and siege units were hurrying to support them, and Mannace sent his flights of Brula ahead to assist. He prepared the flyers with gas and firebombs, knowing they would be invaluable during sieges. The War God's Thunder was also redirected to Adash, being too slow to keep up with Mannace's forced march to Palainth.

After four days of hard marching, the army of the Eastern Colonies arrived at their destination. The Palainth was a massive plain, roughly in the shape of a gigantic oval, with hills surrounding it. From where Mannace's troops entered over the south-western climbs, the hills at the far north-eastern edge were mere wrinkles on the horizon. On the plains and in the northern hills there were enemy camps. Wagon trains were moving north. Divisions of Veldaan troops were already forming in response to Mannace and his approaching troops. Brula scouts were reporting infantry, with some cavalry. From the account they gave, Mannace considered the enemy to be a conventional force. It was an ideal test for his modern soldiers so that even in the face of a numerically superior enemy, he was confident with his plan. As his army formed into a long front in the hills, tens of thousands of allied cavalries arrived and took up position on their flanks. It was a timely and welcome boon to have the Horseclans' aid. The army continued forward.

Mannace commanded from the centre. He was behind the divisions of Colonial Soldiers that formed the vanguard of the attack. To his immediate right, Jayne commanded the Rangers and Brula messengers. Directly to his left was a regiment of Viletri infantry, magnificent in their mechanical armour and magical trappings. Far to the right, he could see Render coming off the hill and onto the plain, riding his disc with his strange entourage in tow. Just beyond that, the Kessik stood out with their pike blocks and war elephants. Mannace remembered fighting the Kessik beasts – the thunder and terror of their stampede. As he looked further in both directions, there was little that was conventional or ordinary about his army. The riders of the Horseclans spread out on the flanks.

The Army of Veldaan was still some distance away. They drew up a front line of spearmen, swordsmen, and heavily armoured infantry with halberds or greatswords. The units moved like veterans, falling quickly into place. On their right and left other troops moved at a run to outflank the Colonial Forces. Even with the Horseclan reinforcements, the Veldaan were too vast in numbers to prevent such a manoeuvre. Rather than worry about it, Mannace left the Horseclan to deal with the threat as best they could. The Veldaan deployed bowmen too, which were always a concern. Since the Dwarves departed the land, Mannace's access to shield discs was limited to the supply he already possessed. He would rely on the long-range of the muskets instead. In contradiction to his steely outward demeanour, his heart was racing.

All the troops armed with muskets: the Colonial soldiers, Yanth divisions, and Arenland infantry - spread out and formed a long line eight ranks deep. Units of bowmen and crossbowmen fell in behind them. The other units dropped back as the march forward continued at a walk. The land underfoot was turned for crops or used as stock land. Sometimes they needed to cross a wall or bypass an abandoned building made of mud and stones. Mannace observed that the people who lived there cared for their land and property, perhaps enjoyed a good life.

The Colonial soldiers stopped. Those in the front rank were kneeling and aiming their muskets. The noise of their firepower echoed across the plains. The next rank fired then they knelt to reload. The third rank fired. At first, the enemy took light casualties and responded by increasing their pace to a jog and then a charge. Still, as the Veldaan forces came closer, the accuracy of the muskets improved and soon their soldiers, even the heavily armoured ones were dying quicker than they could gain ground.

The riders of the Horseclans took a toll on the advancing troops with their bows, but they were forced backwards under the weight of numbers, continuing to harass the Veldaan troops as best they could. They did not prevent the enemy from gathering in numbers on Mannace's flank, and some were now behind the Colonial forces.

As they often rehearsed, four ranks of musket men retreated and took up a position at the rear of the army. The flanks also withdrew towards the centre, so the Colonial army formed a long rectangle with the musketeers, crossbowmen and archers now reinforcing the perimeter. Melee forces gathered at the centre of the formation, anxious to be involved but unneeded for now.

All the while, the muskets roared, and the enemy died. As the Veldaan soldiers attacked from all sides and drew closer, the repeating crossbows, the wizardry of Render and his apprentices, or choke gas, was enough to repel any attack. It was a massacre that caught the enemy by such surprise that they delayed far too long to react, letting their dead form gruesome piles that other attackers clambered over. Eventually, reluctantly, because they knew what a grand prize a victory here would be, the Veldaan generals ordered a retreat. Resisting the temptation to pursue, Mannace held his position. He was proud of his army and how they bared their teeth, giving these Northerners a lesson in modern combat. On the fringes of the battlefield, the Horseclans continued to harass the enemy.

Not a single hand-to-hand blow was struck. Yet tens of thousands of enemy men and women lay dead and dying. In good order, the defeated host of Veldaan retreated North, and only when they were out of sight over the northern hills, did Mannace finally withdraw his forces to the south to regroup and await his allies. After this bloody lesson, he knew the enemy would be much wiser about his capabilities and tactics. For now, he joined his soldiers and their Horseclan allies in celebration, moving between camps and congratulating both his commanders and men.

"Soldiers of the Colonies, you have made history this day. What you have achieved will put the fear of the War God and the thunder of his guns, upon the enemy host. It is a prelude to greater victories to follow."

THE HAND OF FENGAL

Athose enjoyed spending time in the highlands, south of the territory the Wild Elves now called the Hand of Fengal. Today there was a mist over the land and from his treetop perch, Athose relished the view of the valley below; how the forest here seemed to appear out of the mist, with the branches glistening and shadowy, framing the valley as it descended into a haze of light and fog. This valley was one where the spiders made their home, and even at this high end, webs straddled some trees. They too sparkled with moisture and added to nature's magic.

Athose was confused; he was with the Mad King when the call came for the Wengo Orc Tribes to rally. Many did, but where the Mad King influenced the Orcs, they had not heeded the summons. Similarly, the Elves of The Hand talked of battles in the South and the victories of Mannace and the allies, but both they and the Spider Mother took no action. They all seemed content to wait and watch. Even Jaal seemed oblivious; in fact, he seemed determined not to be part of the conflict.

Athose journeyed here to meet Vilera, who he could see approaching. She possessed a knack for finding him, and this time was no exception. Vilera bent forward and scrambled up the tree to perch close to the Elf. "Brother." At first, he didn't respond, and they sat there for a long while watching the mist in the trees.

"I am going south to the land known as Veldaan. I travelled to the border with the Mad King when he visited there. Hu is waiting at the edge of the forest. He will come with me. The Mad King says Hu can do as he pleases, as can I. Come with me, Vilera."

"Why?"

"All of the North travels there, I have watched armies of Orcs and men move south. There will be a great battle. Even the giants in the mountains are gathering. Don't you want to be part of it? To see the giants fight?"

Vilera didn't have the same freedom of action that Athose did, but the Spider Mother said to her that she could spend time with Athose, that he was a person of interest.

"Yes. I will come with you."

Athose jumped to a lower branch, then another before landing lightly on the ground. He started walking toward the hills.

"Let's go."

Vilera was annoyed. Athose always did this, acted on his impulses, and never left time for her to plan. There were many preparations to make that were all left undone. She came alongside and nudged him at just the right time, so he bumped into a tree. He didn't say anything. It was Vilera who spoke.

"Where is Roanna?"

"Busy."

"Why bring Hu. We will not be able to remain hidden?"

"He wants to come. He has no voice, but he is intelligent. He knows what he wants, and it's not to sit back and watch."

"That sounds like what you want."

"We want the same thing."

Athose picked up his pace to avoid further conversation. Vilera matched his stride.

"He will be in danger."

Athose did not think that would be possible. He didn't want to talk about it, remaining silent as he marched on.

"You have been around the Mad King too long. He manipulates everything."

Athose did have an instruction from the Mad King, but any thoughts about sharing it were now gone. He bit back.

"And the Spider Mother doesn't?"

"You are responsible."

Athose wanted to tell Vilera to "Go back then", but he didn't. He liked her company and to keep the peace; he told her what she wanted to hear.

"You are right. I am responsible."

That seemed to do the trick, and they moved on without further conversation.

As they approached the edge of the forest, Hu sat amongst the trees where Athose had left him. Without ceremony, the colossus stood and bashed his way brutally through the woods and onto the open expanse beyond. The land here was flat and wild, with tall grass to waist height and areas of brush or copses of trees. This fertile region was The Ryde, home to the fierce northern horse tribes. Athose had seen the tribesmen; mean, tough-looking men and women who lived and hunted across this vast landscape. He didn't expect to see any here now. They were the first to answer the call of the North and rode hard for neighbouring Veldaan. Athose, Vilera, and Hu charted the same route.

THE RA-ANU

Eya, the Mother of Spiders, was not one to take things for granted and her suspicions this time were well-founded. Her spiders quickly discovered the source of the power of the forest, its protectors, and the reason why a sanctuary so vast might prevail. The Ra-Anu that the spiders came upon were champions of Fengus, who was brother to Fengal, the God of Nature. Fengus was set upon the earth by the God to be his eyes and hand. He was one of the ancient ones thought to have perished thousands of years ago, but here it appeared that three of his servants, and a legacy of his power, lived.

It cost Eya dearly to vanquish the three Ra-Anu, but it was better to deal with them quickly before they could react, or worse yet, have the Elves discover them and ally with the guardians. Together the Wild Elves and the Ra-Anu would be truly formidable. Now though, two of the Ra-Anu were passed from this world and the other Eya personally subdued. The conflict, the many casualties, and the Ra-Anu prisoner were all secreted behind a curtain of webs. The crystal grotto and caves of the Ra-Anu would be her new abode.

The challenge of the Ra-Anu made Eya think back to the days of the Ancient Ones and their minions. In those times conflicts were mostly settled by a clash of champions: beings and creatures of artifice and power. It was the same artifice that created the lesser races. The same untamed power linked the elements and gods themselves. Eya was made of the shadow, and she drew her strength from the elemental darkness. There were so few vestiges of the Age of the Ancient Ones remaining. It was now the Age of Men, but that too was coming to an end.

A CITY TOO FAR

The North was not about to lie down for this Southern incursion. There was still enthusiasm and energy in the Northern camp. Many believed that the southern enemy had poked its head out of their hole, and if that head were to be severed, the body of the south would be defenceless.

The fierce horsemen of the Ryde were the first to join in defence of Veldaan. Initially, they gathered their numbers in the Northwest of that land. Still, it was not long before the Clans of the Ryde moved south in large numbers, flanking the enemy, and reclaiming the territory that the southerners conquered, striking as far south as the defences at the rift itself. At the rift, the horsemen were joined by veteran soldiers from the Young Cities. The Southern Generals were forced to send the Horseclan divisions to counter the threat, which meant compromising their continuous front. The cavalries of the Ryde and the Horseclans were frequent enemies, and once more across Veldaan, bloody battles were being fought. Soon, all the cavalry of the Southern host were deployed just to keep the captured lands secure, and to preserve the supply lines back to the South.

The armies of the South were also compelled to garrison the empty cities they seized, to maintain their lines of communication and deny them to the enemy. Eight large cities were now under Southern control, including the prize of Adash.

For the most part, the Veldaan people withdrew north, continuing to abandon their communities, gathering their strength, and fighting only where it became unavoidable. Mannace and his Colonial army engaged in battle twice more, but they were both delaying actions by the Northerners, easily overcome. With the retreating enemies' scorched earth tactics, rations were already running low.

Rakor, the young King of the Remman, was of a similar mind as Mannace.

"Mannace, we have taken a great swath of land, but we are losing the initiative. The further we advance, the more troops we lose to garrisons, and the longer our supply lines get."

Mannace was nodding.

"When the enemy have gathered their allies, they will grow bolder. Rakor, we must act now if we are to win this war. Angorok is close."

Rakor looked Mannace in the eye to test his mettle.

"Between us, we are nine hundred thousand soldiers. The Brula control the skies. Mannace, there is no better chance to attack the Capital. We can take Angorok."

When Mannace smiled, Rakor went on.

"There are two cities between here and Angorok, but we will need to pass them by. It means we rely on the Galandarians to secure them in our wake. We cannot delay."

"I will let Callos know our plan. He will not forsake us."

"I trust him to protect our backs. We must do this Mannace, strike while the initiative is still ours. We march now!"

The two generals clasped arms in a soldier's grip and then stood back from one another. Rakor was the first to move away, turning purposefully and striding back toward his troops. Mannace took a long pause to let the fire pump through his veins – this moment was thirty years in the making. He could taste destiny upon his tongue, and on closing his eyes, Mannace felt the Oracle's light upon his heart. The leader pulled his shoulders back and drew a deep breath. He was proud of himself for the determination that brought him here, and he felt deserving of the lineage flowing through his veins – worthy of the respect of his immortal Viletri kin. It was time for final victory in the North.

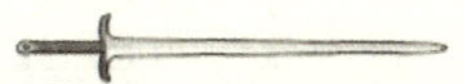

In the capital of their enemy, Tyriah would have liked a few extra days to prepare. Still, she and her people were too proud to consider leaving the Veldaan capital abandoned. With a few more days the armies of May and Ekos would arrive. It would have to be enough that the Wengo tribes, Greshnak, Islani, and the Mountain Giants had come. Importantly they honoured their oaths and came in strength. The Makhon, Sarville, and Granash forces were still camped well east of Veldaan, slowly gathering their numbers. Only minor contingents of the Mago were at Angorok. Other nations hadn't the time to complete the journey or perhaps, did not intend to come to their aid. There was no news from Amon Murn or Churlamen, but it would likely take more than an incursion like this to draw their attention. Rather than send reinforcements, some nations, like the Sarang and Kampatan, responded by attacking across the Rift into the lands of the South. At least this drew some of the Southern armies away from Veldaan. Whatever forces they mustered now would need to be enough; here at Angorok, the Veldaan and their allies would make their defence.

Angorok was bustling with the preparations for war. The Veldaan were dealt a severe and humiliating defeat at the battle at Palainth. But they learned valuable lessons about their enemy and their new weapons. They would not be caught by surprise in the same way again. Already, tower shields were crafted from wood and metal and straw and clay, to protect against the firepower of the muskets.

The Veldaan managed to capture some examples of the enemy's weapons: the guns, repeating crossbows, and gases. It would take too much time to analyse them completely and build their own versions, so for now it was enough to know how they operated. Tyriah could see that the defence of Angorok would not be a numbers game; it required new tactics.

The Usari gathered. They were seated in their traditional

meeting chamber attached to Elderlin's library. The senior apprentices stood around the walls of the room, while the novices gathered in adjoining rooms. Tyriah showed them the weapons, and she asked General Isuman to give an account of the battle at Palainth. The Usari were particularly interested in the Sorcerer that travelled upon a disc. General Isuman told them that the Sorcerer and those with him cast fireballs across their front but played only a minor part in the overall outcome of the battle. Tyriah also shared what she knew; that this enemy sorcerer was named "Render", and that he commanded as many as twenty apprentices. She asked the wizards how they might best aid in the conflict ahead.

"A heavy rain and a fog would blind and slow them", offered one of the Asari.

"And how are we to do that?" Elderlin snorted accusingly at his peer. "Can you suddenly control the weather, Wrathos?"

"Thinking out loud friend. What about darkness, what if we fought at night?"

Tyriah saw where Wrathos was headed.

"The darker, the better. If we can get close to them, we can beat them."

"We can do darkness", a solemn-looking Asari added. "Black as black."

"What does that mean", Elderlin added in his arrogant, accusing tone. "Black as black. Mad as mad maybe."

"White as white", chimed in another mage. "Blinded by light. You can't shoot what you can't see. Darkness and light, it will drive them mad".

There was a nodding of heads that suggested at least they were on the right track.

"What of this enemy sorcerer, Render?" Wrathos liked to cut to the chase, "Is he a threat?"

After an awkward silence, Tyriah chimed in.

"I think we can assume he is dangerous. He acts with confidence. It is not like a wizard to fight from the front."

Rather than take the last comment as an insult, the Asari were simply nodding again in agreement. A dark-skinned Asari named Ferquidan stood to address his peers. His hair was the colour of rust and hung loosely to below his waist. The wizard's long face was sunken so that his eyes seemed to float in their sockets.

"We will send the Drutha to deal with him. Better to end it now."

"Ha! The last time we summoned the Drutha, they ate four apprentices, and when the job was done, they returned for six more. Who would do the rites, you?"

"It would require us all."

There was a resounding "No" from the room. Ferquidan looked at the gathering as if everybody in it were cowards.

"The Shades then, let them deal with him. We can control the Shades."

"I'll not be responsible for letting the shades loose in Veldaan. They have their own agenda."

The Asari who spoke was young in comparison to the others, but he had a wise face and most seemed to agree with his words.

Ferquidan leaned toward the speaker.

"Kel, Shades can be dealt with. If this Sorcerer is powerful, then he is a great threat to Veldaan and us. The Asari were once nineteen, none of them died of old age, they died because they underestimated their foe. Let's end this Mage now and be done with it. We cannot act with confidence in this conflict if we are looking over our shoulders for an attack that could end us!"

Now Wrathos leaned forward.

"I prefer the Drutha. We know what to expect so we can adjust. No more apprentices will be forfeit. We can be certain the Drutha will get the job done."

Tyriah could see a consensus forming amongst those present, and before it took a tangent, she hurried things along.

"Asari, we shall fight the enemy with darkness and light. You will end the Sorcerer before he takes the field against us. Asari, protectors of Veldaan, make it so!"

RISE OF THE SORCERER

Angorok was at the edge of a great plain with hills behind it that formed a ridge stretching far to the east and west. It was a city that had expanded several times so that each concentric ring had its own wall. A veritable fortress protected its main gate and the massive citadel, set back on a hill, towered above the city, casting a sinister shadow over the populace. To Mannace it appeared as if Angorok and the ridge were placed there explicitly to bar them from travelling farther north. The enemy was camped in the hills, safe for now with the advantage of the high ground. There was certainly no panic when the Colonial and Remman divisions set their line well back from the city and ridge and made their camp. It was mid-afternoon. Mannace and Rakor planned to march against the Veldaan capital early the following morning. As a welcome addition to their numbers, two divisions from the Holy Lands and three from Galandar were marching hard to join them during the night.

The Southern forces rested, but the respite was short-lived. As twilight came, the Northern forces moved down from the hills, and as darkness descended over the plains, the Brula reported the enemy were manoeuvring into their battle formations. At the same time, Angorok opened its gates and soldiers issued forth like ants from a nest, forming into tight units. A night offensive, it was unusual, though Mannace could see why the enemy might choose that option, to try and negate the effectiveness of the muskets.

After talking with Rakor, Mannace gathered his commanders; Khing was there, his advisors, Morgan and Milan, Alfar, who was now First Officer of the Colonial divisions, Titus Kane, who commanded the Blood Sea Division, the enigmatic Lord Angelcry, who led the Arenlanders, Castell, of the Blood Legion, and Render.

Many other officers and leaders from the Colonies were present. Of the people he wanted on this journey with him, only Jaal was absent.

The war leaders discussed tactics and each commander knew their responsibilities. Mannace did not want to delay them further from joining their troops.

"Lords and Leaders, tonight we hold the line. This battle will be a defining moment in our history. Go to your stations. Within the hour, we clash in battle."

The darkness of the night intensified, and the moon seemed to be secreted away, possibly behind a cloud, though Render could sense a magic about it. As he made his way past the Blood Legion, Casteel, who was walking with him, patted him on the back before moving off to join her troop.

When the Sorcerer moved on towards his camp, the shadow near him abruptly thickened and then unfolded, taking on monstrous shapes. Render knew demons, and by instinct, he moved into Nearspace. It proved no defence and the demons quickly shifted with him. While everything else from the physical realm faded from Render's view, the demons became more substantial as if they were native to this nether-world. They were the colour of coal, mannish but giant-sized and bull chested. The demon's arms were long and ended in extended claws, while their heads were misshapen, insect-like, with sockets where there should have been eyes. There were two of them, murderous, confident, encircling the wizard.

Fek appeared behind one, leaping on its back and attaching himself with his talons and teeth. The beast screeched and writhed as it tried to toss its assailant free. Render faced the other, and as it lunged at him with exceptional speed, the Sorcerers defences were already present; no demon would find him an easy kill. The beast bounced off an invisible barrier and seemed momentarily stunned. In the language of Demons, with words of ancient power, Render commanded the creatures to cease their attack. Compelled to do as directed, they took a reluctant step away from their prey, circling him menacingly. One screeched at the wizard defiantly. Fek leapt free and scuttled back to observe from the surrounding oblivion. Render spoke more words of power, and now both demons rose and screeched. He had released them from their binding, whatever hold their summoner might have over them. It was a gift, a risk. Render needed the cultists if he were to place his own controls over the devils and in place of that, he took the best option available to him. He set them free. When the demons shifted back into Realspace and then the shadows, Fek also retreated into his hidden state. Render was pleased that Fek proved his loyalty. These northern wizards, the Asari as he had heard them called, would know now that he was not to be trifled with.

In the darkness, the Southerners could hear the rhythmic stepping of hundreds of thousands of troops marching. Amnicles, who commanded the Sorcerers apprentices, launched a great globe of light into the sky. It was a signal to the other apprentices who were dispersed amongst the troops, to raise similar orbs to pierce the night. The bright spheres and the darkness seemed at odds and the night swirled overhead like a tempest washing over the lights and the plains. It was enough illumination, though, to see the outline of troops in the distance, and along the front line, the noise of the muskets erupted as the Colonial troops targeted the advancing foe. Already the enemy was close enough that crossbowmen and archers from both sides started to fill the air with their missiles. Along the Southern lines, the darkness was suddenly replaced by a bright light, coming from behind the enemy troops and shining across the Southern ranks. Soldiers looked away or shielded their eyes, doing their best to continue shooting despite their dazzled vision, knowing that their lives depended on it.

Well above the field of battle, a Brula relaxed as she caught an updraft and climbed even higher into the sky. She was well above the darkness and the lights, high enough that the units below seemed like scuttling insects. Both the Southerners and Northerners formed a long line across the plains, though the Northern ranks were deeper and on both distant flanks, a blackness of Northern reinforcements gathered on the plains. The light washing from the north and across the Southern centre was spectacular, as were the musket flashes as the Southern divisions fired. Her heart raced as the forces below surged together, in places forming a single, writhing mass. Experienced in measuring the flow of battle, the Brula surveyed the enemy reserves and looked beyond for new arrivals.

Render unleashed his prepared magic against the enemy centre, countering the attack of light with a wave of force that washed over the Northern front, tossing soldiers to the ground, and throwing their organisation into disarray. Many thousands of men and women and even the giants lay stunned, injured, and disoriented. Render incorporated Ruu's powers into his magic, amplifying the pain.

The Sorcerer commanded the floating disc to rise further, so he commanded a better view of the carnage he caused. Amongst the fallen, enemy soldiers writhed and screamed in agony.

"HERE I AM," he projected over the noise of battle. These Asari would need to show themselves or back down. He was ready to face them head-on.

The bright light shining into the Southern ranks disappeared, but the darkness again intensified, negating much of the effect of the skylights. Laughing, Render ordered the demons forth. Darkness was the demons' playground.

BATTLE IN THE NIGHT

Lord Fitius Angelcry was at the front of the Arenland line, the High Priestess, Ahmeda, at his side. His regiments of Arenlanders were firing their muskets, but the enemy carried tall shields before them that absorbed much of the impact. Hindered by the poor light, Fitius feared that his troops were causing the enemy little bother. The Veldaan soldiers were slow-moving with the heavy shields, giving him time to order the musket infantry to close ranks, changing from their long line to more compact units. In the spaces created, other infantry moved forward, armed with the repeating crossbows or halberds.

Ahmeda was also issuing commands to her forces, and when the enemy was in charging range, the god-armoured War Priests sallied forth to assault the shield wall with their divine wrath. For a moment, the champions' charge brought the Northern advance to a halt. Where the Priests broke apart the shield wall, the muskets and crossbowmen took a heavy toll on the exposed enemy. However, Ahmeda realised it was like throwing rocks into the ocean, causing some ripples, but unable to hold back the waves of enemy who passed around the champions and came now at a run towards the Arenland line. Many discarded the tower shields as they charged.

Arenland officers tossed their canisters of choke gas, and again it broke the enemy's momentum allowing the musket men and crossbowmen to unleash a hail of death. Already the scene appeared bloody and frantic.

Unexpectedly, the bright light surged again, shining from behind the enemy and blinding the Arenlanders. During the distraction, the enemy, who grew in confidence, hit the Southern front at pace, swinging their axes and swords. Lord Angelcry watched those about him get pushed back, and a giant shape came out of the light to pass close to the

Lord, bashing soldiers aside and creating havoc. The creature fell back suddenly, three long ballista bolts poking out its chest. He could see other giants now assaulting his infantry, spearheading the enemy's offensive. Distracted, Fitius raised his sword just in time as an enemy soldier, a woman, rushed at him and swung down hard with her axe. Fitius caught the weapon on the haft and knocked it aside. Then as he had practised many times, he countered with a thrust that passed above the woman's shield and took her through the neck. It was his first melee and first kill, and his stomach churned as the woman slumped forward, brushing against his side and gushing blood down his leg. Fitius realised it could so easily have been him falling to the ground with an axe buried in his skull. Wisely, the Lord retreated through his troops to join with the reserves. From there he could safely issue commands.

Ahmeda remained in the thick of the fighting. In the poor visibility, she was reluctant to use her full powers and was content to strike down nearby foes with blasts of divine force, god-spears, and dark-rays. Between bursts, residual energy crackled about her outstretched fingertips. With the immediate area cleared, the High Priestess summoned a spirit-wall to hold the advancing enemy back, so that the crossbowmen and muskets nearby could continue their slaughter. A soldier next to her with a shard gun let loose a salvo into the stunned enemy ranks, shredding armour and flesh and adding to the bedlam.

On the far-left flank, Khing faced the Orc hordes of the Wengo. They were lean of build and crudely equipped. However, Khing was familiar with Orcs and the Iron Jaw were some of the best of his soldiers, so he knew not to underestimate them.

As Field General of the Colonial Armies at the Rift, Khing commanded three divisions. They were all veteran troops, mostly from nations outside the Blood Sea, and they did not possess the same technology as their fellow colonials. As always, they relied on the strength of their sword arms, stamina, and wits. He also commanded the Tarash Gormoth division. Khing did not appreciate the value of the slave soldiers until they quaffed their Thog and ran ahead of other troops to meet the advancing Orcs head-on. Many of the slaves were mutated to be larger and tougher - crafted as weapons of war. With the Thog in them, they fought like berserkers and the enemy infantry struggled to counter their wild fury. At Khing's order, units of Belg moved into position amongst the other troops. Khing expected the big warriors would be vital in holding the defensive line.

In this area of the battlefield, the wizard's night-lights were shining brightly, and from horseback, Khing watched enemy engaging along his entire front. The familiar grind of melee commenced. Far to his right, he saw his allies, the Fogmir Elves, also engage with the Orcs. That was no fair contest, and the Elves seemed to surge forward, creating a great swath of death as they ranged deep into the enemy horde. It put a chill up his spine, the ease with which the Elves went about their slaughter. It also reminded Khing that he never chose to be a general, and he did not profess to be good at it. He preferred to let his officers do their own thinking, to take the initiative, and be the decision-makers.

To his left, at the edge of the light, Khing tracked an immense swarm of shapes moving around the Southern army's flank. A Brula landed next to him and spoke with urgency of the vast Goblin hoard circling to be at their rear. When the Brula left to pass on the message to others, Khing ordered his reserves to brace for the attack, and he rode to be with a unit of Kogath cavalry, to rally his troops as he often did from the front. Riding next to him, an apprentice wizard raised another light globe into the sky. They could see the Goblins more clearly now; their numbers seemed endless, stretching past the reach of the bright orb as they wheeled around his forces. Much of the magical darkness hanging over other parts of the battlefield dissipated, and King noticed stars appearing far above. He supposed that the conjured darkness would not suit the enemy either now that hand to hand combat had started.

Not far away, Bollo jogged with the Galandarians. They were close to the battle after picking up the pace when they witnessed the magic lights rise ahead. To Bollo, it appeared like a storm of light and darkness over the vast plain. The prospect of fighting made his blood pulse, and it put fire in his legs, running to be at the fore of the infantry host. Close to the Galandarians, the heavily armoured horsemen of the Holy Lands cantered past, the thunder of thousands of hooves almost deafening.

At the centre, where Render unleashed his sorcery, Colonial soldiers were advancing against a broken enemy. The Veldaan troops retreated from the storm of magic and bullets. Where his demons were active, there were screams in the darkness. Where Ruu used her hellish powers, groups of soldiers froze in poses of agony and fear. As Gax stalked the battlefield, the shadows of the fallen gathered about him and entered the bodies of the living, striking them stupid and turning them around to charge madly at their kin. Those closer, that he touched, burst into flame. Other demons brought their flavours of malice and horror to the uproar. Render moved to be above them and from the flying disc he hurled his malign sorcery wherever the enemy regrouped, yet he held enough energy in reserve to strike hard if he found one of the Asari. Render felt untouchable. At this moment he was indeed The Master and The Sorcerer. Again, his words resounded over the conflict, "ASARI, HERE I AM."

Where Mannace took station, the fighting was brutal. Here the Northern giants joined the Veldaan offensive in large numbers. These giants were not the same as those that attacked Viletri - they were not as well armoured, but possibly were more ferocious - bashing their way through the front ranks of Colonials and causing great carnage and terror as groups of them rampaged. Some carried tall shields for defence or to sweep their enemy aside. Many of Mannace's divisions were in disarray, and he directed the elite Viletri units that were his guard to hurry to where the fighting was most desperate. It left him vulnerable to attack. Mannace learned from the Brula messengers, that against the marauding giants, the Remman divisions fared no better.

It was not until the waves of light and darkness abated and musketeers rallied, that concentrated fire became effective against the assault. The clockwork soldiers that accompanied the Viletri division with their repeating bolt throwers were also helpful. Still, they were too few to turn the tide, and the giants targeted them once they understood the danger. Few of the animations were left. Everywhere, soldiers slashed and bashed and stabbed ... enraged, desperate, determined.

Behind Mannace's divisions, Blood Sea reserves moved forward to lend their blades to the defence. Casteel and the Blood Legion were part of the reinforcements. Casteel was a veteran of many battles, and she considered herself the equal of any challenge, but like many others - the scale of this conflict overwhelmed her senses. Suppressing her anxiety, she led the legion in the direction of a Remman division that held firm despite the terrible casualties they were taking. Giants and armoured infantry with axes, hammered at their shield wall and in those places where the giants were breaking it apart, the Blood Legion threw themselves into the frantic melee. Even with their aid, the best they could do against such an imposing foe was to stand their ground.

In other areas, where the Southern forces fought only the Veldaan soldiers and Chokra, the Colonials and Remman were unbreakable. Where the Chokra dropped their tower shields only a few metres from the southern line to charge, the muskets capitalised on this mistake and cut them down before they could engage. In other locations, where the enemy met the shield wall of the Remman elite, they might as well have thrown themselves against a meat grinder for the bloody slaughter that ensued. More experienced

Veldaan units made good contact, fighting with vigour and passion, knowing that this was the last defence of their lands. As the combat progressed, some Chokra tossed vials of fire or javelins over the front ranks to cause chaos amongst the southern troops. The fierce Chokra from the City of Orroco drove carts drawn by bullocks into the defence. Rakor was wise to such tactics, and he knew that the mettle and resolve of his men would hold firm.

Behind the Southern lines, most of the uncommitted reserves were hurriedly manoeuvring towards the eastern flank where units of Islani appeared and quickly encircled the Southern forces. The Islani were allies of the Veldaan, coming in large numbers from the territories to the east. There was a scattering of other races fighting alongside them.

The Islani soldiers were dark haired, with pointed beards. Their fierce warriors wielded curved blades and donned short-sleeved chainmail coats, with conical helms. Most wore colourful sashes or cloaks, giving them an air of flamboyance. As well as infantry and cavalry, hundreds of Islani chariots and war wagons wheeled to attack the allies where they were most vulnerable. Many of the chariots were small and carried two or three archers who fired from the safety of distance. Some though, were drawn by six horses, with scythes to cut a path through the Southern ranks. At first, the chariots created chaos as they rampaged unchallenged, but once the southerners positioned themselves to counter the attack, the chariots were vulnerable at range. The war wagons were tougher, armoured so that the archers and spearmen riding them could fire or jab from safety. Even the horses wore heavy barding. With the shock of their assault troops and mass of soldiers following behind, it was not long before the allies' eastern flank was overwhelmed.

Render was astonished. Kakos, who was on the disc next to him, manipulated the souls of the Northern dead. Slain enemy scattered across the field, even giants, were rising to his command. Hundreds of them already joined the fighting.

The Sorcerer was too absorbed in his work to think further on it, and when he sensed a magical source behind the enemy lines, he knew he had uncovered one of the hidden Asari. Without hesitation, Render summoned his energy and sent a great sphere of blackness high into the sky before it crashed down on the Asari's location. A storm of dark lightning cleansed the surrounding area, like the tridents of hell stabbing down at the earth and sweeping it clear. As the spell flickered to its conclusion, Render watched intently, sensing fleeting magic then nothing. The small magic was most likely the Asari escaping, and in his heightened state, the frustration that he let his prey get away consumed him. Render's rage required an outlet, and he released a wave of hate across the field below. "RRAAAAAAAAAGGHH!"

To the far left, the Galandarians and heavy cavalry from the Holy States were welcome arrivals. The Holy States cavalry was unstoppable as they charged, sweeping deep into the goblin horde and back out again onto the plains. Bollo and the Galandar infantry were slower to reach the combat. When they did, Bollo was at the forefront of the attack, hacking and slashing his way forward. The troops nearby rallied around him as they often did, knowing him as their champion. A wedge formed with Bollo at its head, thousands of soldiers falling in behind as they ran to join the attack. Into the sea of Goblins, they charged.

Milan Tash oversaw the primary reserves. While most units were sent to the eastern flank to counter the Islani, Milan deployed the Keshik pike and elephants to strengthen the centre. Now only the Charikon mercenaries remained. It was all-in now, so he ordered the Charikon into the fray where the Veldaan and giants were pushing the Southerners back. Milan knew enough about warfare to understand that if push back turned to rout, then the rest of the line would soon follow. The Belg and their hand cannons would be most useful there. It was hard to tell under the magic lights which side was winning. The uncertainty tempted Milan to grab a fast horse and extricate himself to a safer place - but where was safe? He cursed Mannace under his breath and wondered how he was ever convinced to take part in an endeavour with so much risk and so little reward.

Mannace assessed the battlefield. Since his visit to the Oracle, Mannace realised a change in himself; although the armies were vast and spread over a great distance, in his mind he could visualise the formations and shape of battle so that, more than ever, he instinctively knew what actions to take. Messengers gathered about, waiting to carry orders to his commanders.

Mannace saw that the Veldaan fought with skill and bravery. The giants in such massive numbers could have been unstoppable, but the musket men with concentrated fire were gradually taking the creatures down. Defeating the giants was the key to unlocking victory, and as Mannace surmised - when their losses started to mount and they recognized their vulnerability, the Giants were the first to pull back. With the giant's withdrawal, the Veldaan defenders were outclassed by the elite Remman, and colonial units rallied in the Southern centre. It was the most the Veldaan could do to regroup as they slowly retreated - their attack transforming to defence. Mannace was impressed by how the Northerners kept their order and even the Chokra militia did not give over to panic. On the Southern side, the colonial troops and Remman reformed their lines, while a scattering of musket shots helped the enemy on their way.

Towards the flanks, the conflict escalated. At the western end of the line, despite aid from their Galandar and Holy State allies, the weight of goblin numbers was pushing the allies back. The Orcs to the fore and the goblins attacking from behind were smashing Khing's troops. With brutal casualties and no room to manoeuvre, their situation was desperate. The remaining slave soldiers still rampaged, but the Elves who ran short of arrows withdrew. Similarly, at the Eastern extreme of the Southern line, it was a frantic struggle to keep the Islani from annihilating the Southern divisions. Casualties were high, and some allied units were in flight.

While Mannace and his Colonials re-formed at the centre and resupplied the musket men with ammunition, he sent messengers to instruct units from Arenland and Yanth to assist Khing. Rakor hurried what Remman could be spared to help against the Islani. The Rhalec and Iron Jaw who had reinforced the effort at the centre joined them. Soon the reinforced flanks became the new front.

Render commanded the best view of the battle from his floating disc. There was no longer any magical darkness, and the skylights illuminated the whole battlefield. Render saw that the Veldaan were broken, and the Giants and Wengo too. Had they the courage to charge again against the Southern front, they might have overrun the beleaguered defenders. However, the surviving Giants were shifting further away, taking the Northern army's hopes with them. Both the Goblin and Islani must have numbered more than half a million troops each, yet it appeared that the Southern lines were firming up as they reorganised and brought their modern firepower to bear. The Remman were unbreakable, and the Colonial forces remained defiant in the face of their fatalities. Render had witnessed enough conflict over the last weeks to know that, while the fighting would continue for some time, the battle was won.

Beside the Sorcerer, Kakos was still busy, his army of undead growing and spreading out as they continued to harass the Veldaan. The Asari avoided confrontation. Render grinned at the prospect that the enemy wizards were distracted by the very demons they set against him. Render was done and what magical reserves he kept in the statues would be needed if the Asari suddenly found their courage. Even his demons withdrew, satiated.

SIEGE OF ANGOROK

In the morning, the siege of Angorok commenced. The Arenlanders deployed their war machines in range of the city, and the Brula dropped missiles and firebombs from the sky. It was a city of a million people, kept safe behind a sixty-foot stone wall. Siege engines operating from towers on the wall and the forward fortress, aimed flaming salvos at the attackers. The battlements were crowded with archers and other soldiers, tired from the night's conflict but diligently going about their jobs. In the hills flanking the city, the allies of the North regrouped with more on the way, and now they waited; bloodied, exhausted, and deflated, but stoically ready to resume the conflict none-the-less. All took confidence that Angorok had never fallen to siege. The Veldaan had never been conquered.

The Southerners were exhausted too, but at the end of the long night, the victory was theirs. They held the field and earned the luxury of tending to their wounded; the tens of thousands of bloodied soldiers that lay amongst the carnage on the plains. Amid the hurt, Ahmeda dragged Lord Angelcry from the field, less an arm, but after the healers helped him, at least he would survive. Render lost two of his apprentices who were presumed to be among the piles of dead. The Viletri commander, Titus Kane, was among those seriously wounded, as was Dekon Ruel, who's chest was caved in by a giant. It took an age to get the War Priest out of his god-powered armour. Though suffering, they were better off than the hundreds of thousands that lay dead.

A young Elf, a Spiderling, and a creature much larger than the giants, crossed the field of war between the two forces. Mannace knew the creature to be one of the Colossi that the Mad King had recovered. All attention was on the strange trio. Near the city, with the siege missiles arching overhead, they stopped, and the Colossus proceeded alone toward the fortress. At the city's main gate, it picked up speed and with a tremendous crash the gates were thrown aside, blue light washing over the creature so that for a time it crackled and sparked. Missiles bounced off the Colossus. The creature reached out and pulled down a nearby section of the gate tower, then strode across the fortress courtyard to kick aside the smaller gate to the city proper. With the fortress wrecked and the capital open, confidence amongst the defenders was shattered and their resolve with it.

Rakor immediately ordered his Remman warriors forward, thinking this another of Mannace's revelations. Mannace, however, knew differently and rather than move towards the gate, he ordered the musket men to support the Remman by clearing the walls. Other troops he kept in reserve, worried that the enemy in the hills, although defeated, were still superior to his soldiers in numbers. If he presented too easy a target, they might resume the attack.

As the Remman arrived at the gate, the Colossus stood aside and let the soldiers pass. With help from the flights of Brula, they cleared the gateway fortress and then moved into the city. As they marched down the wide streets, the Remman were methodical and ruthless in dealing with resistance. When needed, the Colossus bashed a path for them through the cascade of inner walls. While the Remman still faced large numbers of Veldaan soldiers and Chokra, there was nothing here to give the elite warriors a significant challenge. The Asari were absent.

The gates to the citadel in the hills at the rear of the city were now open. Citizens and soldiers of Angorok poured through it to escape. Neither Rakor nor Mannace dared to enter the hills in pursuit, satisfied that it would be enough to capture the capital this day. By mid-afternoon, the Remman held all but the citadel on the hill. At twilight, they entered the citadel and confronted the last of the defenders at the main hall. Knowing that the enemy commander was holed up there, Rakor and Mannace joined the Remman soldiers for the final assault. It was easy work, with only a few fanatic soldiers and servants to bar their way.

They stood now in the war room. Mannace was impressed with the grand chamber. He spoke coolly to its only inhabitant.

"You are defeated."

Tyriah smiled back. She was very calm and softly spoken.

"There is one final enemy for you to slay. Then you will be victorious, for today."

Mannace spoke plainly.

"Veldaan is the gateway to the North, its bastion. The North is open."

Tyriah laughed.

"You have conquered the land, not its people. These empty cities will be your tomb. You have not defeated the North here, you have awakened it."

Rakor knew the danger of words, so he moved forward to finish the task.

"No!"

It was a voice from the edge of the room. Remman soldiers entered the hall while they had been talking. Mannace saw that amongst them was a young Elf, the one that came with the colossus.

"I am Athose. The Mad King asks that this woman, Tyriah, be spared. He would consider it a great favour."

"Do your job", Tyriah said calmly to Rakor. Turning to Athose, she added, "Tell your Mad King to leave the past where it belongs".

That said she drew her sword and moved towards Rakor with speed. The Remman King did not hesitate before knocking aside her blade with his own then impaling her neatly through the chest.

"A good death", he whispered as he helped the limp body gently to the floor.

COMPANIONS

Mannace and Rakor met with the other generals in the war room at Angorok. They used the map table to recount the retreat of the Northern forces and to mark where the enemy was encamped. The Southern Alliance was in the process of securing the Veldaan borders, and for now, the Northerners seemed content to withdraw and regroup. While the generals took a break to eat and check their own business, clerks were repositioning some of the elements on the map table as information continued to come to them. Rakor, who lingered in the war room, scowled as more Northern reinforcements were placed east of Angorok in Islan.

Mannace, who stood beside the young King, was likewise concerned. Tyriah's last words haunted his thoughts – that these empty cities would be their tomb. When Render entered the room, Mannace pulled him aside into a chamber where they both seated themselves. Mannace was still formulating his thoughts, and Render was patient, browsing a shelf of books as he waited for his friend to speak.

"You brought us to the Oracle, Render. You had the vision too. But we have not achieved the Oracle's purpose, not here at Angorok."

Render shrugged. It was evident to everybody that the war with the North was far from done. He was not as driven as Mannace by the Monastery visions, but he understood the compelling nature of prophecy and the demands it placed on the companions to find that prescribed place in time. It pulled at him too.

"That day will come, Mannace. Take confidence that you have the protection of prophecy until it does. Until that day you are invincible, Mannace, as am I, as is Jaal."

Mannace smiled at Render's self-assurance, though he suspected his friend's assumption was misguided. Mannace's amusement turned to a deep frown as darker thoughts quickly consumed him. For a long while he sat staring intently at the floor, brooding. When Mannace finally looked up at Render, he spoke softly. The wizard could see the turmoil in his friend's eyes and a sense of hurt in his voice.

"Jaal follows his own path. He has forsaken our friendship."

Render was mindful not to roll his eyes. He had watched the tension grow between Mannace and Jaal – they were like brothers; bonded in a way that could not be severed yet grown apart in their philosophy and allegiances. Neither was prepared to see the others point of view.

"He is not in your pocket, you mean. Let him be, he will be there at the final battle – have confidence in the Oracle, Mannace."

"His son is like him. An arrogant shit who follows no Lord but himself."

Render just smiled. The Sorcerer could see that Mannace's views over the last decade were deep-set, which was a strength and a weakness. It was a strength because it drove him to accomplish great things. It was a weakness when his singlemindedness blinded him to other perspectives.

Render remembered back to the campfire when they first journeyed to the Blood Sea under the shadow of The Spine. They came so near to turning back and forsaking this adventure. How things would have been different, so small in comparison to the magnificence of their lives today. Even if Mannace was blind to it, Render could see the greatness of what they already accomplished. He took satisfaction in their elevated status. Render liked the drama of their lives and the prospect of upcoming challenges. He felt alive, relevant, perhaps even pivotal to the future. He stood, and he clasped Mannace on the shoulders and gave his companion a final piece of advice.

"Rejoice that Angorok has fallen. We will confront the next challenge, and the challenge after that, together, my friend."

FIRESIDE

Lord Fitius Angelcry sat in a comfortable lounge chair next to the fire. Saska sat on his lap. Both were naked, and she was stroking the stump where his arm was severed. She licked it and then she licked him on the lips. Saska could feel him rise at the contact.

"What does it mean that the North is awakened?"

Fitius reflected before responding.

"The North is vast, much larger than the South. Since Veldaan was captured, the military has not advanced further. It takes a great effort to hold the territories the South have taken, and as other Northern nations enter the fray, the Southern forces become more outnumbered. Amon Murn is the largest of the Northern nations. It is also known as the Sleeping Nation because it has not been involved in the war at the Rift for many generations, although it did send troops against the Blood Sea. The armies of the North hold back, waiting for Amon Murn to rise. They have a prophecy about it. They think that Mannace is the one to awaken the sleeper."

After a pause to sip his wine, Fitius continued.

"The Eastern Colonies, Arenland foremost amongst them, have shown that invention and industry will set us apart. If we are to win the war, the greater conflict, it will be those qualities that ensure our success."

Saska shifted so that she could handle the Lord better.

"You have done well, Fitius. You deserve a reward."

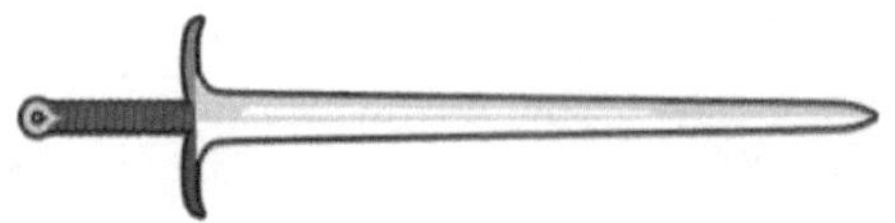

NORTHERN SEA
THE SKERRY
THE SOUTH
THE NORTH

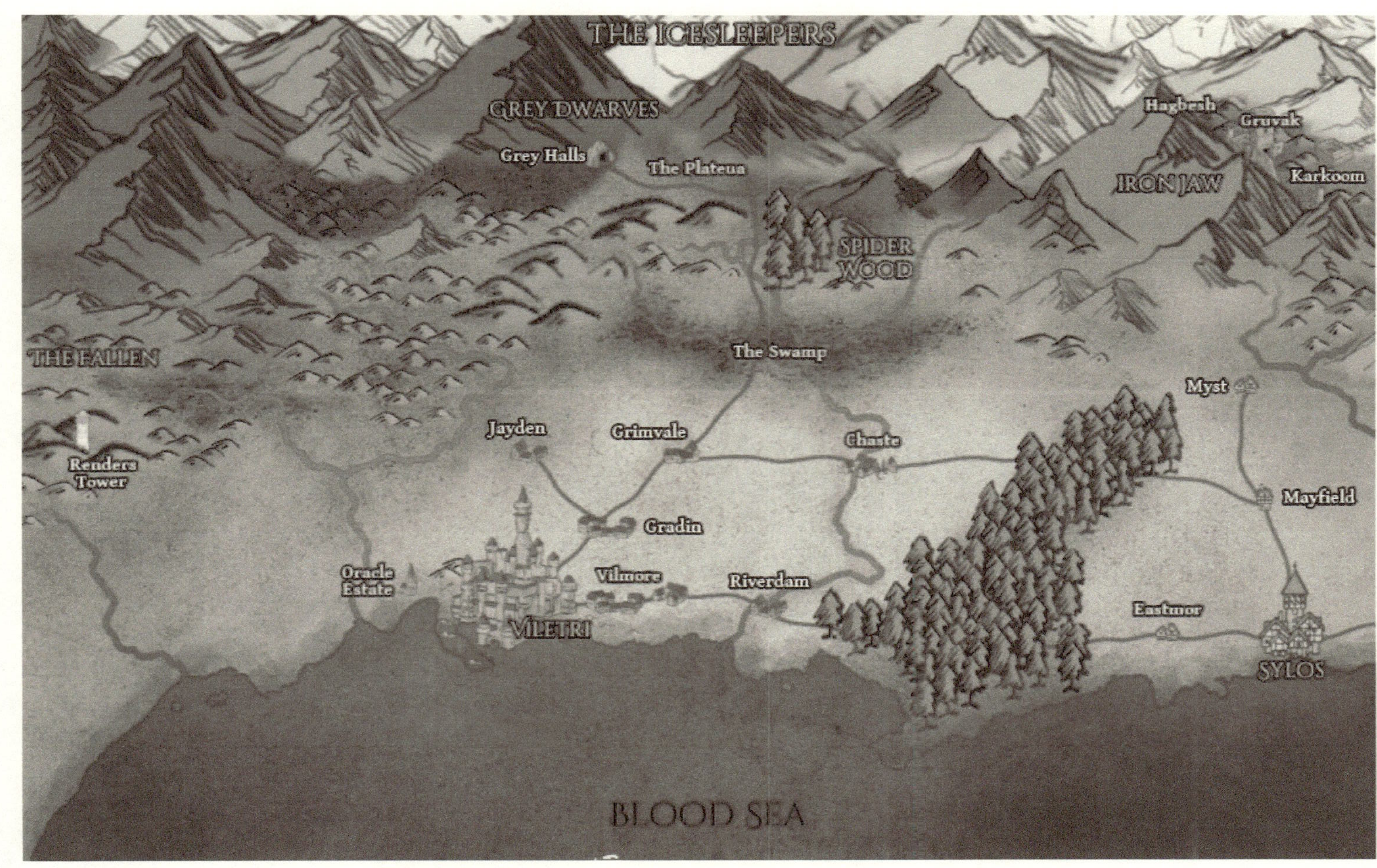
THE ICESLEEPERS
GREY DWARVES
Hagbesh
Gruvak
Grey Halls
The Plateua
IRON JAW
Karkoom
SPIDER WOOD
THE FALLEN
The Swamp
Myst
Jayden
Grimvale
Chaste
Renders Tower
Mayfield
Gradin
Oracle Estate
Vilmore
Riverdam
VILETRI
Eastmor
SYLOS
BLOOD SEA

Immortals Book #2

THE SLEEPER

The companions had done the remarkable, but despite their fame, the destiny that the Oracle promised was not yet within their grasp. Rather, the emergent prophecy of the Sleeper, borne of ancient powers and revered by their enemies, threatens to overshadow their plans and set their destinies to ruin.

To Render, who was resolute of purpose, it seemed that prophecy protected them. That belief emboldened him to take risks as if he were invincible. Such confidence made him a potent foe, elevating him as a sorcerer to be feared, and as a master to the Fallen.

Jaal decided on a different journey, rejecting the Oracle's prediction, and determining to walk his own path. It was a choice with a high price, casting him deep under the shadow, and estranging the Dark Elf from his companions.

Mannace was at the centre, knowing that it was *his* resolve and actions that would determine all their futures. At times, the responsibility was stifling, but always, his purpose motivated him to accomplish what others could not. As a leader of nations, he had achieved enough to recognise that the Oracle was the light and the truth, and that his future was indeed ordained.

More than ever, darkness and light, tradition and invention, wizardry and science, North and South battle for a place in space and time. Long dormant powers stir, and players of the game make their moves, as one Age concludes, and another begins.

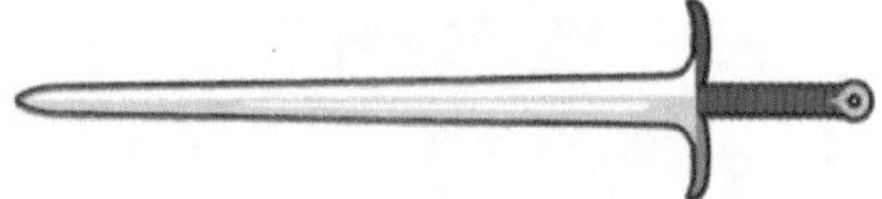

About the Author:

Andrew Wratten

I am a proud Kiwi, living in sunny Australia, with my beautiful Nigerian wife, Tessy, and our six amazing children. Family and friends mean everything ... and good food of course, and dogs, and embarrassingly, reality TV.

One day on the train to work, I took my fantasy daydream and boldly typed my first paragraphs. Since that time, I remain amazed how the words reveal themselves and the tales evolve.

It is a wonderful process to shape a story, witnessing the plot unfold, unexpectedly twist, and surprise even me in its audacious conclusion.

The story belongs to the characters in it, and it is my job to help them be heard, understood, and celebrated for all their glorious traits and flaws. I am indeed a puppet of the Mad King, and like all the others in my books, I am dancing to his manic tune.

I hope others enjoy the characters, their triumphs, and their misadventures, as much as I do.